THE SECRET OF THE DRUIDS

Book 2 of The Mahabharata Quest Series

Christopher C. Doyle is an author who transports the reader into a fascinating world where ancient secrets buried in legends blend with science and history to create a gripping story.

His debut novel, *The Mahabharata Secret,* featured among the top ten books of 2013 and was nominated for the Raymond Crossword Book Award, 2014. He followed it up with the bestselling The Mahabharata Quest series, featuring *The Alexander Secret* and *The Secret of the Druids* and the bestselling The Pataala Prophecy series featuring *Son of Bhrigu* and *The Mists of Brahma,* all of which have won rave reviews from readers.

Christopher can be contacted at:

Website: www.authorchristophercdoyle.com

Email: contact@christophercdoyle.com

Facebook: www.facebook.com/authorchristophercdoyle

The Quest Club: www.authorchristophercdoyle.com/the-quest-club

Other books by Christopher C. Doyle

The Mahabharata Quest Series

The Alexander Secret

The Khandavaprastha Conspiracy

The Pataala Prophecy

Son of Bhrigu

The Mists of Brahma

BOOK 2

THE MAHABHARATA QUEST

THE SECRET OF THE DRUIDS

CHRISTOPHER C. DOYLE

First published by westland ltd in 2016

Published by Westland Publications Private Limited, in 2018

Published by Westland Books, a division of Nasadiya Technologies Private Limited, in 2022

No. 269/2B, First Floor, 'Irai Arul', Vimalraj Street, Nethaji Nagar, Alappakkam Main Road, Maduravoyal, Chennai 600095

Westland and the Westland logo are the trademarks of Nasadiya Technologies Private Limited, or its affiliates.

ISBN: 9789395767286

10 9 8 7 6 5 4 3 2 1

Typeset by Ram Das Lal

Printed at Thomson Press (India) Ltd

While you, ye Druids, when the war was done,
To mysteries strange and hateful rites returned:
To you alone 'tis given the heavenly gods
To know or not to know; secluded groves
Your dwelling place, and forests far remote.
If what ye sing be true, the shades of men
Seek not the dismal homes of Erebus
Or death's pale kingdoms; but the breath of life
Still rules these bodies in another age—
Life on this hand and that, and death between.

Marcus Annaeus Lucanus, ***Pharsalia,*** **I, 450-8**

For
My readers,
For your support, love and appreciation

Author's Note

Have you read *A Secret Revealed*—the mini sequel to *The Alexander Secret,* and the prequel to this book?

If you haven't, then allow me to explain. In October 2015, realising that *The Secret of the Druids* would be released only in 2016, I decided to give my readers a surprise gift: a free ebook that could be accessed on my website. This ebook was published in six parts; one part every month starting October 2015.

This ebook was titled *A Secret Revealed,* and it continued the story from where *The Alexander Secret* ended. Many readers were anxiously waiting to know who the mysterious caller was, who had fixed up to meet Vijay at Starbucks in Cyber Hub, Gurgaon. I thought my readers deserved to know and so I wrote this ebook, which answers some questions that were left unanswered in *The Alexander Secret*.

Subsequently, a significant number of readers wrote to me expressing their interest in a physical copy of *A Secret Revealed*. Since giving away free hard copies of the book was not feasible, I chose a different route. In keeping with the worldwide tradition of authors releasing novellas on World Book Day, I decided I would be the first Indian author to adopt this tradition. On March 3, 2016, therefore, *A Secret Revealed* was published as a paperback, at a reasonable cost.

A word about The Quest Club, in case you haven't registered as a member yet. Membership is free and gives you access to *A Secret Revealed* in electronic form, free of charge. It will also give you access to Quest Club events—where readers interact with me both online and offline—that will be held all over India. There will be more free ebooks over the coming years, in addition to quizzes, puzzles, contests and exclusive previews of my future books for members of the club. Finally, you can join me, as I research my books, and gain free access to images, videos and my research notes. You could even learn more about characters, locations and events in my books. An exciting journey filled with adventure and mystery beckons all Quest Club members. You can register for free at: www.christophercdoyle.com/the-quest-club and start reading *A Secret Revealed* right away for free.

I have included, in this book, the background that is narrated in *A Secret Revealed,* so in case you have not read the mini-sequel, you will still get to know the broad story and the events leading up to the action that unfolds in *The Secret of the Druids*.

But if you can, please do read *A Secret Revealed*—either online, free of charge, or in paperback if you prefer a physical book—before you start reading *The Secret of the Druids*. There are clues in there that will make the reading of this book more enjoyable, as thousands of readers have already discovered.

Happy Reading!

Christopher C. Doyle

Kirkwall
Inverness
Aberdeen
Fort William
North Sea
North Atlantic Sea
Glasgow
Edinburgh
Belfast
Liverpool
Holyhead
Chester
Shefield
Ireland
Cambridge
Oxford
LONDON
Cardiff
Canterbury
English Channel

Prologue

48 B.C.

Alexandria, Egypt

Julius Caesar listened to the centurion, his face grim. The news was not good. His escape route was cut off. While the ship bearing his precious cargo had escaped the siege, the Egyptians had effectively ensured that he could not send for help from his legions in Asia Minor.

He was trapped.

An ordinary man would have cursed his fortune. He would have railed at his miscalculation in bringing two under-strength legions, of 3200 infantry and 800 cavalry, into Egypt in the middle of a civil war. He would have denounced the gods for their fickleness in watching over him, allowing the Egyptians to outmanoeuvre him.

But Caesar was no ordinary man.

And the siege served his plan, even if it was wholly fortuitous. He had reason to thank the gods.

He waited patiently until the centurion had finished. The man was clearly worried. Not scared. That would be most unlike a Roman. But worried, yes. The odds were stacked against them. What was Caesar going to do?

When the centurion had finished, Caesar waited, allowing a few moments of silence to accentuate what he was about to say.

'The Egyptians have not mobilised all the ships,' he began. 'Fifty ships, which were commanded by Gneus, returned to the harbour and are now out there.' He gestured towards the window, towards the Egyptian fleet moored there.

'Twenty-two ships from the Egyptian fleet, as you say, have come into the harbour to reinforce them. They will ensure that they control all seventy-two ships in the harbour.' He paused for effect.

'Here's what you are going to do,' Caesar continued. He swiftly outlined the strategy. The Roman legionnaires were to take up strategic positions, waiting for an opportune moment to set fire to the ships and the docks.

The objective was to destroy the Egyptian fleet, the docks, and the warehouses, even the buildings adjoining them. Nothing was going to stop him from achieving his ambitions...

And, there was one more thing.

Caesar beckoned to the centurion. 'Alexandria must burn,' he said softly. 'I task you with this responsibility.' He told the centurion what he had to do. A posse of soldiers had a specific task to accomplish.

The destruction of a building.

It would cover his tracks and remove all evidence.

The centurion nodded and saluted. It would be done.

As the man walked away, Caesar sat back, lost in thought. It had taken him eight years to get here, he reflected. Eight long years since he first learned, in Gaul, about the great secret that would give him even more glory than he could accomplish by merely ruling over Rome.

He hadn't wasted time. Seven years ago, he had led an exploratory expedition to Britannia but had failed to find the secret. Refusing to give up, he had mounted another expedition to Britannia the following year. This time, he had found success but it was partial. He was only able to get information on where the secret was hidden. The means to put that secret to use, in order to achieve the purpose he had in mind, still eluded him.

And then, it had occurred to him that he might find what he sought here, in Alexandria, the city that Alexander the Great had founded almost 300 years ago.

A week after the completion of the mission, he was now confident that he finally had the secret within his grasp. Now, all he had to do was erase its existence from the memories of men.

That would happen today.

It didn't matter how long it took him to return to Rome. He was its ruler now. And when he got back, he would have control over the greatest secret to rule mankind. One that even Alexander the Great did not have.

Julius Caesar would be the greatest ruler of the world.

Ever.

1305 A.D.

Near Bathgate, West Lothian, UK

Midnight

The man named Jeremy McGregor looked around at his men, who were hard at work, and licked his lips nervously. The tall oak trees surrounded them completely, shielding the light of their lamps from any prying eyes that may have been skulking on the perimeter of the woods. This time of night was quiet and it was extremely unlikely that anyone would be around right now, at this location, right at the top of the hill that was called Kernepopple.

The small group of men had been toiling since early

afternoon when the winter sun had begun to sink below the horizon. It had been hard work, clearing the undergrowth and digging through the layer of earth that covered the cairn, accumulated over the passing of three thousand years.

McGregor's nervousness was palpable. He was the leader of this motley group of cairn robbers, professional thieves who had made it their speciality to dig up the ancient barrows that lay scattered all over this part of Scotland, in search of treasure.

For these barrows were rumoured to be ancient graves, three or four thousand years old if the legends and myths were to be believed, built for important people of those ages, tribal chiefs or noblemen. Very often, these people would have been buried with precious stones and jewellery, for which there was a ready market. And the bones themselves, if they still survived, were also in demand.

Their mission here was to excavate a single grave within the cairn. They didn't know what they would find in the grave, but they did know that the possibility of finding bones was slim. The grave was centuries old and the acid soil would have consumed any human remains buried in it.

But there was a strong possibility that they would find valuables inside—precious stones, even silver from the mines nearby. This was a grave that had stayed untouched despite the passage of the centuries. They had instructions to collect and carry away everything they found within it.

It was not without reason that Kernepopple had been spared by grave robbers in the intervening centuries. Apart from the fact that the silver mines in close proximity to the hill yielded far more treasure than any grave could, the hill itself—and this cairn in particular—was rumoured to radiate a mysterious and powerful energy. For well over a thousand years, the hill had been associated with an ancient fertility goddess, though no one remembered her name any longer. There were also legends, born of ancient myths, that the goddess herself was buried within the cairn.

These ancient legends had been bolstered by the Romans who, when they passed through the area, recorded the cairn as "*media nemeton*"—which meant "central sanctuary"—of the highest order of Druids. And, as everyone knew, the Druids, while they flourished, were the greatest sorcerers of their time. Pliny the Elder, writing in the first century A.D. had, in passing, referred to them as Magi. And almost every eminent classical scholar, Greek or Roman, had written about their power over the people and their knowledge of science and astronomy.

It had been reason enough for McGregor and his ilk to stay away from the cairn on the hill. Until now. The reward on offer this time was so high that he had been encouraged to put his fears aside. He had convinced himself that the stories surrounding the hill were just that; stories.

But now that he was actually at the site, with his men digging away, McGregor wondered if he had let his greed get the better of him...

It wasn't just the fear of being discovered that was unnerving. It was also a fear of the unknown, of the myths and legends surrounding this place. Of the fact that they were actually going to uncover the tomb of the legendary goddess who had been buried here. For it was her grave that they had been tasked to rob.

The identity of McGregor's employer had not been revealed to him. A group of men had summoned him to Linlithgow, where he had been given his instructions along with a purse of gold. And there was more to come once their mission was successfully completed.

But McGregor was no fool. It was easy to guess where

that gold was coming from. Edward I of England had invaded Scotland nine years ago. Three years ago, the English monarch, also known as the "Hammer of the Scots", had built a formidable defence around the royal residence at Linlithgow, called the "Peel". And just this year, William Wallace who had led an insurrection against the English, was captured and convicted of treason against London, after which he was hanged and his corpse drawn and quartered.

The rebellion of the Scots, while brutally suppressed, had troubled Edward I. And McGregor had a feeling that his order to ransack the grave was connected to King Edward's worries. It seemed to him that they were looking for something beyond a treasure of precious stones. If Edward got his hands on whatever was buried in that grave, it would give the English king a hold over the Scots. With the grave goods of the goddess in his hands, McGregor knew that the Scots would be less inclined to repeat their adventure against the English.

While McGregor and his men had no idea about the exact location of the grave, they did know from legend that there were supposed to be three graves in the cairn, of which the largest one was the grave of the goddess. They had spotted a stone protruding from the ground and had decided to start digging there. If everything else in the cairn was under the earth, a stone large enough to be visible above the surface of the ground could possibly mark something very important.

Their guess had been spot on. The stone seemed to be an immense headstone. It was highly probable that this was the grave they sought.

'Come on, then,' he urged his men. 'Let's get inside and take what we came for.'

The top of the headstone jutted out from the stones of the cairn around it; approximately a foot was now visible in the light of their lamps, though even less had protruded above the layer of earth that had covered the cairn.

'Let's get to work,' McGregor said. The men started hauling the stones away; slowly creating a crater within the pile of stones that formed the cairn. Inch by inch, the tall headstone was revealed, shining in the lamplight as its crystals reflected the light back at them.

For a few moments, the men stared at what they had uncovered. From the headstone, smaller standing stones radiated outwards in an ovoid shape, surrounding a smaller cairn within the larger one they had just excavated.

Was this the grave?

Then, something strange happened.

'Look!' someone pointed at the headstone. The sight was terrifying, even though it was tempered somewhat by the light of their lamps.

Bluish flames seemed to be emerging from the ground around the headstone.

A man moaned. 'The fires of hell!'

There was more to come. Above the headstone, four-inch flames of light flickered into existence and then disappeared within a few seconds only to be replaced by orbs of light that floated above the ground.

Another man yelped in fear. 'It's the goddess!'

Even as he spoke, the earth beneath their feet began trembling. Some of the men dropped to their knees and began praying.

For a few moments, the group of men stood absolutely still, looking around them as the earth continued to shiver underfoot.

Then, as abruptly as it had started, the tremor ceased. The balls of light disappeared. Darkness descended on the hilltop once again, broken only by the light of their lamps.

A strange feeling took hold of the men. Whether it was the myths they had been fed or something that truly was within the grave, they could feel an inexplicable sensation within their heads.

One of the men started back towards the path leading out of the grove. 'I can't breathe,' he spluttered. 'I don't feel good at all.' He sprinted back up the path and was lost in the darkness instantly.

'Rubbish!' McGregor declared, repressing his own feelings of nausea and that tingling sensation at his fingertips. The weight of the purse of gold in his waistcoat pocket was a great counterbalance to the experience he and his men were undergoing. 'It was just a small earthquake. Let's get our job done and get the hell out of here! There's gold waiting for us when we get back.'

The men stared back at him doubtfully. A big man ambled forward and glared at McGregor.

'So you say.' He spat. 'An earthquake! And what about the fire and lights? I don't want no gold if the devil's going to come and take my soul! This hill's cursed. We know the legend of the goddess. We are all fools to have come here on a crazy mission like this.' He turned and walked away, muttering a prayer under his breath.

'We haven't even begun digging up the grave,' another man piped up, 'and the earth is shaking and…and…' he spluttered, struggling to find words to describe what he had seen. 'What's going to happen when we uncover the bones?'

The other men murmured their agreement.

McGregor stood there, fighting the urge to join the men. The sensation in his brain that had played havoc with his emotions was beginning to subside. But the fear in his mind was refusing to fade away. The words of his men rang true. The superstitions of the time were too strong for him to ignore. Edward could keep his gold. It was not worth risking the wrath of the goddess for an English king.

'We're done,' McGregor announced, finally, making up his mind. 'Let's leave.'

Without bothering to replace the stones they had moved from the cairn, the men hurried away.

The mysterious grave that had lain untouched and undisturbed for over three thousand years had won a reprieve. The story of McGregor's experience would spread and other grave robbers would learn of it. They would steer clear of the cairn on the hill. The grave would stay that way for another six hundred years before an excavation would uncover it once more.

By then, it would be too late for the world to learn the truth about the tomb and its mysterious occupant.

Too late for the world to stop from hurtling towards its fate. A fate that would be worse than death.

1

November, last year

Intelligence Bureau Headquarters

Imran stared at the agent sitting across the desk from him, a sinking feeling in his heart. He was one of the task force's best, Imran reflected, and if he had drawn a blank, there wasn't much Imran could do.

Still, he persisted. 'Surely there must be some clue,' he pressed the agent. 'Some indication of where they may have gone?'

'I'm sorry, sir,' the agent's tone was contrite. 'I know how important this is for you and we've tried everything. It was a bit of a miracle that we were able to trace Saxena's path to the Al-Sarafa hospital in Abu Dhabi. They did a great job of covering their tracks. It was only because Radha was with them that we were able to get a trace on them. It isn't easy to cover your tracks when you have a dead body that you're trying to pass off as a patient.'

Imran cringed at these words. While the agent knew that Radha had been a task force member, he had no way of knowing how close Imran was to her. After rescuing her from almost certain death two years ago, a unique bond had formed between the two. If Vijay had been devastated while watching the video in which Radha was shot, Imran had not been less affected. And he had been one of the first people to see the video. It was still difficult for him to accept that she was dead. But he knew he had to come to terms with reality, sooner or later.

'So, all we know is that Radha was in that hospital for six days,' Imran reflected on what the agent had told him, to ensure he had understood correctly. 'In that time, the hospital declared her dead. Saxena didn't have a choice but to take her away. Or, as you conjectured, he *wanted* to take her away to a facility that belongs to the Order. If they want to experiment on her ...' he winced again, but steeled himself. He had a job to do. Emotions could not be allowed to interfere. 'If they want to experiment on her, as I'm sure they will, they can't do it at someone else's medical centre. The Order must have their own facility, equipped for such experiments. The problem we have on our hands is that we don't know where this centre is. The trail grows cold and ends at Abu Dhabi.' He looked at the agent. 'Have I summarised it accurately?'

The agent nodded. 'Sir.'

'Fine then,' Imran suppressed the cold, miserable feeling in his gut. 'Great job.'

As the agent left, Imran couldn't help but think about how he would break the news to Vijay. The bad news was twofold. First, the confirmation, from a hospital no less, that Radha was dead. Second, the fact that they didn't know where the Order had taken her body. He shook his head. This was bad.

Very bad.

His phone rang. It was a private number. He frowned. Who could it be?

'Yes?' he connected the call, without identifying himself. Then, he froze. He knew who the caller was. Only, it was the last person he had expected to receive a call from.

Especially in this situation.

2

February, present year

Hertfordshire, England

Ernest Hamilton sat in his favourite chair in his manuscript room and perused the ancient vellum manuscript on the table in front of him. The document was placed under an archival-quality plastic sheet protector to prevent it from deteriorating any further. He took a sip from the glass of whisky at his side from time to time, lost in contemplation of the contents of the manuscript. It was his latest acquisition and, as was his wont with his new acquisitions, he would go through it intimately. He did not collect ancient manuscripts for their value on the antiquities market. It gave him pleasure to know that he had purchased the knowledge of centuries ago; texts written by men now long dead—creations that had outlived their creators by hundreds of years. Even if it was a mundane letter written by an ancient merchant ordering supplies from a distant land, it still gave him a thrill to read the text—the fine script, the objects mentioned, the scratchings on the paper, all had the ability to transport him back in time. It was for this reason that he had mastered five ancient scripts, which enabled him to read almost all the documents in his collection.

A noise from the hall below interrupted his thoughts. He frowned. It was late. Hamilton had dismissed his staff for the night except for Henry, his butler, who had left the room just a short while ago.

'Is that you, Henry?' he called out. There was no reply.

Hamilton pulled off the white cotton gloves he had worn while examining the manuscript and strode towards the doorway of his manuscript room—a specially designed space that contained temperature- and humidity-controlled cabinets to house his manuscripts and preserve them. One wing of the house was dedicated to his collection, with its own state-of-the-art security system.

He stopped short as the door flew open and someone entered the room.

It was a stranger.

A woman.

'Henry!' he called out again, ignoring the woman.

'I'm afraid Henry is in no position to respond,' the woman smiled unpleasantly and held up a wicked-looking, bloodstained dagger with a slim blade. She was around 5 feet 5 inches in height, young, slim and clad in black. Her skin was a mocha colour and she spoke with a clipped British accent.

He stared at her goggle-eyed, seeming to notice her for the first time. He couldn't take his eyes off her face. Not that she was unusually beautiful. Attractive, in her own way, perhaps, but that was not what caught his attention.

Her face seemed to glow.

Hamilton staggered back. His hand shook and he spilt some whisky on the carpet.

'Who…who are you?' he stuttered. A cold fear had begun to take hold of him.

What had this woman done to Henry? The bloodstained dagger made him fear the worst.

There was movement at the door and two men entered the room and stood behind the woman.

The cold dread that Hamilton had been experiencing so far turned into a panic born of certainty.

This was a burglary. They had come for his collection.

He wasn't worried about his treasures. They were safely locked away behind bullet proof, unbreakable, glass cabinets. Each cabinet had its own unique passcode and he had made it a point not to remember any of them, just in case he was kidnapped for ransom.

But he was worried that, in their ignorance, they might torture him to get to the passcodes.

How had they got into a locked house?

'I don't know any of the passcodes,' he blurted out, hoarsely, bumping into a tall cabinet that housed a collection of manuscripts from ancient Rome, as he anxiously backed away from her.

The woman laughed. It was a chilling laugh. Something about it made Hamilton's hair stand on edge. Her voice was cold, like a steel blade.

'Oh, don't worry about that,' she smirked. 'I don't want any of these.' She waved a hand at the ancient texts stored in the room. 'I only want the coins.'

'The coins?' Hamilton echoed, puzzled. 'What coins?'

'The Inverness Hoard,' the woman replied. 'Three coins were unearthed. Your grandfather gave them away.' She shrugged. 'I just need to know who has those coins now. We didn't know where to start looking. So many possibilities, you know. Like hunting for a needle in a haystack. So, I thought I would ask you. It's the easy way out. I'm sure you have a record of who your grandfather bequeathed those coins to. Tell me and you'll live to enjoy your collection.'

Hamilton realised what she was talking about. In 1905, a group of workers had discovered a decaying bag with three ancient Roman coins, while excavating the foundations for a building in Inverness. It was hardly a hoard, but had been instantly dubbed one by the media since the coins were all made of solid gold. His grandfather had purchased the so-called hoard and even published an account of it in 1914, with a detailed description of the coins.

It had been an extraordinary find but had got lost in the news of the Great War that had broken out in Europe that year.

The woman was correct. His grandfather had bequeathed those coins. Two private collectors and a museum had them now. A cold chill ran down his spine. He knew exactly whom the coins had been bequeathed to. And something told him that this woman wouldn't hesitate to use any means to get the information out of him.

'Those coins aren't very valuable,' he said feebly. His mind was racing. *How could he get out of this predicament?* 'They were never meant to be used as currency. They're worthless.'

'Never mind,' the woman told him. 'Their value is far beyond money.'

She gestured and the two men blocked the entrance to the room.

Damn! She had read his mind.

He had been contemplating making a break for it through the main entrance to this room. That option had just been ruled out.

Another thought flashed through his mind. He didn't have an option. He had to try it. And it might even work. Even at forty-five years, he was fit and would swim sixty laps of his pool every morning.

He was not thinking of himself. His thoughts now revolved around his daughter. She, too, could be in danger. She had gone to a friend's place and had decided to stay over for the night at Hamilton's plush apartment in Mayfair. She had to be warned.

Before fear could make him change his mind, he acted.

A quick sprint towards the window directly opposite the cabinet he was standing against.

Swiftly unlatching the window, he threw it open and leaped onto the window frame, perched precariously there for a moment.

Then, he jumped.

3

Out of the window

The window hadn't been a random choice. Directly below was the large heated swimming pool, graded from a depth of six feet to fourteen feet at the deep end. Hamilton was a serious swimmer.

As his feet left the first floor window of the manuscript room, he coiled himself into a tight ball and spun in mid air before opening out into a headfirst dive into the pool, neatly cleaving the water.

He rose to the surface, gasping for breath. It had been years since he had dived into any pool from a height. With quick, strong strokes, he swam towards the far edge of the pool and pulled himself out, dripping wet.

The only problem with this plan was that his phone was now wet.

Would it work?

He didn't have time to check now.

He had to get away first.

Springing to his feet, he dashed away from the pool, towards the garage.

If he could get to one of the cars…

But it was too late.

'Get him!' he heard the woman's voice at the window above.

A shadow loomed before him. There hadn't been just the

three of them up there. The woman had other accomplices. One of them was blocking the way to the garage.

He glanced back at the pool.

Another man was walking towards him menacingly.

Hamilton looked from one man to the other as both men drew guns.

Only one way out now.

The hedge.

It was four feet above the ground. Not low enough to jump over but not too high to vault over either.

It had been ages since he had tried anything like this, but he had to attempt it. He was thankful for his physical fitness. It would come in handy now.

He sprinted towards the hedge to gain momentum and then vaulted neatly over it.

The lack of practice showed. He landed badly, twisting his ankle in the process.

Biting back a shout of pain, he hobbled on. It would have helped if he could sprint away but that was out of the question. He gritted his teeth and soldiered on despite the pain.

They hadn't shot at him. That was good news. They meant to take him alive. That was bad news. It meant they would ensure he gave them the information they wanted.

The phone.

Hamilton pulled it out and checked it.

It was dead. The swimming pool had done it in.

He cursed. How was he to get word to Penny about the danger she was in?

Slowly, painfully, he made his way forward. He could not stop. He had to keep moving.

Forcing himself to suppress the panic that was lurking at the edges of his consciousness, he mentally weighed the options.

There was a phone in the house but someone would certainly be barring the entrance to the building. The staff quarters would also have a phone. He could try and wake up someone and ask for help. But the quarters were in a different direction. If he chose this option and was confronted before he reached the staff quarters, there was nowhere to run or hide.

A familiar silhouette loomed before him in the darkness. He couldn't believe his eyes. His motorcycle. What was it doing here out of the garage?

It didn't matter now. The last thing on his mind at this moment was the question of who was to blame for this transgression.

For now, it was a blessing.

Another option had presented itself to him.

He jumped on the bike and started it. It was a powerful 500cc BMW. He opened up the throttle and the bike lurched forward. A sigh of relief escaped him.

He had a chance.

4

On the bike

The motorcycle's tyres spun on the gravel as he sped down the driveway. The tall, ornate gates came into view. They were shut. But he knew they couldn't be locked. These people—the woman and her henchmen, whoever they were—would have hacked the electronic lock.

Hamilton hopped off the bike and limped to the gates, opening them just enough for the bike to pass through.

Behind him, he heard the sound of a car engine revving up.

They had heard the motorcycle start and had guessed he was trying to make a run for it.

They were in pursuit. He would have to hurry.

He hopped back on the bike and ripped through the gates and onto the tarmac outside.

There was no time to pause and think. He went left, directing the bike towards the bridge that crossed the stream that flowed past the house. It was barely a mile away.

He knew exactly where he was going. A few miles down the road from the bridge was a petrol filling station. There was a payphone there, which he could use.

The rumble of the motorcycle was deafening in the silence of the night.

Behind him, the sound of the car roaring down the driveway came to him and he accelerated.

He was unable to fathom why the woman wanted the coins. Sure, they were made of gold and worth the value of the precious metal. But these coins had never been minted as currency. The experts who had examined the coins had been unanimous in this conclusion. In fact, this feature of the coins had been one of the contributing factors to the mystery surrounding them. The other component of the mystery was the fact that the coins had been found carefully placed in a small rocky chamber that could be accessed only by a narrow shaft. Someone had gone to great lengths to hide those coins away. And they must have had some value for whoever had buried them, since so much care had been taken while burying the coins in their underground tomb.

No one had evinced much interest in those coins after the initial furore over the discovery died out.

Until now.

Their value is far beyond money.

What had the woman meant?

The bike sped down the road in the darkness, the beam from its headlamp cutting a swathe through the blackness of the night.

The wooden bridge over the stream appeared and the bike roared over it as the stream gurgled on its way beneath him.

The country road was dark, and houses flashed by on either side, submerged in darkness, their inhabitants deep in slumber.

The petrol station came into view, shrouded in darkness. It was closed. But it didn't matter. The payphone booth would be unlocked.

Hamilton guided the motorcycle into the petrol station and parked it next to the payphone booth. He slid off the bike and checked the door of the booth, exhaling in relief as it opened without a problem.

He was now faced with a new problem. He didn't remember either Penny's number or the telephone number of the Mayfair apartment. Both were on speed dial on his mobile phone and he had never bothered to memorise them.

It was something he deeply regretted now.

There was only one number that he could recall. The number of a man who shared his interest in ancient manuscripts.

Saul Goldfeld, the historian and expert on ancient scripts.

It was late, he knew, but he didn't have a choice.

Hamilton wiped his credit card dry and swiped it, then dialled Goldfeld's number. It was going to be an expensive call, from a landline to a mobile phone.

'Goldfeld,' the historian answered after a couple of rings.

'Thank heavens!' Hamilton blurted out, hoarsely. 'Listen, I don't have time. Someone has broken into my house and I've managed to get away. Call the police, will you, and let them know that I'm in trouble? And Penny needs to be told that she may also be in danger. She's in the Mayfair apartment. You know the address, don't you?'

'Of course,' Goldfeld's voice came over the line, sounding concerned. 'I'll call the police right away and then go over and tell Penny. Will you be okay?'

'I'll try and keep these people off my tail until the police arrive,' Hamilton responded. 'But there's something that's more important. The coins. It's what these people are after. If something happens to me...'

He broke off as the road running by the petrol filling station suddenly lit up.

5

Tacitus

The car had caught up. Its powerful headlamps cut through the darkness, sweeping the road before it.

Its occupants hadn't noticed the payphone at the back of the petrol station or the bike parked next to it and swept past, intent on catching up with their prey.

'Right then, I have to run,' Hamilton announced. 'There's a safe in the house. Take the diary. Warn the owners of the coins. Tacitus.'

He limped back to the bike and started it. The only direction he could now take was towards the house. Hamilton weighed his chances. The intruders, whoever they were, were bound to have left a few men on the grounds, in case he returned. He would have to ride past the house and hope for the best. Stopping by one of the houses on the way and rousing the residents was too risky. He would only put them in danger. He had to try and get as far as possible from here. That was the only option available.

Hamilton started the bike, grimacing at the pain in his ankle and set off in the direction of the house. He passed the houses cloaked in darkness and crossed the bridge over the stream once more.

But now, he felt more at peace. He knew that Goldfeld was as good as his word. Penny would be safe.

He rounded a curve at top speed and was blinded by the headlights of a car. Cursing, he braked to slow down and hugged the left side of the road, trying to avoid driving off it.

To his surprise, the car moved to its right, continuing straight at him.

He realised that the occupants of this car were also part of the group of intruders.

It was going to be close.

He whipped past the car, almost scraping it in the process. Behind him, the car screeched to a halt and revved up as it reversed and then prepared to pursue him.

The roar of the car engine came to his ears. He switched gears, willing the bike to go faster.

But he knew that it was a battle that he would ultimately lose.

Every second, the car was gaining on him.

He didn't get a warning.

There was a jerk and he found himself thrown off the bike, and flew through the air as the bike fell on its side and slid off the road, its wheels spinning.

The bastards had rammed him!

He fell heavily to the ground and heard the crunch of bone breaking microseconds before the pain manifested itself in his brain.

He heard the cry of anguish and couldn't believe it had come from him.

The car engine had stopped.

The headlamps had been dimmed and a soft glow now lit up the road in front of the car.

The bike, off to the side of the road, lost in the darkness, was also silent.

A death shroud hung over him woven from the darkness of the night and the silence of his doom.

The sound of boots on loose stones came to him and a pair came into view. He tried to look up but couldn't. There was a strange pain in his right shoulder and neck that wouldn't allow him to move his head.

'So,' the woman said, 'you do know where the coins are. But you won't tell us. That's quite a pity.' She turned to one of the men. 'Check his phone. Did he make any calls?'

The man patted him down, searching for the phone, and pulled it out.

'Phone's dead,' the man observed.

'Call Harper,' the woman ordered. 'Tell him I want his daughter. If she isn't in this house, she must be in the Mayfair apartment. I want her brought in tonight.' She knelt down and stroked his hair. 'Let's see how long you will keep your secrets when you watch what we do to your daughter,' she said softly.

The woman rose. 'Take care of him,' she instructed. 'Once we get what we want, I don't want the body to be found. Let them think he's disappeared. Let them search for him for a while. It'll be fun.'

Hamilton tried to rise but his hands wouldn't support him. 'You bitch!' he spat through the haze of pain and numbness that had enveloped him. 'Whatever it is you're after, you'll never get it.'

The woman laughed softly. 'You would never believe what I'm after, Mr Hamilton,' she sneered. 'And I always get what I want.'

The gurgling of the stream came to his ears as silence fell once more.

He could only hope that his confidence in Goldfeld was not misplaced.

Part 1

6

November, last year

The Dorchester Hotel, London

Christian Van Klueck sat at his laptop and carefully rehearsed what he was going to say. His face was grim. He wasn't happy.

After the success of his mission a year and a half ago, he had been assigned to oversee a project for the Order that had its origins in pre-history, over four thousand years ago.

For centuries, the Order had struggled to find all the pieces of the puzzle, but many fragments were lost in the mists of Time. Eventually, the project had been shelved, though the search for the missing pieces continued.

This, he reflected, was the strength of the Order. The patience. The resilience. The ability to keep moving even if things weren't working out; to focus on more immediate projects while never losing sight of those that had to be temporarily sidelined. And the knack to swiftly get a project back on track if a discovery was made that would enable it to move forward, despite the passage of centuries.

Or, as in this case, over two thousand years.

Van Klueck was proud to be a part of the Order. And an important part, he corrected himself. Which other organisation in the world was so well run, so well structured that it could stay on course for over two thousand years?

A few months ago, they had had a breakthrough. And the project was pulled out, dusted down, and handed over to him.

That much was fine. But when he was told who would be the head of operations for the project and supervise it on the ground, much of his happiness dissipated.

And now, he had the unpleasant task of briefing his head of operations for the job ahead.

The doorbell of the suite rang. He exhaled deeply and then rose to cross the ornately furnished sitting room of the suite and opened the door.

'Hello, Dee,' he greeted the woman who stood outside. 'Come on in.'

7

The Dorchester Hotel, London

The woman called Dee followed Van Klueck into the room.

He indicated for her to sit. 'Drink?' he asked, trying to sound as affable as possible.

'A whisky, please. Single malt would be great if you have one.'

The truth was he hated her from the depths of his heart. Not for any other reason than the fact that, unlike him, she was of the true bloodline. That gave her a distinct advantage over ordinary members of the Order like Van Klueck. Whereas he would have to prove himself, and his loyalty, as he and his family had been doing for all these centuries, people like Dee had no such constraints. Their fealty and commitment were taken for granted. It was in their blood.

Their breeding entitled them to the best assignments, especially those that were close to the heart of the Order's goals and carried great strategic risks.

He knew this was the reason that Dee had been chosen to spearhead this project. While he had gained the confidence of the Order by his success in his previous missions, this particular mission was critical to the Order's long-term objectives. It was the reason why this project had survived for over two thousand years.

He suppressed his hatred of her and poured each of them

a large thirty-year-old Macallan. 'Here you go,' he said, handing a glass to her.

'I presume the find was authenticated,' Dee started off without waiting for any preamble from Van Klueck, who grimaced at her matter-of-factness.

He nodded. 'It was a stroke of luck,' he said, then hesitated. 'You know what the find is, of course?'

Dee shook her head. 'I wasn't privy to that information.' She frowned, clearly displeased that such vital information should have been withheld from her. 'I was only told that there was a spectacular find but it needed to be authenticated. And, of course, that I would be called in if that happened.' She looked at Van Klueck. 'I simply put two and two together. It wasn't hard to do, you know.'

Van Klueck clenched his teeth. He was the one running this operation, not this upstart who was talking down to him. Clearly, she was aware of her status within the Order as a member with the bloodline.

But he consoled himself with the fact that, despite all the privilege she enjoyed, she had to come to him to get the information she needed to do her job. Her special status had not given her free access to all the information about the mission.

'Have you heard of the *Commentarii de Bello Gallico*?' he asked.

Dee shook her head again. 'Sounds like Latin,' she remarked. 'What is it? Is that what was found?'

'The *Commentarii de Bello Gallico* is an account of the Gallic Wars written by Julius Caesar himself. How good is your history?' Van Klueck looked at Dee questioningly.

'Not very good,' Dee replied. 'I know who Julius Caesar was, of course, but that's about as far as I go on this particular subject.'

'Fine. Let me bring you up to speed, then.' Van Klueck paused to take a sip of his whisky, then settled back and started explaining.

8

The briefing

'The *Commentarii de Bello Gallico,* or "Commentaries on the Gallic Wars" was written by Julius Caesar himself, one of the rare first-hand accounts written by generals in ancient times. 'If you were a student of history, you would know that Julius Caesar started his conquest of Gaul in 58 B.C. after the Senate appointed him the governor of Gaul—with a little help from his allies, of course.' He glanced surreptitiously at Dee to see if she had noticed the slur.

Even if she had, she didn't respond or react, so he continued. 'Over the next few years, until around 51 B.C., he brought the whole of Gaul under Roman rule, crushing all resistance until peace reigned in 50 B.C., leaving Caesar free to turn his attention to Rome. But that's another story.'

'So Caesar wrote this book about the Gallic wars while he was campaigning in Gaul,' Dee stated, her voice betraying her impatience. Clearly, she wasn't interested in the history lesson that Van Klueck was imparting to her.

Van Klueck sighed. It was amazing, he thought, that most people of the bloodline whom he had met, took the historical heritage of the Order so lightly. It was people like him, he reflected, who truly valued the history behind everything that the Order did today. And history provided very valuable lessons.

He decided to ignore her obvious need to get to the point. 'Actually,' he replied, a bit stiffly, 'Caesar sent reports to the Senate during the campaign, both to inform them about events on the ground as well as to build his own reputation as a general and conqueror, so that when the time was ripe, the Roman people would welcome him as their ruler.'

Dee sat back and folded her arms, as if resigning herself to his ramblings.

'Many experts believe that the Commentaries were published in 52 or 51 B.C. At any rate, they were extant in 46 B.C. when Cicero commented on them, attesting that they were well known in Rome. So, they could have been published any time between 51 B.C. and 46 B.C.'

'So what's my brief?' Dee couldn't help interrupting again. Her impatience was barely hidden. 'It doesn't really matter to me when they were published or who commented on them.'

'You have to understand the history in order to understand the objective and importance of our mission,' Van Klueck told her, gritting his teeth as he uttered the words. It galled him to include her as an owner of the mission. This was a prime mission for the Order and it should have been his exclusively. There should have been no place for someone like Dee, a novice in his eyes, as a leader of this operation.

But he had no choice.

'I'm not interested in what happened two thousand years ago,' Dee said firmly but gently. Bloodline or not, she had yet to prove her mettle and Van Klueck was well respected in the Order. His last mission, apart from being one of the few successful missions in the existence of the Order, had also been a spectacular one, delivering an ancient secret into their hands; one that could tip the balance in favour of the organisation. It would not help her cause if she upset him before this mission even started.

But once the mission was over and it was a success... Dee smiled inwardly. She was going to make this mission even bigger than the one a year and a half ago. And when she achieved success, she would have no time for the likes of Van Klueck.

'Without knowing the history, you won't have a context,' Van Klueck explained, controlling his irritation.

Though Dee suspected that Van Klueck had an inkling of what she was planning, she was not going to give her plans away by any missteps. Not now.

She nodded and allowed him to continue.

'The Commentaries comprised eight books,' Van Klueck resumed after a sip of his whisky. 'Seven were written by Caesar himself. The eighth was written by Aulus Hirtius, one of his generals. The books cover the period from 58 to 51 B.C.' He fixed Dee with a gaze that indicated that what was to follow was the really important part.

'The copy of the Commentaries that we found was an eleventh-century manuscript on vellum that was transcribed by a monk at the Abbey of St. Gildas de Rhuys in Brittany. This copy contained *nine* books. And it has now been authenticated as a genuine copy of the original book written by Caesar.'

Realisation dawned on Dee. So that's why Van Klueck was going on about Caesar and his books. It was the ninth book that was missing from all the other copies of the Commentaries, which contained what she needed to know.

The details of the secret that was at the heart of her mission.

Suddenly, she was interested in what Van Klueck had to tell her. A thrill of anticipation coursed through her being, like an electric charge, energising her.

She put down her glass and leaned forward, her attention unwavering now, her eyes fixed on Van Klueck's face.

He smiled. These novices, with their disregard for history and the larger context. It took them time to understand the importance of the details. It could make all the difference between success and failure.

'Tell me more,' Dee said. 'What does the ninth book contain?'

9

January, present year

Jerusalem, Israel

Alice leaned back in the single-seater sofa in her hotel room and studied the glass of white wine in her hand. She had just returned from the excavation at Tiberias, and wanted to unwind a bit before joining the rest of the team, for dinner.

She had had a whirlwind existence for the last one year, after returning from India. Bill Patterson, the former US Navy Seal, and Director of the Indo-US task force set up to combat technology-based terrorism, had been of the opinion that the best way to ensure her safety was to hide her in plain sight—and watched over by guards round the clock. Kurt Wallace, the billionaire philanthropist, deeply troubled by her experience in Greece at an excavation funded by his trust, had insisted on taking care of the arrangements.

As a consequence of Wallace's extensive network of contacts, she had embarked on a hectic tour of archaeological sites, museums and universities. At her request, she had been included in archaeological excavations, courses and research projects that involved areas of her interest, which she had never had time to explore.

Now, with her enforced sabbatical from her area of specialisation, she had all the time in the world to catch up on the knowledge that she had wanted to acquire. The academic courses at the various universities she visited and the research projects she took on had been interesting, but her heart lay in the field. She would much rather spend her time digging up artefacts and brushing away dirt from ruins, with a soft brush in the hot sun, than sit in an air-conditioned room poring over books.

Which was why she was finally feeling a bit satisfied. A lot of her research and study had focused on ancient civilisations in the Middle East, but field archaeology was out of the question due to the turmoil in Iraq and Syria, where some of the prime archaeological sites were located. As a result, she had to be content with visiting museums and studying artefacts already salvaged from sites in the Middle East, some of them now destroyed, or spending time on research projects with archaeologists who had completed excavations in those areas the previous year. Only now had she been assigned to an excavation at the ancient site of Tiberias, built in 19 A.D. as the new capital of King Herod Antipas and named after the Roman Emperor, Tiberius Caesar.

Her curiosity about Kurt Wallace had also led her to read two of his books. His theories were interesting but too fantastic to be either realistic or believable. While he presented his evidence—based on thorough research, she had to admit—forcefully and logically, his core belief of an ancient civilisation thousands of years ago that had been the genesis of the human race, was as hard to believe as the conspiracy theories about aliens coming to Earth and seeding modern humans.

It all made her wonder why he was writing these books. He was wealthy; among the richest men in the world and his philanthropic activities were appreciated by all. She had not met anyone yet who had a bad word to say about Kurt Wallace. And, she had to admit, if it had not been for him, she would have met a nasty end in Greece the previous year. It was only through his efforts that she had escaped the fate of some of the other members of that excavation.

Her phone rang, intruding on her thoughts. Her heart skipped a beat as she saw the caller identification and connected the call.

'Alice!' Vijay's voice was a pleasure to hear after all these months. He hadn't called her until now though they had exchanged emails at irregular intervals since her departure from India. The correspondence hadn't been very frequent; her hectic schedule and the travel had constrained her from replying with alacrity to his emails.

'It's great to speak to each other after such a long time,' Vijay was saying. 'How have you been and what are you doing these days? Where are you now? You didn't reply to my email last week.'

'Sorry about that,' Alice laughed, unable to conceal her pleasure at hearing an old friend's voice after so many months. 'I was wrapping up a research project on the Assyrians last week and then had to travel to Jerusalem.' She told him about the excavation in Israel after all her search and studies over the last year. 'I feel like I've just been to college again,' she concluded with a laugh. 'But I'm glad to be finally back at a dig. What about you?'

'Oh, I've been good,' Vijay replied. 'Coping.' He paused. 'I've been trying to reach you for a while.'

There was an uncomfortable silence.

'I know,' Alice said, tentatively. 'I've been bouncing around from one place to another.' She wished she could explain in more detail.

'Heh.' Vijay laughed. A nervous laugh.

'Is something the matter?' Alice wondered why he had been trying to reach her.

'I...I need your help.' Vijay seemed reluctant to explain further, so she helped him along.

'Hey, anything will be better than embarking on another research project after this excavation, with my nose buried in books. Tell me what you need.'

'I received an email almost a year and a half ago,' Vijay began. 'After my return from Kazakhstan. At that time, I didn't know who sent it. This guy, a stranger, called me after sending the email and asked me to meet him six months later, in April.' He paused.

Alice waited for him to continue. She was curious.

'We met eventually,' Vijay continued. 'I was initially suspicious, but he turned out to be genuine. His name is KS. He used to work with my Dad in the Archaeological Survey of India. According to him, my Dad gave him an ancient prism shortly before the accident that killed my parents.' He paused again, clearly affected by his memories of that meeting.

'I don't know where Dad got this prism from but it turns out that the prism has some sort of twin,' Vijay resumed. 'A twin that is in the British museum in London. Both prisms bear cuneiform inscriptions. I don't know what the inscriptions say, though. I went to London a few months ago, to see if I could get a peek at the prism at the museum. Maybe it contains clues that will reveal why my parents died.' There was a moment of silence before he spoke again. 'I believe that the car crash that killed my parents was no accident. They were murdered.'

'Oh my god!' Alice was shocked. 'Do you know that for a fact?'

'No,' Vijay confessed. 'But if my hunch is correct, the two prisms conceal something that will reveal whether their accident was truly what it seemed to be or not.'

'And you need my help in getting to that prism at the museum?' Alice guessed. If Vijay was calling her about this prism, then it was clear to her that he hadn't succeeded in gaining access to it at the museum. Why that was the case was beyond her understanding, but it seemed obvious to her that her background as an archaeologist would be useful to Vijay now.

Vijay wrestled with his emotions. This was a struggle for him. On the one hand there was the murder of Radha. On the other there was the need to know what had happened to his parents. He had grown to loathe the man who he held responsible for Radha's death. Yet, today, he knew that this man was probably the only one who could help him learn about his parents' fate. Much as he hated to admit it, he had no other option.

And Alice was the key to obtaining that man's help.

'Not just *your* help,' he said finally, choking on his emotions, as he articulated what would have been unthinkable just a year ago. 'I need you to contact Wallace. I need *his* help.'

10

Intelligence Bureau Headquarters, New Delhi

Vijay sat across Imran's desk and glared at the IB officer, an exasperated look on his face.

'I don't see why I shouldn't be going back to London,' he told Imran. 'This is personal. I don't think Patterson has any right to tell me what to do.'

Imran sighed. 'I know, Vijay. It's just that you are a target for the Order. Patterson is worried about what might happen if the Order tries something in the UK. And after what happened in Gurgaon, he is also worried about the Order learning about the task force.'

The IB Officer was referring to the incident last March, when Vijay had paid an impulsive visit to the Titan Pharmaceutical offices in Gurgaon and confronted Varun Saxena, their Chief Medical Officer. Vijay had told him clearly that he suspected Saxena's involvement in Radha's murder and had threatened to somehow unearth the role that the Titan CMO had played in that tragic incident. Patterson had been furious and had given Vijay a no-holds-barred dressing down, concluding with a clear ban on Vijay having to do anything with the ongoing investigation into Radha's disappearance.

'More than that, Patterson is worried that I may go looking for clues to Radha's whereabouts,' Vijay shot back.

'Will you?' Imran asked Vijay.

'I promised Patterson I wouldn't, after I met Saxena,' Vijay replied, bitterly. 'I'm not going to break that promise. Besides, you promised me that you would go looking for her. And I trust you.' He paused. 'Did you find anything in Abu Dhabi?'

Imran didn't respond. He had still not told Vijay about the latest information regarding Radha. He contemplated the best way to answer Vijay's question. Perhaps it was prudent to be honest.

'We did,' he said quietly.

Vijay leaned forward, an anxious expression on his face. Imran's tone had not been upbeat. 'And?'

'I'm sorry, Vijay,' Imran continued, his voice still low. 'We traced her to a hospital in Abu Dhabi where Saxena had taken her. She was in that hospital for six days, after which she was declared dead.'

Vijay slumped back in his chair, his face registering his shock. Despite the video showing Radha being shot, despite knowing that her chances of survival were very slim, despite continuing to talk about finding her body, somewhere deep down he had hoped that there was just the slightest chance that she may be alive.

Now, even that hope was extinguished.

'Where's her body?' he demanded, gruffly, choking on his emotions. 'Why haven't you got her body back?'

Imran winced. This was the most difficult part of the conversation. It was something he had dreaded and had been putting off for the last two months.

'There's no body, Vijay,' he said finally. 'Saxena took her body from the hospital and disappeared. We don't know where she is right now. But we will find out. I promise you that.'

Tears were beginning to well up in Vijay's eyes. He nodded, unable to speak. It was over a year now and he was no closer to finding Radha than he had been twelve months ago.

Regent's Park, London

Harper waited in the lounge, trying to hide his nervousness. There were sofas in the room that looked quite comfortable, but he remained standing, his arms folded, the fingers of one hand drumming against the other arm.

The other men in the room—his team—were more relaxed. They could be, he thought sardonically. After all, they didn't have to face up to the boss. Harper was a big man, over 6 feet 4 inches, and all muscle. But the boss had a reputation. Few people had met or seen the boss since he had taken over this cell two months ago. It had been quickly established that, if you were summoned by the new boss, you were in trouble. The boss seemed to prefer meeting the men only if they failed to achieve their goals.

And people, once summoned to the presence of the boss, were never seen again.

The trouble was, Harper didn't know why he had been summoned. As far as he knew, he hadn't failed to deliver. What did the boss want from him, then?

The door opened and a swarthy, stocky man emerged. 'The boss will see you now.' He jerked a finger at the door he had just come through.

Harper cleared his throat and crossed the threshold to the room within. The swarthy man looked at the four others accompanying Harper and indicated that they should wait while Harper was inside.

The four men gave each other puzzled looks as the swarthy man followed Harper inside and shut the door behind him.

Harper was still trying to get over the initial shock that had overcome him as he entered the room.

The new boss was a woman!

He had just begun to wonder how this slim, young and good-looking woman of medium height had created such a frenzy of fear around her, when she looked right at him.

And then he noticed. His jaw sagged.

'I have a special assignment for you,' the boss said.

Still amazed, Harper listened as the woman in front of him told him what he needed to do.

'I don't know, boss,' Harper said, tentatively, still unable to take his eyes off her face. It was eerie. 'You want us to find someone on Ernest Hamilton's staff and bribe them to let us into his house in Hertfordshire. Nothing more?'

The boss looked at him sharply. 'That is exactly what I said. And promise any sum of money that will get this done. Once we're in, we'll take care of the contact as well.'

Harper was disappointed. He and his men were known for their skills in hunting and killing. This was a wimpy job. He wasn't interested.

'If you can't do it, I'll find someone else.' The boss fixed him with an icy stare, her voice cold and sharp as a dagger. The air in the room had suddenly become frosty. 'But that will make you dispensable, won't it?'

Harper glanced at the swarthy man and but saw no reassurance on his face.

He nodded, a trifle eagerly. Something about that voice…

It was cold as steel and the undercurrent seemed to suck the very air out of the room.

'Good. You have three weeks to do this.'

Harper was barely able to acknowledge the instruction and stagger out of the room. When he was outside, he took several deep breaths, as if he had been holding his breath inside the room. He looked at his men. They were staring at him, wondering what had happened inside. Beads of sweat dotted his forehead.

The swarthy man had whispered to him before he left the room. A warning. 'We'll be watching you, Harper. Don't screw up.'

Harper steadied himself. He was not going to fail. The picture of the boss's face was still fresh in his mind. The one thing that he had noticed about her, after her sex, was burned into his memory.

Her face. While the features were human, it didn't seem a human face at all. He struggled to find the right words to describe what he thought of her but nothing he could think of made sense. It was unnatural. Unreal. Out of this world.

Her face had *glowed*. There was no other way to describe it.

11

February, present year

The British Museum, London

David Barrows, the Director of the British Museum studied the three people seated before him. It was 6.30 pm and the museum was closed but he had given his visitors an appointment at this specific time for two reasons.

The first reason was their unusual request to examine an ancient artefact that was worthless but for its great antiquity. The second was that their request was backed by an endorsement from two people who were of great importance to the museum. One was Clive Dawkins, a Trustee of the museum who was well respected, and the other was Kurt Wallace, who had contributed generously to the museum, in cash and kind, over the years. Barrows had no doubt that Dawkins's request had been influenced by the fact that Wallace was backing this group, but there it was. It had been difficult for him to turn down this meeting.

'I understand from these letters,' Barrows indicated the documents on his table, 'that both Mr Dawkins and Mr Wallace are desirous that you be permitted to inspect this artefact at close quarters.'

'That's right,' Alice nodded, smiling pleasantly.

'I do hope I'm not being intrusive,' Barrows continued, 'but I'm curious. I have no doubt that you are an archaeologist whom both these gentlemen hold in high esteem. However, Assyrian history is not your area. I did some research before our meeting and learned this for a fact. And I don't understand your interest in this specific artefact.'

Vijay and Alice exchanged glances. It seemed that Barrows was not aware of Vijay's request to see the artefact a few months ago.

'You see,' Barrows explained, 'this artefact is part of a collection that was subject to an attempted robbery last year while it was being brought back to the museum. We didn't lose anything from the collection but we did lose two of our security staff. It was quite unfortunate.'

'I understand, Mr Barrows,' Alice nodded. 'Let me put it this way. I've been doing a lot of research on Assyrian excavations in the last one year, among other things.' It was perfectly true. She had indeed spent a lot of time on the archaeology of the Middle East. It was one of the areas that she had neglected until now. 'And I believe that this prism may provide answers to some of the questions that still remain about that period. Of course, I can't be absolutely sure until I see it.'

'You do realise, Ms Turner, that I cannot permit you to physically remove the artefact from the premises of the museum? So I am curious to learn how you will find the answers you seek.'

'I plan to take high resolution photographs of the artefact.' Alice had rehearsed her responses before the meeting. She had known the questions that would be directed her way based on her request. 'I will then take the help of Saul Goldfeld to decipher the inscriptions.'

Barrows nodded. He knew Goldfeld. The man was eccentric but he was one of the leading authorities on ancient scripts in the Western world.

'Right, then. I won't detain you any longer.' Barrows looked at Vijay and Harry Briggs, the former SAS Mobile Trooper, who had been assigned to Vijay as his partner from the task force in Britain. 'Would both of you like to wait in the security office?'

'I'd prefer if you can allow them to accompany me,' Alice smiled at Barrows. 'Please.'

Barrows nodded and stood up to shake their hands. 'I hope you find what you are looking for.'

Alice and Vijay nodded their thanks and left, Harry striding alongside them, curious to see what they would find.

12

Saul Goldfeld's residence

South Kensington, London

Saul Goldfeld frowned at the inscription on the screen of his laptop. It didn't make sense. He looked at his notes and tapped his pencil on the desk. What was out of place? He couldn't figure out.

He sighed. The inscription was part of a thousand-year-old copper scroll that had just been discovered in a tomb outside Jerusalem. He worked with the Tel Aviv museum, lending his expertise when needed, though he seldom travelled to Israel. The scroll itself was tightly wound into a compact cylinder but the team at the Tel Aviv museum had used a new technique to read its contents without unrolling it. This technology had been a huge blessing for people like Goldfeld, whose job was made more difficult by the damage inflicted upon scrolls like this one when they were unrolled after centuries of being rolled tight.

His mobile phone rang. He looked at the caller identification and smiled. It was one of his favourite archaeologists.

'Alice!' he boomed into the phone. 'To what do I owe the pleasure?'

'I'm in London and need your help,' Alice replied, simply.

'In London and you haven't dropped by to see me?' Goldfeld allowed a hint of indignation to seep into his voice.

'Oh don't worry, I'll be there in an hour.'

'That's quick,' Goldfeld responded. 'And you'll tell me when you get here about the help you need?'

Alice laughed. 'I've already sent you an email. Will you take a look at it while we're on our way there?'

'We?'

'I have some friends with me. I'll explain when I'm there.'

'Oh, all right. I was anyway looking for a diversion from the project I'm working on for Tel Aviv. This is as good as it gets. See you.' Goldfeld disconnected and quickly removed the inscription from the screen, bringing up his email inbox and opening Alice's email.

There were sixteen attachments. All images. He started clicking on each one to see what the files contained. His eyes glinted with excitement as he saw the images on the screen. This was interesting stuff.

Goldfeld began playing with the images, sorting them, rotating them. He had realised what he was seeing and knew what he was looking for. All he had to do was find it.

An hour passed as he patiently tried out every combination he could think of.

Then, things fell into place. He saw the pattern emerge. And his jaw fell open in astonishment as he began reading the inscriptions that jumped out at him from the laptop screen.

What was Alice up to?

13

Ancient inscriptions

'Where the devil did you get these photographs from?' Saul fixed Alice with a curious eye. 'I recognise one set of inscriptions from a prism in the British museum. But the inscriptions on the second prism are new to me. I've never laid eyes on them before and if that prism had been in any museum, I'd have known about it. If I'm not mistaken, these inscriptions are ancient. Really old. Close to 4000 years old, if I know my stuff.'

'And you certainly do, my dear Saul,' Alice responded cheerfully. Goldfeld was an old friend and had been greeted by her with a warm hug when he opened the door to receive them.

Alice, Vijay and Harry were now sitting in the study, sipping wine that Goldfeld had brought out for them. He was a thin, bespectacled man, just over forty-five years of age, and just under 6 feet in height. His hair had begun to grey, giving him an academic look that suited his profession. Solid gold earrings completed the picture, jarring a bit with the academic look. But Goldfeld didn't care. Ancient history, scrolls, inscriptions, carvings and stones were his life and sole interest. Nothing else mattered.

Goldfeld sighed. 'So you aren't going to satiate my curiosity about the source of these inscriptions.'

'I really think you are better off not knowing,' Alice said. 'But did you manage to figure them out?'

'It is really quite simple,' Goldfeld turned to the laptop and angled it so they could all see the screen clearly. 'Of course, you need both the prisms to figure it out. Each prism, by itself, is useless. The inscriptions on them are incomplete. It is only when you have both that you can work out the complete inscriptions.'

Goldfeld clicked the trackpad and two images, placed alongside each other, flashed on the screen. Each image showed one face of the octagonal prisms, with two faces angling away to the back of the image on either side of the face in the foreground. 'You need to know how to read this kind of cuneiform,' he explained. Otherwise you wouldn't know how to place the prisms.'

He pointed with his finger. 'The inscriptions are not to be read with the prisms positioned vertically like this.' He clicked the trackpad again and the images seemed to rotate and flip over on their sides, so that the long edges of the prism were now horizontal and parallel to the laptop keyboard.

'Now, the inscriptions can be read. Horizontally.' He ran his finger along the lines of the cuneiform script indicating the direction in which the script was supposed to be read. 'But even now, each face has incomplete inscriptions on it. Now if you do this...' He clicked again and the two images seemed to merge so that the two prisms were now positioned end to end, with the bottom of one prism touching the top of the other. 'And, voila, you get a complete story, inscribed on all the eight sides!'

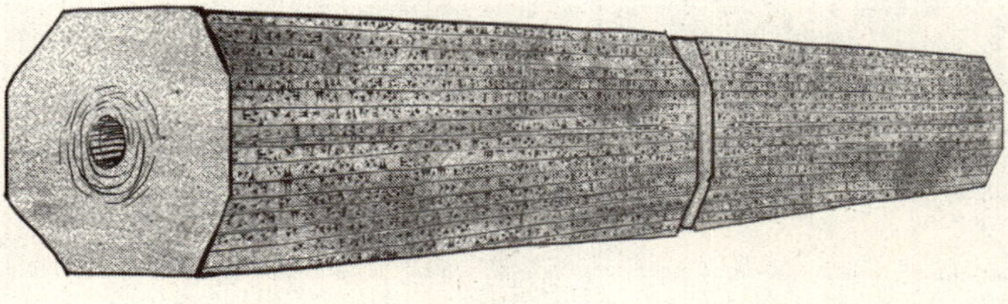

Reading the inscriptions on the prisms

'Wow!' Vijay and Alice looked at each other. They had seen instances of ancient inscriptions earlier, that needed to be read in specific ways to make sense. Every time, those inscriptions had concealed a deadly secret.

What deadly secret did this prism conceal?

14

Saul Goldfeld's residence

'And what's the story, Saul?' Alice wanted Goldfeld to elaborate.

Goldfeld beamed. 'Now this is where it really gets interesting. Have you heard of Semiramis?'

Vijay shook his head. Harry looked puzzled. Only Alice had a gleam in her eyes. She had read about Semiramis in detail during her research into Assyrian legends over the course of the last year.

'Are you saying that the prisms contain a story about Semiramis?' She couldn't believe the possibility. 'That would mean this is the first possible piece of evidence that she was not a mythical figure but a historical one.'

Goldfeld held up his hands. 'Not so fast, my dear. I believe this story is about Semiramis. But that doesn't have to mean I am right. The name of the central figure of the story inscribed on the prism is actually *Samí-Rámési*, which I am interpreting as Semiramis; a plausible translation in English. And even if I am correct, this really cannot be taken as historical evidence. It still is just a story, like all the other myths about her. Until we find more artefacts that support the existence of Semiramis, we really can't be conclusive about whether she was a historical figure or just a myth.'

'Will one of you please explain who you are talking about? Harry and I have no clue,' Vijay complained.

Goldfeld gestured to Alice. 'Would you like to do the honours?'

'Sorry, we got a little carried away in our excitement,' Alice smiled sheepishly. 'As you would have figured by now, Semiramis is a mythical figure, so no one really knows who she is or where she came from. There are also conflicting versions of the myths surrounding her. What the myths do agree on is that she was a great queen of the Assyrian empire and conquered Egypt, Ethiopia, much of Asia and even waged a battle in what is today India, where she suffered a massive defeat on the banks of the Indus against a ruler who we know as Strabrobates, which is the name the Greeks gave him.'

The reference to the banks of the Indus seemed to set off a recollection in Vijay's mind. 'Hang on, didn't you mention her name to us when we were talking about Alexander the Great and his march through the Makran desert? You had said something about Cyrus the Great and Semiramis crossing the Makran before Alexander did.'

Alice knew that Vijay had a prodigious memory so she was not surprised that he would remember a conversation like this. 'That's right,' she agreed. 'Semiramis had crossed the Makran desert when she waged her ill-fated war against Strabrobates.'

Harry looked confused. 'Maybe I'm missing something here but if you chaps know so much about Semiramis and where she went and what she did, isn't all that history?'

'I'm afraid not,' Goldfeld clarified. 'History is not just an aggregation of events or the deeds of people. At least it should not be that way. History is about verifiable facts. If there are deeds and events, there should be evidence to support them—either documentary evidence in the form of credible historical accounts or artefacts that prove that the events took place and the people involved existed. Take this prism, for example. There's an impressive story here. But that doesn't mean it is true. We had a wonderful story on a Sumerian tablet, which we now call the Epic of Gilgamesh. It doesn't necessarily mean it is true. But if we find evidence to back it up, it becomes factual and, therefore, history. Until then, it stays a legend or a myth. Interesting, entertaining, even spellbinding. But not history.'

'Like Asoka the Great,' Vijay mused. 'A legend that no one believed was true until Princep deciphered the first edicts and established the fact that Asoka did exist.'

'Exactly,' Goldfeld beamed, happy that there was understanding in the group now.

'You know,' Alice said thoughtfully, 'that is exactly what Kurt Wallace has a problem with. I've been reading his books.'

'Not you, too, Alice! You're an archaeologist, for god's sake. How can you go about believing that drivel?' Goldfeld groaned.

'He does have a point, though,' Alice countered. 'As archaeologists and historians, we have a tendency to make assumptions that may not necessarily be true. Take the Asoka example that Vijay gave. If Princep had never discovered the edicts, we would never have believed that Asoka even existed. Who knows what other discoveries we have cast by the wayside just because we want to stick to our academic dogmas? Or because most of us are too afraid to challenge them?'

Vijay coughed. 'Uh, guys, we're digressing. You were telling us about Semiramis.'

It was Goldfeld's turn to look sheepish. 'Alice gave you a pretty good background about Semiramis,' he took up the narrative. 'Much of what we know about Semiramis comes from a Greek historian called Diodorus Siculus, who lived around the same time as Julius Caesar. He, in turn, is said to have taken his material for the Semiramis story largely from Ctesias of Cnide. But today, many historians believe that much of his writings, especially the stories concerning Semiramis were a mix of fantasy and legend and had little to do with historical facts. According to Diodorus, King Ninus of Assyria built a city that became Nineveh, which you are familiar with from the Bible. Of course, the Bible attributes the building of Nineveh to Nimrod, a descendent of Noah, better known as the chief instigator of the Tower of Babel. Scholars have placed Ninus or Nimrod at around 2180 B.C. and assumed that both are the same person. There is no historical basis for this.'

Goldfeld paused and looked at Vijay to see if there were any questions. Seeing that there were none, he continued. 'Nineveh is also a historical city, mentioned during the reign of Shamsi Adad I, around 1800 B.C. The city has long been associated with the worship of Ishtar, the Akkadian goddess of fertility and love, war, rain and thunderstorms. According to Diodorus, when Ninus was campaigning against Bactria, he called upon his general, Onnes, for help since the Bactrians had the upper hand. Semiramis was the wife of Onnes and she suggested a battle plan to help salvage the battle. The Assyrians implemented her strategy and the battle was won. Ninus was impressed with her intelligence and overwhelmed by her beauty and wanted to marry her. Eventually, he did and Semiramis became Queen of the Assyrians. After Ninus died, Semiramis ruled until her son Ninyas is said to have plotted against her and overthrown her. Her rule, some say, lasted forty-two years. When Ninyas came to the throne, Semiramis disappeared. No one knows where she went. Just as no one knows where she came from, unless you believe the myth about a goddess giving birth to her and abandoning her, after which doves in a place called Ascalon brought her up. Later, she was associated with Astarte of Ascalon—the moon goddess, who is also a version of Ishtar.'

'Okay, that's a lot of information. She does sound like a mythical figure to me,' Harry remarked. 'I don't remember seeing anything about Semiramis in the British museum.'

Vijay was silent. From his own experience, he knew better than to jump to conclusions. After all, hadn't he discovered secrets from the Mahabharata that had long been assumed to be myths, only to learn that at least some of the so-called myths had a kernel of truth in them, wrapped in mysticism and fantasy? Who knew if this wasn't the case with Semiramis? A queen forgotten by history, her story buried in obscurity, maybe even deliberately ignored for some reason? It wouldn't be the first time this had happened.

Goldfeld pursed his lips. 'I guess you could say that,' he replied. 'Though historians have taken a stab at trying to place her historically. Speiser, for example, believed that the Assyrian king Tukulti-Ninurta was a possible prototype for Ninus. Other historians believe that Semiramis was actually Sammu-ramat, the mother of the Assyrian king Adad-Nirari III, and the wife of Shamshi-Adad V. The stela of Sammu-ramat has been found at Ashur and there is also an inscription at Nimrud, which shows that she ruled after the death of her husband and before the rule of her son, probably when he was a minor. These historians have placed her rule at around 810 to 805 B.C. Interestingly, there is also a wall between the ancient old and new palace which has a detailed carving of Semiramis hunting a leopard using a javelin, while on horseback, and Ninus, her husband, hunting a lion.'

'So, what does the prism say about this mysterious queen who may have existed either around 2180 B.C. or 800 B.C.?' Vijay enquired.

Goldfeld glanced back at the laptop screen. 'It's a great story,' he said. 'But I'm not sure whether this one really indicates that she did exist, or just adds to the myths surrounding her. Okay, here we go.'

15

The story on the prisms

'I'm not going to translate the inscription on the prism line by line,' Goldfeld clarified. 'I'm summarising the story it contains. There's a lot of stuff in there about how great and glorious Semiramis was and how she was the moon goddess and the goddess of fertility and so on. Stuff that we already know from the myths. And from the writings of Diodorus.'

He consulted his notes. 'The story on the prism starts with a meeting between Semiramis and a priest of some sort from the north-west, an elderly man who is described in quite a bit of detail actually. He's bearded, with long hair, fair skin and blue eyes and is dressed in white robes. This priest tells Semiramis about a secret legend that has been passed down for generations by an ancient people referred to as the "Lords of Light". The legend describes an ancient and powerful device, which is hidden in a secret location in the land where Semiramis was born. He asks her, as the all-powerful ruler of the world, to go back and find this device. He tells her that the "brothers in the east", whatever that means, guard this device. And he also, quite conveniently, gives her the location of the device—a secret that has been transmitted orally for generations and is known to none but the "brothers".

Goldfeld looked up. 'Then, the story gets into more familiar territory, though it goes against the grain of the legend narrated by Diodorus. It narrates how Semiramis musters a large army and marches to the banks of the Indus, which is where the device is hidden. She is challenged by the "brothers of the east" led by a priest king called Sthavarapati who rules a kingdom on the banks of the Indus. A fierce battle follows, in which Semiramis is missing in action. She is nowhere to be found on the battlefield. The inscriptions say that she disappears into the desert without an explanation, leaving her generals to lead the Assyrians into battle. Her army, dispirited by her absence, begins to wilt under the aggression of the opponent. Eventually, they are routed and flee back across the Indus in retreat. This is when Semiramis makes a dramatic appearance, with the device that she has come all this way to find. She reveals her possession of the device to Sthavarapati and the "brothers of the east", who shrink back and allow her to return in peace. Semiramis returns to Nineveh, defeated in battle but victorious in her mission.

'Her joy, however, is short-lived, as her son has been plotting against her in her absence and decides to stake his claim as the true ruler of Assyria. According to the story, Semiramis had once consulted the Oracle of Jupiter-Ammon in Ethiopia and was told that her reign would end when her son rebelled against her. She realises that the prophecy has come to pass and travels to the land of the priests in the northwest, carrying the device with her. The story ends with a description of her death and burial on a hill that is sacred to the priests. There is no mention of what happens to the device.'

'Does the story say what the device is?' Alice wanted to know. 'None of the myths about Semiramis mention any kind of device though they all seem to agree that Semiramis was routed and almost lost her life in India.'

'Not really,' Goldfeld perused his notes once more. 'The only clue to the nature of the device lies in what the priest tells Semiramis. He calls it a...' Goldfeld hesitated as he looked at his notes and then again at the laptop screen. 'Yes, I guess that's the best translation I have for what's on the prism. It says, "sceptre of light". That's odd and doesn't really make sense. The priest says that the "sceptre of light" will enable his people to regain the power that the Lords of Light once possessed in their lands.'

There was silence in the room once he had finished speaking. Alice looked at Vijay. He looked crestfallen. She knew what he was thinking. He had pinned all his hopes on deciphering the inscriptions on the prism. This had been his sole means of possibly learning what the truth was behind his parents' accident. And the story they had just heard didn't seem to lead anywhere.

Vijay brooded over the dead end they had reached. His father may have been killed for the prism he had possessed. He had thought that he would finally discover why. He had been certain that, once he had both sets of inscriptions, he would find what he was looking for. Yet, all that they had unearthed was a fairy tale. A myth about a long-dead queen, whose existence itself was in doubt, and a fantastic story about a sceptre of light.

Like tales from the Arabian Nights.

He laughed a hollow laugh. 'I guess that's it then,' he said. 'End of the road.' He rose and shook Goldfeld's hand. 'I owe you a lot for clearing this up for me,' he told the historian. 'At least I now know there's no point pursuing this further.'

Goldfeld nodded. He didn't know what Vijay meant, but he could sense his disappointment. 'If there's ever anything else I can help you with, Vijay, let me know.'

Vijay nodded and opened the front door and stepped out into the cold London night. A light rain was falling but he ignored it as Alice and Harry joined him. He pulled his overcoat tight and walked faster. All he wanted now was to get back home as soon as possible.

He couldn't shake off his despondency. This trail was cold. His thoughts turned to Radha. Imran hadn't had any luck in finding where Saxena had taken her. Was that trail going to end the same way?

16

Outside Saul Goldfeld's residence

'They're leaving Goldfeld's place now,' Petrovsky muttered into his microphone. 'Should I follow them?'

'Of course,' Harper's voice came back over Petrovsky's earphone. 'Don't let them out of your sight for even a second. Even if you have to pee.'

Petrovsky grimaced. He had been out in the rain for the last few hours, following Alice and Vijay to the British Museum and then to Goldfeld's house. It had been a cold, wet mission for him. And now it looked like it was only going to continue.

Well, if it had to be done, he'd better do it. He turned up the collar of his overcoat and began following Vijay and Alice at a discreet distance.

He hadn't gone more than a few yards, when his path was blocked by a large black man.

Petrovsky was no pushover. Standing at 6 feet, 3 inches, he was well muscled and had served in the Ukranian military before deserting when the political problems began in Ukraine. Rather than fighting the rebels, he found it more lucrative to serve as a mercenary. There were plenty of opportunities for people with military training in all kinds of dark, nefarious activities around the world.

And they paid in dollars.

But he still baulked at the sight of the man who stood in his way. The man stood a good five inches taller than Petrovsky and wore a sleeveless leather jacket that revealed his muscled arms, which glistened in the light of the street lamps and the rain.

'Turn back.' The man had a distinctive British accent.

Petrovsky understood. This was some sort of security assigned to the two people he had been tasked to shadow. But he hadn't been told that they had a security cover. Had their intel failed?

'Get. Out. Of. My. Way.' Petrovsky uttered each word with a distinct emphasis. He wasn't about to give up on his assignment.

His opponent shrugged. 'Looks like you want to do it the hard way.'

Petrovsky realised with a start that there were now three other men standing around him.

'Mayday,' he hissed into his microphone. 'I need back up. Now!'

Two men grabbed his arms and the big man who had spoken to him lashed out with powerful punches to Petrovsky's face, head and body.

Petrovsky was a tough man but the ferocity of the assault was something few could have withstood. He felt himself slipping into an abyss of darkness.

The men holding him let go and he crumpled to the ground.

'Stay away from them. Or, next time, I'm gonna kill you,' he heard the black man say as the darkness overcame him.

17

2002 B.C.

Near the River Indus, modern-day Pakistan

Semiramis stood on the bank of the Indus and stared out across the river at the army that had assembled on the opposite bank. For the first time in her life, she wondered if she had underestimated the enemy.

Her thoughts flitted back to her meeting with the priests two nights ago. She had sent a messenger to Sthavarapati and asked for an audience with him and his priestly brothers. She had been confident of securing the audience. Her confidence came, not from the fact that she was the most powerful queen of her time, but the fact that Sthavarapati knew who she really was. And where she came from. Surely he wouldn't refuse her?

She had been correct about that. The messenger had come back with an assurance of safe passage across the river to the court of the priest-king.

But that was the only thing that had gone according to plan.

Sthavarapati had greeted her and welcomed her cordially enough. 'You have come a long way, Queen *Samí-Rámési*,' he smiled, using her true name, and bowed. 'What is it that you seek in these lands?'

He left his question incomplete but she knew what he was asking.

Why have you come back to the lands that you forsook so many years ago?

She returned his smile. 'I seek something special. Something that is precious to your people. But only I know where it is.'

Sthavarapati frowned. 'And what is that? I can think of nothing that is dear to us that you would know of and we would not.'

Semiramis told him.

Sthavarapati's reaction had been immediate and unexpected. His face grew dark with rage. 'Of all people,' he thundered, 'you have the least right to possess a celestial weapon! You do not belong here anymore. You may have become a queen, for that was your destiny in this life, but our people will never forget that you turned your back on us. And now you come back only because you wish to possess what will never rightfully be yours!'

The queen's beautiful face creased with lines of worry. She had hoped for the cooperation of the priests. With their help, finding the celestial device would have been child's play. If they were going to be antagonistic, it would be much harder. Not impossible, but she could have done without the additional complication.

'Understand this,' she told the king in a calm voice. Years of experience dealing with soldiers, commanding them, leading them in battle, had taught her how to deal with men, how to ensure that they listened to her. 'I will find the celestial device without your help, if necessary. I came here with the intention of acquiring it and I will not return without it. If you don't wish to help, don't. You can watch me find the device and march away with it.'

Sthavarapati's rage seemed to increase at her words. 'So you think we will stand by and allow you to loot our precious treasure? Hear this, O Queen. You will have to battle us before we allow you to search for it!'

The queen's heart sank. It was bad enough that they would not help. A war was something she could not afford. True, she had brought her army in full strength on this journey, in anticipation of this situation. But she had hoped with all her heart that it never would come to pass.

She tightened her lips. 'As you wish, your Majesty,' she said coldly. 'Do what you will. My army will be ready for battle.'

Semiramis swept out of Sthavarapati's palace and rode back across the river to her army. She roused them and instructed them to prepare for war.

But she was worried. For the first time since she had become the ruler of Assyria, she would not be there to lead her soldiers into battle. Never before had it happened that Semiramis was missing from the battlefield.

She turned away from gazing upon the enemy's troops and gave last-minute instructions to her generals. They looked as doubtful as she felt.

'Don't worry,' she said. She was taking a small band of trusted soldiers with her. 'I know where I am going. It will take me not more than three days to return. Engage with the enemy. Ensure that you do not give ground until I am back, no matter what happens. Once I am back, we will be victorious, I promise you.'

The generals nodded. But their confidence levels were low. For them, as it was for the people of Assyria, Semiramis was more than a queen. She was Ishtar, the goddess of fertility, war and storms. She was the consort of Baal. If the goddess of war was going to abandon them just before a battle, what chance did they stand?

Semiramis rode away, filled with misgivings. She knew where to look for the device. The Makran desert was large. But the priest from the northwest had given her clear instructions. His knowledge was derived, through generations of oral transmission, from the time of the Lords of Light. And maybe even before them. From the days of old. When gods, not men, ruled the earth.

She was going to find the celestial device. And when she had it in her possession, she was truly going to be a goddess.

Part 2

18

February, present year

Wiltshire, England

'I still don't know why I allowed you to talk me into this,' Vijay grumbled as the car swept down the A303. Goldfeld had offered to drive him and Alice down to the Salisbury plains, after Alice had suggested that Vijay needed a break in the countryside. She was worried about his dark mood since that evening a week ago, in Goldfeld's study. The last week had been spent with Vijay largely shutting himself up in his room, emerging only for meals, which were spent in silence.

Alice had been uncomfortable and unsure of what she should do. A part of her wanted to return to the US and get on with her life. And another part of her was telling her that her place was here, by Vijay's side. In this hour of darkness, she could not abandon him.

Last evening, over a drink with Goldfeld, when Alice found herself engaged in conversation with him, with Vijay playing the part of a listener, she had suggested this excursion and Goldfeld had promptly offered to play chauffeur.

'That is why,' Alice pointed out of the window of the car as the circle of stones came into view; giant protrusions that stood out in an otherwise largely featureless plain that stretched out on all sides as far as the eye could see.

Despite his morose mood, Vijay could not help but be enthralled by the sight of Stonehenge. Somewhere inside, a sense of excitement awakened. Over the last two years, he had become so involved with ancient history that a sight like this could not fail to stir him.

Goldfeld parked the car and they walked across to the Visitor Centre, which was just opening. They were among the first few people in the queue and quickly boarded the minibus that would take them to the stone circle.

The sky was overcast with angry black clouds hovering low over them, casting a dismal gloom over the stones. With his connections, the historian had got them access to the inner circle of stones, where semi-darkness lurked in the shadow of some of the larger stones, reflecting the mood of the sky above.

'Would you like me to explain the structure and layout to you?' Goldfeld asked.

Both Vijay and Alice nodded. Vijay was now eager to learn more about the ancient site. He had heard a lot about Stonehenge but had never visited it.

'Right,' Goldfeld began. He gestured around them, to the circular banks of earth, which were clearly delineated, surrounding the circle of stones at the centre, interspersed at intervals with gaps in the structure where the ground was flat rather than concave. 'This is the original henge. A henge, by the way, refers to the circular banks of earth with a parallel internal ditch, and not to the stones themselves. The stone monument was built around 4500 years ago and was modelled on a timber structure that was built much earlier.'

'How do you date stone?' Vijay wanted to know. 'I've heard of radio carbon dating for organic matter and thermo luminescence dating for shards of pottery, but never of any technique to date stone.'

'We don't actually date the stone,' Alice explained. 'We look for organic material—bones, remains of hearths or fires—and pottery shards in the ground under the stones, if they can be lifted; or at the site if the stones are too heavy to lift, as in the case of Stonehenge. If we find animal or human bones or even pottery under the stones, we can date those and since they would have to have been there before the stone was placed at that spot, the structure, rather than the stone, can be dated to the time the organic remains or pottery were buried there.'

'But the stones could have been placed there later,' Vijay observed. 'For example, if you found bones that you could date to 2500 B.C., the stones could have been put over the bones in 1000 B.C. but you would date the structure to 2500 B.C. That would mean an error of 1500 years in the dating of the structure.'

'It is a bit approximate,' Alice admitted, 'but that's the accepted manner of dating all sites where stone is used in construction.'

'Not just that,' Vijay persisted. 'For something like Stonehenge, if you found organic matter in a ditch and dated it to 2000 B.C., that doesn't mean the stones were placed there at the same time, right? The stones could have been erected in, say, 5000 B.C. but the organic matter could have been buried 3000 years later. How does that help?'

'Actually it isn't that random, Vijay,' Alice clarified. 'It isn't just about finding organic matter anywhere. For accurate dating, you need organic matter that is closely associated with the stones. For Stonehenge, there was an excavation a few years ago—the first excavation permitted since 1946—when a small patch of turf between the two circles of the sarsen stones was dug up. The objective was to collect organic matter from the original bluestone sockets that are now buried under the monument. A selection of samples from the organic matter was then carbon-dated using modern techniques and a date range of 2400 to 2200 B.C. was arrived at.' She looked at Vijay and laughed. 'Does that convince you, Mr Sceptic?'

Alice's mind flashed back to their college days. Vijay had always been curious, willing—almost eager—to challenge established conventions. She could see that he hadn't changed in that respect, at least.

Vijay shrugged. He didn't look entirely convinced. 'I guess so,' he said, sounding non-committal. 'You would know better. This is your field, not mine. I was just a bit confused, that's all.'

Alice prodded him in the ribs with an elbow. 'Come on, then, let's listen to Saul. You interrupted him just when he was warming up.' She flashed a smile at Saul, who picked up the narrative once again as he returned her smile.

'This monument, at least the way you see it today, was constructed in three phases,' Goldfeld resumed his commentary as they reached the outer circle of trilithons—two upright stones capped by a horizontal stone. 'The first phase was the construction of the encircling ditch which consists of a high internal earth bank with an exterior bank encircling the inner bank. Inside this ditch, fifty-six holes were dug. These are now called Aubrey holes after John Aubrey, the first antiquarian who discovered them. It is speculated that timber posts may have been implanted in these holes.' He pointed out a few, which were clearly visible and helpfully marked out with labels.

'The second phase,' Goldfeld continued, 'is still the subject of debate and speculation. But the conclusion seems to be that the final Stonehenge mirrored the wooden circle that existed prior to the erection of the stones. The problem lies in the fact that the postholes are scattered at random, not in a perfect circle, while the stones are arranged very thoughtfully. The last phase was when the stones arrived. The final plan of Stonehenge, when it was complete, consisted of an inner horseshoe formation of bluestones, surrounded by a horseshoe formation of sarsen trilithons. This was further encircled by a circle of bluestones, which, in turn were encircled by a complete circle of trilithons.'

Stonehenge as it would have looked in 2400 B.C.

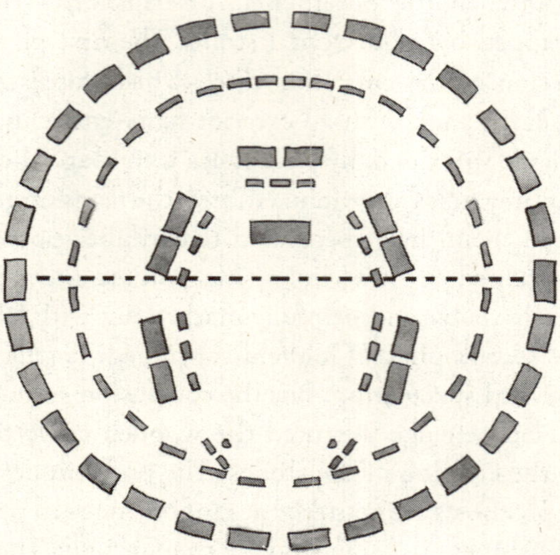

Plan of Stonehenge viewed from the top, as it would have looked in 2400 B.C.

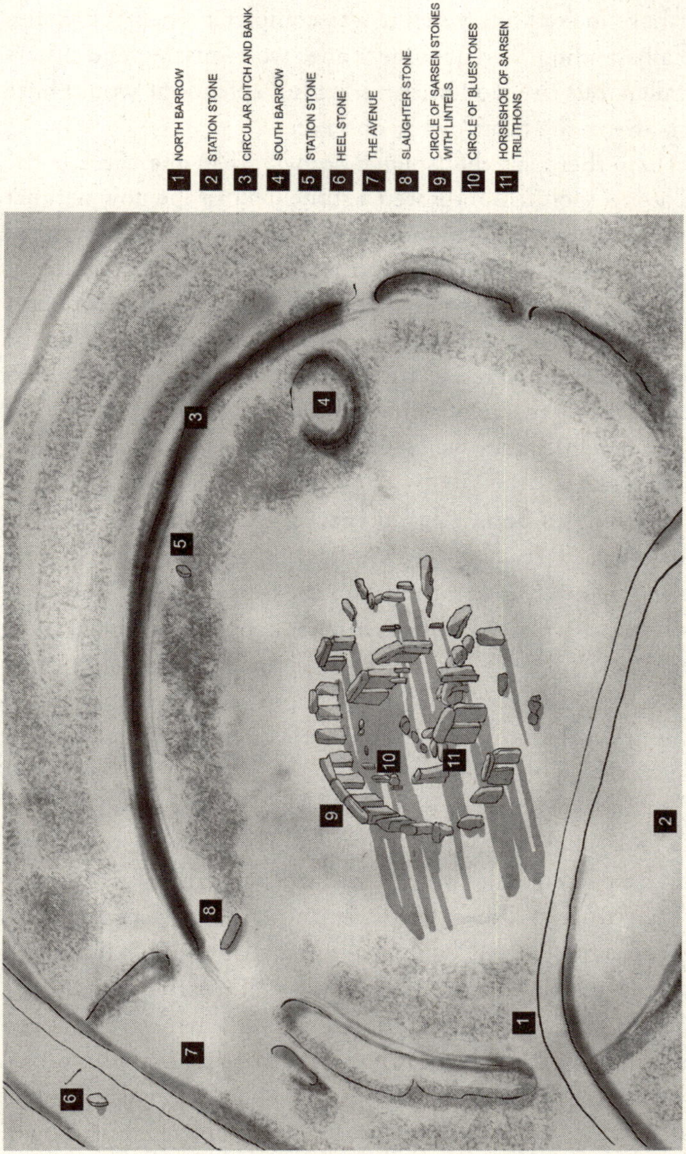

Layout of Stonehenge as it stands today

There was silence as they contemplated what this monument must have looked like when it was complete; when the stones were all standing. Today, some stones were missing and others had fallen, but the monument in its full splendour would have struck awe in the heart of any observer.

'Then, there are the isolated stones. That one there is the Heel stone,' Goldfeld indicated a stone next to the now defunct A344. 'There lies the "slaughter stone,"' he continued pointing at a horizontal slab embedded in the ground. 'And lest we forget the Station stones!' he said as he gestured beyond the outer circle of Stonehenge, at some distance. Vijay strained to see the smaller stones outside the circle but within the ditch, placed on the corners of a rectangular formation.'

For a while, they walked among the stones, as the day grew darker.

'It's going to pour,' Alice observed, looking at the sky. The clouds seemed to have grown heavier and appeared to be lowering themselves as if to rest on the tops of the trilithons.

Goldfeld grimaced. 'This is England, my dear. It pours most of the time. And when it isn't pouring, it is drizzling.' He pointed to the bluestones. 'If it rains, you'll get to see why they're called bluestones. When they're wet, they reflect blue light and appear to gleam with a blue shine.'

He unfolded a sheet of paper he had been carrying. 'Here, take a look,' he said, handing it to Vijay. 'This is what Stonehenge would have looked like when it was still standing.'

Vijay took the sheet of paper and studied it. A few large drops of rain spattered on the sheet and he hurriedly folded it and tucked it away safely. They were all wearing waterproof jackets in anticipation of the downpour, which had been imminent from the time they had left London.

Thunder crashed in the heavens and lightning flashed as the clouds released their burden and the rain came crashing down.

Within no time, the landscape had turned blurry and the few tourists who had ventured here had fled to the car park. Only the three of them lingered. Vijay was curious to see what the bluestones looked like when they were wet.

'Let's go,' Goldfeld said, finally, realising that Vijay had no intention of leaving soon. 'It's coming down pretty heavily.'

Vijay was staring at the bluestones, mesmerised. They had an almost magical appearance when they were wet. Reluctantly, he tore himself away from the sight of the stones and followed Alice and Goldfeld back to the car.

As they drove away, Vijay wiped his hands dry and took out the sheet of paper Goldfeld had given him earlier. He stared at the drawing in his hands. He hadn't got a good look at it earlier. Now that he could study it closely, he frowned.

He had never been to Stonehenge before. While he had seen images of the famous stone circle in photographs and on the Internet, those had always shown the stones the way they were now. Some standing, some fallen, many missing.

The drawing Goldfeld had given him showed the complete structure. He had never seen this before.

Yet, something struck him as being familiar in the drawing.

How could something he had never seen before look so familiar? He couldn't figure it out.

But he was now sure of it.

While he had never seen this drawing before, he knew it from somewhere.

Only, he didn't know where. Or why.

19

Picadilly Circus, London

The fluffy white clouds flitted across the summer sky as the sun hung low over the western horizon. Vijay stood in the centre of the stone circle and watched as the rays of the dying sun lit up the stone pillar that stood in the very centre of the circle.

The pillar was notched at regular intervals and Vijay gazed from the sun to the pillar, watching as the light shone through the immense trilithons and moved from one notch to the next as the sun sank lower.

He floated, rather than walked, beyond the outer circle of trilithons and gazed at the countryside around him.

As far as the eye could see, a verdant plain spread, gently undulating in places. But that was not the sight that caught his breath.

Dotting the plain all around the stone circle that he had just left were enormous stone structures—circles, straight avenues lined with stones on both sides, dolmens and mounds built from stone.

Vijay's field of vision changed abruptly as he found himself in near darkness. Glancing around, he realised he was inside one of the mounds he had been gazing upon just a moment ago. As he looked on, a narrow ray of sunlight lit up the chamber he stood within.

He realised that he was standing within a circular

chamber and the light from the sun lit up a pillar in the centre of the chamber. This pillar, too, was made of stone and had notches on it, which were lit up one by one, in turn, by the light of the sun.

His perspective changed again. He was now looking down upon the plain from somewhere high in the sky, gazing down upon the field of stones below. It was an awe-inspiring sight.

The plain and stone structures below morphed into a sheet of paper with line diagrams similar to the sheet that Goldfeld had given Vijay earlier that day at Stonehenge.

Vijay sat up with a start, blinking as he looked around, disoriented.

Where was he?

Then, he realised. He was in one of the bedrooms of the serviced apartment Alice and he were staying at in London.

He slowly rose and wore his slippers. The dream still lingered in his mind even though parts of it were already beginning to fade.

Vijay emerged from the bedroom and headed for the small kitchen where he opened the refrigerator and took out a beer. He sat at the wooden dining table and sipped the beer as he thought over the strange scenes his dream had revealed to him.

There was a sound outside the kitchen and Alice ambled in, her hair dishevelled, stifling a yawn. She stopped as she saw the bottle of beer and frowned.

'Are you all right? Drinking beer in the middle of the night?'

Vijay tried to look contrite, though he welcomed the company. 'Sorry, did I wake you up?'

Alice yawned again and, pulling up a dining chair, sat down next to Vijay. 'I heard a noise and thought I'd check.' She looked at him seriously. 'What's wrong?'

Vijay couldn't help but recall the times when they were shacking up together in college. He would wake up at times in the middle of the night when some idea would strike him and, uncannily, Alice would somehow know it. She would wake up and join him. And her first question would always be, 'What's wrong?'

For that moment, time stood still.

He shook his head and smiled. It was all so long ago. So much water under the bridge. They had been so deeply in love. And how did it end?

'Nothing much,' he responded, then remembered that this was exactly the response he would give her all those years ago.

'I've heard that before,' Alice chuckled. Clearly, she, too, remembered. 'Come on now, spill the beans.'

Vijay narrated his dream to her.

He still didn't understand what it was all about. It was definitely inspired by his visit to Stonehenge; that was for sure. But what about the other stone structures he had seen? What did they mean? They had seen nothing else around Stonehenge. Only a few barrows and mounds and flat plains stretching on all sides of the stone circle.

Alice frowned again. 'You say you've seen this design before somewhere. But you don't remember where.' She yawned again. 'Look, if it was me, I wouldn't know where I would have seen it. I've been doing so much research over the last year that I have diagrams and photographs coming out of my ears. I'm quite sure I'd see something today and think, hey I've seen that somewhere before! But I'd have no clue which source or reference material I'd actually seen it in.' She looked at him. 'Maybe that's what has happened to you. I don't know what you've been up to the last one year but maybe you saw the Stonehenge design in some book or magazine that you read somewhere, sometime? And your dream,' she stifled another yawn, 'that's just your subconscious mind running wild.'

Vijay felt a cold feeling come over him. It was a mix of

fear, apprehension and excitement. Something Alice said had triggered a cue somewhere in his mind.

He looked at Alice, gazing deep into her eyes. It was a scene from all those years ago. She had always been there for him when he needed help. And, somehow, even though she never understood his subject, she was a catalyst that enabled him to work out stuff. And that was what she was doing now.

How could something so good have turned out so badly? He couldn't figure it out. He had been an ass. Wrapped up in himself, he had lost her.

Alice gazed back at him, unsure. Somewhere, deep down, she still loved Vijay. But she had been hurt too many times to be sure. She was wary.

They both sat there, looking at each other, each one unsure. Feelings bubbled below the surface but both of them suppressed them. Too much had happened in the past.

Too many wounds.

Time was a great healer but even Time couldn't make the pain go away forever.

Abruptly, Alice rose from her chair. 'I'm going back to sleep,' she said, ruffling Vijay's hair. 'Don't stay up late now. I know you.'

Vijay watched her leave. A part of him wanted to go after her, take her by the hand and sit her down on the chair. But there was another part of him that held him back, made him feel guilty. It had been just over a year since Radha's death. And he was already harbouring feelings for someone else. It didn't make him feel good at all.

'You okay?' Harry stuck his head through the kitchen door. He occupied the third bedroom in the apartment. Clearly, he had woken up but had not interrupted Alice and Vijay while they were talking.

Vijay nodded. 'Thanks, I'm good.'

Harry flashed a thumbs up sign and retired to his bedroom, leaving Vijay by himself in the kitchen.

Vijay looked at the beer bottle. It was empty. He rose and opened another.

His thoughts turned back to his dream. What had Alice said that had struck him? He thought hard and long.

Then it dawned on him.

The drawing of Stonehenge as it would have looked when it was first built.

It had seemed familiar. But he hadn't been able to figure out why.

He now knew. There was a reason behind the feeling of déjà vu he had experienced earlier today.

Vijay had seen the same drawing before. Only, at that time, he hadn't realised he was looking at Stonehenge.

20

Saul Goldfeld's residence, London

'I'm curious,' Goldfeld said. 'Why do you want to make this trip? It is quite out of the way, you know.'

When Alice had woken that morning, Vijay had told her his plan and they had headed for Goldfeld's place, accompanied by Harry, as soon as they finished breakfast.

Both of them had steered away from mentioning the interaction of last night. It had been too keen, too sensitive to talk about. Neither of them was ready yet to discuss their emotions.

'Are there other stone circles around Stonehenge?' was the first question Vijay posed, even before they could all seat themselves comfortably in Goldfeld's study.

'Well,' Goldfeld had mused, 'there's Avebury which is also on the Salisbury plains, not too far from Stonehenge. And there's Woodhenge and Durrington Walls. The latter isn't really a stone circle, more a henge. But there have been some recent surveys which indicate that there may have been an enormous stone structure at Durrington Walls.'

'What about mounds?' was Vijay's next question.

Goldfeld eyed him quizzically. 'There are a few barrows around Stonehenge, on the plains,' he replied.

Vijay shook his head. 'Not barrows. Mounds which can be entered through a narrow passageway. Where the light from the sun shines through the entrance passage and lights up the chamber within the mound.' The mound from his dream was still a vivid recollection for him.

Goldfeld pursed his lips. 'Can't think of anything near Stonehenge. There are quite a few megalithic burial chambers, though, in Scotland, especially in the Orkney Islands.'

'Can we go there?' Vijay's response was immediate. He had been thinking about this ever since his realisation during the night about where he had seen the diagram of Stonehenge. It had been just one of many diagrams he had seen and he was keen to validate the theory that was beginning to form in his mind. It wasn't really relevant to his main purpose for visiting London, but since that had proved fruitless, this was a welcome distraction for him. And if his theory was correct, then he would have discovered an interesting connection which might prove significant, though he couldn't say in what way. But something told him this puzzle was worth pursuing.

'The Orkney Islands are quite far,' Goldfeld replied. 'Maybe two hours by plane. But if you want to see some good megalithic burial chambers, we could go to Bryn Celli Ddu and Barclodiad y Gawres in Wales. That's closer. We can take a train to Holyhead, which is on the island of Anglesey, where the most famous mounds are located. We can hire a car there and look around.'

'Can we go now?' Vijay was itching to see the mounds Goldfeld was talking about.

It was then that Goldfeld had asked Vijay about the reasons for his trip. He couldn't understand the sudden bug that had bitten Vijay.

Neither had Alice, for that matter. But she knew Vijay better than to ask questions like this. If he had a reason for doing something and didn't want to reveal it, wild horses wouldn't get him to part with the answer. He would share his reasons in time but only when he decided to do so. When Vijay had told her what he was planning, she had simply agreed to go along with it and had refrained from questioning his objectives.

'Just want to check out something,' Vijay muttered, unhelpfully.

Goldfeld was about to ask another question but he caught Alice's eye and stopped himself. 'Very well, then,' he said, suppressing his curiosity with great difficulty. 'We can start right away.'

'I'll organise the logistics,' Harry offered and pulled out his mobile phone. He proceeded to speak to someone and make arrangements for their train journey and car hire in Holyhead. 'Done,' he said when he had finished. 'Let's go.'

They decided that Goldfeld would drive them to London Euston station where they would board a non-stop fast train to Holyhead.

As they set off for the station, Vijay was silent. He found himself wondering what he would see today. And how the mounds they would see would compare to what he had seen earlier. While he was reasonably sure about his theory, he wanted to be absolutely certain.

And this trip would tell him if he was on the right track.

21

Bryn Celli Ddu

Anglesey, North Wales

Goldfeld eased the Land Rover onto the shoulder of the road, where it widened to form a kind of an informal car parking space. There were no other cars. The sun had been veiled since the moment they had landed in Holyhead and a grim chill was in the air. It was not surprising that no one else had ventured out to the farm, which housed the famous site of Bryn Celli Ddu.

Vijay was out of the car first, followed by Harry and Alice. Goldfeld brought up the rear as they walked in single file down the narrow track that led from the road towards the site where the burial chamber was located.

On their left stretched a hedge, beyond which they could see water, sheep and cows. It seemed that a stream ran along the hedge and the animals flocked here to quench their thirst.

They followed the signposts indicating the location of the mound, almost constantly walking between hedges on either side of the path until finally they arrived at the gate that gave them access to the field, which contained the mound.

It occupied the centre of the field, a rather modest-looking mound of earth covered with grass.

As they approached it, Vijay felt a bit let down. It was nothing like the mound he had seen in his dream.

But then, he reproached himself, his dream was not based on a true-life burial mound like this one. It had been created from his imagination, from the mysterious processes of the brain that create the images we see in our dreams, a pale reflection of our true lives.

'This is the rear,' Goldfeld remarked, as they gazed upon a slit in the mound facing west. 'The entrance will be on the other side.'

Exterior view of Brynn Celli Ddu, viewed from the east

Vijay observed that a barely visible ditch and small standing stones surrounded the mound. A ring of stones marked its base.

They rounded the mound and the entrance revealed itself to them—a narrow gash in the earth, lined with stone slabs forming a rude doorway leading into the inner chamber.

Vijay took the lead and entered the narrow entrance passage, bending to do so since the doorway was quite low. The others followed.

The passage opened up into a small rocky chamber. The rock that had been used to build the walls clearly contained crystals of some sort, since it shone even in the dim light that penetrated through to the chamber.

Vijay sucked in his breath as he noticed a tall pillar. Only, this pillar was not at the centre of the chamber, but positioned off to the side of the entrance passage. It bore notches, like the pillars he had seen in his dreams.

'See these carvings here,' Goldfeld pointed out the cup marks carved into one of the rock walls. 'These cup marks and this spiral here,' he indicated a spiral carved into one of the slabs forming a wall, 'are very common in these megalithic monuments.'

Had he visited here a day earlier, Vijay would have marvelled at how he had dreamt of the notches.

But now, with the realisation that had dawned on him during the night, he had no doubts about where he had gleaned that information.

He looked around and nodded with satisfaction. He would have to cross-check to validate his hypothesis but he seemed to be on the right track.

'Let's see the other one,' he said, briskly.

Goldfeld looked at him in surprise. 'We just got here,' he began, but broke off as Alice jabbed him with her elbow. 'Oh, okay,' he conceded and followed Vijay who was already making his way out of the chamber, leaving the room of gloom for the muted light outside.

22

2002 B.C.

Near the River Indus, modern-day Pakistan

Semiramis looked upon the scene, grim-faced. Her long hair, tied in a fine braid, was streaked with dust. Her beautiful face, usually composed and youthful looking, was now lined with stress, anxiety and the physical exertion she had just undertaken.

For the first time in decades, she looked her age.

But that did not bother her. She had known that her soldiers would not last long against the army of Sthavarapati without her to lead them, inspire them, goad them to victory as she had done countless times before. They were so accustomed to her presence on the battlefield, to her strategies and generalship that they would wilt in her absence like flowers without rain.

What did bother her was the fact that her army had been routed faster than she had expected. And with far greater losses than she had planned for.

She pursed her lips. The great queen would win this battle. Just like many others. But at a very high cost.

This was the second jolt to hit her on this day. The first had been the news she had received from Nineveh earlier.

'Round up the army,' she commanded. 'Get them back. I don't need them now. But we will leave with our heads held high.'

Two riders immediately headed off in the direction of the dust cloud that showed where the Assyrian army was retreating.

Followed by the rest of the soldiers who had accompanied her deep into the desert, and the wagon bearing her treasure, Semiramis rode towards the river.

Bodies of soldiers, Assyrian and native, lay strewn on the battlefield. Blood had flowed freely and the air reeked with the stench of death.

The small group reached the banks of the Indus and looked across the river. The bridge across it was in shambles. Bodies floated in the river, testimony to the fierceness of the battle that had been fought here.

Semiramis read the situation immediately. The final charge of the Assyrian army had been across the bridge, a courageous attack on the camp of the natives. That had been a folly.

Outnumbered or outflanked, she didn't know which, the Assyrians had been routed and forced to retreat across the bridge. Many of them had not made it back, cut down by the enemy, in their panicked stampede to safety.

Then, there had been a pitched battle on this bank of the river. Her men had fought bravely. The innumerable corpses of Sthavarapati's soldiers bore testimony to the stand her army had taken. But they had been overwhelmed. Eventually, the absence Semiramis and, perhaps, the fear that she may not return had probably overcome them and they had turned and fled.

Semiramis sighed. She couldn't blame them. She had promised that she would be back in three days.

It had been well over a week since she had left her army to face Sthavarapati's wrath.

'Go to them,' she instructed. 'Tell the king I wish to speak to him. Tell him I have their precious treasure. I am willing to give him the chance to see it with his own eyes if he wishes...'

One of the soldiers nodded and hastily contrived a white flag using a branch and a scrap of linen.

With the flag borne high, and with no small amount of trepidation, the emissary from Semiramis rode slowly over the bridge towards the camp of the natives.

23

February, present year

Jaungarh Fort

Vijay sat in the secret chamber housing the microfilms that contained the Library of the Nine.

Two and a half years ago, his uncle, Vikram Singh, had been brutally murdered, minutes after a call with Vijay as he sat in his office in San Jose. Barely moments later, Vijay had received five emails from Vikram, a recluse who had retired as a nuclear scientist working with the Indian government, and lived in a remote fort in Rajasthan.

The emails had confounded Vijay, appearing to be a little more than gibberish. It was only after he travelled to India to conduct the last rites of his uncle that he had suspected that Vikram Singh had been trying to communicate with him through the weird emails. He realised that there were messages concealed in the emails, which he would need to decode.

With the help of his friends, Vijay had followed a trail of clues across India, through two-thousand-year-old ruins, and uncovered a secret from the time of Asoka the Great; a secret linked to a secret society called the Brotherhood of the Nine Unknown Men, which Asoka had created.

Only, the Nine—as they were commonly known—hadn't restricted themselves to writing nine books on advanced scientific subjects, as the traditional legend went. Vijay and his friends had discovered that the Nine had been formed by Asoka to protect—and conceal from the world—a secret from the Mahabharata, that Asoka had decided was too dangerous to reveal. It was a secret that could destroy the world, and the emperor wanted to ensure that it never fell into the wrong hands. The traditional legend of the Nine was just a smokescreen to hide their real purpose. The world would believe the story of the nine books and never know the true secret that the Nine had been created to protect and hide away forever.

Vijay and his friends succeeded in locating the secret, in the process leading a group of terrorists to the place where the secret had remained hidden for almost two thousand three hundred years. Eventually, the cavern where the secret was concealed had been destroyed, and along with it the secret from the Mahabharata that Asoka had wanted to conceal.

However, there had been one last surprise for Vijay. He learned that Vikram Singh had been the last surviving member of the brotherhood in contemporary times. Vikram Singh had also been the custodian of the secret Library of the Nine, a trove of ancient texts containing knowledge from an age lost to time and forgotten by humanity. Vikram Singh had captured the texts on microfilm and stored them in a secret chamber in his fort. He had been engaged in translating them into English when he was murdered.

Vijay didn't know where the texts had come from, but he guessed that there was a connection between the Library and the Mahabharata. What that connection was, he hadn't discovered yet.

What he had unearthed, however, was the existence of a shadowy organisation called the Order, which had been referred to by Asoka in an ancient text recovered as part of the search for the secret of the Nine two and a half years ago.

His hands trembled with excitement as he went through the containers of microfilm one at a time.

Alice's words when she had heard about his dream had triggered a memory. The recollection of where he had seen the diagram of Stonehenge, Bryn Celli Ddu, Barclodiad y Gawres and the stone circle at Avebury, had struck him like a bolt of lightning.

The secret Library of the Nine! He had been perusing the microfilm records for months now, hoping to find some clue to the origins of the Order. Over the months, he had gone through most of the records but had drawn a blank. He was no closer to knowing anything more about the Order than when he had started.

But he was sure of one thing. The entire scene in his dream had not been conjured up out of thin air. There was a very real basis for everything his dream had contained.

The first stone circle that had appeared in his dream. The plethora of stone monuments on the plain surrounding this stone circle—stone-lined avenues, dolmens, lone megaliths and more stone circles—had featured in his dream. And he had seen diagrams of all of these while sitting in this very chamber, months ago.

All he had to do was locate the correct microfilm container. He didn't know how long that would take but he was determined to get to the bottom of this mystery.

Why were the bird's-eye views of the stone monuments on Salisbury Plain and the mounds in Wales part of the Library of the Nine?

24

Regent's Park, London

Dee stared at her computer screen with grim satisfaction. When she had heard from the tail she had put on Vijay and Alice that they had gone to the British Museum and then called on Saul Goldfeld, she had had a hunch. And her suspicions had turned out to be true.

It all seemed to be coming together now. She had been briefed earlier regarding Vijay's meeting with KS in India. The Order had suspected that KS had shared something with Vijay about the missing prism. When Vijay had first come to London nine months ago, another member of the Order had been assigned the task of tracking their movements. But that mission had come to naught. Not only had the Order failed to shadow Vijay and his friends effectively but Vijay himself had suddenly, and inexplicably, returned to India.

Things had been quiet after that until a few weeks ago, when Vijay had turned up suddenly once more in London, this time with Alice in tow.

Dee had suspected that something was afoot. The fact that an archaeologist, Alice, was accompanying Vijay to the museum had to mean something. Especially since Alice had also been involved in the search for the Alexander Secret the previous year.

What had complicated the situation was the fact that there

seemed to be a security cordon around the two of them. Starting with Petrovsky, every time Harper's men had attempted to shadow Vijay and Alice, they had been forced to beat a hasty retreat. The attempt at surveillance had been unsuccessful yet again.

Dee didn't know if Vijay and Alice realised the importance of the prism and whether they were following the same trail as the Order, but to her that didn't matter. It was clear that Vijay and Alice were doing something that was important enough for someone to hire professional help to protect them.

For her, it was critical that the mission stayed low profile. She could throw more men at the task but it seemed inefficient when the objective was just to follow the two around and see what they were up to. And more men meant a high probability of an encounter escalating into an armed conflict on the streets of London, which would draw unnecessary attention to the mission.

So she had decided to withdraw her surveillance team. Whatever Vijay and Alice were up to, as long as they didn't get in her way, she didn't care. And if they did get in the way, she wouldn't be as kind to them as Van Klueck had been. For two years, he had allowed Vijay to create hurdles for the Order. It had certainly posed challenges. That Van Klueck had succeeded in his mission a year and a half ago didn't mean that Vijay could be let off so easily.

The code of the Order had been violated. It was not for her to pursue Vijay and his friends and eliminate them. Not only did her brief exclude this, but doing so might put the mission at risk, which she was loath to do.

She realised that she had to find another way out.

After much thought, Dee had ordered her tech team to hack into Vijay and Alice's email accounts.

That had been interesting. Her team came across an email

sent a year and a half ago from KS to Vijay asking for a meeting, but, more importantly, they had discovered an email sent by Alice to Goldfeld, with photographs as attachments. And the photographs were no ordinary images. They were of the prisms that the Order had been hunting for all these decades.

The Order had known that one prism was at the British Museum. A botched attempt at trying to steal it last year had led to it being stored in a secure facility within the museum. Dee had spent a lot of time trying to work out how they could acquire the prism, but had failed to come up with a plan that would work.

But now, that wasn't required any more. Not only did she have the images of the prism at the British Museum, but she also had the images of the prism that had been missing for all these years. The Order had always suspected that KS knew something about its whereabouts and that had now been confirmed.

At last, the Order could start working on one of its most ambitious projects.

Now, all she had to do was find someone to decipher the inscriptions.

Part 3

25

February, present year

Day 1

Saul Goldfeld's residence, London

Goldfeld was incredulous. 'You are asking me to believe that the blueprints of Stonehenge, Brynn Celli Ddu, the Avebury stone circle and some other megalithic sites which you are not familiar with, were made over two thousand years ago?'

Vijay nodded and sighed. 'I know it's hard to believe. And I wish I could tell you how I came across this information. But it is true. I have seen the blueprints with my own eyes.'

Goldfeld shook his head as if trying to shake his disbelief away. 'What's more, you say there are elements in the diagrams that are not present in the sites today—at least for the sites you have visited.'

Vijay nodded again to affirm the statement. 'I've only been to Stonehenge, Brynn Celli Ddu, Barclodiad y Gawres and I've seen photographs of the Avebury stone circle. For at least these sites, there is a distinct difference between what I saw at the sites, what archaeologists say the sites originally looked like, and the two-thousand-plus-year-old blueprints that I have seen back in India.'

'How do you know the blueprints you have seen are authentic?' Goldfeld challenged Vijay.

Vijay hesitated. How was he to explain without disclosing the fact that he had access to secrets protected by the Nine? He had pored over the microfilms, sleeping barely two hours every night; staying up all night at times, to find the diagrams of the megalithic sites that he remembered having seen last year.

He shrugged. 'It's....it's confidential,' he said finally. 'You'll just have to trust me. All I can tell you is that the blueprints are part of a private collection. A very private collection.'

Goldfeld looked at Alice, confused.

Harry looked on impassively. He knew something was going on but it was none of his business.

'I believe Vijay,' Alice said promptly. She knew Vijay too well to suspect him of dissembling in matters like this. She shot Vijay a glance to reassure him and also to reassure herself.

There was silence for a few moments.

'It sounds crazy,' Goldfeld said after a while. 'The stone-lined avenues you describe exist at Avebury. But how is it possible that there was a blueprint created two thousand years ago that depicted these sites and we don't know about them but you do?'

'Saul, does it matter?' Alice intervened. She could see that Vijay was growing uncomfortable. She was as curious as Goldfeld was. But she knew that no amount of probing for an explanation would elicit one.

She looked at Vijay. 'You have something in mind, don't you?' Even as she asked the question, she knew she had hit the nail on the head. Nothing seemed to have changed from all those years ago. Vijay was as frustrating as he was predictable.

'It's crazy,' Vijay admitted, 'but I have some ideas I wanted to bounce off you guys.'

It was at that moment that Goldfeld's mobile phone rang.

26

A call for help

Goldfeld listened with horror to the voice of Ernest Hamilton. The man sounded like he was in deep trouble.

Hamilton was asking him to call the police. Someone had broken into his house. He was asking for his daughter to be warned.

'Of course,' Goldfeld reassured his friend. 'I'll call the police right away and then go over and tell Penny. Will you be okay?'

Hamilton's response wasn't very reassuring. But there wasn't much Goldfeld could do from here. And there was more. Hamilton was saying something about coins, a safe, a diary...and a warning to be given to someone.

'Tacitus,' Hamilton concluded, and the line went dead.

Goldfeld stared at his phone for a few moments.

Vijay and Alice were looking at him.

'Something wrong?' Vijay enquired, concerned. Goldfeld was looking troubled.

'Yes,' Goldfeld said slowly. 'I'm sorry, but I have to leave immediately. It's an emergency.'

'Can we help?' Alice asked. Something told her that Goldfeld needed support.

He looked at her, relief writ large on his face. 'Will you?' he asked. 'I could do with help.'

'Sure,' Vijay assured him. 'Tell us what we can do.'

Goldfeld swiftly explained the situation. 'So, we need to get to Mayfair immediately,' he concluded.

'Let's go, then,' Vijay swept up his overcoat and headed for the exit. 'Let's get Penny back here and safe.'

Harry was up already, having read Vijay's thoughts.

'I don't know what it is, really,' Goldfeld confessed as he followed Vijay. 'Hamilton sounded pretty confused. But what worries me is that he sounded scared. And I've never known that man to feel fear.'

Alice followed the three men out into the dark night made gloomier by the rain, a deep foreboding rising within her.

Something told her that trouble lay ahead.

27

Mayfair, London

Goldfeld eased the car into a vacant slot and killed the engine. He had called Scotland Yard while they were en-route to Mayfair and informed them about Hamilton's call and the break in.

Now it was time to get Penny to safety.

They looked at the silhouette of the apartment building rising above them. It was dark, except for the penthouse, which had a light on in one of the rooms.

'Let's go,' Vijay opened the door of the car and jumped out, striding swiftly towards the main entrance of the apartment block, followed by Harry.

He pressed the buzzer. A girl's voice responded.

'Who is it?'

'Saul Goldfeld.' Goldfeld had hurried up behind Vijay, accompanied by Alice.

'Saul!' the girl's voice instantly changed to a more welcoming tone. 'Come on up!'

A buzzer sounded and the door swung open.

Goldfeld silently thanked their luck. It seemed that no one else had reached here yet.

Harry ensured that the door swung shut and was locked behind them before they entered the elevator.

Within minutes, they were at the top floor of the building.

The front door of the apartment was open and a young

girl, not more than twenty years old, was silhouetted against the doorway.

She flung her arms around Saul and greeted him like an old friend. 'So good to see you. It has been so long!'

'Your college keeps you busy, my dear,' Goldfeld replied, looking pleased. He was very fond of Penny.

'Who are your friends?' Penny enquired, looking curiously at Vijay, Alice and Harry.

Goldfeld did the introductions and soon all five of them were safely ensconced in the sitting room of the apartment.

'We have to leave here fast,' Goldfeld informed Penny, as they sat on the comfortable sofas. 'Pack some of your things and we'll get out of here.'

'What's the hurry, Saul?' Penny asked, wide-eyed and confused. 'You've just got here.'

'You're in danger,' Vijay said. He felt there was no other option but to be direct if they were to get moving fast. 'There are people who are after you and your father. He called us and asked us to get you to safety immediately. We can't linger much longer.'

Penny's eyes widened even more. 'Is Papa okay?'

Goldfeld nodded. 'I spoke to him just a while ago. Now pack up.'

Penny nodded and disappeared. The sounds of a suitcase being packed came from within.

The buzzer sounded from the front entrance of the apartment block leading to the street.

Vijay, Goldfeld and Alice looked at each other, fear on their faces.

It was late. Who could it be?

Alice decided to answer, pretending to be Penny. 'Yes?' she enquired. 'Who is it? I was sleeping.'

'Sorry to bother you, ma'am,' a polite voice came through the speaker. 'We have an urgent delivery for Miss Penelope Hamilton.'

'It's late,' Alice replied. 'Come back tomorrow. I'm Penelope and I can't take the delivery at this time of night.'

There was no response and she took her finger off the speaker button.

'It's them,' Vijay said, grimly. 'No one in London delivers anything at this time of night.'

Goldfeld nodded his agreement. 'Penny!' he called out. 'We have to leave now!'

'Just a minute, Saul!' Penny called back. 'Just a few things more to pack.'

Vijay rose from the sofa and disappeared into the bedroom.

There was a bit of a commotion and Vijay re-appeared carrying a large suitcase, with Penny behind him, looking distressed.

'He threw out half my stuff!' she complained to Goldfeld. 'I can't leave without…'

She broke off as there was a sound at the door.

'What...?' She looked from Vijay to Goldfeld.

Harry put a finger to his lips, indicating that they were all to be silent. He took a quick look around the room, noting the layout of the furniture.

An open area by the large windows looking onto the street.

A seven-seater sofa set arranged in a rectangular formation opposite the windows.

Occasional tables bearing cut glass ornaments and vases scattered across the room.

This was not going to be easy.

He nodded to Vijay, who understood. The two of them would have to hold off the intruders long enough for the others to make a getaway.

'Lights off,' Vijay whispered to Alice.

Alice quickly located the light switch and the room was bathed in darkness.

28

Intruders!

Vijay and Harry crouched on opposite sides of the room, as Goldfeld, Alice and Penny hid themselves behind the sofas.

They had hoped to get Penny out before anyone else got here.

That hadn't worked as expected.

Now there was no plan.

Neither did they know how many men were at the door. It was clear that the people who were masquerading as couriers had come after Penny. When Alice had rebuffed them, they would have forced their way into the apartment block and were now breaking their way into the apartment.

Vijay's heart was in his mouth. It was all right for Harry to stay calm in the face of adversity. He had served in tougher situations, facing gunfire and bombs in Iraq and Afghanistan.

Vijay had also had experiences similar to this before and none of them had turned out well for him. Of course, things were different now. As part of the task force for the last two years, he had undergone training in unarmed combat and weapons handling. But those were simulations.

This was real.

This was different.

The front door swung open silently.

It was obvious that these men were professionals. The swiftness with which they had reached the penthouse and the ease with which they had entered the apartment was testimony to their skills.

Vijay's mouth was dry. His palms were sweaty.

Bloody hell.

London in February and sweaty palms.

Reflected light from the street several floors below streamed in through the open windows. That was how Harry had planned it.

Their eyes were acclimatised to the darkness and the dim lighting.

The men coming in from outside would not have that advantage.

Or so they had thought.

Now, Vijay noticed that the landing outside was shrouded in darkness. These men had anticipated trouble. They would be as comfortable in the darkness as those inside the room.

The only advantage that was left was the few seconds that Vijay and Harry had had to take a good look at the room they were in and the pattern of furniture arrangement.

Vijay hoped it would be enough.

29

Trouble

Vijay and Harry watched as two men, dressed in suits, entered the apartment, treading cautiously.

The fact that the living room was dark would have triggered alarm bells in the minds of the intruders.

There wasn't much time available to act.

They had to do it now.

Two men. The odds were still stacked against them, Vijay thought grimly. These two men were professional killers.

He wasn't and neither was Harry, even though the latter had been involved in armed combat.

All he could hope for was that he would not be a handicap for Harry.

Vijay saw Harry emerge from the shadows where he had been skulking and charge at one of the men. There was no warning, no sound. It was clear that he expected Vijay to follow his lead.

Within seconds, the second intruder had rushed to his companion's aid.

The two men tackled Harry, though it was tough going for them. Harry was built like a bull and his experience showed. The three men wrestled hard, the sofa legs scraping against the wooden parquet flooring, as the men bumped into the furniture.

An occasional table went over with a crash, the vase that was placed on it shattering as it hit the floor.

Vijay steeled himself to enter the fray.

This was not something he was accustomed to. He had always regarded himself a thinker, not a physical person. Quite apart from the fact that he and Colin relished engaging in outdoor exertions and action-packed holidays.

But those were for fun. Those were getaways. A break from the routine of everyday life.

This was different. He urged himself to move. But his feet felt like lead.

What was happening to him?

Harry was now on his back, virtually overpowered by his two assailants, but still wrestling with them, keeping them at bay.

From across the room, Goldfeld, Alice and Penny watched with horror as one of the men held a dagger aloft, in preparation to plunge it into Harry.

Time seemed to slow down.

Vijay saw the dagger glint in the light streaming in through the windows.

He found himself thinking of Radha. He had helplessly watched the video of her getting shot. He had wanted to save her. But he knew there was nothing he could do.

The pain surfaced again.

The scene where she was shot flashed before his eyes.

Radha being shot multiple times.

Radha falling to the floor, blood gushing from her wounds, staining her clothes, pooling on the floor as she collapsed.

Now, he was watching as Harry's attackers prepared to kill him.

Something snapped within him.

He had promised Shukla he would get Radha back. Even if she was dead. And now there was no way he could fulfil that promise.

But Vijay wasn't helpless. He wasn't worthless. He had failed to save Radha. But he would not fail to help Harry.

We watch each other's backs.

He was still capable of delivering on his promises.

30

Fight in the night

Alice watched, horrified, as Vijay stood rooted to the spot. He seemed to be immobilised.

Was it fear? Was it inexperience?

She couldn't tell.

Harry was having a rough time. He had waded into the men, but Vijay hadn't backed him up as expected.

While Harry was strong, the two men were more than a match for him. They were coordinated and swiftly overpowered him.

One of the men brandished a dagger.

Alice stifled an involuntary gasp and placed her palm over Penny's mouth as a precaution.

Suddenly, she saw Vijay move.

Something had happened to spur him into action.

Vijay moved with lightning speed towards the three men who were grappling with each other.

Even as he moved forward, he had decided he would tackle the man with the knife. That was the immediate danger.

In one swift motion, he grasped the wrist holding the dagger and bent it backwards with all his strength, forcing the man's elbow to touch his back.

The man cried out in pain as something snapped with the sudden pressure.

Simultaneously, recalling his training, Vijay attacked the man's legs.

As the attacker with the knife lost his balance, Vijay pressed home his advantage and twisted the man's arm further, causing the knife to drop from his grasp.

Harry immediately responded to the respite and swung at the other intruder, catching him on the cheek with a roundhouse punch. He followed it up with a jab and a hook to the man's head. As Harry pressed home his advantage with a flurry of hooks and cross punches, the man tried to fend him off, retreating towards the windows.

Vijay's adversary was now sliding to the floor, writhing, trying to force his way out of his grasp.

Without warning, he twisted around, cried out in pain, and went slack.

Vijay tried to haul him to his feet but his inexperience let him down.

The intruder twisted around again and freed himself from Vijay's grip, which had loosened as a result of the effort to pick the man off the floor.

Even with one useless arm, the intruder counter-attacked Vijay. His fist shot out and connected with Vijay's jaw, jarring his teeth and throwing him off balance.

As Vijay backed away, trying to defend himself, his attacker sprang to his feet and lashed out with a powerful kick to Vijay's sternum.

Vijay flew backwards through the air for a few feet and landed with a thud against one of the sofas, hitting the floor hard as the sofa gave way beneath the momentum of his contact. He bit off a cry as a jolt of pain coursed through his tailbone.

Harry saw Vijay's predicament, but was in no position to rush to his help. He was having a difficult time with his own opponent who was proving to be as tough as nails.

Not only was he standing up to Harry's punches but he had also got in a few good shots of his own. Harry's left ear was ringing and his left eye had begun to swell up.

His adversary tackled him and both men fell to the floor, locked in a tight embrace, each trying to get a stranglehold on the other. A second occasional table toppled over, the ornaments on it crashing to the ground and tinkling as they spread out across the floor.

Harry could only hope that there were no sharp-edged objects strewn around the floor now.

He struggled wildly. Vijay was clearly out of his league in this fight. He had to overpower his opponent and help Vijay.

But his opponent was in no mood to oblige.

As the two men rolled around on the floor, Harry saw Vijay's attacker slug him repeatedly, as Vijay frantically tried to haul himself to his feet.

He knew it was just a matter of time before Vijay went down.

31

2002 B.C.

Near the River Indus, modern-day Pakistan

Sthavarapati couldn't take his eyes off the contents of the wagon.

Over the course of the last week, his spies had confirmed that Semiramis had, indeed, disappeared from the battlefield. The news had bewildered him. It wasn't like Semiramis to desert her army. The Semiramis he knew would never do that. She would lead from the front.

And Sthavarapati knew Semiramis well.

Very well.

Ever since her childhood days, she had demonstrated strength of character and determination that he had never seen in anyone before. The yearning to make her own place in the world, unfettered by the compulsions of society and independent of the status of her parents or her social standing, had been powerful and perceptible.

The young Semiramis had been defiant to the point of being rebellious. Wild and uncontrollable, she had decided, at the age of fifteen, that she would not be held back anymore. Her life, she had declared, was stifled by the customs of her society, and the obligations of her social standing, where women were veiled and kept behind screens. Never to be seen, only to be heard—little more than possessions for the men to fight over.

At least, Semiramis had reasoned at that time, the women of the lower strata of society still had their independence. They could walk around freely, unfettered by the customs of the upper echelons of society.

She had had enough and was leaving, she had announced to her parents, to seek status that she would achieve, not by the rules of society, but by her own efforts. Semiramis would lay down the rules and society would abide by them. And she would ensure, she had added, that she would elevate herself to such a position that the rules of society, no matter how liberal, would cease to apply to her.

Sthavarapati had kept a close watch on the progress of the young girl after she had vanished one day, shortly after her announcement. Her disappearance had not come as a surprise to anyone, given her vocal pronouncements on her ambitions and her dissatisfaction with her current life.

The king had heard, over the past forty-five years, of how Semiramis had mysteriously re-appeared in Assyria, in the town of Ascalon. He had learned of how Onnes, a general in the army of King Ninus, had met her while inspecting the flocks of the king in Syria. Onnes had seen the beautiful maiden who was the foster-child of Simmas, the keeper of the king's flocks and, smitten by her beauty, had married her.

When Ninus had attacked the Bactrians, he was able to take most parts of Bactria without much trouble, but Bactra—the main city where the palace of Oxyartes, King of Bactria lay—was unassailable. Ninus had besieged the city but could not prevail. It had been at this time that Onnes, who had accompanied Ninus on the campaign, had sent for his wife to be by his side.

It had not surprised Sthavarapati when he heard that Semiramis had seized this as an opportunity to display her intelligence and power. She had arrived in the Assyrian camp attired in clothing that made it hard to discern if she was a man or a woman. On her arrival, she had swiftly perceived a weakness in the defence of the Bactrian citadel and had led a small group of soldiers in a daring attack on it. They had ascended from a deep ravine, captured a part of the citadel, and then signalled the rest of the Assyrian army, which was engaged in assaulting the city walls on the plains. It had not been difficult to overcome and subdue the Bactrians after their citadel was taken.

Ninus had been infatuated with the beauty of the young Semiramis and impressed by her courage. In addition to showering her with costly gifts, he had attempted to persuade Onnes to give up Semiramis to him as his queen. Ninus had even offered his own daughter, Sosana, in marriage to Onnes as compensation for giving up his wife.

Sthavarapati had been told of how Onnes, under threat by the king, had taken his own life. The words of Semiramis had come back to him at that time—her words that reflected the status of high society women in her time as being possessions for men to fight over. But he knew that, on this occasion, it wasn't a passive role that the woman at the centre of this saga was playing. On the contrary, she wielded the power, and continued to do so after she married Ninus and became Queen of Assyria. Ninus was a great king and his successes were owed in no small measure to the intelligence of his queen.

Sthavarapati had not been surprised at this last development. It was merely the fulfilment of what Semiramis had always aimed for. It wasn't that she wouldn't have achieved something similar in her own native land. It was just that it wouldn't have been on her terms.

It was what happened after the death of Ninus that had really surprised Sthavarapati.

32

February, present year

Day 1

Mayfair, London

Abruptly, Harry broke free of his opponent, and kicked him away. His adversary was taken by surprise.

The split-second hesitation, as the other man wondered what Harry was doing, was sufficient. Even as Harry rolled away, the man rose swiftly, ready to attack, his body outlined in the dim light that was coming in through the window.

But before the man could move, Harry was on his feet, at the edge of the open space between the windows and the sofas.

As his adversary looked on in wonder, Harry hopped forward and then twisted sideways, putting his whole weight behind his right leg which shot out in a powerful kick that caught his attacker in the ribcage. There was an audible crunch as the man's ribcage shattered, and he flew backwards with the momentum of the kick, sailing out of the window, dropping to the street below.

The ferocity of the attack took everyone by surprise, including Vijay's attacker, who paused momentarily, distracted.

Vijay took advantage of the moment to roll away, too exhausted and groggy to do anything else. His attacker had no time to pursue him. Within seconds, Harry was upon him, delivering a deadly uppercut and a cross punch to the ribs and head, knocking him out.

There was silence in the room. The horrifying sight of the man going through the window was difficult to forget.

Alice flicked the light switch.

The sofas had been displaced and were now at awkward angles to each other. Two of the occasional tables had been knocked over and the shards of a ceramic vase covered the floor, mixed up with the set of ornaments that had adorned the second table.

Both Vijay and Harry had swollen and bloody faces, puffed eyes, split lips and bruised cheeks. They looked like they had been run over by a train.

'Wow,' Vijay muttered through swollen lips. 'I don't want to rub you the wrong way.' He tried to smile at Harry but it was too painful.

Harry jerked a thumb towards the window. 'These men were trained professionals. I'm willing to bet they're from the services as well. They were tough. It was a close call and we got lucky.'

'I'll call the police,' Goldfeld said. 'We need to report this.'

Harry shook his head. 'Let's get out of here first. There may be more on the way. And anyway, this is now something that the task force needs to handle. There's a dead man on the street below. There's been a break in here. And we got assaulted. How are we going to explain this to the police?'

Vijay wasn't very happy with this proposition, but he grudgingly agreed that this was the best course of action.

'Right,' Goldfeld said, looking uncomfortable with this unorthodox approach that Harry and Vijay were pursuing. 'Off to my place, then.'

33

Saul Goldfeld's residence, London

Harry and Vijay sat holding ice packs to their faces. As soon as they reached Goldfeld's house, Harry had called in and reported the incident to the task force's US Headquarters. Within minutes, Patterson had called back and asked for a detailed brief. Harry and Vijay had closeted themselves in Goldfeld's kitchen and had put Patterson on the speaker so that both men could brief him and answer his questions.

Patterson had sounded quite relieved that Vijay had not been the instigator of this violence.

'We'll take care of this,' he had assured the two men. 'See if you can get a doctor in confidentially and treat you guys. We don't want a police report filed for this until we know what is happening out there and who is responsible for this. It may turn out to be a simple case of a kidnapping for ransom, but now that two members of the task force are involved, we can't let the police handle this. Good job, guys.'

After Patterson had hung up they had returned to the living room to learn that Goldfeld had called a doctor friend of his to take a look at their bruises.

The doctor had concluded that there were no serious injuries and advised applying an ice pack for two days, followed by a heat pack to promote healing.

'A fine sight you two are,' Alice grinned at the two men holding ice packs to their faces, after the doctor had left. 'But I don't know what we would have done if you guys hadn't tackled those men the way you did.'

'Your dad was right,' Goldfeld said gravely to Penny. 'He thought you might be in danger. Those men had come for you.'

'Is there any news of Papa?' Penny asked anxiously.

Goldfeld hesitated then decided it was best to be truthful. 'I got a call from the police,' he answered. 'Your dad is missing. There are no signs of a break in, but they found the body of the butler and another member of your dad's domestic staff. The police suspect that one of them had let the intruders in and was then killed by them, since there was no forced entry. The other one was simply unfortunate to be around when the intruders arrived. They're looking for your dad and we'll drive up to the house tomorrow to talk to them. I've arranged for them to meet us at eleven o'clock in the morning.'

He looked at Vijay and Harry. 'Not you two, though,' he told them. 'I think you both need to take it easy for some time.'

'You bet,' Vijay agreed through swollen and cut lips. All thoughts of the discovery in the Library of the Nine were forgotten for now. They could wait. All he wanted, for now, was to feel normal again.

34

Regent's Park, London

Dee stared at Harper, her eyes flashing with anger. 'Your men were supposed to bring that girl back here. Not get beaten up or killed. Is there nothing you can do right?'

Harper tried to remain calm though his heart was beating wildly. 'She had professional help,' he suggested tentatively. 'My men were good, fighting men. If someone was able to overpower them, it could only be men with military training. My men would not go down so easily.'

Dee's eyes bored into Harper. 'Who was with the girl?'

'Bill didn't get a good look at them,' Harper replied. 'The room was in darkness. These people knew we were coming for the girl. I don't know how, but they were prepared. They were lying in ambush and the moment Bill and Frank walked into the room, they pounced on them. All Bill saw were two silhouettes. Both tall, well-built men. He couldn't make out anything else. They didn't utter a word, so there was no way to identify them. Professionals.'

Dee contemplated this. 'Very well then,' she said. 'I think I need to call in some extraordinary help. If we come across trouble again, we need someone who can take care of them and get them out of our way quickly and easily.'

Harper wondered what this extraordinary help was. But Dee was speaking again.

'In the meanwhile,' she continued, 'I want you to hunt for that girl. I want her dead. We'll get the dope on the coins from Hamilton himself. With all his injuries, he is going to be particularly sensitive to pain. It won't take us long to get him to cough up what we need. But I don't want that girl running around loose either.'

Harper left and Dee turned to the only other man left in the room. 'Call Boris,' she instructed. 'I want Yeti here as soon as possible. I don't know what we're up against but we may need him. And let me know when Hamilton breaks. I want that third coin.'

Part 4

35

Day 2

Hertfordshire

The Vauxhall Insignia swung into the drive of the Hamilton mansion with Goldfeld at the wheel and Penny in the passenger's seat.

Nothing seemed amiss except for the weather, which was, as was customary this time of the year, wet and windy. Grey skies glowered overhead as the car came to a halt at the porch.

A policeman hurried out to meet them and they quickly entered the house, dusting off the rain from their overcoats.

A member of Hamilton's staff came up and took their coats as an affable-looking man, tall and gaunt, came up to them.

'Inspector Galloway?' Goldfeld enquired.

'Indeed, Dr Goldfeld,' Galloway replied and nodded to Penny. 'Miss Hamilton.'

'Where's my father?' Penny asked, wide-eyed with worry.

Galloway pursed his lips and rocked on his heels. 'Well, Miss, I'm sorry, but I really don't have any news for you, good or bad.' He gestured, indicating that they should move into the study where they could speak privately.

'Please sit,' Galloway indicated the high-backed leather reading chairs, as the study door shut behind them. A burly policeman stood on watch outside, ensuring that they would not be disturbed.

'Now, then,' Galloway resumed, when they were all seated. 'I understand Mr Hamilton called you last night.' He looked at Goldfeld.

'Indeed, yes he did,' Goldfeld replied. 'And I wish I could have done something to help Ernest.'

'You did what you could, Mr Goldfeld,' Galloway reassured him. 'There was nothing else you could do from so far away except for letting us know. We got here as fast as we could, but that wasn't good enough.' He paused. 'What exactly did Mr Hamilton say to you?'

'He told me that someone had broken into his house. That Penny may be in danger and I should contact her and remove her to safety immediately. And he asked me to retrieve something from his safe, should something happen to him.' Goldfeld frowned, trying to recall the conversation of the previous night. He had been so intent on Penny's safety that much of what Hamilton had said to him had not really registered. 'Oh yes, and he said something about the coins.'

'The coins?' Galloway was puzzled. 'He seems to be more of a manuscript collector than a numismatist.'

'I'm really not sure what he meant,' Goldfeld scratched his head. Again, he had been too focused on what he should do to help Penny to have asked Hamilton what he was going on about. And, of course, he had been worried about Hamilton's safety, too. The thought that something would actually happen to Hamilton had not seemed as real as it did now.

'Well, then, I would suggest that you retrieve whatever he asked you to,' Galloway's face was grave. 'We've hunted high and low for him all of last night. We've put out an alert. But nothing's turned up yet. The strange thing is that, though Mr Hamilton told you that someone broke into the house, it really wasn't a break in. We found two bodies. One of them had to be an accomplice of the intruders and had let them in. We don't know if it was the butler or the other staff member. And nothing seems to have been stolen. We've checked everything. There's been no attempt to try and force open any of the cabinets. Whoever they were, they weren't after the manuscripts. Maybe they were after these coins Hamilton mentioned to you.'

He turned to Penny. 'Do you have any idea about these coins, Miss?'

Penny shook her head, bewildered. 'Papa never mentioned any coins to me,' she said. 'I know about the safe in the house. It's where he keeps his papers. But he didn't collect coins.'

Galloway nodded. 'We'll keep searching, then,' he said briskly and rose from his chair. 'I will keep you informed of any developments in our investigation. Until then,' he addressed Goldfeld, 'I suggest that you keep Miss Hamilton in a safe place. If Mr Hamilton said she may be in danger, he could be quite right.' He nodded to them. 'Good day and thank you for driving up here.'

Goldfeld looked at Penny. 'Where's the safe?'

'Right here in the study.'

'Great.' He looked at Penny. 'You don't happen to have the combination, do you?'

'No,' Penny said. 'But Papa did tell me something. He said that the combination was hidden in one of the cabinets in the manuscript room. I have the passcode for that cabinet.'

'Now we're getting somewhere,' Goldfeld said. 'Which cabinet?'

Penny stared at him. 'I don't remember. I never really thought I'd need it anytime.' Her lower lip quivered. 'I'm going to let Papa down.'

'Now, now,' Goldfeld put an arm around her shoulders in an avuncular gesture. 'There's no need to get upset. We'll figure it out. Shall we walk around the cabinets and see if you can remember?'

Penny nodded tearfully and they made their way to the manuscript room.

Row upon row of cabinets lined the room, ancient manuscripts imprisoned within their glass walls.

'They're labelled,' Goldfeld remarked as they began examining the cabinets one by one. 'Look—Plutarch, Arrian; my word, he has quite a collection.'

'They're labelled by the authors of the manuscripts within each cabinet,' Penny sniffed. 'Except where authorship was not established. For that he had a set of cabinets labelled "Anonymous".'

'That's it!' Goldfeld exulted. 'So that's what he meant!'

Penny looked at him, not understanding.

'Before your father disconnected the call last night, he gave me the name of a Roman historian—Tacitus, the son-in-law of Agricola. I was wondering at the time what he was trying to say. Now, I know. He was referring to the cabinet, knowing that you would know the passcode for that cabinet.'

Penny smiled through her tears. 'Papa and his sense of drama,' she said. 'I do hope they find him soon.'

'The police are doing their best,' Goldfeld reassured her. 'Now, let's find out what's in this diary of his.'

36

Picadilly Circus

The little sitting room of the apartment was quite crowded. Vijay, Alice and Harry—the residents of the apartment—were there. Penny was there too.

Goldfeld had dropped Penny off at the apartment after their return to London in the afternoon and had requested that she be allowed to stay with them for now.

'I feel she will be safer here with you than anywhere else,' he had said and the others had immediately agreed. Harry had offered to vacate his bedroom and sleep on the couch and Penny had gratefully taken him up on the offer to use the third bedroom.

It was late evening now and the streets of London glistened in the light of the streetlamps as the rain continued to fall in a steady rhythm.

Goldfeld had just returned, shaking the rain off his overcoat and stamping his boots on the doormat.

The other occupants of the room looked at him enquiringly. The swelling on the faces of Vijay and Harry had begun to subside and bruises had begun to manifest themselves as evidence of their adventure of last night.

Before Goldfeld had left them in the afternoon, they had tried to work out exactly what Hamilton had asked him to do.

In the safe in Hamilton's study, Goldfeld and Penny

had found a diary, exactly as Hamilton had said they would. Following his instructions, they had taken the diary and Penny had studied it while Goldfeld drove back to London.

By the time they had arrived in London, they had worked out what Hamilton had referred to in his last call.

Ten pages of the diary dealt with the subject of the coins, under the title "The Inverness Hoard". There was a detailed description of the coins along with drawings of both sides of three coins. There were also names written against each coin.

Two were the names of people. J. Foster Esq. and S. Holmes Esq.

The third was a museum.

The British Museum.

None of the people in the room had heard of the Inverness Hoard, so they had spent some time researching the subject on the Internet.

When they finally learned what the Inverness Hoard was, Hamilton's instructions became clearer. The intruders at the house had been after these coins. And, according to the diary, Hamilton's grandfather had bequeathed these coins, shortly before his death. There was a unanimous conclusion that one coin had been bequeathed each to the British Museum and the mysterious Mr Foster and Mr Holmes.

Hamilton had perhaps realised that the intruders would get the information out of him and learn who possessed the three coins. He had wanted them to be warned.

Goldfeld decided that he would try and locate the two men mentioned in the diary after which they could decide their course of action.

Now, as he returned, the others were eager to know what he had achieved.

'I guess we'll need to call Patterson again,' Goldfeld said wearily as he flopped down on a sofa. 'This is bigger than we thought.' He turned to Penny. 'I'm sorry, my dear,' he said gently, 'but the police have not made much headway. They're still looking for your father.'

Penny bit her lip and fought back her tears as she realised what he had left unsaid.

After twenty-four hours of searching and no clues to his whereabouts, it was going to get more difficult from here onwards for the police to locate Hamilton.

Alice noticed the young girl's reaction and put an arm around her. Penny closed her eyes and leaned against Alice, her head on Alice's shoulder.

'Do you want to go inside and rest for a bit?' Alice whispered to her, but Penny shook her head. She didn't want to be alone and was grateful for the company of the others.

'Glass of wine?' Vijay enquired, to break the uncomfortable silence that had enveloped the room. The historian nodded gratefully and waited as Vijay poured out the wine and handed him a glass.

'Thank you, Vijay.' Goldfeld took a sip of wine and set the glass on the centre table.

'I reached out to my connections in the antiquities and archaeological circles, assuming that both Foster and Holmes were collectors. It took the better part of the day but, luckily, I was correct and some people I knew had heard of them. Of course, both men have been long dead—they were probably contemporaries of Ernest's grandfather—but their descendants knew about the coins. For the simple reason that, in both cases, there was a break in last night and the coins were stolen. Whoever was after the coins got two of them, probably because they were easy pickings. These people had no inkling that someone would come for the coins.'

'Which leaves the third one,' Alice said slowly. 'The one in the British Museum.'

'That's right,' Goldfeld assented. 'They're probably preparing a break in there as well, but that will take time. The coin in the museum is much better protected than the other two.'

'We have to warn the museum,' Vijay said. 'They...'

He broke off as Penny let out a wail. She couldn't control her emotions anymore. She was struggling to be brave but, as the discussion progressed, it became clear to her that the odds were stacked high against her father returning safely. If there were people who wanted the coins so badly that they could plan to burgle the British Museum, they were dangerous folk. And it had also struck her, as it had no doubt struck the others, that only one person could have given these people the information about the owners of the coins.

Ernest Hamilton.

37

A plan

Alice led Penny into her bedroom and sat talking to her, comforting her as the others continued their discussion.

Penny was still crying, her thin frame wracked by sobs, as the bedroom door closed behind them.

'They'll kill him!' she blubbered. 'They must have tortured him to get the names of these people from him! I'm never going to see him again.'

Alice wordlessly held the young girl as she continued to shed tears. There was nothing she could say to make Penny feel better. The truth was that Hamilton's chances were bleak. If he was still alive at all.

Presently, the flood of tears abated and Penny dropped to bed, physically and emotionally drained. The past twenty-four hours had been a nightmare for the young girl. Her father had been kidnapped, two men had broken into her apartment with the clear intention of abducting her, if not worse; one of them had been killed, Harry and Vijay had sustained injuries in the skirmish and now it was apparent that her father had been tortured and probably killed.

Alice sat silently by Penny's side until the girl dropped off to sleep, fatigue eventually overcoming her stress and anxiety, which had kept her awake the entire night before.

Silently shutting the door of the bedroom, Alice returned to the others in the sitting room.

'She's sleeping now,' Alice informed them.

Vijay updated her on their discussions. 'We've decided to speak to Patterson and see what he says. Harry's on the phone with him right now. We think we should inform the British Museum but we need Patterson's clearance for that.'

Harry emerged from Vijay's bedroom, looking grim. 'Patterson's been working the lines,' he reported. 'They got a positive ID on the dead man. I was right. Special Forces.' He touched his face ruefully. 'I should have been more careful. Never thought that we would get into something like this.' He looked accusingly at Vijay. 'You're supposed to be here on holiday. On personal work. Whatever. Not an official task force mission.'

He sat down. 'Patterson agrees with us. We need to inform the museum. He'll take care of that. But we'll need to go to the museum tomorrow and brief them. They need to know what to watch out for.'

'Looking like this?' Vijay grimaced.

Harry grinned. 'That's what the boss says.'

Vijay looked at Alice. 'Harry and I will go. You need to meet Wallace, anyway.'

Earlier that evening, Alice had received a call from Kurt Wallace. He was arriving tonight in London and wanted to meet her the following morning.

Alice caught Vijay's eye and shrugged. She knew what he was trying to convey to her without the others catching on. Wallace didn't need to be told everything. They had had a long talk about her meeting with Wallace after his call.

'He doesn't need to know the story on the prisms,' Vijay had insisted, when Alice had informed him about the meeting.

'Vijay, you knew that we'd have to share some information with Kurt,' Alice had remonstrated. 'When I approached him for help with the British Museum, I had to tell him what we wanted so that the letter he sent them was specific to our requirement. And you had agreed to that.'

'I had agreed only to tell him that we wanted to see the prism at the museum,' Vijay had argued. 'We never discussed sharing the story on the prism with him.'

'I know we didn't explicitly discuss that,' Alice had replied. 'But Kurt was very clear about the terms of his assistance. He was curious and had asked me to share with him what we found once we examined the prism. And that includes the story. I can't withhold that from him. I had sent him an email thanking him and expressing my gratitude after we got to examine the prism. So if he still wants to meet me, I'm quite sure he's going to ask me for details tomorrow.'

Vijay was reluctant to accept her point of view, but had grudgingly conceded some ground after hearing her final argument.

'Don't forget, Vijay, that he helped us out despite knowing that you were the one who met Saxena in the Titan office a few months ago. He told me that he was upset about that and had complained to Patterson. I don't want us to get into any further trouble over this. And what's the harm of sharing the Semiramis story with him anyway? It didn't get us anywhere and we all agreed that it is just another myth.'

'Fine then,' Vijay had grumbled. 'But just the basic story. Nothing more.'

'I'll play it by ear, Vijay,' was Alice's final word on the matter.

She found herself wondering how the meeting would go. For her own sake and Vijay's, she hoped that Kurt Wallace would not be too inquisitive about the prism.

Part 5

38

Day 3

The Dorchester Hotel, London

Kurt Wallace beamed at Alice as their tea was poured out for them at the Promenade.

Alice had been overawed by the sheer opulence of the setting: marble columns crowned with gold, elegantly set tables, inlaid marble floors, gorgeous flowers and soft illumination from the table lamps.Even though it was a public space, the high-backed sofas and the marble pillars with curtains created a sense of privacy.

Wallace was quite obviously a regular at the hotel since he was recognised by the courteous staff, who knew exactly what his preferences were.

Alice had been too awestruck to choose from the many varieties of tea on offer and Wallace had ordered for her.

'I'm glad you got what you wanted from the British Museum,' Wallace came straight to the point. He had already enquired after her when they met in the lobby and he was a man who didn't believe in wasting time on formalities. 'Dawkins' word carries a lot of weight around there.' He shrugged modestly.'And I just happened to have helped them out a few times, so they were obliged to me.'

Alice smiled back at him. 'Vijay and I are grateful for your help, Kurt. There was no other way we could have got access to the prism.'

Wallace's face darkened for a fleeting moment at the mention of Vijay's name. Then, the shadow passed and he was back to his usual gracious self. 'I am glad,' he said, sipping his tea. 'You never did tell me why you wanted to take a look at the prism. Or why Vijay was interested in it.'

Alice launched into an explanation of how she had sharpened her knowledge of the archaeology of the Middle East, especially the Sumerian, Babylonian and Assyrian civilisations, which she had not been well acquainted with before. 'The projects and programmes that you helped arrange for me were really interesting,' she concluded. 'And the chance to see this prism up close was too good to pass up. Vijay just happened to be in London on vacation at the same time and he, too, is interested in ancient history so he decided to accompany me to the museum.

She hoped that her story was convincing.

To her relief, Wallace nodded. 'So you're now an expert on the ancient Middle East?'

'Not exactly,' Alice laughed.

'What was on the prism?'

The question caught her by surprise. Even though she had been expecting it, the timing threw her off balance.

'I'm sorry?' was the best she could muster in response.

'The prism you examined,' Wallace persisted. 'What did the inscriptions say? I'm sure you had them deciphered.'

Alice decided to come clean. There was no point in concealing anything from Wallace. He was just too sharp. And she didn't want to rub him the wrong way. Vijay didn't really bother about things like this. He wouldn't have cared about whether he was upsetting Wallace or not. But Alice was more pragmatic.

She told him about the story that Goldfeld had shared with

them. The story of Semiramis and the priest who had asked her to go East and get something back for him and his brethren. She decided not to tell him about the second prism—the one that KS had given Vijay, since that didn't seem necessary—but she held nothing back from the story on the two prisms.

There was silence when she had finished.

Alice felt a bit foolish. Was the truth stranger than fiction? Was Wallace thinking that she had woven a story out of thin air? It was, after all, a spectacularly fantastic story.

'That's really interesting,' Wallace said finally, looking thoughtful. Then, he looked Alice in the eye. 'What if that story were true?'

39

The British Museum, London

'Welcome back to the British Museum,' Atkins greeted Vijay and Harry without the slightest trace of humour. 'Shall we sit in my office? It is more private there and we can talk freely.'

'Shall we take a look at the coin first?' Vijay countered. 'I didn't see it the last time I was here.'

'Yes, of course,' Atkins replied. 'The last time you were more interested in the Assyrian exhibits, as I recall.'

Atkins gestured to one of his men. 'He'll show you where the coin is exhibited. Once you're done, please come to my office and we'll talk. I need to ask you some questions.'

'Sure, thanks,' Vijay said and they turned to follow the security guard who had been deputed as their guide.

'Level 3, Gallery 49,' the guard informed them as they headed up the staircase in the East Wing.

On the third floor, they passed through various galleries containing exhibits from ancient Arabia, Iran, Britain and Europe, finally entering the gallery with artefacts from Roman Britain.

Their guide led them to the glass case where the coin rested on one face, with the other face visible. This face bore a profile of Julius Caesar, as was noted by the small plaque next to the coin.

Vijay and Harry stared at the seemingly ordinary coin that had inspired such violence and bloodshed.

But clearly, there was something about these coins that they couldn't see. And didn't know.

What was it?

40

The Security Office

'Right,' Atkins said, as Vijay and Harry sat across his desk and one of his guards shut the door to the office. 'What's so bloody important about this coin that we've got to do a lockdown of the museum?'

Vijay and Harry looked at each other. They had no answer.

Atkins divined their thoughts. 'Great,' he said. 'You say that someone is after the coin but you don't know why.'

Clearly, Patterson had kept his cards close to his chest. The museum had not been told why they thought there was a threat to the coin. All they knew was that there was reliable intelligence that someone would try and steal the coin.

'Are you working for an intelligence agency?' Atkins queried suspiciously. 'You told me you were interested in history. Now you tell me you have intel reports on a possible theft. How on earth do you have information like this?'

Vijay shrugged. 'I don't know any more than you do,' he replied. 'Believe me, I wish I did.' It was the honest truth.

'So when do you expect this burglary to happen?' Atkins continued his line of questioning. 'The attempt to steal the coin, that is.'

'We don't really know,' Vijay found himself in the awkward position of not having much of the information that Atkins was requesting, and unable to share with Atkins the information that he did have. 'All we know for certain is that this coin will be targeted soon. They will certainly take some time to prepare for the break in. But I don't think they will wait too long. All signs point to a sense of urgency for these people.'

'And what are those signs?' Atkins pressed.

Vijay shook his head.

'Okay... Who are these people who want the coin?' Atkins came back.

Vijay shook his head again and Atkins let out an exasperated sigh.

'Do you know what a lockdown of the museum entails? We will have to restrict entry during the daytime. Increase security during the night.' A thought struck him. 'I don't suppose you know what the chances of a daytime burglary are vis-à-vis a night time break in?'

Vijay at last found himself able to partly answer a question. 'We can't be certain. We don't know much about them.'

'Very well, then.' Atkins had reached a decision. 'I can't go around shutting down the museum without any concrete information. I'll double the night watch. But I can't do more. If they are planning a burglary, it will probably be at night. I have to have more to go on if anything further needs to be done.'

Vijay's heart sank. This didn't sound very promising. Would doubling the night security really be a deterrent?

But he realised he wasn't going to get anything more out of Atkins.

Atkins rose, indicating that the meeting was over and held out his hand. 'If you get any more information, let me know and we'll act immediately on it.'

'Sure,' Vijay mumbled and they left the security office.

'That didn't go too well,' Harry muttered as the two men left the building.

'I don't blame him,' Vijay replied. 'I guess he's also doubting us because he doesn't know who we are working for and why we are asking for increased security over one little coin. That's accentuated by the fact that I came here eight months ago trying to get access to a prism, which was also the target of a burglary over a year ago. Wouldn't you be suspicious if you were in his shoes?'

Vijay's phone rang. To his surprise, it was a number from India.

'Vijay?' It was Imran.

What was Imran calling for?

'I got a message from Patterson,' Imran continued, without waiting for Vijay to respond. 'He's trying to keep a tight lid on the events in the UK but it isn't easy. You're in charge of this one. You've got to figure out what's happening with the coins and who is behind the attack on Hamilton. You're on the ground, so I told Patterson I'd give you this job.'

'There isn't much to go on,' Vijay said. 'I just had a look at the third coin. It is very ordinary. But I'll try my best.'

'I've asked Colin to join you,' Imran told him. 'You guys work well as a team. I've seen that in the past. He's already on a flight to London. You'll need all the help you can get. Patterson can only hold out for a week. After that, the police will go public and the media will be all over this case. The disappearance of a wealthy collector will make headlines. And if anything happens at the British Museum, that, too, will make national headlines in the UK. You have a week to find out what's happening.'

'A week?' Vijay was incredulous. 'That isn't enough time.'

'No choice,' Imran responded. 'Rise to the challenge. Bye now.'

Vijay stared at the phone in his hand. What was Imran thinking? How could he find out anything within a week?

Even if Colin was coming to help him. He didn't even know where to start!

His phone rang again.

This time, it was Alice.

'Hey, Alice,' he greeted her warmly. 'How was your meeting with Wallace?'

Her voice had an urgency to it that startled Vijay. 'Can you come right away to the Dorchester Hotel? You need to meet Kurt.'

41

On the streets of London

Vijay was nervous. Imran had just thrust a tremendous responsibility upon him. It hadn't struck him during the call but was beginning to sink in now.

He was in charge. Which meant that he had to deliver the goods. Solve the case.

The problem was that he had absolutely no experience in intelligence gathering or case cracking. He was no professional investigator or intelligence agent, unlike Imran. True, over the last two years, he had been instrumental in resolving the two big challenges that had arisen as a consequence of the Order's activities in India. But he had been lucky most of the time. There had been no structure to his actions in both cases. Things had just…happened and he had reacted to them.

This was different. This was a formal responsibility. With a clearly defined outcome.

Vijay was never one to run away from responsibility. He loved solving problems and was happy to rise to the challenge, as Imran had urged. But it was one thing to solve problems in engineering college or in the business he had set up with Colin after graduating from MIT. And it was quite another thing to find out why unknown people were hunting down ancient Roman gold coins, and to probe the disappearance of Ernest

Hamilton. Added to this was the fact that there was the strong possibility of a break in at the British Museum.

Was he up to the task? Vijay wasn't sure. Was he the right person for this job? He didn't think so.

But Vijay hadn't protested when Imran had announced his decision to hand over this case to him. And it was too late to do anything about it. The case was his. For better or for worse.

This, however, was not the only source of his trepidation.

He was on his way, with Harry, to meet Kurt Wallace. Alice had made it very clear that Vijay had to meet Kurt. She hadn't explained why, but the tone of her voice had convinced Vijay that there was a good reason behind it. And Vijay had known Alice long enough to not question her judgement.

The problem was that Vijay didn't like Kurt Wallace. For one thing, he held Kurt responsible, directly or indirectly, for Radha's death. It was in a medical centre associated with a pharmaceutical company owned by Kurt Wallace that Radha had met her end. He had never been convinced that Wallace could be completely absolved of the responsibility for her death. His own personal opinion was that Saxena would have done nothing without Wallace's approval since Wallace was the Chairman of Titan Pharmaceuticals, the company for which Saxena worked.

Unfortunately, there was no evidence to pin down Wallace and Patterson had made it clear that Wallace and Saxena were not to be hounded. They had the law on their side and Wallace had the connections to make life very difficult for the task force, should he wish to.

The other reason for Vijay's antagonism towards Wallace was his action following Vijay's meeting with Saxena a year ago in the offices of Titan Pharmaceuticals. Vijay had always known that there was no logic behind that meeting and it had turned out to be futile anyway. The only outcome of that meeting had been the complaint lodged by Wallace with Patterson, in which Wallace had falsely accused Vijay of threatening Saxena.

Vijay's resentment towards Wallace had grown after that episode and had not abated since.

Things had grown more complicated when Vijay had realised that Wallace was the one person who could reliably help him gain access to the prism in the British Museum. He had overcome his resentment of Wallace with great difficulty while asking Alice to speak to Wallace and request his help.

And now, he was about to meet Wallace in person for the first time.

Throughout the cab ride, Vijay had to keep telling himself that he had to watch his temper. There was no way that Patterson would overlook any missteps on Vijay's part with Wallace today.

The cab pulled up at the Dorchester Hotel and Vijay handed the driver the fare.

'Keep the change,' he told the cab driver, as he stepped out and prepared to enter the hotel.

He wondered what it was that Wallace was going to speak to him about.

42

The Dorchester Hotel, London

Vijay sat uncomfortably at the table with Wallace and Alice and tried hard not to fidget. The billionaire had been cordial, if not warm, in his greeting, though it was obvious from his demeanour that the suggestion for Vijay's presence at the table had been made by Alice, not Wallace.

Alice looked from Vijay to Wallace and back, sizing up the situation and sighed inwardly. Men! Both were visibly reluctant participants and she would have to manage the situation.

'Kurt had something very interesting to tell me about the prism we saw at the British Museum.' Alice broached the agenda for the discussion without any further delay. She knew how important this meeting was for Vijay, even though he didn't know it himself yet. She emphasised the word "prism" slightly, so Vijay would know that she hadn't disclosed the existence of two prisms to Wallace.

'Ah, yes,' Wallace took up the narrative, as Alice looked at him meaningfully. 'Alice told me about the story on the prism you saw at the museum. Semiramis and the war in the East and so on.'

It was Vijay's turn to look at Alice, who simply nodded her acknowledgement that she had shared the Semiramis story with Wallace.

'I know the story seems like just another of the countless myths surrounding Semiramis,' Wallace continued, now warming up to the subject. 'But something struck me as she was narrating the story. It concerns a codex that was acquired a few years ago by a friend of mine, a collector in the US.' He looked at Vijay. 'Have you heard of Cicero?'

Vijay pursed his lips as he searched his memory but could find no recollection of the name. He shook his head.

'Then allow me to explain a bit about Cicero. Marcus Tullius Cicero was a Roman statesman, lawyer, scholar, orator and writer. He was a contemporary of Julius Caesar and, after his assassination, of Octavius—who later became Augustus, the first Emperor of Rome. Cicero wrote a number of books, most of them comprising letters to and from different people including Julius Caesar, Octavius, Brutus and Pompey.'

'Brutus was one of the assassins of Julius Caesar,' Alice interjected, not sure how good Vijay's knowledge of ancient Roman history was. 'And Pompey was the general Caesar defeated to become the dictator of Rome.'

Vijay nodded his thanks to Alice.

'Thank you, Alice,' Wallace took up the thread again. 'Many of his collections of letters have been lost, including the books containing correspondence with Caesar, Pompey and Brutus. The books that do exist are well preserved and documented. Bear in mind, of course, that these are all copies made during medieval times and not the original books, none of which have survived. The codex I refer to is a previously unknown book, consisting of letters exchanged by Cicero and his brother Quintus who was a legate in Caesar's army during the conquest of Gaul.' He paused.

Satisfied that Vijay was following the thread of the narrative, Wallace resumed. 'Apparently, this codex was discovered by Francesco Petrarca, better known as Petrarch, a self-avowed fan, as we would term him today, of Cicero. Petrarch had one of the largest collections of Cicero's works in medieval times. We knew earlier of two discoveries made by Petrarch, in 1333 at Liège and in 1345 at Verona, of previously lost texts by Cicero, which had disappeared from circulation since antiquity. Both those manuscripts, unfortunately, have not survived, despite being major discoveries, which are well documented. It seems that this third codex, which we have named the "Quintus Codex" for ease of reference, was less famous, but was unearthed by Petrarch in the chapter Library of Verona cathedral in 1340. It disappeared after that but turned up at a private auction where my friend acquired it.'

Vijay didn't know where this was leading up to but he had an inkling about the significance of this codex.

'I'm guessing that this Quintus Codex contained something related to the Semiramis myth,' he volunteered.

Wallace raised an eyebrow, surprised at Vijay's perspicacity. 'That's right. And interestingly, it meshes very well with the story you found inscribed on that prism.'

Alice felt a pang inside her as Wallace repeatedly spoke of a single prism. She was never very comfortable with dissembling and, though she hadn't really lied, she had distorted the truth somewhat and Wallace's unconditional acceptance of her story made her feel guilty.

Vijay was suddenly very interested in Wallace. 'I'm sorry, I didn't mean to interrupt,' he said. 'Please go on.'

He wondered what revelation Wallace would disclose to him. The prism had already disgorged its secret.

What did the Quintus Codex say?

43

56 B.C.

Gaul, modern-day France

Julius Caesar frowned at the man sitting in the chair opposite him. He was not happy. But if there was someone who could help Caesar get to the root of the problem, it was this man.

Divitiacus was no ordinary man. He was a chief of the Aedui and elder brother to Dumnorix, their ruling king. More importantly, he was also a Druid, albeit a young one. Caesar estimated that Divitiacus was no more than thirty-five years of age.

The Druid had first made Caesar's acquaintance on a visit to Rome four years ago, when Divitiacus had appeared before the Roman senate to appeal for help after the conquest of the Aedui by the Sequani who were allied with Ariovistus, the king of the invading Teutonic tribe of the Suebi.

Divitiacus had met Caesar and Cicero during his stay in Rome and, while his own mission was unsuccessful, the Druid had developed a loyalty to Rome, and Caesar, that had served the Roman general well during his campaign in Gaul. This was despite the fact that Divitiacus' own brother, Dumnorix, hated both Rome and Caesar and led the resistance against the Roman occupation of Gaul.

Two years ago, Caesar had let loose his ten legions on Gaul after cutting off the migrating tribe called the Helvetii, despite the Roman army being outnumbered by more than six to one.

It had been during this campaign that Dumnorix had asserted his own power and authority among the Aedui and attempted to thwart Caesar's plan, by joining Orgetorix, the head of the Helvetian nobles.

When Caesar finally emerged victorious, Dumnorix's anti-Roman activities had been detailed to Caesar.

It had been at this juncture that Divitiacus had intervened. The Roman general well remembered that conversation, which he had documented in his reports to the Senate in Rome.

'I ask for pardon for my brother,' Divitiacus had said, holding Caesar's gaze even as he pleaded for his brother's life. 'It was with my help that my brother, Dumnorix, came to power. If you punish Dumnorix, as he deserves to be punished, justice will be served for Rome. But I am your friend and all of Gaul knows that. I will lose the goodwill of every inhabitant of Gaul. I beg of you, Caesar, pardon Dumnorix. There is no other way out. You cannot rule unless Gaul is behind you. And you well know that I am the only one who can help you to bring Gaul under the sway of Rome, and Caesar.'

Caesar had astutely realised the truth of Divitiacus's words.

'It shall be as you ask, then,' Caesar had nodded gravely. 'Your friendship and love, your loyalty and my faith in you are more precious to me than anything else in Gaul. And I would not lose any of those for anything in the world. I will pardon Dumnorix. But hear this, Divitiacus. He will be watched by my spies day and night. No action of his, no thought, will go unnoticed or unreported. I will do everything to enhance your prestige among the Aedui and the tribes of Gaul. You will be foremost among their chiefs.'

Next, Caesar had turned north to the river Rhine and defeated the German chieftain Ariovistus. The loyal Divitiacus had been of immense help in this endeavour. Caesar had summoned the Druid while laying out his strategy to fight Ariovistus.

'We need to keep apart the two main bodies of the enemy—the Belgae and the Bellovaci,' Caesar had told the Druid. 'This can only be done if the Aedui lead their own forces into the borders of the Bellovaci and begin to lay waste their lands.' The conversation that had followed went into details of battle strategy, defence positions and manoeuvres.

The strategy had succeeded. The Belgae, who continued their resistance, crumbled on hearing of the approach of Divitiacus and the Aedui against the borders of their allies, the Bellovaci. This had helped Caesar defeat them and establish Roman supremacy in the war to conquer Gaul.

The conquest of Gaul had followed soon after, with most of Gaul falling to the Romans. Only pockets of resistance remained. It was these oases of resistance in the desert of submission that posed a problem for Caesar.

And Caesar didn't like it. The conquest of Gaul was the stepping-stone for him to his ultimate objective.

The outright control of Rome.

When he was governor of Farther Spain, he had come across a statue of the Macedonian general, Alexander the Great. The Macedonian had conquered much of the known world by the time he was 30. The young Caesar, in Spain, was of the same age and felt that his achievements were trifling when compared to those of Alexander. He was governing a mere province of Rome, and Alexander had ruled most of the world at the same age.

The realisation struck him that he needed to be in Rome and close to the fountainhead of power. That would enable him to achieve his ambitions.

Caesar had returned to Rome, where he became a high priest first and then a high-ranking judge. This was followed by a return to Farther Spain, but this time as a Pro-Consul.

Before returning to Spain, he had formed an informal alliance with the great Roman general, Pompey, and Crassus, who held the distinction of being the richest man in all of Rome. Caesar offered the hand of his daughter in marriage to Pompey to strengthen the alliance between the three men, which was the first triumvirate of Rome. And the world.

But he always knew this was not enough. He had to build a reputation for himself as a great general. And for that, he had to lead a campaign against one of the unconquered lands beyond the Roman frontier.

Gaul.

With the conquest of Gaul, Caesar knew that he would command power as a victorious general—a natural outcome of the support of the army.

And, now that he was so close to achieving his goal, he was not going to allow a few tribes of Gaul to come in his way.

The problem was that a few of these tribes were consistently confounding the Romans. A well-led Roman legion was the world's ultimate fighting machine. And none of Caesar's legions were anything but well led. These were battle-hardened soldiers, unafraid of anything and virtually unbeatable in battle. The four major battles the Romans had won in the last two years, including a naval battle, were testimony to the bravery and tenacity of the legionnaires.

Yet, there were some parts of Gaul where he had visited and met with the legionnaires and discovered something that was as inexplicable as it was bizarre.

Especially Brittany, where the Armorican tribes had recently revolted.

The legionnaires had been afraid. Something strange had been happening during their battles with the Gauls. The Roman army, which normally worked with the precision of a well-oiled machine, had been falling apart. Carefully crafted battle plans, normally followed to the letter, would be discarded inexplicably.

The Gauls would immediately seize the opportunity and waste no time in inflicting heavy losses on the enemy.

The Romans had no idea what was happening or why the highly trained and hardened legionnaires were losing their wits during these battles.

The only thing that they knew was that, a few hours before the Gauls would attack in guerrilla style, the drumming would begin. Slow beats—sonorous and low-pitched, in an unnerving, regular rhythm.

Initially, the Romans had paid no heed to the drums. But they had soon learnt two things.

The first was that, even though the drum beats were faint—sounding as if they were coming from far away—they were actually being generated within a mile of the Roman encampment.

The second was that the drumbeats were not the dead giveaway the Romans had presumed them to be. The first few times the drums were heard, the Roman camp was on alert, not sure what to expect, but wary and watchful. It had seemed silly, if the Gauls were planning an attack, to alert the enemy in this manner.

But this illusion had been quickly disabused from their minds. When the attack finally came, as it always did, the Romans, alert as they were, quickly found themselves floundering, unable to defend themselves.

The Gallic attacks were swift, short and debilitating. They would sweep through the Roman defences and then disappear.

The drums would stop thereafter.

This could not be allowed to continue. Caesar had ordered that a few Gauls be captured alive for interrogation. He wanted to know what the secret of their success was. What was it that enabled them to destabilise his army and instil a fear in their hearts that was unnatural?

But the endeavour had failed. In the chaos of battle, it had proved impossible to capture any of the Gauls. They would mount short strikes and then vanish.

It was then that Julius Caesar had turned to the one man in Gaul whom he had complete faith in.

Divitiacus the Druid.

Caesar had just finished his litany of complaints against the Gallic resistance. 'I need your help, Divitiacus,' he concluded. 'There is something happening here that is beyond the realm of military warfare.' He paused.

'Last year,' he resumed after a few moments, 'you had appealed for a pardon to be granted to the Bellovaci. And I, keeping in mind my respect towards you and the Aedui, had agreed to receive them into my protection. You had also assured me that the chief troublemakers among the Bellovaci had fled to Britannia and would cause no more bother to me.'

He leaned forward, his eyes boring into the Druid. 'So what is happening to my troops? Explain this to me.'

44

February, present year

Day 3

The Dorchester Hotel, London

'In order to understand the significance of the Quintus Codex,' Wallace continued, 'you need to consider the history of Julius Caesar's campaigns in Britain.'

'Um, I don't know much about that,' Vijay admitted.

'No problem,' Wallace replied. 'Let me give you a brief snapshot. Julius Caesar mounted two invasions of Britain, in two consecutive years—55 B.C. and 54 B.C. While his own reports to the Roman Senate somewhat played up his accomplishments during both campaigns, the truth is that he accomplished little on both occasions. The first one was a near disaster and he only just managed to salvage his reputation as a general. The second one was better, simply because he managed to subdue the Celts through subterfuge. But the nature of the treaty they signed gave Rome no significant benefit either by way of tribute, access or even sovereignty. After Caesar left Britain in 54 B.C., while there was cultural and commercial interaction between Rome and Britain, it took a century before Rome finally brought Britain within the ambit of the Roman Empire. Lots of explanations have been advanced by historians trying to explain Caesar's motivations, and Rome's, for his adventures in Britain. Different schools of thought have ascribed widely divergent motives, but personally I find none of the explanations very satisfying.'

'You have your own theory about why he went to Britain?' Vijay couldn't help asking. Wallace was perceptibly sceptical about what the historians said.

'As it happens, I do,' Wallace grunted. 'If you read any of my books, you will see that I have a very strong aversion to the explanations being trotted out by the historical establishment for the gaps and mysteries that exist in the historical record.'

'I read a couple of your books,' Alice confessed. 'Your theories are...interesting.'

'But you don't really believe them,' Wallace caught on to what Alice had left unsaid.

Alice looked sheepish. She had not intended to convey that message. 'I meant that I know what you mean about the theories of the establishment. You present a very strong case in your books for challenging the conventional historical explanations, especially in cases where they are based not on archaeological data, but on ideas and opinions of people who carried weight in academic circles.'

'Don't worry, I didn't take offence,' Wallace waved a forgiving hand at her. 'I stopped getting offended a long time ago when I realised that people weren't going to easily give up beliefs instilled in them through long years of indoctrination in schools, even if those beliefs were not backed by data and evidence. And it is going to be a long time before people start realising, on a large scale, that absence of evidence doesn't mean evidence of absence.'

He checked himself and paused. 'But I'm digressing. Yes, I have a theory—an idea, actually—about Caesar's invasion of Britain. But, I don't have any evidence to back my theory. Most of all, my theory isn't even conclusive.' He leaned forward to emphasise his point. 'I believe that Caesar went to Britain for a purpose that was not related to either securing his position in Gaul or for acquiring wealth for Rome. With the sea as a natural defence, Gaul was hardly facing a threat from anyone; leave alone an obscure island off the west coast of Europe. And it certainly didn't yield any great mineral wealth or tributes for Rome.' He paused for effect.

Vijay waited. He had no idea where Wallace was going with this or what the connection was with the story on the prism. But he liked a good mystery and this was as good as any.

'I believe,' Wallace said, emphasising each word, 'that Julius Caesar went to Britain seeking power. He had learned of an ancient source of power that was hidden in Britain that would make him mightier than he already was or ever would be. And this power was associated in some way with the Druids of Britain.'

Wallace looked at Vijay, expecting scepticism. But Vijay had seen too many ancient secrets unearthed over the last two years to disbelieve an idea like this. A year and a half ago, they had uncovered an ancient secret that was being pursued by Alexander the Great, which brought him all the way to India. It was not hard for him to believe that Julius Caesar went to Britain searching for something that would make him one of the greatest generals of all time.

'What was that power?' Vijay asked.

Wallace shrugged. 'That's the problem,' he replied. 'I don't know. Like I said, it is just an idea. It isn't conclusive.'

Vijay digested this for a moment. 'And the Quintus Codex? Where does that fit in?'

Wallace smiled. He had anticipated this question. He had wanted Vijay to ask this question.

'The Quintus Codex,' Wallace declared, 'provides evidence that my idea about Caesar's invasions of Britain could be more than just a theory. It actually explains why Caesar went to Britain. It says that he went to Britain to stop the Druids from enslaving the Romans.'

45

The Quintus Codex

Wallace smiled at Vijay's shocked expression. He was a natural orator, flamboyant and dramatic, using pauses and silence to good effect, and it always gave him satisfaction to see the impact of his words on an audience, even if it comprised just one person.

'You see,' Wallace boomed, 'Quintus the legate accompanied Julius Caesar on his invasion of Britain in 54 B.C. And in a couple of letters to his brother, Cicero, he talks about the reasons for the second invasion. Of course, he does it in a roundabout manner, couching it in clever language and dismissing certain ideas as myths. It wouldn't have done for him to openly talk about his general's motives, especially when you see what he says.'

He paused to order some more tea before resuming. 'According to Quintus—once you distil the essence of what he is saying—Caesar was facing resistance from some pockets in Gaul. That was only to be expected, but it seems the Gauls were giving the Romans a tough time and Caesar somehow discovered that it was the Druids of Britain who were helping them. During the first invasion of Britain, Caesar finally discovered what the secret of the Druids was. Apparently, centuries ago, the Druids had sent an emissary to Semiramis, the Assyrian Queen.'

Vijay straightened in his chair at these words.

'Semiramis, Caesar learned, came back to Britain and gave the Druids an ancient divine weapon that she had picked up somewhere in the east,' Wallace didn't miss a beat even though he was mindful of the impact of his words on Vijay. 'Quintus doesn't say where in the east Semiramis got the weapon from; but that isn't important to his account. The Druids had used the weapon to subdue the warring Celtic tribes and establish their authority over the Celts; and then, a few centuries before the Roman invasion, they hid the weapon away. Quintus says they didn't need it any more. But when Caesar started his campaign in Gaul, the Druids began having second thoughts about keeping the weapon concealed. So, they decided to bring it out again to use it once more to establish their power and supremacy. Only, this time it would be used against the Romans. Against Julius Caesar.'

He paused to allow the waiter to pour another round of tea for all of them.

'So you're saying that Caesar went back a second time, in the following year, to stop the Druids from retrieving their weapon and setting it up to challenge the Romans?' Vijay asked thoughtfully, after the waiter had withdrawn.

'That's what Quintus says,' Wallace clarified.

'But why would it take so long for a weapon to be deployed?' Vijay was puzzling over this mystery. 'I mean, Caesar's campaign in Gaul would have lasted several years. And then, even a year after his first invasion of Britain, they had obviously not deployed the weapon.'

Wallace found it interesting that Vijay had not questioned the existence of a divine weapon. He was challenging the story about the Druids but not the fact that they did have an ancient weapon that was capable of destroying the mighty Roman army. But he said nothing, merely making a mental note for himself.

'You're right,' he answered Vijay. 'The conquest of Gaul had been ongoing for three years when Caesar first invaded Britain. And, according to Quintus, the weapon had still not been deployed when the second invasion happened.' Wallace shrugged. 'There's nothing in the letters to explain this and Quintus doesn't seem to think this important.'

'Does he say what the weapon is?' Alice enquired. She had been silent all this while, having already heard this account from Wallace. It was when Wallace had disclosed the contents of the Quintus Codex to her that she realised that Vijay had to know about this. She had immediately decided that it was best that Vijay meet Wallace and get the information first hand. She was relieved that her decision had been the right one.

'Not really. All he says is that the weapon was capable of rendering the entire Roman army ineffective. That sounds like a pretty tall claim to me, but if it was true then it isn't surprising that Caesar was worried enough to mount two invasions of Britain. Quintus ends his story by telling Cicero that Caesar's second invasion ended with a deal he made with the Druids. In return for leaving them alone and never returning, the Druids gave Caesar the location of the weapon and the means to deploy it. Quintus is a bit ambiguous about the deployment but that isn't surprising since he wouldn't have had access to all of Caesar's meetings or negotiations with the Celts.'

'And that's why Caesar left the Celts no worse off than they were before his invasion, and never returned to Britain,' Alice concluded.

'Exactly.' Wallace sat back and waited for the questions to come.

'How sure are we about the authenticity of this codex?' Vijay wanted to know. 'After all it is, as you say, a medieval copy and not the original. How do we know all this is true? Wouldn't Cicero have gotten into trouble with Caesar for publishing letters that revealed the true nature of his invasions? If this story is true, that is.'

'That's a fair question,' Wallace agreed. 'We first authenticated the codex. It isn't a forgery. It is genuinely old. And, to be quite honest with you, we weren't very sure if the story that Quintus tells within its pages was true. It does sound quite fantastic. But the content of the letters is something we had no way of validating. Until now. You approached me with the story of a prism with inscriptions that tell us how Semiramis was asked to bring a celestial weapon from the east. The inscriptions describe the war she wages to secure the weapon, her return to her kingdom and her eventual retirement to a land in the north where she is worshipped as a goddess until she dies. The two stories—the one on the prism and that narrated by Quintus— are independent of each other, yet they seem to be describing the same events. That would be a major coincidence, especially since the prism is a couple of thousand years older than the letters written by Quintus. Unless he got his hands on the prism and was able to read cuneiform, which seems to be highly unlikely. And not all of Cicero's letters were published when Caesar was alive. Some were published even after Cicero's death in 43 B.C. Caesar died in 44 B.C. This codex could have been among them because it certainly isn't among the existing manuscripts that we have of Cicero's correspondence with Quintus.'

'It certainly seems more than a coincidence,' Vijay agreed.

'It isn't just that,' Wallace insisted. 'Semiramis has been relegated to a myth by historians. Even those historians who try and find a place for her in history, place her in the ninth century B.C.; centuries after the ancient traditions claim she existed. Why do you think that happened? Was it just an accident? Or was her role in world history more important than the official historical records make it out to be? If the story on the prism and the one in the letters of Quintus are true, then there seems to have been a deliberate attempt to cover up the true story of Semiramis. I am quite familiar with the tricks of the establishment. Many of these ancient myths are rooted in truth. Why, take your own Vedic traditions.' He was addressing Vijay directly now. 'The Mahabharata, for instance. I don't know Sanskrit, but those who do tell me that it claims to be a historical account. Yet, how many Indians believe that the events described in the Mahabharata could have actually occurred? Hasn't the possibility that the epic has a historical base been effectively stamped out by years of colonial rule and western interpretations and theories about the epic?'

Vijay didn't respond. His own experience with the Mahabharata and its so-called myths had been a revelation. Wallace's words resonated with him, but he couldn't reveal that to the billionaire.

'Is it possible to get a copy of this codex?' Vijay asked Wallace instead. He wanted the opportunity to study this manuscript first hand and see exactly what it contained.

Wallace gestured to a waiter, who placed a manila envelope on the table. 'That's a facsimile of the manuscript. I got it emailed here and printed out while we were waiting for you to arrive. But it is in Latin. You will need to get someone to translate it for you.'

'Thank you, Mr Wallace,' Vijay was sincerely grateful. It seemed that finally the lead from the prisms was going to lead him somewhere. What had seemed to be a dead end had suddenly transformed into a path ahead.

But what would he find at the end of the road?

46

56 B.C.

Gaul, modern-day France

Divitiacus hesitated. 'Will you believe me, Caesar?' he asked, finally.

'Why shouldn't I? I have complete faith in you.'

'It is the Druids of Britannia, O Caesar,' Divitiacus replied.

Caesar's eyes lit up. So this was the secret behind the fight that the Gauls were putting up. Arms and, perhaps, even men from Britannia, crossing the narrow strip of ocean that separated them from Gaul, reinforcing the small bands of armed men who were proving to be such a thorn in his side. All aided by the Druids of Britannia.

But the more he thought about it the less sense it made. 'How are arms and men from Britannia helping the Gauls?' he voiced his doubt. 'That doesn't explain why our soldiers are afraid. Why their discipline, their battle formations are falling apart in these minor battles.'

The Druid nodded. You're right Governor Caesar,' he replied. 'It isn't men or arms that are coming from Britannia. It is the Druids of Britannia. Some of them have crossed over to Gaul. That much is certain from what you tell me.'

He paused again.

Caesar waited for an explanation of how the Druids of Britannia were involved.

'From what you describe, they have retrieved their secret. Or at least a part of it.'

'What secret do you mean?' Caesar was mystified.

'A secret that is thousands of years old. Our teachings, memorised and passed down orally from generation to generation, speak of this secret and its hiding place. Until now, however, the Druids have never needed to retrieve it. It is possible that, with the conquest of Gaul and your military successes, the Druids of Britannia have decided to bring back their legacy and use it against you.'

Caesar frowned. 'Explain yourself, Divitiacus. I don't like riddles.'

The Druid provided his explanation.

There was silence when he had finished. Caesar's eyes narrowed to two points as he gazed upon the Druid.

'You swear that what you have just told me is the truth?' he asked.

'May Jupiter strike me dead if I have lied,' Divitiacus replied. 'I have told you exactly what I know from my years of training as a Druid.'

Caesar frowned. 'So how do we counter this power of theirs?'

Divitiacus shook his head. 'You cannot,' he replied, holding Caesar's gaze. 'This is a power bestowed by the gods on the Lords of Light—a power that was passed on to the Druids. There is no force on earth that can stand against it.'

'What do you mean?' Caesar demanded.

The Druid hesitated once more, then spoke slowly, emphasising each word. 'If they have retrieved their weapon, the Druids in Britannia will enslave us all. It is only a matter of time.'

47

February, present year

Day 3

Regent's Park, London

Dee's eyes bored into the man who sat in the chair, his left hand wrapped in a bloody bandage, his eyes wide with terror.

She knew that under those bandages were two stumps of his fingers. Dee had sliced them off personally when the man had refused to accede to her demand. Of course, at that time, he hadn't known whom he was dealing with. He wouldn't make such a mistake again.

Once he had lost those fingers, he had quickly become very compliant, willing to do anything she asked.

'Are you sure about this translation?' She jabbed a finger at the papers on the desk before her. 'Dead sure?'

The man nodded, his head bobbing like that of a bobblehead doll.

Dee perused the translation once more. 'And the grave lies on the top of this hill. That is what the inscriptions say?'

The man's head bobbed up and down again.

Dee sat back, deep in thought. Caesar's diary—the ninth book of the version of the Commentaries that the Order had uncovered—had told the story of Semiramis, the Assyrian Queen, bringing a divine weapon back from the east for the Druids of Britain.

While the diary didn't say where that weapon was now hidden, it corroborated the story that this man had translated for her from the images of the prisms that she had obtained from Alice's email to Goldfeld.

It had to be more than a coincidence, she thought, that two independent sources told the same story.

The diary itself had been quite clear on several counts. It had given a detailed account of the story of Semiramis, which matched perfectly with the story she was reading in the translation before her.

The diary had also explained in detail the nature of the divine weapon that Semiramis had brought back for the Druids. Apparently, as part of the deal that Caesar had struck with the Druids in 54 B.C., they had tutored him in the art of activating and deploying the weapon and also given him the location where the weapon had been hidden a few centuries before the invasion of Gaul.

Finally, Caesar had mentioned that he had, during his stay in Alexandria after the Alexandrian civil war, requested Cleopatra—who was, by then, Pharoah—to mint three coins especially for him.

These three coins were the key to finding the location of the weapon.

How was she going to locate those three coins? Who even knew if they had survived the centuries, especially the years of turmoil after Caesar's death?

It had seemed that her mission was destined to fail even before it started.

The situation was complicated by the fact that Caesar had, surprisingly, been very ambiguous in his description of the coins. While he had been quite detailed in his other accounts in the diary, there was very little information about the coins.

All that the diary said was that the coins were gold and they bore the image of Julius Caesar on one side and the distinctive image of an elongated, oval shaped, Celtic shield on the other, accompanied by a single inscription. It also had a map that showed the location of the megalithic sites that represented the geographical interpretation of the inscriptions.

It wasn't much to go on.

But Dee had never been one to give up. She had put her team on the job to locate all Roman coins that had been traded or unearthed in recorded history. If these coins were not among them, then she would have to find another way.

But, as luck would have it, they had come across a news article from 1914, which mentioned the Inverness Hoard, along with a description of the coins that seemed to match the description that Caesar had given in his diary.

From there, it hadn't been too difficult to track down Ernest Hamilton and learn the whereabouts of the three coins.

Now, she had two of the coins in her possession. The third looked like it was going to be a challenge. She had never anticipated that it would have been bequeathed to the British Museum of all places.

Without the third coin, she had no way of beginning the search for the weapon.

The prisms, however, recorded where Semiramis was buried. Perhaps there were clues there?

While she and her team prepared for the task of breaking into the British Museum, it would be worth seeing if there was anything to be learned from the tomb of Semiramis.

If nothing else, a visit to the tomb would give her a sense of connection with the ancient queen.

There were similarities between the two of them. Both had been born in the land of the Indus. They had both left their birthplaces and travelled to distant lands to seek their fortune. Both women were ambitious and sought power.

The difference was that Semiramis had achieved everlasting fame as a goddess.

It would be good to see her tomb, Dee decided.

But there was one small detail that she had to take care of first.

The man in the chair. The expert on ancient scripts who had been kidnapped from Florence and brought here especially for this task. Now that he had given her what she wanted, he was of no further use.

She faced him, her eyes gleaming with anticipation, and gestured.

One of the men in the room moved over to the linguist and slipped a dagger between his ribs, straight into the heart. The man in the chair jerked with shock and the spark of life faded away from his eyes even as Dee gazed straight into them.

She had no reservations about watching people being killed. Truth be told, she quite relished it. On the odd special occasion, she took delight in delivering the deathblow herself.

As she had done with Ernest Hamilton and countless others.

Now, she had a job to do. A mission to complete.

It would start with the grave of Semiramis.

48

August 26, 55 B.C.

Present-day Dover

The Romans aboard the galleys gazed upon the sight that greeted their eyes. The chalk cliffs that loomed high above the waters of the channel separating Gaul from Britannia were lined with Celtic warriors.

'What a sight, Governor!' Marcus Arius, a centurion standing at Caesar's side, had exclaimed on first sighting the line upon line of Celts. 'A welcome fit for an emperor! See how the tribes of Britannia are waiting for their conquerors!'

But that elation had swiftly turned to concern as the Romans had realised that the men on the cliffs were armed to the teeth with stones, javelins and swords.

This was no welcoming party.

Docking in the face of such hostile intent was impossible and the Romans were forced to change their plans.

'We will stop further up the coast, then,' Caesar had instructed, through clenched teeth. He was angry for allowing himself to be deceived by the Celts.

He should have suspected that something was afoot when Commius, the chief of the Gallic Atrebates, had gone to Britannia earlier as his emissary to negotiate peace with the Celts. There had been no word from Commius ever since he set foot on that forsaken island. Some of his generals had murmured doubts about Commius being taken prisoner by the Celts. But Caesar, in his arrogance, had brushed all such concerns aside. It was impossible for him to entertain the thought that the primitive Celts would dare to spit in the face of Roman military might.

Instead, with two legions—the seventh and the tenth—he had set sail from Portus Itius and reached the coast of Dover after an overnight journey, expecting the Celts to submit to his superior forces without a battle. Clearly, this was not to be.

Battles would be fought.

Caesar was not happy. Not just because he had just ten thousand men with him between the two legions. Not because his cavalry was back in Gaul, due to join him tomorrow.

But because his mission here had not been to wage war, even though that was his ostensible intention, well documented in the reports he was sending back to Rome.

The truth was that Caesar had no interest in this island with its piteous weather and even more pathetic inhabitants.

He was after bigger things. Divitiacus had revealed that the Druids of Britannia harboured an ancient secret—a secret that gave the Druids the ability to overcome even the Romans, if they so wished.

It was this secret that Caesar had come to unearth. A secret so powerful that Rome would submit to him without the petty political intrigues that he knew he would have to otherwise weave in order to achieve his objective.

A goal that had been born in Farther Spain all those years ago.

An ambition to match Alexander the Great in his achievements.

A desire to rule the world.

49

February, present year

Day 3

Picadilly Circus

The apartment was a hotbed of activity. Vijay and Alice had dropped in at Goldfeld's house on their way back from the meeting with Wallace and handed over the copy of the Quintus Codex to him.

Goldfeld had been thrilled to see the codex and hear about how it had been discovered by Petrarch. He had been even more excited when Vijay shared with him the details of the conversation he had had with Wallace a short while ago regarding its contents.

'I had no idea something like this existed,' he murmured as he opened the envelope. 'Imagine finding another set of letters by Quintus!'

He readily agreed to Vijay's request to review the contents of the codex and prepare a translation of the relevant letters for them, while Vijay and Alice returned to the apartment. Vijay wanted to read up on Semiramis and put in a call to Dr Shukla in India before it got too late. He was curious about the divine weapon that Semiramis was supposed to have given the Druids and thought that Shukla may have some thoughts on what it could be.

Alice had volunteered to study the diary they had recovered from Hamilton's safe and see if there were any clues to this mystery available there.

If they were going to find out who was behind the attack on Hamilton and why they were searching for the coins, they first needed to figure out what these people were after.

Vijay and Alice had discussed what they had learned from Wallace and had come to the conclusion that it was worth investigating a possible link between the coins and Caesar's invasions of Britain. Now that they knew that the coins were minted by Caesar, and that they had been discovered in Britain, it seemed possible that there was a connection there. Whether it was related in any way to the story of the Druids was not clear, but they decided to probe further and see what they could unearth.

They had decided to meet at Goldfeld's house later in the day to discuss what each of them had found.

Harry and Penny were busy organising lunch while Alice pored over the diary and Vijay sat with his laptop and a notebook, furiously scribbling away.

The doorbell rang.

'I'll get it.' Harry opened the door.

Colin stood there, a big grin on his face. He had been flown here in a private jet specially chartered by the task force, after a quick briefing by Imran. He was delighted to be back with his friends.

'Hey guys!' Colin whooped as he entered the apartment, his suitcase in tow. 'Good to see you again, Harry!'

Alice got a peck on her cheek and Vijay got the customary warm hug. Colin stopped short as he saw Penny.

'Hi, there,' he said. 'We haven't met. I'm Colin. You must be Penny.'

Vijay brought Colin up to speed on the story of Semiramis and the divine weapon on the prisms, the meeting with Wallace, the revelations of the Quintus Codex and their assigned tasks for the day.

'I've got work for you, too,' Vijay told Colin. 'Research the Druids. See if you can find anything that may point us to what they had asked Semiramis to get back from India.'

'This is great,' Colin said excitedly. 'Another adventure. More ancient mysteries. And, this time, no threats from any terrorist organisation or any riddles to solve that can get us into trouble. My kind of adventure.'

Vijay smiled, as much at Colin's enthusiasm as his happiness at the relative tameness of their assignment. He had to agree, it seemed to be much less dangerous than their earlier entanglements with history and mythology. All they needed to do was find out what Semiramis had brought back with her from India, whether it was related to the coins and then use that information to work out who was behind Ernest Hamilton's abduction.

But he also knew that it was easier said than done.

And one thing still nagged at him. He hadn't shared it with Alice since he wasn't sure if she would agree or even understand; but he had found it impossible to get it out of his mind.

It had struck Vijay as strange that Wallace had not only shared the story of the codex and its contents—something he didn't have to do—but had also given Vijay a copy to work on.

Why had Wallace been so pliant and cooperative?

50

Saul Goldfeld's house

The little group settled down in Saul Goldfeld's comfortable study. It hadn't been designed to house so many people, but each of them found a chair, a cushion, part of a couch or a niche.

Only Penny was missing. Shortly after lunch, Hamilton's sister had come and picked her up. Susan Hamilton-Rogers lived in California and she had been informed of Hamilton's disappearance just the day before. She had hopped onto the first available flight to London. Susan had insisted on taking Penny with her and had been genuinely grateful to Vijay and his friends for looking after the young girl. The aunt and niece had then departed for the Hamilton estate, where Susan intended to stay until the police were able to find Hamilton.

Goldfeld looked at Vijay. 'Would you like me to start with what I found in the codex?'

'I think that's best,' Vijay assented. 'The codex seems to be the key to unlocking this mystery.'

'Right, then.' Goldfeld cleared his throat and began. 'To start with, Wallace covered most of the contents of the letters with respect to Caesar's invasions of Britain. He was right about Quintus being discreet in his descriptions and conclusions but there's no mistaking the meaning of his words. I suppose it is easier for us to interpret them in the context of Caesar's invasions of Britain because we know so much about them from other sources. The people of those times, not being privy to the information we have about Caesar, would have found it more difficult to read anything more into his letters than a description of the myths of Britain and how Caesar handled the Celts by making the Druids give up their secret to him. The Druids were viewed as sorcerers by many—Pliny the Elder called them "magi", which is derived from the word "magus", which means possessing magical powers. So Caesar's victory over the Druids would have only cemented Caesar's reputation as a great general who was unbeatable.'

Goldfeld referred to his notes before resuming. 'I think Wallace gave you a fairly good summary of the contents. There's a fairly detailed narration of Semiramis' story, which is an almost perfect match with the story on the prisms if you look at the facts presented in each case. But you know the story so we don't need to go into that. There are, however, two interesting things that Wallace didn't mention to you. Perhaps he didn't think they were important.'

His audience listened with rapt attention as he went on. 'The first is that Quintus refers to the prisms in an oblique manner. He doesn't really speak of prisms, but he does say that Caesar was told in Britain that a puzzle was created which told the story of Semiramis and the Druids. He also says that this puzzle describes the location of the grave of Semiramis. The Druids kept half of the puzzle and sent the other half to the king of the eastern kingdom from where Semiramis had obtained the divine weapon. This was done both to protect the location of her grave as well as to honour a promise made by Semiramis to that king.'

'That certainly sounds like the two prisms,' Vijay agreed. 'Two parts of a puzzle.'

'That kind of confirms it, doesn't it?' Colin added. 'If the prisms and the letters are separated by two thousand years, then the story on the prism and the letters must be true. Quintus certainly would not have had access to both the prisms even if he was able to read cuneiform, which he probably wasn't. So there was no way he could have copied the Semiramis story from the prisms.'

Goldfeld nodded. 'Independent corroboration by two different sources,' he replied. 'As fantastic as it seems, there must be some truth to the story. It would be difficult for a myth to perpetuate unchanged in all its details for two thousand years.' He looked at Alice. 'And I can now safely say that you were right when you referred to the inscriptions as the Semiramis story. The *Samí-Rámési* of the inscriptions is clearly the Semiramis that we were talking about.'

'But when you translated the story for us, there didn't seem to be anything about the location of the grave of Semiramis,' Alice said to Goldfeld.

Goldfeld clicked his tongue, indicating his disagreement. 'My dear,' he said, 'if you recall, I had told you that I would give you a summary of the story in the inscriptions, not a line by line translation.'

Alice nodded, remembering. 'So what you're saying is that the location is described in the inscriptions but you didn't go into the details because we all thought that it was such a crazy story that it just couldn't possibly be true.'

'What does the prism say about the grave?' Vijay wondered.

Goldfeld turned the pages until he was looking at his notes from three weeks ago, when Alice had first sent him the images of the prisms.

'Here we are. The inscriptions describe a few landmarks that lead to a hill, which was sacred to the gods of the Celts. From the top of the hill, across the land, the sea was clearly visible both to the north and to the west. On the summit of the hill stood a stone circle with a north-south alignment and two entrances along the north-south axis. In the very centre of the stone circle, a grave was dug with its head in alignment with the moon, for Semiramis was the moon goddess, and the goddess of fertility. Her body was wrapped carefully and her face covered with a burnt wooden mask.'

Goldfeld looked up from his notes. 'She was buried with a wooden club in the shape of the divine weapon that she had brought back for the Druids. Her grave was then strewn with flowers and an oval formation of stones was created to surround it with a large headstone to mark where she lay.'

There was silence when he finished. It all seemed to be so unreal. They were talking about a queen who had lived four thousand years ago; a queen who had been consigned by history to the dustbins of mythology, dismissed from the memories of men and her very existence erased.

Yet, here were two accounts that provided evidence that Semiramis had lived, fought and died.

A queen who had died as a goddess.

Vijay broke the silence. 'What was the second thing which you said Wallace hadn't mentioned?'

51

The Quintus revelations

'Ah, now here's the other interesting fact,' Goldfeld declared. 'According to Quintus, when Caesar struck his deal with the Celts, the Druids told him the location of the weapon in the only way they knew. They rarely wrote anything down, especially when it related to their knowledge or their secrets. Even the location of the weapon had been passed down the generations orally, like the rest of their learning, in the form of a verse. They shared this verse with Caesar and even explained what it meant so he would not have to decipher its meaning.'

'Does Quintus say what the verse is?' Colin asked.

'No, he doesn't. Apparently, he wasn't privy to the discussions with the Druids. He only got bits and pieces of information which he quite excitedly conveyed to Cicero in these letters.'

'So where does that leave us?' Vijay asked. 'I think the only thing that we've established so far is that Semiramis did go to India and she did bring back something from there.' He looked at Colin. 'Anything useful about the Druids?'

'There is a whole load of information about the Druids on the Internet,' Colin replied, 'and I didn't have time to go through all of it. God knows how much of it is accurate anyway. But I got some interesting stuff which, in some ways, reinforces what we've been discussing so far.' He flipped open his laptop and brought up his file of notes on the screen.

'Go ahead,' Alice said. 'Spill the beans already.'

'Okay, so the first thing is that there is an uncanny similarity between the Druids and the people of Vedic times in India.'

Vijay looked sharply at Colin. 'You're kidding.'

'No I'm not. In fact, many of the websites I visited actually stated that the Druids were the Brahmins of the West. There is a very strong correlation between the beliefs of the Druids and those of the Vedic people. I'll come to that in a bit. Let's start with the meaning of the word "Druid". The origin and meaning of the word is disputed. Some say it means "*those familiar with the oak*". Others say that it means "*those whose knowledge is very great*."'

'So it doesn't really mean magician or sorcerer?' Alice was surprised.

'Not really, though, as Saul mentioned, Pliny had referred to them as magi. The earliest people to write about the Druids are Strabo, Diodorus Siculus, Posidonius and Julius Caesar. Though it is now believed that a lot of Caesar's material was based on the writings of Posidonius, a Greek writer who was a contemporary of Caesar and Cicero.' Colin paused to grin. 'You won't believe how many names I've suddenly become familiar with in the course of a few hours. It's like a new education for me.'

'Go on,' Vijay said impatiently. 'Save us the personal asides for later.'

'Fine, fine,' Colin returned to his notes. 'The other thing that there doesn't seem to be unanimity about is when the Druids first appeared on the scene. In fact, I'm a bit confused by all the theories here. It seems most common to believe that the Druids first appeared around 300 B.C. But then, there are those who say that the Druids were an intrinsic part of Celtic culture and the Celts came into Ireland and Britain around 1000 B.C. So, shouldn't the Druids have been around then? There certainly seems to be evidence that the Druids were pretty well established and powerful by 200 B.C. A Greek writer called Diogenes Laertius used sources on the Druids from 200 B.C. which means that they would have had to have been well established by then to have such a wide reputation outside the Celtic world. In fact there's another school of thought that believes that the Druids pre-dated the Celts. When the Celts arrived in 1000 B.C. the Druids were already well established, according to this theory.'

'If we go by the story on the prism and the Quintus Codex,' Goldfeld interjected, 'and if we believe that Semiramis did exist, then it would mean that the Druids were around in 2000 B.C. Because that is around the time that Ninus or Nimrod is said to have existed. That is well before any of the timelines you have mentioned.'

'And the codex mentions that the Druids used the weapon that Semiramis gave them to subdue the warring Celtic tribes and bring peace in the land,' Vijay commented. 'How they achieved that I can't guess, but that would give credence to what Saul just said.'

'You could be right,' Colin replied. 'The Druids were very powerful, more powerful than even their kings. All disputes were settled by them. And,' Colin looked at them, 'you're not going to believe this. Apparently, they had the power to stop battles. If two tribes went to war, and if the Druids wished, they would step between the two armies about to commence battle and stop the fighting before it could begin.'

'That certainly sounds like it ties in with what Quintus said,' Alice observed.

'Then there's the bit about human sacrifice. Apparently, they would stab a sacrificial victim in the back and read the future from the twitching of his limbs and the flow of blood.' Colin made a face. 'Rome really hated the Druids. Julius Caesar made it mandatory for anyone taking Roman citizenship to publicly renounce Druidism. And Augustus Caesar passed a measure prohibiting Roman citizens from practising Druidism. Rome left Britain—and the Druids—alone after Caesar's second invasion in 54 B.C. But when the Romans finally occupied Britain, it seemed that they were out to destroy Druidism at its roots. The Roman army went all the way to Wales, where they defeated the Druids at Anglesey in 60 A.D. Not content with that, they pursued the Druids across all Druidic sites in northern Scotland until, in 84 A.D. the last Druid stronghold was destroyed.'

'Good stuff, Colin,' Vijay remarked. 'What about the Vedic connection you spoke of?'

52

August 26, 55 B.C.

Present-day Deal, Great Britain

The legionnaires gazed nervously at the Celts who had been pacing alongside the Roman galleys as they slowly sailed northwards in search of an alternate landing place.

It had finally been decided to berth the galleys just off a pebbly flat shore near Deal, a few miles north of the cliffs of Dover.

Caesar was grim-faced. This was not an ideal situation. His calculations had not worked out.

The tide was low. The ships had been forced to anchor more than six hundred feet offshore. Their deep keels would not allow the galleys to anchor any closer to the beach.

The water was, at the very least, waist deep. And the Celts still lined the shore, though they lacked the advantage of height that the cliffs of Dover had afforded them.

It was still a terrifying sight. Thousands of Celts stood along the shore. The Roman legions held back, hesitating, despite Caesar's command to attack the Celts. The odds were stacked against them. Stacked high.

To everyone's surprise, the Tenth Legion's standard-bearer suddenly appeared in the water. Bearing the Roman standard aloft, he struggled to wade through the waist-deep water.

Apparently, even the Celts were taken aback by this sudden appearance of a lone legionnaire. They simply stood and watched.

The standard-bearer turned and faced the galleys. 'Leap forth, legionnaires!' he shouted. 'Unless you wish to betray your standard to the enemy! I, at any rate, shall have performed my duty to my country and to my general!'

Turning around, he continued his progression to the shore. His challenge was not in vain.

The Romans would not allow their standard to fall to the enemy.

With loud cries, the Roman army dispersed from the galleys and began wading to the shore, despite being weighed down by their arms and the heavy mailed leather jerkins they wore.

They were still some distance from the pebble-strewn beach when the Celtic cavalry charged them, their swords cutting through the ranks of the Romans, accompanied by loud battle cries.

Romans fell to the left and to the right and the water turned bloody as the swords of the horsemen, reinforced by the stones and javelins hurled by the men on the beach, took their toll.

But they were not daunted. Despite their losses, they persevered and soon the Celts had to flee. They were not interested in engaging the Roman machine in a full-out battle that they could never win.

They had inflicted losses. This was enough for today. They would return to strike another day.

53

February, present year

Day 3

The Vedic connection

'Oh, there's plenty of that,' Colin said. 'Let's start with the fundamental beliefs of the Druids. According to them the human soul is indestructible and so is the universe, although at some time, fire and water will prevail over them. They believed in Four Ages: Aiuestu Nemeti, Aiuestu Uirionas, Aiuestu Danuion, Aiuestu Miletonion.' He looked at Vijay. 'Sound familiar so far?'

'Wow,' Vijay couldn't believe what he was hearing. 'That is amazing. Do the Four Ages correspond directly with the Vedic *yugas?*'

'Directly,' Colin replied. 'Golden, Silver, Bronze and Iron. In fact, at least one author I came across—Clement of Alexandria, a Greek who lived in the 5th century A.D.— claimed that Pythagoras and the Greeks acquired their philosophy from the Gauls and other barbarians. Apparently, Pythagoras also believed in the transmigration of souls. Clement apparently says,' he paused to look at his laptop, 'that Polyhistor—another ancient scribe who lived in the second century B.C.—claimed that "Pythagoras hearkened to the Galatae and the Brahmins." That's yet another Vedic connection for you, quite explicitly stated in the ancient writings. Moreover, the original teachings of the Druids emanated from the Seven Sages, the stars of Ursa Major. And I understand that there are seven sages in the Vedic scriptures as well.'

'The Saptarishis,' Vijay answered.

'There's more,' Colin scanned the laptop screen. 'The gods of the Vedas are referred to as "*deva*". Apparently, in Sanskrit, that means "Shining One". The Celtic term for their gods is "deuos", which also means "Shining Ones". Fire pits seem to play an important role in the Druidic religion, as they do in the Vedic one. And, finally, the Druids studied for twenty years to master their knowledge which was passed down orally from generation to generation, as Saul just mentioned. They never wrote down anything connected with their scriptures, science or astronomy. All their learning was orally transmitted in much the same way that knowledge, learning and the scriptures were orally transmitted in Vedic times in India.'

He looked around. 'When I was listening to you guys discuss the codex and the story on the prisms, I couldn't help thinking how it all ties in. A brotherhood of priests in the west—the Druids. A brotherhood of priests in the east—the Brahmins. A weapon of the gods that lies in the east. A divine weapon belonging to the "Shining Ones", who were worshipped by both sets. The connection is hard to miss.'

'True,' Goldfeld agreed. 'And, according to the prisms, Semiramis was born in what is today called India. So she was a natural bridge between the two.'

'There's one more thing that clinches it,' Colin added.

'What's that?' Alice asked.

'It doesn't concern the Druids directly, but it seems to tie in with all the facts we have with us so far.' He consulted his notes.

'This is about Ireland. According to Irish legend, the *Tuatha de Danann* came from the north of the world. They were skilled in Druidic lore and magic and brought a lot of objects of power into Ireland.'

'Objects of power?' Vijay latched onto Colin's words immediately. 'You mean like the divine weapon in the Semiramis story?'

'I don't know,' Colin replied. 'That's a mystery. But the interesting thing is this. The *Tuatha de Danann* were known as the Lords of Light. There could be a possible reference to them in the story on the prism. Doesn't that story say that the Druid who approached Semiramis told her that there was a legend passed down by the Lords of Light? And that the Druids hoped to regain the power that was once possessed by the Lords of Light in their lands?'

'That certainly seems to tie in,' Goldfeld was now very interested. 'It would really make the existence of this divine weapon, whatever it is, sound much more realistic.'

'And finally,' Colin grinned, unable to resist the drama of the moment, 'the connection between the *Tuatha de Danann* and the Vedic people.'

Vijay looked surprised. 'There's a connection there?'

'Of course.' Colin was enjoying himself. It wasn't very often that he found himself in a position where he was educating Vijay. Normally, Vijay was the one who had a head for research and would drill deep until he got all the information he wanted. '*Tuatha de Danann* means "people of the Goddess Danu". Ring a bell?'

'Sounds familiar,' Vijay admitted sheepishly, a bit embarrassed that he wasn't as well versed in his own mythology, as Colin seemed to be. 'Who is Danu?'

'I've no idea,' Colin said. 'As I told you, I didn't have enough time to go into all the details. But she had something to do with Vedic mythology. This is as much as I was able to gather.'

'Good job, Colin,' Alice smiled at him. 'This has really helped.'

'Yes,' Goldfeld agreed. 'It does seem like we're getting somewhere, though we still have a few missing links.'

Vijay's phone rang. He looked at the number. 'It's Dr Shukla.' He switched on the phone. 'Hi, Dr Shukla. I'm going to videoconference you. That way you will be able to see everyone.'

He disconnected the phone and picked up his laptop. Goldfeld took the laptop and adjusted it on the desk so that the screen as well as the camera faced the group.

'Wait a minute.' Goldfeld hurried out of the room and returned holding a pair of speakers. 'Here,' he said, 'this will help.'

'Great idea.' Vijay took the speakers from him and connected the USB cable to his laptop and checked the volume of the speakers. 'Good to go,' he affirmed.

He called Shukla via the encrypted video conference software belonging to the task force and the linguist appeared on the screen.

'Hi Vijay,' Shukla's voice came over the speakers. 'Hello everyone.'

'Actually, you called just in time,' Vijay said. 'We were discussing something and I had a question for you, apart from what I requested earlier today.'

'Go ahead, son,' Shukla responded.

'Who is Danu in Indian mythology?'

54

Videoconference with Dr Shukla

Shukla peered out of the laptop screen at his audience. 'Not all of you will be familiar with Indian mythology,' he said. 'So I think I should give a more detailed explanation.'

'Sure,' Goldfeld said. 'Please go ahead. I'm curious.'

'Give me a minute, please.' Shukla rose and disappeared for a few moments. He returned and brandished a hardbound volume of the Mahabharata. 'I'll need this for reference,' he said as he opened the book and settled down in front of the camera.

'As described in the Mahabharata,' Shukla began, 'in the *Sambhava Parva,* which is the seventh book of the *AdiParva*—the first book of the Mahabharata—Brahma had seven sons who were created from his mind. They were Marichi, Atri, Angiras, Pulastya, Pulaha, Kratu and Sthanu—the seven great *rishis*.' He consulted the copy of the epic before him.

'The *shloka* that talks about the first six *Rishis* is:

ब्रह्मणो मानसाः पुत्र विदिताः षण्महर्षयः।
मरीचिरत्र्यङ्गिरसौ पुलस्त्यः पुलहः क्रतुः।।

And the *shloka* that mentions Sthanu is:

ब्रह्मणो मानसाः पुत्रा विदिताः षण्महर्षयः।
एकादश सुताः स्थाणोः ख्याताः परमतेजसः।।

Now, Marichi had a son called Kashyapa, who is considered the progenitor of all the worlds because his offspring were the *Suras* and the *Asuras*:

मरीचेः कश्यपः पुत्रः कश्यपस्य सुरासुराः।
जज्ञिरे नृपशार्दूल लोकनां प्रभवस्तु सः।।

And this is where Danu comes in. The great *rishi*, Daksha, had thirteen daughters, all of whom were married to Kashyapa. Danu was one of Daksha's daughters and she begot forty-four sons. The *Danavas*.'

'The bad guys of Indian mythology,' Vijay added, for the benefit of the others in the room. 'I know that's a rather simplistic way of putting it,' he looked at Shukla apologetically, knowing that he would not approve.

Shukla nodded, though he didn't look too happy. 'Unfortunately, that's the way the *Danavas*, and the rest of the *Asuras*, are portrayed,' he told the group. 'This portrayal tends to ignore several nuances that are clearly observed in the narrative of the Mahabharata. These nuances tend to blur the distinction between the *Devas* and the *Asuras* that has been created based on whether their natures were good or evil. But I know this is not the time or place to get into a discussion about this.'

'I thought there may be a connection between the Danu of the Vedic scriptures and the Lords of Light.' Colin sounded disappointed. 'But from what I understand, the *Tuatha de Danann* seem to have been the good guys.'

Vijay quickly briefed Shukla on what Colin had researched about the *Tuatha de Danann*. The information that Shukla had just given them did seem to be at odds with the Irish legend that they had just been discussing.

'Well, if you consider the fact that the *Danavas* and the *Devas*—who are simplistically considered to be the "good guys"— are actually half brothers, and if you do take into account the nuances in the Mahabharata that demonstrate the virtuous side of the *Asuras* and, conversely, the disreputable side of the *Devas*, then you could speculate about a connection between the *Tuatha de Danann* and the *Danavas* based on the fact that the names of their mothers were the same,' Shukla responded. 'But there doesn't have to be a connection.'

'True,' Vijay conceded. 'But if there was a connection between the Druids and the Vedic people, it is worth considering that there could be a connection between the beings whom they considered to be superior. The *Tuatha de Danaan* definitely weren't the gods of the Druids or the Celts. But they were considered to be superior beings, which can be gleaned from their sobriquet.'

'What is the connection between the Druids and the Vedic people?' Shukla enquired, interested.

Colin briefly repeated what he had already told the others.

Shukla pondered this information for a few moments. 'Fascinating,' he said, finally. 'I can't see any holes to pick in the comparison you have drawn,' he said.

There was another moment of silence. Vijay whispered something to Colin.

'Would you like me to brief you on what I found?' Shukla asked.

Realising that Shukla was speaking to him, Vijay tore himself away and faced the laptop. 'Yes, please.'

'You wanted to know if I had any thoughts on what the celestial weapon could be—the one that Semiramis came looking for in India. I spent some time thinking and also going through the Mahabharata, because that is one source that lists most of the so-called celestial weapons. The main problem that I faced was that I don't know to what use this weapon was put. Every celestial weapon had a unique and distinct purpose.

While most of them were, according to the Mahabharata, operated by the use of mantras, or even the mind, there were no generic celestial weapons. They all had specific functions. So it is difficult to even speculate which weapon Semiramis came looking for.'

Vijay was disappointed. 'That means that there is no way of working out what that weapon could be. I was hoping for more.'

'Well,' Shukla said, hesitantly, 'I may be going out on a limb here, but, while we can't know what the weapon was, we may be able to hazard a guess regarding its genesis.'

'I don't understand,' Alice spoke up. 'How are we supposed to do that?'

55

Genesis

'As I said, I'm speculating wildly here,' Shukla reiterated. 'But I'm willing to stick my neck out if what Vijay told me is true.'

Vijay frowned. 'What did I tell you?'

'You told me that Semiramis went into the Makran desert to find the weapon.'

'That's what Alice had told me and the inscriptions on the prisms corroborated it.'

Shukla nodded. 'That gave me a clue. Let me show you. I'm going to share my screen with you, so you aren't going to be able to see me.' His face disappeared and was replaced by a geographical map of India and Pakistan. Shukla zoomed in on a region that encompassed north-western India and Pakistan.

'I had a thought that might be way off the mark, but I decided to pursue it anyway,' Shukla's disembodied voice came from the speakers. 'Once again, the Mahabharata is the point of reference. This time it is the penultimate book of the epic—the *Mahaprasthanika Parva*—which describes the final journey of the Pandava princes as they leave Hastinapur and fall by the wayside one by one until only the eldest Pandava, Yudhishthira, is left, along with a dog who follows him all the way to *Swarga Lok*—the region of the gods.' The cursor jiggled on the screen. 'Can all of you see the cursor?' he asked.

'Yes,' his audience replied with one voice.

'Good. Now, we're not going to quibble over the ancient location of Hastinapur. We do know that it was in north India. Modern-day Hastinapur is in Uttar Pradesh, close to the city of Meerut. The location of Hastinapur is not important. Let's now follow the Pandavas on their journey from Hastinapur. Let's assume they start somewhere here. The cursor hovered around a spot not far from New Delhi on the map. Now, I'm going to read out the *shlokas* one by one and then show you what may be the corresponding route on the map. The first clue to their path is this *shloka*:

पाण्डवाश्च महात्मानो द्रोपदी च यशस्विनी।
कृतोपवासाः कौरव्य प्रययुः प्राङ्मुखस्ततः।।

'It says: "*Meanwhile, the great Pandavas, O you of Kuru's race, and the illustrious Draupadi, having observed the preliminary fast, started with their faces towards the east.*'

'The next *shloka* talks about them reaching a sea of red waters, but I couldn't find anything that matched that description, so I'm skipping it and moving on to the next one, which is important to the idea that I had.

गाण्डीवं तु धनुर्दिव्यं न मुमोच धनञ्जयः।
रत्नलोभान्महाराज ते चाक्षय्ये महेषुधी।।

'This one says: "*Dhananjaya had not thrown off his celestial bow Gandiva nor his couple of inexhaustible quivers, actuated, O king, by the cupidity for valuable things*". Dhananjaya is Arjuna, the supreme archer. This *shloka* is interesting and I will come back to it a bit later. Let's talk about the route the Pandavas are taking for now.' He paused. 'I hope this is not too confusing?'

Goldfeld spoke up. 'I'm actually quite fascinated by this. I know you're building up to something and I'm really curious to see what it is.'

Shukla continued. 'The next few *shlokas* talk about their encounter with Agni, the god of Fire, who instructs Arjuna to cast off his bow, Gandiva, and return it to Varuna, the god of the Ocean, for it belonged to him. Agni had presented the bow to Arjuna when he had requested help to burn the forest of Khandavaprastha. So Arjuna throws his bow and the quivers into the sea. The next *shloka* tells us:

ततोऽग्निर्भरतश्रेष्ठ तत्रैवान्तरधीयत।
ययुश्च पाण्डवा वीरास्ततस्ते दक्षिणामुखाः।।

"After this, O chief of Bharata's race, the god of Fire disappeared then and these the heroic sons of Pandu next went out with their faces turned towards the South."'

The cursor moved eastwards from the starting point and then southwards.

'The distances are not important, but the general direction is,' Shukla explained. 'The next five *shlokas* are self explanatory:

ततस्ते तूत्तरेणैव तीरेण लवणाम्भसः।
जग्मुर्भरतशार्दूल दिशं दक्षिणपश्चिमाम्।।

"Then, by the northern coast of the salt sea, those princes of Bharata's race, went to the south-west."

ततः पुनः समावृत्ता पश्चिमां दिशमेव ते।
ददृशुर्द्वारकां चापि सागरेण परिप्लुताम्।।

"Turning next towards the west, they saw the city of Dwarka covered by the ocean."

उदीचीं पुनरावृत्य ययुर्भरतसत्तमाः।
प्रादक्षिण्यं चिकीर्षन्तः पृथिव्या योगधर्मिणः।।

"Turning next to the north, those foremost ones went on observant of Yoga, they were desirous of going round the whole earth."

वैशम्पायन उवाच
ततस्ते नियतात्मान उदीचीं दिशमास्थिताः ।
ददृशुर्योगयुक्ताश्च हिमवन्तं महागिरिम् ।।

"Vaishampayana said: Those princes of controlled souls and devoted to Yoga, proceeded to the north, saw Himavat, that huge mountain."

तं चाप्यतिक्रमन्तस्ते ददृशर्वालुकार्णवम् ।
अवैक्षन्त महाशैलं मेरूं शिखरिणां वरम् ।।

"Crossing the Himavat, they saw a vast desert of sand. They then saw the powerful mountain Meru, the foremost of all high-peaked mountains."'

As Shukla read out the *shlokas,* the cursor moved southwest, towards the modern-day state of Gujarat, then west towards the Arabian Sea, after which it moved north, crossed a mountainous area in present-day Pakistan and then stopped.

'I must confess,' Shukla said, 'that the mention of Himavat and Meru threw me off a bit. But the rest of the geography, as you can see, matches pretty well with the route that is described in such detail. There is a mountain range to be crossed before you come to the Makran desert. Which is where the cursor stands now.'

Light dawned on them all as they made the connection. Alice was the first to speak up. 'So you think that this journey of the Pandavas is somehow connected to the mission Semiramis was on when she came to India?'

The map disappeared from the laptop screen and Shukla's face reappeared. 'Not just somehow connected,' he smiled. 'I have a theory. As I said earlier, it is a wild one, but it is worth putting on the table. My theory is based on this route the Pandavas took and another *shloka* in the book preceding the *Mahaprasthanika Parva,* which describes a specific event that involved Arjuna.'

56

Of Celestial Weapons

'In the *Mausala Parva,*' Shukla continued, 'which tells the story of the death of Krishna, there is a *shloka* which talks about the failure of Arjuna to deploy his celestial weapons. According to the *shloka,* Arjuna tries to deploy his celestial weapons by bringing them to mind but they refuse to appear. This *shloka* and a few others in the same *Parva,* which describe Arjuna's failure to call his celestial weapons to action using his mind, are the last we hear about the weapons given to him by the gods. There is no mention about these weapons thereafter—only the bow and the quivers are mentioned in the *shloka* that I just read out to you a while back.'

Vijay realised where Shukla was going with this. 'So you're thinking it is possible that Arjuna left his celestial weapons in the Makran desert?'

'Why not?' Shukla replied. 'The Mahabharata doesn't say he does, but it doesn't say what he did with his weapons either. As I told you a while ago, most of the weapons described in the Mahabharata are activated by mantras or by the mind. Suppose the *shloka* that mentions his failure to deploy the weapons is actually talking about Arjuna forgetting the mantras that activated them? He was so overcome with grief at Lord Krishna giving up his earthly body, that it could have affected his memory. Who knows? Suppose he hid his weapons in the Makran desert, which they appear to have passed. There is no explicit reference to this but that doesn't preclude the possibility.'

'That would explain why Semiramis decided to go to the Makran desert even while her army was waging war with Stabrobates,' Goldfeld mused. 'And since we now know that the Semiramis story is based on historical events, if she found a divine weapon in the Makran desert, it would have been placed there by somebody. Which could easily have been Arjuna, going by what you have just told us.'

'There are a lot of connections all around,' Alice admitted. 'Normally, I'd be looking for archaeological evidence to prove our speculation but this is different. The similarity between the Druids and the Vedic people, the fact that a goddess called Danu exists in both the Celtic and Vedic mythologies, and the Semiramis story's apparent link with the Mahabharata; there seem to be too many coincidences for them to be explained by pure chance.'

'I dug up some more information on the *Tuatha de Danann,*' Colin spoke up. He had been busy on his laptop all this while, pausing now and then to keep abreast of Shukla's report, but it was clear that he was researching something. 'You were right, Vijay. I found two very interesting things about them.'

Vijay waited. When Shukla had mentioned that there wasn't much to connect the *Tuatha de Danann* with the *Danavas,* apart from the fact that both had a mother named Danu, he had asked Colin to check on a couple of facts. It seemed that his hunch had paid off.

'Here's the first one,' Colin continued. 'It is said that the *Tuatha de Danann* lived underground. And I'm no expert, but I did a quick google search and it seems that even the *Danavas* are supposed to have lived underground.'

'That is interesting,' Shukla said thoughtfully. 'You are right, Colin. In the *Udyog Parva*—one of the books of the Mahabharata—the underground city of the *Danavas* is described in great detail. Give me a minute.' He rose and returned with another hardbound volume of the epic, which he leafed through until he found what he was looking for.

'Here it is,' he said. 'I'll read out a *shloka* to you:

नारद उवाच
एतत् तु नागलोकस्य नाभिस्थाने स्थितं पुरम्।
पातालमिति विख्यातं दैत्यदानवसेवितम्।।

'It means: "*Narada said—this city, situated in the very heart of the region of the Nagas, is known as* Patalam, *inhabited by the* daityas *and Danavas.*"'

He flipped a few pages then stopped. 'And this *shloka* is interesting in this context too,' he said. 'Listen:

अत्र मायासहस्त्राणि विकुर्वाणा महौजसः।
दानवा निवसन्ति स्म शूरा दत्तवराः पुरा।।

'It says: "*Here the Danavas, endued with great spirit and energy, practising a thousand kind of different illusions, reside. They were, in the days of old, heroes who had received the grant of boons.*" I'm not going to say that this is the connection you seek between the *Tuatha de Danann* and the *Danavas*, but it is as close as you can get. The heroes of Irish mythology and the heroes of old from the Mahabharata. Both live underground. Both have a mother named Danu. Interesting bit of speculation.' He put the book down and stared out at them from the laptop screen. 'But even if this is not mere speculation and does turn out to be history in the disguise of mythology, we only manage to establish a connection between the ancient Celts of Ireland and the *Danavas*. What you're looking for is a connection between the Druids and the Vedic people, beyond the similarities that Colin has already listed.

'Actually, there does seem to be a connection that also links up to the *Tuatha de Danann*,' Colin said.

57

September, 55 B.C.

Present-day Kent, Britain

Caesar sat in his tent and brooded. Things had not gone well for him and his men.

He had envisioned a quick journey into Britannia, negotiations with the Celtic tribes and a simultaneous reconnaissance to gather more information about the secret of the Druids. Nothing had prepared him for either the resistance of the Celts or the vagaries of the weather.

Four days after their costly landing at Deal, the much-awaited Roman cavalry had arrived. Caesar knew that his infantry would have to face an uphill task—challenging if not impossible—of battling the Celts with their war chariots and javelins. He had to have the support of his cavalry if his troops were to get the better of the Celts.

But a fierce storm had arisen and forced the galleys bearing the cavalry back to Gaul.

Caesar's misfortunes had not ended there. The same storm and changes in the tides had damaged the bulk of his anchored fleet. Their food supplies were depleted and it looked difficult for the two Roman legions, and Caesar, to return to Gaul.

The indomitable spirit of his soldiers had prevailed then.

One legion had set to work salvaging and repairing the fleet. The other went inland to reap corn from the local fields, which were lying untended since the Celts went into hiding in the forests.

It was then that Caesar had a first-hand demonstration of the secret power of the Celts. Until now, there had been no sign of it, and Caesar had been wondering if Divitiacus had been right in his speculation.

The legionnaires in the cornfields had been ambushed by the Celts, who had been watching them from the shelter of the forests.

Word had come to the camp about the ambush, and more. The news spread—the Romans were unable to fight their enemy in the disciplined style in which they were trained for battle.

Worried about a rout of his legion, Caesar had rushed there with reinforcements.

Far above the din of the battle Caesar heard the drums. Until now, he had only heard of them from his legionnaires in Gaul. They had told him stories about the range of feelings those drumbeats evoked—from terror, to self-doubt, loss of confidence and panic. He had never doubted his legionnaires. They were brave men and would not resort to fables to justify their failure against the Gallic resistance. But neither had he understood just what they had experienced.

Now, he was face to face with the drumbeats.

For the first time in his life, Caesar had been petrified. An inexplicable terror had seized him when he arrived at the scene of the fighting and he could see that his soldiers were also in the grip of this madness. It was impossible to think straight. His mind had refused to calm down, preferring to stay in a state of panic and raw terror.

The Celts were cutting down the Romans with ease.

Ironically, it was the weather that saved the Romans. Without warning, a heavy downpour started and the Celts withdrew. Their chariots and horses would not be able to manoeuvre swiftly in the mud underfoot that was swiftly turning to slush.

Caesar found that his panic-stricken state of mind had also begun to clear and he led his forces back to their camp.

It had rained for three straight days after that and Caesar had been able to withdraw to the beach and his other legion.

There had been no fighting as long as the rain lasted. The Romans had used this reprieve to set both legions to the task of repairing the ships.

The lull in fighting had also given Caesar time to think and strategise. Not for nothing had he gained the reputation of being one of the best generals in the world.

He decided that he would not allow the Celts to choose their time for battle any more. He had had enough of hiding and defending. He and his troops had not been trained to fight in this manner.

When the rain ended, Caesar had gone on the offensive. The Celts had no time to regroup and were swiftly defeated.

Now he was sitting and pondering his next move.

Julius Caesar arose from contemplation. It was time to be decisive. He had realised that his resources were inadequate to complete his task. He had underestimated the enemy and their power.

He would not make that mistake again.

'Board the galleys,' he commanded and his men immediately went to work, organising the troops for an orderly boarding of the Roman ships.

From the shelter and protection of their forests, the Celts watched as the Roman galleys set sail. They had forced the conqueror of Gaul to abort his mission and return to Gaul.

Standing on the deck of his galley, Caesar's face was grim and determined. He would be back the following year.

And, this time, he would bring a larger force with him. More cavalry. A bigger fleet.

Julius Caesar had been in Britannia for less than three weeks. His reports to Rome painted the invasion of Britannia as a success. He depicted it as a preliminary mission to prepare for a much bigger invasion the following year.

The next time, he would triumph. And then he would have the secret of the Druids in his grasp.

58

February, present year

Day 3

Another Vedic connection

'When Vijay was here a couple of weeks ago,' Colin explained, 'he visited megalithic sites in Wales, with Alice and Saul. He had written to me about his visit since he was quite impressed by what he saw.'

Vijay nodded his agreement.

Colin referred to his laptop. 'One of the things I stumbled upon while researching the *Tuatha de Danann* just now is the Welsh connection. There are old Welsh legends that tell the story of a Druid called Gwydion ap Don,' he grimaced, not sure if he had got the pronunciation correct.

'His name is interesting. "Gwydion" means man of learning, magician, philosopher or even scientist; and apparently there are meanings attached to the name, which come down from antiquity: giant, monster, wizard, sorcerer. "Ap Don" means "son of Don". Don is an important female in the collection of old Welsh legends called *Mabinogion*. Don is married to Beli ap Manogan, who is often referred to as the god of the dead. Don, through her marriage with Beli, gives birth to children who are known in mythology as the Children or Lords of Light. Gwydion was the eldest son, known as an astronomer and a master of light; sometimes even referred to as a man of science. And listen to this.'

The little group waited expectantly, as Colin mentally summarised what he had read so he could be succinct.

'Celtic scholars believe that "Don" is a variant on the name "Danu". And we all know who Danu is,' he concluded.

'Let me get this,' Harry spoke up for the first time. He had been sitting quietly all this time, listening to the discussion but not contributing. Now, he summarised the discussion, trying to cut through the mass of data they had just been presented with by Colin and Shukla. 'You're saying that the *Tuatha de Danann* are the original Druids—the Lords of Light—who populated Ireland before the Celts arrived there. These guys were the sons of Danu, who is also the mother of *Danavas* from Indian mythology. The *Tuatha de Danann* brought to Ireland the original Druidic practices and, possibly, the beliefs of the Druids, which were the same as the beliefs of the Vedic people. A variant of the myth exists in Wales, which means the Lords of Light were also in Britain. Somehow, somewhere, they faded away and were replaced by the Druids, as we know them; and when the Celts arrived, the Druids, using their power of the weapon brought by Semiramis, established their authority in Celtic tradition and society. Finally, the Druids were connected to the Vedic priests by virtue of the connection between the *Tuatha de Danann* and the *Danavas*.'

'That's a pretty good summary, Harry,' Vijay said, impressed. 'As crazy as it sounds, all the evidence we have seems to point to exactly the conclusions you just stated.'

'I wouldn't have believed it if it wasn't for the story on the prisms and the Quintus Codex,' Goldfeld stated flatly.

'Neither would I,' Alice agreed. 'But they seem to corroborate the links in mythology that we've discovered.'

'There's another very interesting thing,' Colin spoke up.

'Oh, right, you had said you discovered two things about the *Tuatha de Danann*,' Alice said.

'I don't know how this information helps,' Colin began, 'since it doesn't seem to fit into any of the links that we've explored so far. But it is interesting nevertheless. Celtic scholars believe that Druidism was imposed upon the Celts by the megalithic people. And the *Tuatha de Danann* are closely associated with the megalithic complexes in Ireland's Boyne Valley.'

There was silence as they all digested this.

'Are you saying that the Lords of Light built the megalithic complexes that are scattered all over Ireland and Britain?' Harry asked.

Colin shrugged. 'Scholars of Irish legend have drawn a parallel between them and sites like Newgrange in Ireland. If they existed in Wales, then it is possible that they also built the sites in Britain. And, as Harry rightly put it, they disappeared at some time. No one seems to be able to date when they existed, but there it is. It is a compelling story.'

Alice was looking at Vijay who had a strange expression on his face. She knew that look. It came on whenever he was trying to put facts and instinct together—an uncanny ability of his. She knew better than to interrupt him while he was thinking, analysing, sorting data and working on his gut feel to reach a conclusion. He would share his thoughts when he wanted to and not earlier.

'You know, Colin,' Vijay said, slowly. 'You may just have solved the mystery.'

59

Another mystery

'Really? What do you mean?' Colin pressed Vijay.

'Let me work it out in my mind,' Vijay replied. 'I want to be absolutely sure before I share it with you.' He looked at Alice. 'Let's see what you found in the diary.'

'Right,' Alice opened up the diary, which she had marked with sticky notes. 'It isn't as exciting as what we've been discussing, but it is interesting, nevertheless.'

She scanned the sticky notes, working out where she should start, and finally decided to talk about the history of the coins first.

'According to the notes in the diary, experts who inspected the coins were of the opinion that these coins were not minted to serve as currency but rather to commemorate something. Probably a victory like Julius Caesar's conquest of Gaul or his invasions of Britain. They felt it was likely that these are the only coins of their type ever minted, though there is no way to be sure. The coins were minted in Alexandria in 48 B.C. This, apparently, is quite unusual because coins for Rome were not minted in Alexandria until 30 B.C. when Egypt was formally conquered by Rome. That is when the Alexandrian mint was officially pressed into churning out coinage for Rome. It was speculated that, since Caesar was in Alexandria in 48 B.C.—

once Cleopatra had prevailed over her brother with Caesar's help, and become Pharoah—he may have asked for these to be made especially for him.'

She turned over the page, looking over her notes. 'In 1905, a group of workers in Inverness were excavating the foundations for a building when they came across a narrow shaft going into the ground. They realised that there might be an archaeological discovery in store and got a local archaeologist to take a look. When the shaft was cleared of rubble and dirt, it was found to lead to a small rocky chamber where a rotting leather bag was found, with the three coins in it. There was nothing else in the chamber. It was bare. No artefacts, no inscriptions. Just the coins.'

'Sounds like someone went to an awful lot of trouble just to bury three coins,' Colin remarked.

'Which means that whoever put them there intended them to remain hidden forever,' Goldfeld surmised. 'Never to be found.'

'Possibly,' Alice responded to their remarks. 'There are quite a few unanswered questions here. How the coins got to Inverness in the first place. Who hid them there? And why?'

'Anything special about the coins?' Vijay asked, frowning.

'Well, there are pretty detailed descriptions of all three coins, accompanied by diagrams,' Alice replied. 'All three coins had a profile of Julius Caesar on one side. On the other side of the coin, they all had the same outline of what looks like a Celtic shield, along with some random shapes; and one of the coins has a few knots on it—probably imperfections during the process of minting it. The random shapes and the inscription on each coin are different for some reason.'

'Inscriptions,' Colin was immediately interested. 'Do you think they mean anything?'

Alice shrugged. 'I'll read them out to you. I can't make them out in the diagrams and, anyway, the lines are in Latin, but there's a translation here for each coin. The first inscription says: "*Twenty-four to four is the first of the squares.*" The second one is: "*Four to twenty-eight is the second of the squares.*" And the third inscription: "*Twenty-four to twenty-eight is the sum of the squares.*"

'Blimey,' Harry said. 'That makes no sense at all. Sounds like one of my mathematics examination questions. I was never very good at those.'

'That's right,' Alice affirmed. 'It does sound like mathematics.'

'Maybe it refers to the measurement of areas,' Goldfeld ventured. 'Perhaps that is why "squares" have been used? But I agree with Harry. It doesn't seem to make any kind of sense at all.'

'So why is someone after these coins?' Vijay wondered. 'If these inscriptions are as meaningless as we believe they are, why go to such lengths to acquire them?'

The profile of Julius Caesar on the coins

60

Next Steps

'Here's what we need to do,' Vijay decided to outline the plan he had been mulling over. He was still not quite sure about the hunch that had struck him during the conversation so he decided against sharing it until he was certain it made sense. What they would do next would either confirm or reject the idea that had taken shape in his mind.

'We're missing two things,' he continued. 'The first is the location of the grave of Semiramis. I think that is important. If we can work that out, we can visit the grave and see if we can find any clues there. The second is the significance of the coins. Alice, will you and Saul work on checking out the location of the grave? You two are best suited for the task.'

'Sure,' Alice said. 'I guess we could make a start by searching for ancient sites where graves have been found.' She looked at Goldfeld for validation.

'That would be a good place to start,' he agreed. 'We can then narrow down the sites based on age and any human remains found there that indicate that a female was buried there. And if there are any traces of the burial mask and the club that were described in the inscriptions on the prism.'

'Great.' Vijay looked at Colin. 'Will you and Harry work on checking out Roman history in Britain and see if there is any information available on Romans in Inverness? If we can work out who may have hidden those coins there, that may help us figure out why someone wants them so badly.'

'Me?' Harry sounded surprised and confused.

'Yeah, why not?' Vijay shot back. 'If Colin can do it, so can you.'

'Hey!' Colin protested. 'Come on, Harry, ignore him. And what are you going to do?' He looked accusingly at Vijay, though he already knew the answer to his question.

'I'm going to check out my hunch,' Vijay replied, as Colin had guessed. 'I need some more facts before I can crystallise my thoughts and be sure.' He turned to Alice. 'Can I have the diary please? I will need to refer to the drawings of the coins.'

Alice handed over the diary, wondering what Vijay had in mind.

They bent over their respective laptops. 'Is there another room I can use?' Vijay asked Goldfeld. 'I need to be alone to work on this. And if I could have your printer that would really help.'

'Sure, you can use the guest room. I'll set up the printer for you.' Saul led Vijay out of the room. Presently he returned and silence reigned as they went about their respective tasks.

The minutes passed, an hour, two hours, the silence broken only occasionally by murmurs and the rustle of paper as they discussed what they saw on the screen or made notes. Saul left the room a few times to make some calls. Otherwise, no one stirred.

Shukla had logged out of the videoconference. They would call him back when they regrouped to discuss what each of them had found.

The only other interruption was when Vijay had rushed into the study, wild-eyed, asking for a pair of scissors, which Goldfeld had handed to him. He hadn't given any explanation for his strange request and no one had asked him for one. They were all curious but they knew they would have to wait.

Outside, darkness fell and the streetlights came on, even though it was only late afternoon. A light rain began to fall, the raindrops tapping at the window in a steady beat, providing a background rhythm to their thoughts.

61

New information

'Anyone for tea or a glass of wine?' Goldfeld enquired, tearing himself away from his laptop. He had been so engrossed in his research and comparing notes with Alice that he had quite overlooked the fact that he was the host here.

Everyone opted for hot tea. Goldfeld disappeared into the kitchen.

'We're done,' Colin said. 'How are you guys doing?'

Alice flashed him a jubilant smile that obviated the need for words to answer his question.

'I wonder how Vijay is doing,' she said.

As if on cue, Vijay entered the room, his hair dishevelled, as if he had been running his hands through it all the while he had been away.

Goldfeld returned with a tray bearing cups of steaming tea and they gratefully helped themselves, adding milk and sugar before settling down again.

'Right, then,' Goldfeld said, his excitement palpable, 'shall we begin?' He glanced at Alice. 'We believe we know where Semiramis was buried.'

Alice nodded, her eyes gleaming.

Colin looked at Harry. 'Sure,' he said, as Harry shrugged, indicating his indifference to who went first. 'Go ahead. This will be interesting.'

'Cairnpapple Hill,' Goldfeld announced. 'Near Bathgate, West Lothian. Not very far from Edinburgh. That's where we think she's buried. Alice?'

'We searched for sites where ancient graves had been found, as we had decided earlier,' Alice took up the explanation. 'We looked only for graves which showed evidence of being located within stone circles. It turns out that there are quite a few, from Avebury to the burial mounds in the Orkney Islands. But many of them are communal graves, where more than one person was buried. So we first shortlisted those graves where a solitary skeleton was found. That list, too, had quite a few locations. It seems that Britain has an abundance of burial mounds, which were found, on excavation, to contain human remains. Then we searched for skeletons, which had been identified as female. Saul had to call some of his friends for help here.'

'There wasn't a terribly large amount of information on the sex of the skeletons,' Goldfeld explained. 'And, apparently, a lot of the bones have disappeared over the years, since many of these sites were excavated anywhere between 60 to 150 years ago. People took the bones for research and many of them went missing. So I had to ask some friends to look up the information for me. But we did manage to get a fair amount of data.'

'Enough to get by,' Alice observed. 'While we weren't able to identify the gender of every skeleton on our list, we were able to get quite a few. Our shortlist was now down to five sites. So we examined the reports of excavations from these sites to see what was recovered from each grave apart from the bones. Again, Saul's friends came in handy. Where reports were not available on the net, they were able to find them and email them to us.'

'Yes, indeed,' Saul rubbed his hands together, barely able to contain his excitement. If they were right about this, it would be the find of the century. 'I guess we were plain lucky. In one of the graves, there wasn't much left of the skeleton itself, but the remains of a burnt wooden face mask and a burnt wooden club were found. Just as it says in the inscriptions on the prism.'

'Even the location matched the description on the prisms,' Alice added. 'From the summit of Cairnpapple Hill, or Kernepopple as it was called centuries ago, you can see the Firth of Forth to the north and, on a clear day, the Isle of Arran to the west. The sea to the north and to the west, just like it says on the prisms.'

'And the ancient cairn at the summit of the hill has been recorded as *media nemeton*, or the central sanctuary of the highest order of the Druids, by the Romans who passed that way in the first century A.D.' Goldfeld said. 'The inscriptions said that her burial place was a sacred spot for the Druids. It all adds up.'

'Sounds like you hit the jackpot,' Colin remarked. 'Incredible.'

'This is a cairn that was excavated in 1946 by Professor Stuart Piggott,' Alice went on, reading from her laptop. 'It is located within a stone circle that is surrounded by a henge. Now, there is a concrete dome that has been built to protect the three burial cairns inside the stone circle. The earliest grave is the North grave, which consists of a standing stone, a rock cut grave at its foot and an ovoid setting of ten small stones around the grave. Before the excavations started, the standing stone, which is eight feet high and pear shaped, barely projected above the surface of the cairn. The grave's long axis is approximately west-east, aligned with the moon—again as described in the inscriptions. When the grave was excavated, they found an area of carbonised wood in the under surface of which were the enamel crowns of adult human teeth, the only part of the body to have resisted dissolving in the acids within the soil. The rest of the body and bones had dissolved a long time ago. The conclusion was that the wood area represented a wooden object placed over the face of the corpse at burial. They also found two crushed beakers and a large carbonised object made of a single piece of oak wood. It was 3 feet 6 inches long and 3 inches thick at the middle, expanding into an oval shape 6 inches thick at one end. The other end had partially disintegrated but it also appeared to have been an expanded section of the wood. The excavators concluded it was a massive club.'

'Remember,' Goldfeld interjected, 'the inscriptions say that Semiramis was buried with a wooden club in the shape of the divine weapon. This could be it.'

'According to Piggott's report, the grave is unparalleled in its contents and structure, which means that someone really special was buried there,' Alice concluded.

'Semiramis,' Colin breathed, hardly able to believe that, sitting in this room, they had been able to locate the grave of this mysterious queen who lived four thousand years ago; who had, until now, been considered to be no more than a myth.

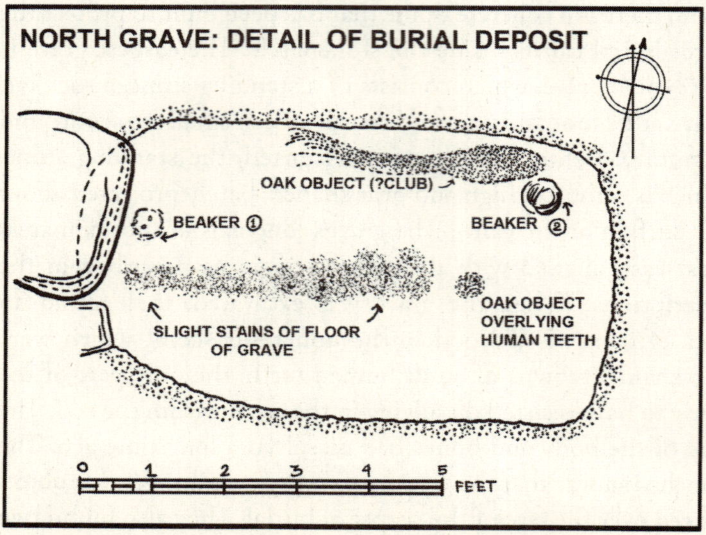

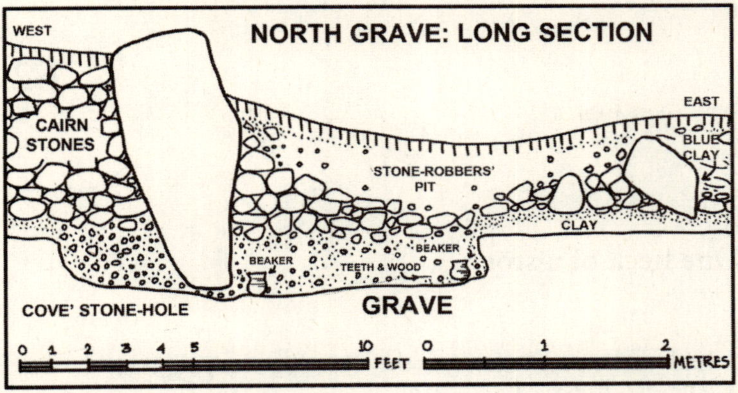

Detail (top view and side section) of the grave at Cairnpapple Hill (source: Excavation report of Prof. Stuart Piggott, 1946)

Vijay frowned. 'So we're looking for a divine weapon that is in the shape of a club, bulbous at either end, and fairly large in size.' He addressed Shukla who had joined them once again via videoconference. 'Does that sound familiar, Dr Shukla?'

Shukla shook his head. 'I can check, but I can't recall any weapon that has been described in the Mahabharata with this kind of shape.'

Vijay looked at Colin. 'Your turn.'

'Okay, we've got one heck of a story,' Colin declared and even Harry had to smile at his exuberance.

62

One heck of a story

'I had earlier summarised the Roman campaign to destroy the Druids,' Colin began. 'If we get into a bit more detail, we find some more answers. After Caesar's second invasion of Britain, the Romans didn't return until 43 A.D. when Claudius was the Emperor. This led to the conquest of England. In 60 A.D. the Roman general Suetonius Paulinus invaded the Druid stronghold on Anglesey in Wales. Nero was the Roman Emperor at that time. It took Paulinus a year to capture Castell Ior in Anglesey, where the Druids put up a fierce stand, until the mighty Roman army overwhelmed them. Castell Ior was razed to the ground and all its defenders were killed.'

'So the Druids apparently believed in Caesar's promise to leave them alone,' Alice murmured. 'They never suspected that the Romans would come back. And when they did, they didn't have time to retrieve their weapon to fight the Romans.'

'Remember that a hundred years had passed without the Romans troubling them,' Goldfeld replied. 'A hundred years is a long time; enough to create complacency born out of trust.'

Colin waited. When he was satisfied that there were no more comments or questions forthcoming, he continued. 'Around that time, Queen Boudicca of the Iceni tribe rose in rebellion in the south of Britain. Paulinus had to abandon Anglesey, leaving his campaign incomplete, and rush to quell the rebellion, which he did. He was subsequently recalled by Rome. When Vespasian took Rome and crowned himself emperor in 69 A.D., he made Gnaeus Julius Agricola—who had been a young officer under Paulinus in Britain—commander of the 20th legion in Britain. In 78 A.D., Agricola was sent back to Britain as governor, with an explicit instruction to overrun all the Druidic sites and destroy the Druids once and for all.'

'This reinforces our suspicion that the Druidic sites were not just in Wales, even though the *Tuatha de Danann* connection is limited to Wales,' Harry observed. 'The megalithic sites in Scotland were also part of the Druid culture.'

'Agricola first returned to Wales and established full Roman control over North Wales, building the fort of Segontium,' Colin continued. 'He then attacked Anglesey, where the Druids, vanquished earlier, had regrouped. This time, he completed the job that Paulinus had left incomplete and built a fort at Holyhead to control Anglesey.' He looked at Harry. 'You want to talk about Scotland? You're the one who made the connection.'

Harry looked uncomfortable, but he took up the narration. 'The Druids still had a stronghold in Scotland. Agricola advanced into Scotland and built a line of forts from the Firth of Forth to the Firth of Clyde.'

'This was probably when the Romans passed Cairnpapple,' Colin interjected.

'By 84 A.D., Agricola had gone up to the Moray Firth while his fleet sailed the seas between the mainland and the Orkney Island and the Hebrides,' Harry carried on. 'This was his expedition to Inverness. The final battle was fought somewhere around Inverness and the last Druid stronghold was destroyed. As far as the Romans were concerned, the Druids had been wiped off the face of the earth.'

'So someone in Agricola's army buried the coins in Inverness during this expedition,' Goldfeld mused.

'That's what we thought,' Harry said. 'This would seem to be the Inverness connection. But that's where we hit a roadblock. We couldn't figure out who it was that buried the coins and why they did it.'

'Great job, guys,' Vijay said. 'This is just what we needed. But I think we are asking ourselves the wrong question. We should be asking why they were carrying coins minted in Alexandria all the way to Inverness in the first place.'

'What do you mean?' Colin looked puzzled. 'How can we guess why they were carrying the coins?'

'I'll explain,' Vijay said, smiling. 'First tell me this: was Agricola's mission successful?'

'Yes, it was,' Harry replied. 'After the battle near Inverness, he controlled all the megalithic sites at Salisbury Plain, Anglesey and Northern Scotland.'

'So what happened to him after that?' Vijay enquired.

'Nothing good,' Colin replied. 'These Roman emperors were a nasty lot. Evil as hell. Vespasian died in 79 A.D. and was replaced by Titus who was himself replaced after just one year by Domitian. This guy, by all accounts, was a real mean guy. And he didn't like Agricola because the general outshone the emperor in his achievements. Agricola was recalled to Rome before he became too powerful. It is said that Domitian had Agricola poisoned to get rid of a possible rival and what he perceived to be a threat.'

He looked suspiciously at Vijay, knowing how Vijay's mind worked. 'Why did you want to know about Agricola? Surely you don't believe he buried those coins there? Why would he?'

'Let me tell you what I've found,' Vijay offered in reply, 'and then you'll understand.'

63

Vijay's hunch

'Let's start by going over what we have learnt so far,' Vijay began. 'The inscriptions on the prisms, the Quintus Codex, the mysterious coins, the legends surrounding the Druids and, of course, the *Tuatha de Danann*. I'm leaving the *Danavas* out of this for now since the focus is on Britain.'

He ticked off the points on his fingers. 'One: Going by the story on the prisms, Semiramis knew exactly where to look for the weapon. She disappeared from the battlefield and came back with it. Clearly, she had been given very precise instructions on how and where to find it. How did the Druids know where to find the divine weapon?

He paused, waiting for an answer.

'Well,' Goldfeld ventured, 'according to the prisms, the Druids knew of an ancient legend passed down by the Lords of Light, which told them where the location lay.'

'Correct. And we've established that the *Tuatha de Danann* were the Lords of Light, who preceded the Druids and created their beliefs. We've also explored a possible connection between the Lords of Light and the *Danavas* of Indian mythology, which possibly explains how they knew about a weapon hidden in ancient India. And if Dr Shukla's hypothesis about the weapons from the Mahabharata being buried in the Makran desert is true, then that reinforces this explanation. That brings us to the second question. The Druids clearly knew how to use the weapon. And, according to the Quintus Codex, they also instructed Caesar in the means to deploy the weapon. Now, if this was a weapon from the Mahabharata it is possible that the so-called means of deployment were *mantras*. I know we're speculating but it doesn't matter right now if we're right or wrong. The question is: how did the Druids know the *mantras* or the means to deploy the weapon?'

'Again, this could be a result of their oral tradition—wisdom and knowledge passed down from generations ago,' Goldfeld remarked.

'Very possible,' Vijay agreed. 'So we have a situation in 2000 B.C. where the Druids know where a weapon is hidden in the Makran desert and how to activate it. This knowledge has been inherited from the *Tuatha de Danann*. The logical conclusion is that the *Tuatha de Danann* were using this weapon in the time before the Druids. That is the only way they would know how to use it. Are we in agreement so far?'

They all nodded. Vijay had summarised the conclusions they had reached through all their discussions so far.

'The third question is: what did the *Tuatha de Danann* use the weapon for?'

There was silence as everyone mulled over this.

'The weapon is called a sceptre of light in the inscriptions,' Alice said slowly, thinking hard. 'Dr Shukla, is there any weapon like this in Indian mythology?'

'Not in the Mahabharata,' Shukla replied. 'But in the Ramayana, Lord Rama uses the *Suryastra* which is as brilliant as the sun. But I'm not sure you could call it a sceptre of light. I'd need to read up on this weapon to say anymore. I'm not as familiar with the Ramayana as I am with the Mahabharata.'

'There's also the shape of the weapon,' Colin reminded them. 'We know what it looks like, thanks to the grave of Semiramis, if we're right about that. And Dr Shukla has already confirmed that he can't think of any celestial weapon of that shape. So we can't seem to match any weapon that Arjuna carried with the description of the weapon that we have come across so far. How do we figure out what it was used for?'

'That's where your research about the association of the *Tuatha de Danann* with the megaliths comes in,' Vijay answered. 'If they really did build the megalithic sites, then two things are clear. First, those sites are more ancient than the dates currently ascribed to them. I've always been sceptical about the dating of stone monuments since we really can't be sure when they were built. But if the Lords of Light built them, they would have done so much before 2000 B.C., since they definitely weren't around when the Druids asked Semiramis to fetch the weapon for them. Second, it is possible that they used the weapon in conjunction with these sites.'

'Whoa, hang on there!' Colin interjected hurriedly. 'Are you saying that the *Tuatha de Danann* built the stone circles and the burial mounds to deploy this weapon? That doesn't make sense.'

'I know,' Vijay admitted. 'Until we know the exact nature of the weapon and we're able to identify it, we really can't be sure. But humour me for now, will you?'

'I agree with Colin,' Alice frowned. 'We've made some leaps in our thinking today, but it has all been based on information we've had access to that wasn't available before, like the inscriptions on the prisms and the Quintus Codex. But you're now making a really big leap and there's absolutely nothing to justify it.'

'But there is,' Vijay argued. 'We just haven't spoken about it in detail yet.'

64

New evidence

'You remember I was telling you about the ancient drawings I saw of Stonehenge, Barclodiad y Gawres and Brynn Celli Ddu?' Vijay asked Goldfeld.

'Ah, yes,' Goldfeld recalled the conversation they had been having just before Hamilton had called. 'I also remember that I wasn't very convinced about the diagrams you spoke of.'

'I know,' Vijay agreed. 'But let's assume for a moment that those blueprints are real and accurate, even though they are thousands of years old. *I* know that they are, but I'm asking you to agree with me for just a moment. After all, we've established that the Druids, who were in Britain, knew about the weapon hidden away in the Makran. If that was possible, then it was equally possible that people in India, at that time, knew about the megalithic monuments in Britain.'

'Fair point, Vijay,' Goldfeld conceded. 'I'm curious to see where you are going with this.'

'This is the strange thing about every diagram I saw which corresponded to the sites I visited with you and Alice,' Vijay continued his explanation. 'The blueprints pretty much matched the reconstructions done by modern archaeologists to show what these structures would have originally looked like. There was, however, one major difference. Every one of these sites had a single additional element: an additional stone that was placed either within a stone circle or within a so-called burial mound. And this additional stone was not placed at the very centre of the structure. It was always displaced to one side.'

'So what does that indicate?' Goldfeld asked.

'It doesn't indicate anything as long as you assume it is a stone,' Vijay replied, 'as I assumed when I first saw the blueprint of Stonehenge. But what if it wasn't a stone at all?'

It finally dawned on Colin. 'You're saying that the additional stone in every blueprint isn't really a stone but the weapon?'

'But what would the weapon be doing there?' Alice asked, puzzled. 'And that would mean that there would have to be many weapons, not just one!'

'Correct,' Vijay conceded. 'The interesting thing is that, while I saw blueprints of several sites, not all of them had the additional stone. Only a few of them did. So, while there are lots of sites in Britain, there wouldn't be lots of weapons. Just a handful, I'd reckon based on what I've seen.'

'So what you're saying,' Goldfeld said, 'if we assume your ancient blueprints are accurate, is that Semiramis was not asked to bring back one weapon. Or she was asked to bring back one weapon but she brought back a cache of them?'

'It is possible,' Vijay replied. 'We'll only be able to corroborate this once we know what the weapon actually is.'

'But the Druids gave Caesar the location of just one weapon,' Goldfeld persisted.

Vijay shrugged. 'If you were the Druids, would you hand over all your weapons to the Roman conqueror? Or would you prefer to give him just one—enough to satisfy him and buy you peace—and keep the rest for yourself just in case?'

'How does your theory about the weapons and the megalithic sites tie in with the coins?' Harry piped up, curious.

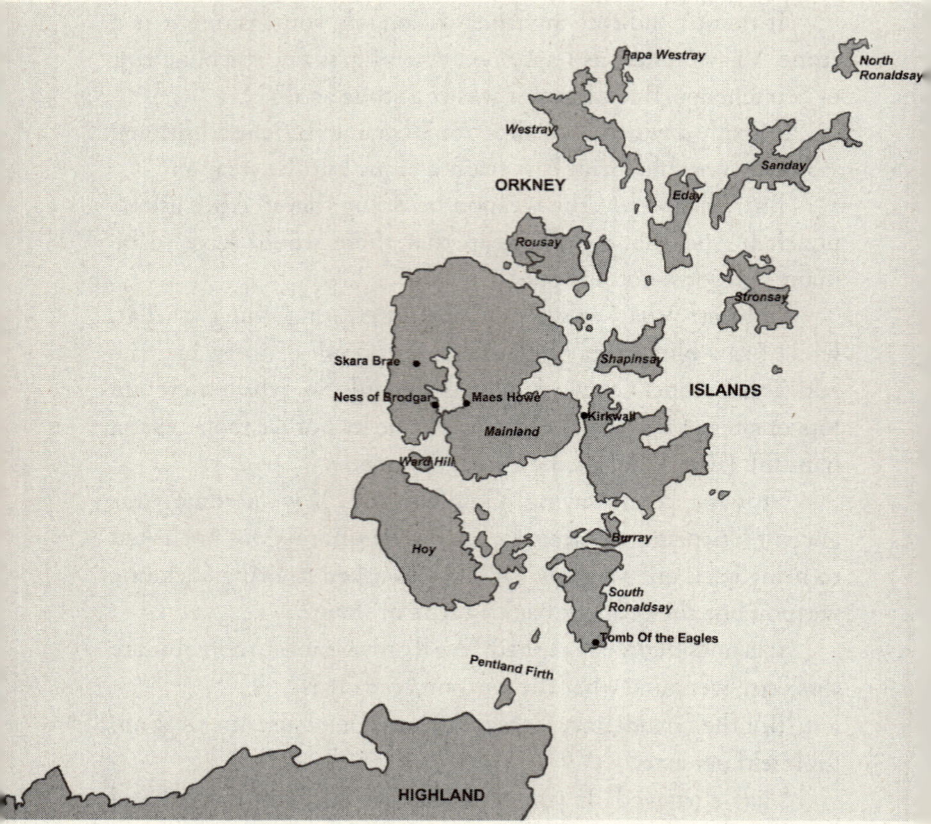

The Orkney Islands, showing the location of major megalithic sites

'That's where my research comes in. Dr Shukla, I'm sharing the screen with you so you can see this, too.' Vijay opened up a map of the UK, which filled up the screen.

He zoomed in to the north of the island, beyond Inverness, to the northernmost tip of Scotland. Beyond the highlands, across the Pentland Firth, lay a cluster of islands.

'What struck me about the coins were the random shapes on them,' Vijay began. 'They are crude, but they occupy most of the side of the coin on which they are inscribed. Why? I wondered if it was possible that these shapes aren't truly random. Could they be there by design?'

He placed on the table three circles of paper cut in the shape of the coins.

The others realised why Vijay had asked for the pair of scissors. He had been cutting out the paper coins.

'Seriously?' Colin quizzed Vijay. 'You took shots with your phone and printed out the coins?'

Vijay grinned back at him. 'The ole grey cells at work, pal.'

He wordlessly moved the paper printouts of the coins around until their edges touched.

The resulting image jumped out at all of them.

It was amazing.

65

July 10, 54 B.C.

Present-day Canterbury, Britain

Julius Caesar surveyed the scene with grim satisfaction. Four days back, he had led his legions to a successful and unopposed landing on the shores of Britannia, unlike his previous attempt a year ago.

But then, on this second expedition to Britannia, he was better prepared. With eight hundred ships, five legions and two thousand cavalry, this was the largest naval landing operation in history; and one that would not be rivalled until almost two thousand years later.

Leaving one legion and three hundred cavalry at the beach camp, the bulk of the force had pushed inland, pursuing the retreating Celts.

Enroute, they had subdued many of the local tribes. More importantly, Caesar had captured prisoners who were being interrogated regarding the secret that was his real motive for arriving in Britannia. And, for the first time, they had succeeded in capturing the men Caesar had wanted to meet and question.

The Druids.

He was making progress. This time, he would succeed.

66

Day 3

Saul Goldfeld's residence

The secret of the coins

The coins were metal—gold. The minting technology available two thousand years ago would not have been able to ensure perfect circular shapes. And the edges of the coins were not smooth. They had ridges and troughs.

But even that fact did not disguise the truth that stood out now. The three coins had been designed like pieces of a jigsaw puzzle.

And the result was startling.

They were looking at a map of the Orkney Islands, including the northern tip of Scotland. The random shapes on each coin, while roughly drawn, corresponded to the location and approximate shape of the larger islands in the archipelago.

'Wow,' Colin said, 'now that's something.'

'It certainly is,' Goldfeld agreed. 'Who would have guessed? The Orkney Islands of all places!'

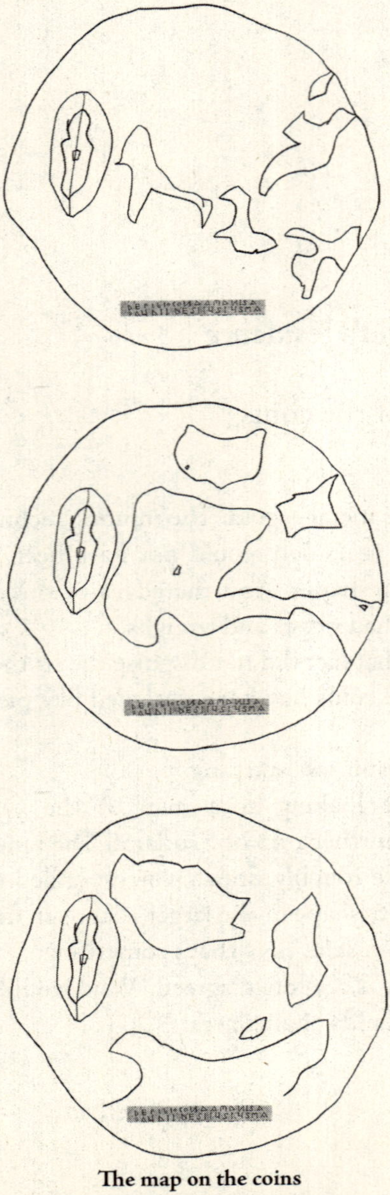

The map on the coins

'Blimey,' Harry added, then looked at Vijay. 'How did you even think of this?'

'It was Colin who set me on the right path,' Vijay admitted. He looked at Colin. 'When you mentioned that the *Tuatha de Danann* were associated with the megalithic sites in Europe and probably built them, something clicked in my mind. I remembered the ancient drawings of the megalithic sites that I had seen earlier. Then, Alice told us that the coins were unusual, according to the diary, and not just because of what was inscribed on them. It was speculated that Caesar had asked Cleopatra to mint these coins especially for him. Why would he do that? Then, I asked myself why these coins were carried all the way to Inverness. And it hit me like a bolt of lightning. We know from the Quintus Codex that the Druids had shared the location of the weapon with Caesar. What better way to remember the location, without anyone getting suspicious, than minting three coins ostensibly to commemorate his battles in Britain or Gaul, but in fact describing the location of the weapon? So, I researched the megalithic sites in Britain and discovered that the oldest sites are located in the Orkney Islands. Then I looked at the map to see where the sites were and discovered that there are over seventy megalithic sites that have been discovered there. No one has an idea of how many are still to be discovered or have been dismantled over the centuries to make way for farmland on the islands. And that was when I noticed the similarity between the shapes on the coins and the map I was studying.'

'That certainly explains why someone is after these coins,' Goldfeld agreed. 'If your line of reasoning is correct, and I don't see any reason why it should not be, given all the facts we have with us now, then someone wants that weapon badly. And they know that the coins are the only clue to find it.'

'Er, silly question,' Harry said, raising his hand. 'How would anyone know about the map on the coins? It took the five of us to research the facts that led us to this conclusion. And we were helped along the way by the Quintus Codex and the fact that Vijay had seen two-thousand-year-old blueprints of the megalithic sites. Who would have all of this information with them?'

Silence greeted his question. It wasn't silly at all. They had all been so caught up in the excitement of solving this puzzle, researching the facts and trying to make sense of all the information they had gathered, that no one had given thought to the question Harry had raised. But it was pertinent.

Somebody would have had to have access to all this information much before they unearthed it.

But who had the capacity and ability to gather this information, working silently and unobtrusively, so that no one else, until now, even knew that this information existed?

'There's only one possibility,' Vijay said grimly. 'And it isn't good news. The only other people who could have any knowledge of this, and the motive to seek the weapon, would have to belong to the Order.'

'Bloody hell.' Harry's face grew serious. He had been briefed about the Order and Vijay's encounters with them in the past. 'No wonder those blokes at Hamilton's apartment almost took us apart.'

Alice and Colin, too, looked grave. If the Order was involved, every move they made would be fraught with danger.

'Who or what is the Order?' Goldfeld enquired.

Vijay briefly explained their adventures of the last two years and their experience with the Order. Goldfeld was deeply and inextricably involved in this. He had to know.

Goldfeld's face paled. 'So we're all in danger of being killed?'

'Yes,' Vijay stated frankly. 'This explains why we've been followed for all these months. I don't know why they haven't tried to move in on us, though, if they had us in their sights all along.'

'They probably knew that you had one prism and that you had access to the second prism at the British Museum,' Colin reasoned. 'They don't have either one. Perhaps they were waiting for you to get the information that they were missing before making a move?'

'In that case,' Harry said, 'we need to keep Imran and Patterson updated on every move we make and all our plans. We have to be prepared for anything.'

There was silence again as everyone digested the reality of the situation they now found themselves in.

'We'd better move fast, then,' Colin said finally. 'And find the weapon before the Order does. We've already lost one round to them. We can't lose another one now.'

Vijay nodded his agreement. 'There's a problem though. We have both the prisms and the diagrams of the coins. Yet, apart from the fact that we've zeroed in on the Orkney Islands, we still don't know the exact location of the weapon. Are we missing something?'

'If the Order knew about the prisms, then the grave of Semiramis could have something to do with identifying the location of the weapon,' Alice suggested.

'You could be right,' Vijay looked thoughtful. 'In that case, we have a lead over them since they don't have the prisms. We should visit Cairnpapple Hill.'

'Sure,' Colin replied. 'First thing in the morning.'

'No,' Vijay shook his head. 'Now. You have a jet waiting at the airport. Let's use that and fly to Edinburgh and see what we find there.'

'They'll tail you there,' Harry pointed out. 'It might be better to split up. Some of us can go to Cairnpapple. The others can serve as a diversion to distract the guys shadowing us.'

'Fine,' Vijay said. 'You and Alice go to Cairnpapple,' he addressed Colin. 'I'm booking myself and Harry on a flight to Orkney tomorrow.' He turned to Goldfeld. 'You can come with either of us. Your choice.'

'I'll go with Colin and Alice,' Goldfeld replied. 'I'm curious to see the grave of Semiramis. And I'm not too keen to freeze in Orkney. It will be miserable at this time of year—more windy and rainy than London and also much colder.'

'All the best,' Shukla said, then hesitated. 'Vijay, I need to talk to you privately, whenever you can spare some time,' he signed off.

Vijay could guess what Shukla wanted to talk to him about. But there were more pressing matters at hand. His face was set. 'Let's give our shadows something to chase.'

67

South Kensington, London

Colin and Alice watched from behind a curtain as Vijay and Harry hailed a cab and got in. They were the decoys, aiming to draw the men tailing them away from the house so that the other three could make their way to the airport, with Goldfeld driving them.

Patterson had been called and briefed, along with Imran, and they had both endorsed the plan. The need for extra security for the team visiting Cairnpapple had been discussed but Patterson advised against it.

'In any case, you can't carry guns,' he had argued. 'British laws don't allow it. An unarmed security escort would be of no use against armed attackers but would definitely attract attention. If the Order doesn't know what's on the prism, then your best bet is to get there before they realise what's happening and get out fast after finding what we need.'

The leader of the task force had also been unhappy about Goldfeld and Alice accompanying Colin, since neither of them was, technically, a member of the task force. But he also realised that, if the plan to lure the shadows away was to succeed, splitting up was the best way. So if Vijay had decided to go to Orkney, it had to be Colin who would go to Cairnpapple. And it was best that he didn't go alone. Patterson accepted the situation and wished them luck.

He also made it clear that Alice and Goldfeld were accompanying Colin at their own risk.

Colin's phone rang. It was Vijay. 'All clear?'

'Not really,' Colin replied. 'We've been watching since you left and there's no sign of anyone following you.'

'That's strange. I would have thought that they would have suspected something was up since only the two of us left. They should have come after us.'

'Maybe we are giving them too much credit?' Colin suggested.

'Watch for a while longer and then we'll decide.'

Colin reported his conversation with Vijay to Alice and Goldfeld. They continued to watch for another twenty minutes. Then Colin called Vijay. 'Nothing yet. Silent night.'

Vijay sighed. He hated it when things didn't go according to plan. 'I guess we have no choice then,' he said. 'You guys leave. But keep your eyes peeled for any sign of pursuit. If you're followed, let me know.'

'Roger.' Colin conveyed the instructions to Goldfeld and Alice and they stepped out. No one was in sight.

They got into Goldfeld's car and looked all around as it pulled away from the kerb. Alice kept a watch at the back to see if anyone was behind them while Colin looked left and right, as Goldfeld concentrated on driving.

After half an hour of driving, Colin called Vijay again. 'Looks like we didn't have a tail tonight,' he reported. 'We're clear.'

'Great,' Vijay replied, though he was baffled. 'Good luck.'

But the question continued to bother him. *Why wasn't the Order watching them tonight?*

68

Saul Goldfeld's residence

Vijay sat in Goldfeld's guest room and watched Shukla's face on the laptop screen, as the linguist spoke. While his voice sounded calm, there was just the hint of a tremor that betrayed the older man's emotions.

'You made me a promise, Vijay,' Shukla was saying, as he got straight to the point. 'What happened?'

Vijay knew what Shukla was referring to. On his return from Kazakhstan over a year ago, he had promised Shukla that he would get Radha's body back, no matter what it took.

Shukla waited. The silence weighed heavily on Vijay as he wrestled with his emotions.

Even though it was born from an emotional reaction to Radha's death and, more significantly, the circumstances of her death, Vijay had been sincere about delivering on his promise. His intentions had never wavered.

But two things had thwarted him. First, the fact that the trail ran cold after Abu Dhabi. Even Imran had failed to track Radha after the hospital in Abu Dhabi had declared her dead and Saxena had disappeared with Radha's body.

The second was his preoccupation with solving the mystery behind the death of his parents. His helplessness in pursuing the trail beyond Abu Dhabi, and Patterson's clear admonitions regarding his personal involvement with Titan Pharmaceuticals, had led to him immersing himself in the search for clues that would reveal why his parents had died.

Even now his emotions jostled with each other, as he regretted not having been more adamant about the search for Radha and his obsession with following the trail that the prism had led to.

Was he becoming less human? More emotionless? Did Radha no longer mean anything to him? Was the thrill of the chase, the pursuit of the secret of the Druids, elbowing out the need to pursue the trail that would lead to his promise to Shukla being fulfilled?

He struggled with the unpleasant questions that crowded his mind, trying to grapple with the possibility that a horrible reality was at play, as Shukla waited patiently for his answer.

'I don't know,' Vijay hunched up as he managed to answer. It was the truth. He wasn't sure of anything any longer. 'I'm…I don't know what happened.'

Even across the distance of thousands of miles and the uncertainty of the image transmitted by the laptop camera, Shukla discerned Vijay's emotional state.

'I'm not judging you, son,' he said gently. 'I know it hasn't been easy for either of us. But I want closure for my daughter and myself. And also for you.'

Vijay nodded. He wanted to cry but the tears wouldn't come. How could he explain himself when he didn't understand in the first place?

'I'm sorry,' he said finally, fighting to regain his composure but knowing that he was failing miserably to do so. He told Shukla about how Imran tracked Saxena and Radha to Abu Dhabi and then lost scent of the trail. 'I guess I just gave up with everything that happened,' he admitted. 'Maybe I ran away from the situation. Perhaps it got too much for me to bear.' He shrugged. 'I really don't know. I have no idea where to go from here. Or what to do.'

The two men sat in silence, looking at each other. They shared a common grief, yet a yawning gap seemed to separate them now; a gap that hadn't been there when Vijay had made his promise.

What had changed since then? How could he close the distance between him and Shukla?

Vijay found himself unable to find an answer.

69

Cairnpapple Hill, Bathgate, West Lothian

Colin eased the Land Rover onto the extended shoulder of the road, which served as a small car park and cut the engine.

There was another car parked there. A BMW X5.

Goldfeld frowned. 'It is well past visiting hours. Who could be here at this hour?'

'It isn't that late,' Alice observed. 'It could be random tourists not interested in paying for looking around. According to the website of Scottish Heritage, this is on a working farm, so access is free. But the guided tours—which are paid tours—have specified timings.'

'Or someone could be visiting the farm,' Colin added. 'Either way, it doesn't matter. Let's look around and then get out of here. This is way out in the countryside and it's cold and wet.'

While they were driving up it had started to rain and it hadn't let up until now.

They turned up the collars of their overcoats and passed through the gate at the top of a short flight of steps to gain access to the hill. Great tufts of grass, spongy and wet, covered the hill.

It was dark all around and they switched on their torches. There seemed to be a glow at the top of the hill where the cairn stood.

'Oh crap.' Colin had discovered that there was more than

grass covering the hillside. He shone his torch down. Dung, some of it fresh, was spread around in patches.

'It's a working farm, after all, Colin,' Alice giggled. 'There must be sheep and cows around here.'

Colin scowled at her and wiped his shoes on a tuft of grass. He trained his torch on the ground now and began picking his way carefully through the grass. Alice and Goldfeld followed him, both grinning widely at his indignation.

'I wonder what that glow is?' Alice remarked as the grassy mound that covered the concrete dome came in sight. The glow seemed to be emanating from the very top of the dome.

To their left, a tall telecom tower loomed like a giant skeleton in the night, all metal bone.

Goldfeld shrugged. 'Maybe it's some sort of lighting at the site. We'll find out.'

Presently, a wire fence gleamed in the light of their torches. A gate led into the area within the fence, which enclosed the entire site.

A large earthen bank loomed before them, giving way to a shallow ditch.

'The Henge,' Goldfeld murmured.

Beyond the bank and ditch was a circular area of loose rock surrounding the concrete dome that covered the central cairn. A gravel-lined path had been cut into the bank and ditch, leading to the bed of loose rocks around the dome.

Light streamed into the night sky from the top of the dome.

'Did you hear that?' Alice said suddenly. 'Sounds like voices.'

They stood still and listened.

The sound of voices came to them. The words were indistinguishable, but they were unmistakeably uttered by humans.

Colin put a finger to his lips. He gestured to Alice and Goldfeld to stay back.

The grass-covered concrete dome at the summit of Cairnpapple Hill

The ring of loose rock around the dome, with large circular holes dug in it

'I'm going ahead and climbing the dome,' he whispered in Alice's ear. 'These may be tourists for all we know, but I'm not taking any chances.'

Alice nodded and Colin approached the dome cautiously. He decided that walking on wet gravel might pose a risk of being heard, so he avoided the path and walked over the turf instead. His next challenge was not to disturb the loose rock or stumble over the large circular holes dug into the bed of rocks that surrounded the dome.

He reached the base of the dome and switched off his torch. Though the light streaming from the top of the dome was not very bright, it was sufficient to show him the flight of stone steps set in the concrete, leading to the top of the dome.

Slowly, silently, he walked up the steps. Two stairs before the summit, he crouched down to survey the top of the dome, clinging to the steps to avoid being detected.

There was no one visible at the top, but he could see that a trapdoor lay open in the very centre of the concrete dome. The light was emanating from a hole in the roof of the dome.

The voices came to him clearly now and he could make out what they were saying.

Colin froze. He couldn't believe what he was hearing.

In the car park

Outside the henge, Alice and Goldfeld stood in the rain and waited for Colin to return.

Goldfeld nudged Alice and nodded towards the car park.

A car had just arrived, clearly noticeable by the headlights.

It stopped at the car park for a few moments.

Alice's heart was in her mouth.

What was happening here? On a dark, wet night like this,

how many people were visiting Cairnpapple? It didn't seem likely that all of them were tourists.

She only hoped that the Order had not caught up with them.

70

At the summit of Cairnpapple Hill

'We've been here three hours,' a man was saying angrily. 'We've overturned every bloody stone in this place but there's nothing apart from those squiggles on the headstone. I'm wet and tired and I think we've come on a wild goose chase.'

'Shut your whining, will you?' a woman's voice came to Colin. She sounded cold and harsh. 'The inscriptions on the prisms clearly indicated that this is where the grave of Semiramis is located. And Caesar's diary specifically mentioned the Semiramis connection. There has to be something here that will give us the clues we need.'

'Waste of bloody time if you ask me,' the man murmured. 'We've dug up the grave, moved the stones, checked them all. There's nothing here to be found.'

'I agree with Harper, boss,' another man said.

Colin frowned. *How many people were down there?*

'Give it another lookover.' The woman sounded disappointed. 'If we don't find anything then it'll just mean that our plans for securing the third coin get advanced.'

'But boss, we aren't ready yet,' one of the men protested. 'When do you want to attack the museum?'

'We return tonight. Call the helicopter. Tomorrow morning, we hit the museum. I want that coin. If this grave has yielded nothing, we need to examine the coins if we have to find the weapon.'

Colin had heard enough. He was shocked. They had all believed that the Order had no idea about Cairnpapple Hill. But, somehow, the Order was two steps ahead of them.

How could they have known what was on the prisms?

But there was no time to ponder this.

They had to get out of here.

Fast.

Colin slithered down the stairs, almost falling in the process, grasping at the sides of the stone steps to break his slide.

His knee hit the edge of one of the stone steps and exploded in red-hot pain. It was all he could do to stop himself from crying out.

He hit the bottom of the dome and slipped again, this time on a flat stone slab at the bottom of the stairs.

'What's that?' the woman asked sharply, her voice still clearly audible. 'Did you hear that noise?'

Colin stood up gingerly and tested his knee. He still saw stars, but he could walk. He would have a nasty bruise tomorrow.

The ring of loose rock awaited him. If he walked slowly across, he could make it.

But he wouldn't get the chance.

Colin heard someone scrambling up the ladder through the hole in the roof. Glancing back, he saw a man silhouetted on the top of the dome.

The man gave a shout.

This was no time to be subtle.

Colin decided to run for it. He dashed across the ring of loose stones surrounding the dome, switching his torch on as he ran to avoid the large holes in the bed of stones that were scattered around the site.

'Run!' He called out to Alice and Goldfeld. 'Now!'

71

Run!

Alice watched transfixed as the car at the foot of the hill stayed stationary, its headlights on. Who was it? And what were they doing here?

Goldfeld was at her side. Though he didn't say anything, she knew that the same thoughts were running through his mind.

She recalled her experience last year in Greece, when she was hunted by members of the Order. The trauma of that night had not completely gone away. It lingered and there were still nights when she would wake up, sweating and terrified.

Was this going to be another night like that one?

To her relief, the car finally moved on up the road and then disappeared into the night.

Probably some people looking for a farm, she thought to herself.

With the immediate scare gone, her thoughts turned to Colin. What was happening at the top of the dome? What had he found?

Then, all hell broke loose.

She saw a man emerge at the summit of the dome.

The man, spotting Colin, shouted.

Colin's dark figure materialised, running across to where she stood.

Alice didn't know if the man on the dome had seen her and Goldfeld, but this wasn't the time for analysis.

Even before Colin started shouting, she was jolted into action by Goldfeld, who gave her a push and began running himself.

They dashed down the hill, Colin catching up with them, ignoring the sheep droppings and cow dung.

They had to get away.

That was all that mattered now.

71

Pursue!

Within the concrete dome, Dee was exasperated and disappointed. She had been so sure that there would be clues to finding the weapon in this cairn.

But now she knew she had been wrong. Caesar hadn't mentioned the Semiramis story in his diary because there were clues there. He had merely recorded the means by which the weapon had come all the way from India to Britain. She was angry with herself. She had been so stupid. Caesar had clearly written in his diary that the coins were the key to finding the weapon. And here she was, on a wild goose chase, looking for clues where there weren't any. She tried to convince herself that the visit to Cairnpapple Hill was useful, if only to eliminate the possibility that something was concealed here.

A noise made her start. It had come from outside the dome.

'What's that?' she asked sharply. 'Did you hear that noise?'

Harper and the three men with him had evidently heard the noise as well. It couldn't be sheep or cattle ambling across the loose rocks surrounding the dome. The metal fence surrounding the site would keep them out.

One of the men scrambled up the ladder, through the trapdoor opening, and on to the roof of the dome.

A shout came to them.

There was someone outside.

Who was it?

She found it hard to believe that it could be tourists at this time of night, in the rain and cold.

But who else would visit Cairnpapple now? They hadn't posted a lookout on top of the mound only because it was extremely unlikely that anyone would be about in this weather and at this hour. The hill was not the sort of place that people would venture out to on just a whim.

'Get them,' she said. 'I want them alive. I want to know who they are and what they are doing here. And what they've heard. We can kill them after that.'

Harper nodded and led his remaining men up the ladder. As he emerged on the roof, the staccato beat of the helicopter's rotors came to his ears.

Dee's transport had arrived.

72

Fear

They reached the foot of the hill. Colin fumbled with the latch on the gate, which was wet and slippery.

So far, things had gone in their favour.

He had been surprised that no one was shooting at them. These people were clearly from the Order. They had talked about Semiramis, Caesar and the coins. And, to top it all, they had mentioned a weapon. If he had needed proof that their deductions had been spot on, here it was.

But the Order wasn't given to letting people go. Especially when people overheard their secrets.

So why weren't they shooting?

Behind them, they heard the men thudding down the hill in hot pursuit.

The gate opened and Alice and Goldfeld slipped through, with Colin bringing up the rear.

Colin unlocked the car using the remote and they all dived in. He started the engine, not bothering to fasten his seatbelt.

There was no time for safety measures.

The car lurched forward as Colin pressed the accelerator to the floor and the powerful engine of the Land Rover kicked in.

The road was wet, but Colin didn't have the luxury of caution.

In the rearview mirror, he saw three men dash onto the road and jump into the other car that had been parked there.

Then, the Land Rover rounded a bend and they disappeared from sight.

But he knew that they would be back in his rearview mirror again.

They would not give up the chase so easily.

73

Shock

The helicopter lowered two harnesses, one each for Dee and Harper, who were swiftly winched up into the cabin. Then the chopper banked to the left, towards the road leading away from the hill.

From the helicopter, Dee could clearly see the Land Rover speeding away.

She could also see Harper's men boarding their own car to give chase.

But there was something more.

Another car.

It came out of nowhere, from the opposite direction, its headlights off, like a phantom in the darkness.

Dee could see the car coming.

But her men in the car park below couldn't.

Even as the car with Harper's men began to pull out of the car park, the mystery car came plunging down the road and overtook them, screeching to a halt in front, blocking their way.

The three men jumped out, shouting angry curses, only to be greeted by gunfire.

Dee watched, shocked, as Harper's men were shot before her eyes. She watched them collapse on the road.

What was happening? Who were these men who dared to carry guns on them? Certainly not the police. They would not violate the law.

'Take us there,' Dee instructed the pilot. She was damned if she was going to let them get away after inflicting losses on her team. She turned to Harper. 'Get those men.'

Harper nodded. From the back of the cabin, he pulled out a long-range sniper's rifle. It would do.

But Dee had not counted on one thing.

The mystery men who had taken out her team heard the chopper coming. Before Harper had a chance to line them up in his sights, the men on the ground were shooting at the helicopter, which was flying low.

Bullets whizzed past as the pilot banked and dived to evade them.

'I have to pull out!' he shouted above the din of the rotors. 'This is a light chopper. It isn't armoured. If one of those bullets hits our fuel tank, we're goners!'

Dee pursed her lips. She hated to admit defeat.

But tonight she had no choice.

'Pull out,' she ordered and the pilot swiftly banked away from the road and over a wooded section of hillside, affording some cover to the helicopter.

As they began the flight back to London, Dee reflected on the events of the night. Slowly, she came to an inescapable conclusion.

The Order didn't know whom it was dealing with. All along, it had thought that no one knew its plans. But someone did.

And she thought she knew who it was.

Warning

Half an hour had passed and, to Colin's surprise, there were no signs of pursuit. Had the men pursuing them fallen behind? Had they developed engine trouble? He had no way of knowing what had befallen them.

It didn't matter. He would keep driving. There was no slowing down now.

'Call Vijay,' he told Alice, who was in the front passenger seat. 'He has to be told. They're going to attack the British Museum tomorrow and steal the third coin.'

Reflection

Dee sat in the helicopter and collected her thoughts. She was furious with herself. Her focus on the goal—finding the clues to the weapon and then locating it— had been so strong and single-minded that she had neglected to watch her back.

She was guilty of complacence. And her lack of experience in missions of this nature, coupled with her obstinate refusal to solicit advice from Van Klueck didn't help. She had assumed that only the Order had access to all the information that could help locate the weapon. It was clear now that that assumption had been fallacious.

Someone else knew.

Nothing else could explain what had happened tonight. She might have dismissed the intrusion at the cairn as an accident. Tourists happening upon them by chance and then getting frightened away. That could have explained it.

But what had followed—the car appearing from out of thin air; her men being mowed down, while the intruders made good their escape—underlined the fact that someone else was after the weapon. Nothing else could explain anyone's interest in Cairnpapple Hill.

Dee realised that Van Klueck would have to be told. She cringed mentally at the prospect. Not only would it give him pleasure to point out how careless she had been, but it would also affect her credibility as a strategic planner.

She set her jaw, determined to find out who was behind the events tonight. And she knew where she would start looking.

Before the British Museum, she had one more stop to make.

The Hamilton estate.

Part 6

74

Day 4

Regent's Park, London

Dee glared fiercely at the two women sitting in the room, bound to their chairs, fear oozing from every pore in their body.

Harper's men had picked up the two this morning from the Hamilton estate. It had been easy to subdue the lone constable provided in the name of security, at the Hamilton residence in Hertfordshire.

Dee ignored Susan Hamilton-Roger's snivels and concentrated her full attention on Penny.

The young girl's tear-stained face was white with terror.

Dee liked that. She brandished an evil-looking dagger at Penny and smiled, a cruel smile born out of pleasure in watching the women cringe.

'A simple question,' Dee told Penny. 'That's all I have. Give me the answer and I'll set you free and never bother you again.' She brought her face close to Penny's. 'Do you understand?'

Penny nodded, grateful for the opportunity to escape with her life.

'Tell me the truth,' Dee continued. 'Lie or hide the facts and both you and your aunt will regret it.'

'I'll tell you whatever I know,' Penny sobbed. 'I swear. Just don't harm us.'

'Apart from your father and yourself, who else knew about the coins?'

Penny hesitated.

Susan Hamilton-Rogers spoke up, her voice quavering. 'Go on, dear, tell her!' Her voice broke.

Penny was in a quandary. On one hand, her life, and her aunt's, was at stake. On the other hand if she disclosed their names, Vijay and his friends would be in danger. What was she to do?

'Listen to your aunt,' Dee urged. 'I can get the information out of you in more painful ways. I will have what I want.'

Penny believed her. This woman was not to be trifled with. And she would not stop at anything to get what she wanted.

The young girl broke. She revealed the names of the little group with whom she had spent the last two days. Ashamed at her own helplessness and overwhelmed by guilt at her betrayal, she broke down, her body wracked with sobs.

Dee stood straight, a satisfied look on her face. She had suspected that Vijay Singh and his friends were involved in this affair. It had been a mistake to call off the surveillance. But it had been a tough call. The security cordon around Vijay and his friends would have compromised the mission.

Last night, she had informed Van Klueck about the incident at Cairnpapple Hill. As expected, he had been caustic in his remarks and critical in his assessment of her competence in handling the mission.

But it had been necessary to report her conclusions to Van Klueck. It was clear to her that the Order was not dealing with random individuals but a well-organised force.

Dee had kept her suspicions about Vijay's involvement to herself. For one thing, she wasn't sure if she was right about him. For another, if she even voiced her suspicions, she knew Van

Klueck would want to get involved. And she didn't want that to happen.

She wanted the glory of killing Vijay for herself.

By the time Van Klueck mobilised the intelligence machinery of the Order to find out who their unseen, mysterious enemy was, she would have validated her hunch about Vijay and, perhaps, have even found the weapon.

And then, she would have gone after him and eliminated him before Van Klueck got to know.

Now that Penny had confirmed her suspicions, Dee knew it was a matter of time. The organisation Vijay was working for, whatever it was, also wanted to find the weapon.

Which meant that her path would cross Vijay's at some point in time.

That was when she would kill him.

And take pleasure in it.

Dee smiled at the thought and brought her attention back to the two women.

She didn't need them any longer. She smiled at Penny. 'Thank you, my dear,' she said as she walked behind the young girl. 'You did the right thing. And I'll keep my promise to you.'

Abruptly, she pushed Penny's head forward so that the girl's chin was pointing at her chest.

The blade of the knife flashed as Dee drew it swiftly across the young girl's throat.

Susan screamed as Penny slumped in her chair, blood gushing out of the cut and pouring down her chest.

Dee handed the blade to one of the men in the room. She wasn't interested in Susan. Her men could take care of the woman. It was the girl who had been her prey.

Now, she had a coin to steal.

75

The British Museum, London

Ben Atkins frowned at Colin, who was sitting in the security office and had just given him the news about the Order's plans to attack the museum this morning. Colin hadn't disclosed who was behind the attack; all he had revealed was that he had a reliable intelligence report regarding an attack by a terrorist organisation.

Alice, Colin and Goldfeld had returned to London this morning. While the others had headed to Goldfeld's house, where the task force had organised security for them, Colin had headed directly for the museum. He had hoped he wouldn't be too late.

'And you're sure about this?' Atkins grunted, finding it hard to believe that any terrorist would want to attack the museum just to steal a worthless coin. 'I still don't know what they're going to achieve by stealing that coin,' he opined. 'The museum experts say it has no worth, apart from the value of the gold in it, which isn't enough to inspire anyone to steal it.'

Colin shrugged. 'I can only tell you what I know about the intel we have,' he replied. 'Anything else would be speculation.'

'Come on then,' Atkins rose. 'Let's go upstairs to the Roman gallery. I'm putting extra people on duty there.'

Aberdeen Airport, Scotland

Vijay sat on one of the red faux leather airport row chairs and sipped his coffee thoughtfully.

Last night, when Colin had called him from West Lothian to inform him about the Order's plans to steal the coin, he had been stunned. It had come as a shock to him that the Order knew about the inscriptions on the prisms and had worked out the location of Semiramis's grave before they did. Clearly they had all underestimated the Order. It had been a foolish thing to do. It was going to be a race against time. The Order was after the coin. And Vijay, like Colin, had no doubt that they would go to any lengths to get it from the British Museum.

There had to be a change in plans.

'You guys fly back here first thing tomorrow morning,' Vijay had instructed Colin. 'I want you to take charge at the museum. The Order has to be stopped.'

'Fine,' Colin said. 'Does that mean that you're not going to be in London tomorrow morning?'

'I'm going to take the first flight from London City Airport to Kirkwall,' Vijay replied. 'There's a flight at 7 am that lands in Kirkwall, via Aberdeen, at 10.50 am. I'll book it right away.'

'I'd rather we went together,' Colin said.

'So would I,' Vijay responded. 'But we have to do both things tomorrow morning—the Museum and Orkney. I don't want to take a chance. We don't know what else the Order has up their sleeves. Even if they fail in their attempt to get the coin, they may figure out by some other means, that the weapon is hidden in the Orkney Islands. We made a mistake earlier in assuming they didn't know about Semiramis or Cairnpapple Hill. We have to assume they know all that we do. Right now, we may be ahead of them because we had Hamilton's diary. The

Order doesn't have all the coins yet. And I'll need at least a day to go around Orkney and figure out how to find the weapon. We don't have a choice. We have to split up.'

Colin hadn't been happy with the situation. But he knew that Vijay made sense. Besides, Harry would be going with Vijay, so he relented.

One thing was clear now. Cairnpapple Hill was not a part of the puzzle that led to the weapon. The coins were the key.

Vijay had spent most of last night, as well as the ninety odd minutes on the flight from London to Aberdeen, trying to resolve what he believed was the key to unlocking the mystery of the coins.

The three inscriptions.

He was convinced that, as meaningless as they sounded, they were instructions to find the secret location. There was no other reason why Caesar would have had them inscribed on the coins.

But despite the hours of thinking and analysing, he was no closer to solving the puzzle.

Vijay looked at his watch. Five minutes to go before his flight to Kirkwall—the airport on the largest island of Orkney, called the Mainland—started boarding.

Harry came up to him, coffee in one hand, two packed sushi meals in the other, from the Boots outlet at the airport. 'Better than buying food on the plane,' he grinned. 'This will keep us going until Kirkwall.'

Vijay accepted one of the plastic boxes gratefully and they quickly ate. They hadn't had time to have breakfast in the morning and both of them had a dislike for airline food, so they hadn't purchased food on the flight either.

The departure of their flight was announced and they walked through the bridge that connected the main terminal to the gate that would lead to their aircraft.

As they boarded their plane, a Fairchild 340, a sense of trepidation gripped Vijay.

He was embarking on the final leg of their search for the weapon, engaged in a race against time with an organisation that had no scruples.

And he was going to be in Orkney within the next hour.

The problem was that he had no idea what he was looking for in Orkney. Neither did he know where to start looking.

There was no way he could afford to fail in his mission. Yet, he could see no way of making it a success.

Unless he was able to figure out what the inscriptions meant.

76

The British Museum, London

Colin looked around the gallery. It was a Saturday and there was a decent crowd in the room. He wondered how the Order planned to pull off this robbery. It wasn't going to be easy. Moreover, it went against the grain of everything they had learnt about the Order until now. One of their main principles was to carry out their operations away from the glare of the media. They sought the darkness of anonymity, not the limelight. They stayed away from attacking public places or high profile locations for this reason, preferring not to draw attention to themselves.

It was how the Order had survived, unknown and invisible, through the centuries.

Yet, Colin had overheard an operative of the Order, no less, claiming that a place as public and high profile as the British Museum was going to be attacked to steal a coin.

The coin in question rested at the bottom of a tall glass case that stood against one wall of the gallery, housing other artefacts from the Roman period in Britain.

Atkins had deployed five security guards in the room and promised to be in constant touch with Jim, a red-haired young guard who was in charge of the security team assigned to this gallery. It was obvious that Atkins didn't think much of the threat that Colin had outlined; yet he didn't want to take any chances.

Colin wasn't very happy with what he felt was a lackadaisical attitude on the part of the security chief, but he didn't have a choice. He was strongly tempted to stand next to the glass case with the coin but Atkins had warned him against interfering with the security operation.

'If anything happens here, my team will take care of it,' Atkins had said before he stomped off. 'Stay clear and don't try to help. You'll just get in the way.'

So Colin hung back, finding himself a vantage point in the gallery from where he could surreptitiously observe the coin, and waited.

There was a motley crowd of people in the room—teenagers, a few elderly people, some Japanese tourists, two British families with young children.

His attention was drawn to a young woman who was studying the artefacts kept with the coins. She had short hair and was around 5 feet 5 inches in height, with an unusual complexion. Her face practically shone and he was quite entranced by it. She glanced at her watch and then continued her study of the artefacts, her nose almost pressed against the glass.

Colin had noticed her the moment she entered the room because of the unnatural glow on her face.

The woman must have felt his eyes on her. She looked around and their eyes met. She smiled at him and he smiled back, embarrassed to have been caught in the act of staring at her. He quickly looked away and the woman went back to studying the artefacts.

Colin looked at Jim and saw his expression change from stolid to that of worry.

Now what?

Security Control Room

The British Museum, London

Ben Atkins frowned at the drama being played out on the video monitor—one of a bank of monitors receiving live feed from the multitude of CCTV cameras placed all over the museum.

His team in the control room had summoned him, just as he returned to his office after leaving Colin and his five guards in the Roman gallery.

A lone man had suddenly created a commotion in the Great Court. Atkins had rushed to the control room when he heard the news.

'He says he is a suicide bomber,' the security officer in charge of the control room briefed him. 'George Thurwell is down there giving us updates. The man suddenly started shouting in Arabic, then apparently took off his coat, displaying *that*.' He pointed to the screen and Atkins saw the explosive belt attached to the man's torso. 'He then said in English that he was going to blow himself up.'

'We've called in the Blue Berets,' the security officer continued, referring to the occasional nickname for SCO19, the specialist armed force of the Greater London Metropolitan police. Though they no longer wore blue berets, having traded them in for helmets or baseball caps, they comprised the branch of the police equipped with firearms, unlike the rest of the police force who were unarmed.

Atkins grunted. 'Hope they get here before the bugger blows himself up.'

'Islamic State,' another guard manning the control room spoke up. 'Thurwell just reported that the bomber mentioned IS in English amid his rant in Arabic.'

Atkins pursed his lips. This didn't look good. He hoped the Blue Berets would show up in time.

The Roman Gallery

Jim hurried up to Colin. 'We have to rush downstairs,' he said. 'We have a terrorist situation in the Great Court. We need to evacuate the gallery in case there are any other terrorists in the building.'

A chill gripped Colin. Had the assault begun?

There was no time to ask questions.

The guards in the gallery began shepherding the people towards an exit, gently informing them that there was an emergency and the gallery needed to be evacuated.

As Colin left the gallery, the crowds thickened as people from all the other galleries on the floor converged on the staircase, following the museum guards.

77

Security Control Room

Atkins watched as the screens showed men in SCO19 uniform spreading out across the museum. They had arrived in remarkable time.

He felt a sense of relief. The situation had been beyond the control of his security team. Now that the professionals were here, they would take charge.

But what would they do?

The suicide bomber fell silent. He dropped to his knees, his head hung. Then, he raised his head and seemed to cry out loud.

He rose and stood, his pose menacing and threatening.

The little group of men in the control room watched in horror.

They knew what was about to come.

A lot of people were going to die.

The Roman Gallery

Colin found Jim by his side and decided to quiz him as they jogged downstairs. 'What's happened? Gunmen?'

'Not that bad,' Jim replied. 'A single man. But he's wired with bombs. He's threatening to blow himself up in the name of the Islamic State.' The guard shook his head. 'It's crazy. There are families down there. Children...' He looked at Colin. 'I'm sorry but this takes priority over everything else.'

Colin nodded his agreement. He felt a strange sinking feeling in his stomach; a feeling of helplessness, like a void. How many people would die today?

It was ironic, he thought. They had been expecting the Order to strike and a suicide bomber had struck instead.

'Oh great,' Jim perked up as a team of men dressed in black, wearing helmets, visors and carrying automatic weapons rushed up the staircase, heading towards the galleries on the third floor. 'The SCO19 have arrived. That was quick.'

'Who are they?' Colin enquired.

'The British equivalent of the SWAT in America,' Jim explained. 'They are the Metropolitan Police's Specialist Firearms Unit. We can feel more reassured now that they are in the building.'

Security Control Room

The suicide bomber fumbled at his waist, reaching for the detonator.

The group in the control room collectively held their breath.

Without warning, the bomber jerked, flew backwards a couple of feet and crumpled to the floor.

The anticipated explosion hadn't happened.

A cheer went up in the control room.

They hadn't seen anything but it was obvious that an SCO19 sniper's bullet had found its mark.

On the way down

Jim listened to something on his earpiece and then beamed at Colin. 'They got him. The suicide bomber. Shot him dead.

They're now securing the rest of the building in case there are any accomplices around.'

Colin was relieved. This meant that the plans of the Order were thwarted, if only temporarily. Surely they wouldn't try anything as long as the SCO19 personnel were in the building? They weren't that foolhardy.

Security Control Room

On the rest of the screens, the SCO19 teams were regrouping and returning, converging on the entrance to the museum.

'What's happening there?' One of the guards pointed to a screen where three SCO19 officers seemed to be clustered around an exhibit in a gallery.

'Which gallery is that?' Atkins asked.

'The Roman gallery,' the security officer replied. 'Maybe something up there caught their interest.'

One of the SCO19 officers in the gallery nodded and the three men turned around and walked out of the gallery, followed by a woman.

Atkins looked at the security officer. 'Weren't all the galleries evacuated?'

The security officer looked puzzled. 'Yes, they were. I got a confirmation on that.'

'Then what was she doing there?' Atkins pointed at the woman who disappeared from the screen as she walked past the camera, then appeared a bit later, on the staircase, still following the SCO19 men.

'Maybe she got left out...I don't know,' the security officer shrugged. 'But she's with the specialists, and the threat has been contained, so I guess there's no need to worry.'

Atkins wasn't satisfied. 'Ask a team to report to the gallery immediately and do a sweep.'

Something about this situation troubled him.

78

July, 54 B.C.

Near the Stour River, England

Julius Caesar would have wept, had he been a man who was given to showing his emotions. But he suppressed his frustration and maintained an outward calm as he listened to the bad news.

A coastal storm had wreaked havoc among his fleet. Forty ships had been completely wrecked. Many others had been devastated but not beyond repair. Either way, his plans for Britannia had to wait.

'Build a land fort,' Caesar had instructed. 'Move the entire fleet of remaining galleys—all seven hundred and sixty of them—into the fort. And send word to Laeienus to build more ships in Gaul to replace the ones that were wrecked.'

The Roman army had spent ten days building the land fort and transporting the remainder of the fleet as instructed.

The passage of time had given the Celts the opportunity to regroup under a tribal chief named Cassivellaunus.

And Caesar's interrogation of the prisoners had, so far, unearthed no clues about the whereabouts of the secret that he pursued.

This operation was faring no better than the disaster of the previous year.

79

February

Day 4

Entrance to the British Museum

Colin stood with Jim and watched the SCO19 men jog away to the accompaniment of grateful applause from the museum guests. Two of the officers carried the dead suicide bomber's body. But for them, many people could have been killed today. They were true heroes.

In the background, the chatter of a helicopter's rotors came to their ears, growing louder by the minute.

'Quiet heroism,' Colin observed. 'In the US, our SWAT teams are a bit more dramatic. They arrive in black trucks and knock down doors. At least that's what they do in the movies and TV shows.'

'These guys have a pretty mean-looking truck,' Jim countered. 'I guess they didn't want to alert the terrorist—he probably had accomplices in the crowd.'

The helicopter was overhead now and fairly low. Everyone looked up, wondering. It was a sleek, black machine, slowly disappearing from sight even as they watched. The continued sound of the rotors indicated that it was hovering, unseen, over the roof of the Great Court.

'That's probably one of their choppers,' Jim said. He put his hand to the earpiece. 'Right-oh,' he spoke into his microphone. I'm on my way now.'

'What's the matter?' Colin asked, as he followed Jim back into the Great Court.

'Atkins has asked for a sweep of the Roman gallery,' Jim replied absently, as he signalled to the rest of his team.

The sound of engines rumbling and tyres screeching made them turn in surprise.

Four black Ford 650 Jankels—enormous trucks with the word "Police" in capital letters blazoned on the sides, pulled up beyond the museum's front courtyard.

Men in black SCO19 uniform, armed to the teeth, poured out.

Security Control Room

'The SCO19?' Atkins frowned at the news delivered to him in the control room. Word had just come from the museum entrance that the SCO19 men had returned. 'What do they want now? Give me that headset.'

The headset used to relay instructions to the guards was handed over to him. 'What the devil's happening down there, Thurwell?' he demanded. 'Why are the counter terrorism guys back?'

A look of surprise crossed his face, giving way to concern.

'Where are those three SCO19 men who were in the Roman gallery?' he asked, taking off the headset. 'Yes, the blokes with the woman.'

The control room team swiftly scanned the screens.

They were nowhere to be seen.

The three men, along with the woman, had disappeared.

The Great Court

Jim broke into a run as he received another communication on his earpiece, his face contorted with worry. He was closely followed by the other guards from the Roman gallery.

'Now what?' Colin asked, between breaths, as he kept pace with the younger man who was darting up the staircase two steps at a time.

'Problem,' Jim replied, without missing a step. 'These SCO19 officers say that they came as soon as they got the alert. They've only just arrived. And there are three SCO19 men still inside the museum. They've disappeared.'

'You mean…?' Colin's voice faltered as the implication of Jim's words struck him. A cold dread gripped his heart.

'Yes,' Jim replied. 'The earlier lot were apparently imposters.'

They were at the third floor now and the group rushed through the row of galleries until they reached the one they had been guarding just a while ago.

Colin's worst fears were true.

The coin was missing.

Security Control Room

'Dammit!' Atkins spat. 'Find those men and that woman. That's what they were doing in the gallery. Stealing the bloody coin!'

'Jim Brady's going to the roof. He's asked for back up,' the guard with the headset reported.

A quick message was despatched to the SCO19 team downstairs.

Their target had changed. It was no longer a suicide bomber.

It was a thief.

80

The Roman Gallery

Colin and Jim stood and looked at the round hole in the glass case. It had been a professional job. Cutting a hole like that using a diamond-tipped glasscutter would have taken just a few minutes. There had been enough time to cut the glass and purloin the coin while everybody else was distracted with the suicide bomber.

It was a smart move, Colin thought. There would be no big story for the media who would be more interested in the suicide bomber angle, especially after the recent attacks in Paris and Brussels.

He also wondered if they had really killed the so-called bomber or had that, too, been an act?

'The helicopter!' A thought struck Colin. 'Are you sure it belongs to the SCO19 guys? The real ones, I mean?'

Jim looked at him. 'Good thought. We should check it out.' He spoke into his microphone. 'I'm heading for the roof. The fake SCO19 men are armed. I can't tackle them by myself. I need back up. Now.'

Without waiting for a reply, he sprinted out of the room and was gone before Colin could react.

For a second, Colin hesitated. Like Jim, he, too, was unarmed. But Jim was trained in security procedures; he wasn't.

The rest of the guards had followed Jim's lead and Colin was alone in the gallery now.

He made up his mind and dashed through the galleries and up the stairs, following the last of the guards.

The roof of the British Museum, London

Dee stood on the rooftop of the British Museum and surveyed the city, which lay sprawled below her, with grim satisfaction.

Her plan had been executed to perfection. The state of panic that had ensued at the discovery of the "suicide bomber" had helped. No one had thought to suspect that the SCO19 men who had responded so swiftly to the alarm could be anything other than what they claimed to be.

It had been the perfect cover. The galleries had been emptied of guests and guards and everyone's attention was focused on the suicide bomber, enabling her to steal the coin with remarkable ease. Of course, she had been unable to disable the CCTV cameras but that didn't matter. By the time the museum security realised what had happened it would be too late.

The real SCO19 officers had arrived now, but, in just a few moments, she would be transported away from here. Her immediate destination was the airport.

Right after killing Penny, she had ensured that her team started monitoring all airports and all flight manifests.

If Vijay Singh was also in search of the coins, and the weapon, then he would have to travel out of London.

She had wondered if it had been Vijay at Cairnpapple Hill. But even if it hadn't, he was sure to know by now that someone apart from him was also after the weapon. And the man was smart enough to join the dots and realise that it could only be the Order. He would be in a hurry to get there first, before they did. He would have chosen the fastest means of travelling out which precluded car or train. Unless the weapon was hidden near London. But she didn't think that was possible.

While at the museum, she had been informed that Vijay Singh was on a flight to Orkney via Aberdeen.

The Orkney Islands!

It was the last place she would have suspected. But if Vijay had gone there, then that was where she would go.

She had an advantage over Vijay: her private jet, which would get her to the Orkney Islands in two hours flat.

Had Vijay figured out what the secret of the coins was?

Dee smiled to herself. She didn't need to speculate. She would soon find out for herself.

81

The rooftop of the British Museum, London

The harnesses were lowered by the helicopter. Four harnesses, for Dee and the three fake SCO19 men.

As Dee fastened her harness, Jim appeared in the doorway of the exit hut that led to the rooftop from the stairway.

Jim spotted the fake SCO19 men and gave a shout. His team was still a few steps behind him, followed by Colin.

Realising that the thieves were getting away, Jim rushed out onto the roof. His back up hadn't arrived yet. No doubt, they were on their way. But by the time they would reach, these people would have got away.

Somehow, he had to stop them.

The rest of his team had also reached the rooftop.

Jim was now halfway between them and the thieves, who were being winched up.

The guards, with one accord, charged Dee and her men, right behind Jim.

Dee stared at the museum security guards charging towards her. She was angry. Her plan had been to get away from the museum without any violence. No bloodshed.

Not that she disliked spilling blood.

But a clean break in and getaway would make less news. If she was right about an organisation being at work behind Vijay Singh, the news of the theft of the coin and the fake SCO19 exercise would be suppressed. The only thing the media would be fed would be the suicide bomber and his death.

But dead guards were another matter, especially when they were from the museum.

On the other hand, she reasoned, neither the museum nor Vijay's organisation would want to publicise the deaths of the guards.

After all, news of the attempted theft last year, aimed at stealing the prism, had never seen the light of day.

So, perhaps, things were not that bad after all.

That didn't exonerate these guards, though. They had to be taught a lesson.

'Glock,' she said, and the man standing next to her handed her his handgun.

The harnesses jerked as the winch cable became taut and the four of them slowly rose from the ground, pulled up towards the helicopter.

Dee took aim at the leader of the security guards. She was a good shot but she wasn't planning to shoot him between the eyes.

Not yet.

He thought he could stop her from getting away.

She'd show him.

Her first shot was to his right knee.

Dee watched the guard in the lead stumble and fall. A gesture to her men and automatic fire cut down the rest of the guards, even as the man Dee had shot struggled to raise himself.

The winches had now raised them to a height that was barely a few feet away from the helicopter.

One last shot. Now that he knew.

She stared straight into Jim's eyes as he lay there, his body half raised, supported by his hands.

Then she shot him in the forehead.

The stairway to the rooftop

Colin paused as he heard the shots. He was just a few stairs away from the rooftop exit.

A single gunshot followed by staccato gunfire. Then another single shot.

He feared the worst.

The sound of the helicopter's rotors began to fade out.

There was a rumbling of boots on the stairway and a posse of SCO19 officers came sprinting up the stairs.

Colin flattened himself against the wall, making way for them, as they rushed out to the rooftop, their guns ready.

He followed them out, only to see Jim and the other security guards lying in a pool of their own blood.

The helicopter was a rapidly shrinking dot in the sky.

Good men were dead.

And the coin was gone.

82

The Mainland, Orkney

Vijay heaved a sigh of relief as they touched down at Kirkwall airport, drops of rain spattering against the aircraft windows and streaking across them as the plane decelerated and taxied towards the parking bay.

The short thirty-five minute flight had been a bumpy one amidst dark clouds, and the little turboprop plane had been tossed around by the high velocity winds that resulted from the atmospheric and pressure conditions, making it a rather unpleasant flight despite the cheerful demeanour of the airhostess on board the aircraft.

Vijay and Harry hurried down to the tarmac, turning up the collars of their windcheaters against the wind and the rain. Vijay's research on Orkney had indicated that they should come equipped with waterproof and windproof clothing. They had bought windcheaters and waterproof trousers along with tough industrial boots that would serve them for any heavy-duty walking or climbing.

Once inside the terminal, Vijay switched on his mobile phone as they walked towards the Hertz desk near the exit.

There was one message. It was from Alice, asking Vijay to call her back when they landed.

Harry went ahead and completed the formalities for renting a vehicle, while Vijay called her number.

'We think we may have found something that will help you,' Alice said, as soon as the call connected. Vijay's last request to Colin last night had been to ask Alice and Goldfeld to spend the morning trying to see if they could come up with any other useful information or ideas on the coins.

'Go on.'

'We spent a lot of time looking at maps of the Orkney Islands, especially those which showed the major megalithic sites on the islands. It finally struck us that the three imperfections—the knots—on the coins might be a clue. One knot seems to be located on the island of Rousay and the other two knots seem to be on the Mainland. After a lot of discussion, Saul and I got to wondering if the three knots were not just imperfections, but were deliberately placed there.'

'You mean the knots are markers of some sort to indicate specific locations?'

'Possibly. After all, if the coins were supposed to be a guide to the location of the weapon, shouldn't there be some sort of marker to indicate where one should start? There are 70 islands in the archipelago. Even if Caesar was told where the weapon was hidden, he hadn't been to Orkney. How would he know which island was which? Suppose the three knots are a way of triangulating the area within which the secret location lies? Or maybe they indicate three of the many megalithic sites in Orkney—and any one of those three could be the hiding place of the weapon? We really can't be sure which one to go with, or if we're even right, but I thought I should mention this to you.'

Harry led them to the car and got into the driver's seat. He started the engine and pulled away from the airport and onto the road leading to Kirkwall.

'That's an interesting thought,' Vijay agreed. 'Certainly a possibility. Let me take a look when I get to the hotel. You say that one of the knots is on Rousay? If I recall correctly, that's the island immediately to the north of the Mainland, right?'

'Yup,' Alice confirmed.

'Good job, guys. At least I have a starting point now. I was beginning to get worried.'

It wasn't long before Harry pulled into the small car park of the picturesque Ayre Hotel. They lugged their overnighters from the boot of the Land Rover and hurried into the little reception of the hotel.

'Welcome,' the young woman greeted them from behind the reception desk. Mr Singh and Mr Briggs? You're booked with us for three nights so we've given you rooms with the harbour view.'

'Thanks a lot,' Vijay smiled at her. 'Let's go,' he said to Harry. 'Julie Dickens should be here any time now.'

The Orkney trip, while necessary, had been organised in a rush. It had not been very well planned, primarily owing to the lack of any conclusion on how best to locate the weapon. Goldfeld had called up an archaeologist friend, Julie Dickens, who lived on Orkney and was part of the team currently excavating the Ness of Brodgar site on the Mainland. Julie had agreed to meet Vijay and Harry at their hotel at 11.30 am.

Vijay and Harry quickly took the lift to the second floor, dumped their bags in their respective rooms, and headed back downstairs, to find a pleasant-looking middle-aged woman with a ruddy face, waiting for them at the reception.

'Hi, I'm Julie,' she introduced herself. Vijay and Harry shook hands with her amid introductions.

'Saul told me you needed some help but he wasn't very specific,' Julie smiled at the two men, as they sat down in the cosy restaurant in the hotel. 'But I'm happy to help in any way. He did mention something about the megalithic sites.' She handed a thin book to Vijay. 'For you. I thought it might be of use.'

'Thank you, Julie,' Vijay said, glancing at the title of the book as he placed it on the table. It was an official visitor's guide to Orkney. He was glad that Alice had given him the tip about the knots. Without that, this conversation would have been fairly aimless and definitely unfocused. Now, armed with the possibility that Alice had raised, he had something specific to talk about. 'We could use your knowledge of the sites in Orkney to help us solve a puzzle.'

'Oh, a puzzle,' Julie smiled. 'That sounds interesting. I'm curious now. What does archaeology have to do with a puzzle?'

Vijay had come prepared for this meeting. He had taken a printout last night of the coins. But, after speaking with Alice, he had realised that he may not need the entire map on all three coins after all. He took only a single sheet of paper—the map on the coin with the knots. 'We were wondering if you could help us identify these three sites on Orkney.' He indicated the three dots on the paper that represented the knots on the coin.

Julie studied the map intently. 'The shape of the islands are pretty indistinct,' she remarked finally. 'This isn't really a map, is it?' She looked at Vijay enquiringly.

'No, it isn't,' Vijay admitted. 'We found this drawing on a coin which we believe is associated with Orkney. And we thought that the shapes strongly resembled Rousay and the Mainland.'

'On a coin,' Julie murmured, her attention focused once again on the paper before her. 'Interesting. Yes, I can see what you mean about the shapes corresponding to Rousay and the Mainland.' She looked up again. 'Quite honestly, if you hadn't told me that, I wouldn't have seen the similarity. But, if this was on a coin, then it explains why the map, if it is one, isn't quite accurate.'

Vijay wanted to tell her that she was correct. The purpose of the coin had been to disguise the true nature of the drawing.

Only Caesar would have known that the Orkney Islands were depicted on the coins. No one else would have realised that this was a map. Vijay had only realised it after a lot of research, deep thought, and the gift of hindsight. He knew that Caesar had not only been cunning as a general but his talent had extended to other areas as well.

Julie was back to studying the map. 'I can't be very sure about this,' she said after a few minutes of silent thought. 'But, I think I can identify one site, and give you an educated guess about a second site. The third one, however, is difficult to identify.'

Vijay's phone rang. It was Colin. He excused himself from the table and stood in the little parlour that lay between the restaurant and the small banquet hall that extruded into the car park of the hotel. He listened intently as Colin briefed him about the heist at the museum.

'Smart,' Vijay observed, when Colin had finished. 'Sneaky, actually. If we had any doubt, I think this just confirms that the Order is involved. No one else would have the kind of resources to pull off something like this.'

Colin was a bit taken aback by Vijay's response. He had expected Vijay to respond more sensitively to the mass panic in the Great Court. But Vijay seemed to be focused only on the Order. He pushed the thought aside. 'This also means that the Order will be in Orkney sooner than we thought,' Colin told Vijay.

'True,' Vijay agreed. 'They'll probably be here today. I'm sure they've been watching my movements and yours. They won't waste time in trying to figure out the clues by themselves.'

'Good luck,' Colin signed off. 'I hope you find the hiding place before they get there.'

83

Map of coins

'Please remember,' Julie cautioned, 'that my guesses are based on the assumption that these dots correspond to sites that are extant or that we know about. If these are sites that have either been lost to history or have not been discovered yet, then I could be way off the mark.'

She pointed to one of the dots, which was in the lower left quadrant of the map. 'Take this one for example. This could be any of the sites in and around Stenness. The Ring of Brodgar, the Standing Stones of Stenness, Maes Howe, Barnhouse village... It could be any one of them. Or, it could be the Ness of Brodgar, a recently discovered site, which we didn't know about for decades. If this is the Ness of Brodgar, then we wouldn't have been able to identify this if you had shown me the map, say, fifteen years ago. That's what I mean.'

She jabbed a finger at a site in the lower right quadrant of the map. 'This one, however, seems pretty clear, if we assume that we are lucky and the dots represent only extant sites. There's just one site out there, in Tankerness. It's called Mine Howe and is a rather mysterious site. No one has been able to figure out what its purpose was.'

'And the third one?' Vijay enquired, excitedly. 'The one on Rousay?'

'Well,' Julie considered for a moment for replying. 'It could be either of two sites which are adjacent to each other but dating from different periods. Mid Howe Broch, which is from the Iron Age. Or Mid Howe Cairn, which is from the Neolithic period. It has to be one of them. If it is a site we know about, of course.'

Vijay looked at his watch. 'Do you think there is time to hop across to Rousay and check out the Mid Howe sites?'

Julie consulted her watch. 'You can't make it to the 11.50 ferry to Rousay. But you have enough time to plan for the 2.45 ferry.'

'Maybe we could check out Maes Howe and the sites at Stenness and then catch the boat to Rousay.' Vijay looked at Harry. 'Then, we could come back and take a look at Mine Howe.'

'Sure,' Harry replied with an air that indicated that he didn't have much choice in the matter.

'You'll need help if you're planning to go to Mine Howe that late,' Julie smiled. 'Would you like me to take you around and show you these sites? I've got a fairly free day today as I did try to avoid scheduling any major work. Saul said you needed help and I didn't know how much of my time you'd need.'

'That's really thoughtful of you.' Vijay was touched. 'Are you sure? We'd really appreciate your taking us around. We don't know the place and your expertise would be really useful.'

He nudged Harry, who quickly chimed in. 'Yes, yes, that would be great!'

'Right, then,' Julie said, 'let's go!'

Tingwall, Orkney

Vijay watched as the ferry docked, the front section of the boat unfolding to create a ramp, which was used by the cars on the ferry to disembark.

They had spent the afternoon visiting the sites in Stenness, all of which had been awe-inspiring. The Ring of Brodgar, with its twenty-seven standing stones—survivors of a circle of possibly sixty standing stones; the four Standing Stones of Stenness—remnants of a circle of twelve, with a hearth within the circle; the Barnhouse village—one-foot-high ruins of a settlement near the Ring of Brodgar. And finally, the Maes Howe burial tomb—a marvel of architecture and astronomical knowledge. Luckily there weren't too many people around and they were able to gain entry into Maes Howe despite not having made an advance booking. The interior of the tomb with its three chambers off to the sides of the central chamber—the four enormous standing stones towering above them at the corners of the central chamber—combined with the fact that the winter solstice sun shone through the entrance passage to light up the rear of the tomb, all contributed to the sense of awe that Vijay and Harry experienced.

But, for all it had been worth, the tour of the sites had contributed very little to advancing their knowledge about the link between the sites and the coins. As Julie had explained, any of these sites could have been represented by one of the knots on the coin.

The ferry staff indicated that the cars could begin loading, and Harry drove the Land Rover onto the boat, where they got off and entered the cabin.

The sun was beginning to sink below the horizon and the first tendrils of darkness were feeling their way around as the ferry moved away from its moorings.

The twenty-five-minute trip was uneventful, though the sea was a bit choppy, and they soon disembarked at the Rousay ferry terminal.

It wasn't difficult to work out the best way to get to Mid Howe. There was a road that ran in a large circle around the island and Mid Howe lay just off the road.

'Mid Howe, like all the cairns on Orkney, was discovered without a roof. Apparently, at some point of time—we estimate around 2500 B.C.— there was a trend of destroying the roofs of all the tombs. It probably wasn't a concerted effort, but it certainly seems to have been part of a pattern. Perhaps a new religious order taking root and displacing the old cultural and religious norms of the time.' Julie kept talking as they drove, pointing out smaller tombs that they passed—the two-storeyed cairn at Taversoe Tuick, the cairn at Blackhammer and the Knowe of Yarso.

Finally, they reached a small car park on the shoulder of the road, overlooking the sea. As they clambered out in the thickening darkness, Vijay and Harry observed that they were around halfway up the hillside, which was covered with heather. Far below, near the rocky beach, stood a large building that resembled an aircraft hangar.

'Come on,' Julie said. 'The cairn is within that building, which was erected by William Grant to protect what remained of it when it was excavated.'

They started the long trek down to the hangar, crossing three levels of terraces on the hillside.

'These are natural terraces,' Julie explained. 'A unique feature here. If we had time and if there was light, we could have gone around the island and you would have seen more terraces like this.'

They reached the bottom of the hill and entered the building that housed the cairn. Even in the semi-darkness the magnificence of the structure did not fail to impress.

The cairn stretched out for a hundred feet, its ruined dry-stone walls rising before them, enclosing a narrow passageway,

The interior of Mid Howe

broken only by standing slabs of stone that divided the passage into stalls.

'This is why it is called a stalled cairn,' Julie explained, as she walked up the stairs leading to a ramp above the cairn from where visitors to the site could view the structure. Access to the cairn at ground level was not permitted.

The grandeur of the cairn filled them with awe. They followed the ramp above the structure as it encircled the cairn several feet above it, suspended from the roof of the building.

'This was supposed to be a communal tomb,' Julie explained. 'The bones of twenty-five individuals were recovered from the tomb when it was excavated. The roof, of course, had fallen in and filled up the passage, as I'd told you earlier. There were benches in the stalls, presumably to lay out the corpses while the flesh decayed. Though, the report of the excavation says that at least some of the bones were placed in the cairn after the tissues had wasted away.'

They were now standing directly above the central point of the cairn looking down on the stalls below.

'There were twelve stalls on each side,' Julie continued, 'a total of twenty-four stalls in the cairn.'

Vijay looked at her, stunned, as something went off in his brain.

Finally, he thought, he had found the link between the sites and the coins.

84

The Ferry to Tingwall

'You seem a bit thoughtful,' Julie observed.

They were on the ferry back from Rousay to Tingwall, having explored Mid Howe Cairn and the adjacent Broch.

The Broch had turned out to be the remains of a circular tower with two hearths on the ground floor and what seemed to be fortifications—ditches and banks—around it.

Vijay had been preoccupied through most of the tour, even as Julie had maintained a commentary on the ruins, their history and the speculations of archaeologists and historians regarding the purpose of the Cairn and the Broch, which had been built by people who had lived two thousand years apart.

'It's just that everything we've seen so far is so amazing,' Vijay replied with a smile. He realised that it must seem rude to Julie that he had been brooding over his own thoughts for most of the time she had spent with them. 'Lots of these sites are even older than the Egyptian pyramids.'

'True,' Julie said. 'And the most amazing thing is that these were built by people with no knowledge of iron tools. Except for the Broch you saw. That was built in the Iron Age—somewhere between the fifth century B.C. to the third century A.D.'

'It is mind boggling,' Vijay agreed. 'Quarrying and transporting stones, each weighing forty to fifty tonnes, setting them precisely in the ground—precisely enough for astronomical features to exist—pulling them upright; all this without iron tools. Why, digging some of those ditches using stones and bones would have taken decades!'

Julie smiled. 'I'm glad you're enjoying the sights of Orkney,' she said. 'Of course, I wish the weather were better. But at least it isn't raining today.' The day had been overcast, with dark grey clouds hiding the sun all day.

'We really appreciate your showing us around, Julie,' Vijay said. 'I had a question regarding Maes Howe.'

'You're welcome,' Julie replied. 'Anything for Saul, he's an old friend. Go ahead, what do you want to know?'

'Just this,' Vijay said. 'When we saw Maes Howe, the guide from Scottish Heritage told us that the four standing stones at each corner of the central chamber had no load-bearing function. In fact, he said that they didn't seem to have any specific function at all. Yet, they are in sharp contrast to all the other stones in the central chamber.'

'True,' Julie admitted.

'I was just wondering if it is possible that Maes Howe was a circle of four standing stones to begin with. The four corner stones. And then the rest of the chamber and the smaller cells off to the sides were simply built around them.'

'Interesting thought,' Julie smiled. 'You aren't the first one who has wondered about this. There has been considerable speculation about the four corner stones; and one of the theories is exactly along the lines that you have just mentioned.'

'Great, thanks,' Vijay smiled back. 'Another mystery of Maes Howe, then.'

The mystery of Mine Howe

The sky had darkened when the Land Rover pulled into the sliver of a car park on the shoulder of the road.

Interior of Maes Howe. One of the side chambers is visible as are two of the corner standing stones

The landscape was fairly unremarkable. A low mound rose beyond the road and the faint outlines of a henge—the familiar bank and ditch—were just discernible from where they stood.

They had stopped on the way from the ferry at Julie's office, to pick up construction helmets and electric torches, which Julie had insisted they would need.

'Can't have you knocking your heads on the stones at Mine Howe,' she had told them jocularly. Now, she handed out the helmets.

'Only two people can fit in the chamber,' she told them. 'So only one of you can come with me at a time.'

'That's okay,' Harry said, handing back his helmet. 'I don't need to see the place. He's the one who is really interested in this sort of stuff. I'll just wait outside.'

They zipped up their protective clothing against the wind, which was whipping at them now.

'I must warn you,' Julie informed Vijay, 'that it can get a bit uncomfortable down there when it is as windy as it is now. The wind, blowing over the surface of the entrance shaft, prevents air from circulating within the chamber; breathing can become difficult. If you start having trouble breathing, let me know immediately and we'll get out of there right away.'

Vijay nodded his understanding and they made their way to the mound.

'This is part of the ditch that was excavated,' Julie said. 'It is extraordinary, really. Look at the depth. There was a definite purpose to this ditch.'

'You mentioned that this is an Iron Age site,' Vijay recalled.

'That's correct. In fact, there are the remains of a metal workshop and a settlement around the mound, all dated back to the Iron Age.'

They had reached the top of the mound, where a circular hole gaped in the ground, just wide enough for one person to enter, leading into a dark abyss.

An iron ladder dropped down from the surface for a few feet after which a series of rough stone steps began a downward descent, disappearing into the darkness that enveloped whatever lay below, within the mound.

Inside Mine Howe

'Come on, then,' Julie said, as she turned around so that she was facing the steps, and started climbing down the iron ladder. 'This is the only way to go down,' she told Vijay. 'You can't walk down the steps the way you would a normal stairway. I must warn you about the stone steps. They are irregular both in height and width. So be very careful where you place your feet. And hold onto the iron rail at all times.' She indicated a sturdy iron rail that had been attached to the wall as a support to climb down.

She switched her torch on and disappeared.

Vijay looked at Harry who grinned at him as if to say, 'You wanted to do this, not I,' and then sighed and followed her.

As Vijay reached the stone steps, he realised the truth behind Julie's words. Each step was not just a different width and different height but also a different shape. Some were rectangular; others were almost triangular, narrow at one end and wide at the other.

It was tough going. The shaft was narrow, almost touching him as it enclosed him on all sides.

He heaved a sigh of relief as he reached a small landing. He heard Julie chuckle below. She had evidently reached the underground chamber.

'Those were just the first seventeen steps,' she said. 'The next eleven are more treacherous. Some of them are barely even there. Be careful.'

Vijay paused. Something about what Julie had just said had struck a chord.

What was it?

He couldn't focus properly after the climb he had just made and with his attention on the climb that he now needed to make.

Deciding to work it out later, he continued on his way and soon found himself climbing the last few steps down an iron frame. The second flight of stone steps had ended in a small sill that protruded around three feet above the floor of the chamber. The modern iron frame had been put in to facilitate entry into the chamber, as an alternative to having to jump the last three feet down to the floor.

The chamber itself was nearly four feet in diameter, though irregular in shape.

Vijay was breathing hard by now, and he noticed that Julie was also out of breath. She hadn't been joking about the air quality down here, even though the mouth of the shaft was open.

Julie shined her torch around the chamber, talking all the while. 'The floor of this chamber is just under twenty-eight feet below the surface of the mound. When you go back up, pause at the landing to see the two galleries which I am sure you missed while coming down.'

'I was too busy trying not to fall off the steps,' Vijay laughed. 'So I didn't notice any galleries. I'll check them out on the way back up.'

'The ceiling is corbelled, like all the tombs in Orkney,' Julie continued, shining her torch on the roof of the chamber. 'It stands around twelve feet at its highest point—the capstone—from the floor of the chamber. The floor, as you can see, has been dug out of the bedrock. Now let me show you something. Switch off your torch. And just keep still. Very quiet. Listen.'

Vijay complied, switching off his torch and controlling his breathing. Julie abruptly switched her torch off as well, plunging them both into a darkness that was blacker than the blackest colour Vijay had ever seen in his life.

He realised what Julie wanted him to experience.

It wasn't just the darkness.

It was the silence.

Absolute silence.

Even the air in the chamber seemed to stand still.

This was the most perfect silence he had ever experienced in his life. The builders of this chamber had not only ensured that no light would ever penetrate it, but they had also ensured that no sound would ever enter this chamber.

Even if the mouth of the shaft was not sealed.

It was more than unnerving.

It was scary.

In fact, after a few minutes, he knew it would be downright terrifying.

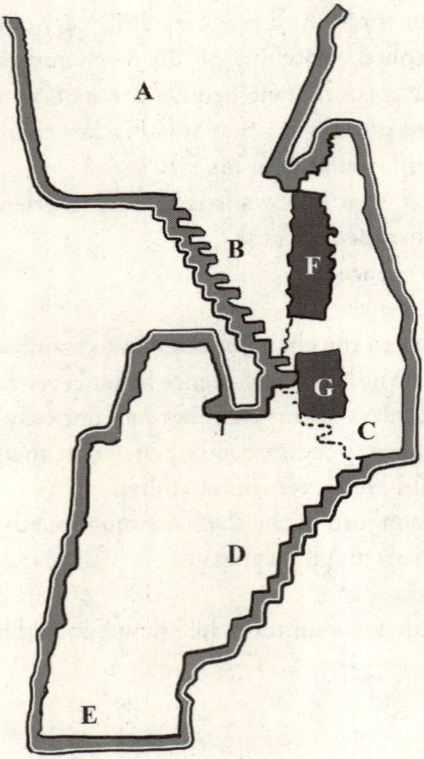

Plan of Mine Howe

A: Pit from the surface to the entry of the actual structure. This is where the iron ladder rests.
B: First flight of steps
C: Landing
D: Second flight of steps
E: Bottom of the chamber
F: Upper gallery
G: Lower gallery

86

Kirkwall Airport

Dee disembarked from her private jet and stormed through the airport terminal. She was livid.

It had been her plan to head to Kirkwall immediately after acquiring the coin. The knowledge that Vijay had left for Orkney had meant that work on deciphering the inscriptions on the coins was going to be so much easier.

Caesar, in his diary, had very helpfully disclosed that the drawings on the coins corresponded to a map of a specific region in Britain; though he had not specified which region. He had also mentioned that each of the three inscriptions on the coins was a separate line of a riddle that the Druids had shared with him. He had explained how he couldn't make sense of the inscriptions until the Druids helped him understand. This had led him to think of a means to record the details of the location of the weapon in a manner that would not arouse suspicion, yet would remind him of the exact location. He intended to go back to Britain to retrieve the weapon and had wanted to ensure that he found it. So he decided to mint the coins in Alexandria. And Cleopatra, eager for his support in her newfound status as Pharaoh, had been only too willing to oblige.

But Dee didn't want anyone to know how she had hit upon Orkney. Least of all Van Klueck. That had meant additional complications since Dee needed to organise and plan for the retrieval of the weapon once she found it. That would require resources that only Van Klueck could arrange at such short notice.

Quite naturally, the Austrian had been curious to understand the reason for her sudden desire to visit Orkney.

'Why Orkney?' he had asked Dee. 'What makes you so sure you will find it there?'

Dee had been hard pressed to explain. Finally, she had to resort to leveraging her bloodline.

'If you doubt me,' she had told Van Klueck, 'then take me off this mission now. But I will report my findings and if I am correct, then you will be responsible for our failure. Think about it, Christian. Do you really want me to do that? You know the Order won't take kindly to someone with the bloodline being left to fend for themselves.'

Van Klueck had grudgingly relented. But she had lost a lot of time in the process.

Now, she had to make up for it. On the positive side, the delay meant that her preparations were complete as she arrived at Kirkwall. She could hit the ground running.

But she was still angry. Someone with the bloodline should not need to struggle so much. Not against the likes of Van Klueck.

Dee slowed as she passed the Hertz desk. 'There,' she commanded Harper. 'You know what we need.'

Harper nodded to two of his men, who made their way to the Hertz counter.

Dee walked on, lost in her thoughts, once again reflecting on her humiliating conversation with Van Klueck.

She was going to find the weapon.

And then she would take care of the Austrian.

Underground

Thankfully, Julie switched her torch back on just before Vijay was about to. 'Well?' she asked him, her teeth glinting in the torchlight.

'Wow,' was all that Vijay could muster. 'What was this place built for? I mean, it isn't a tomb...'

'We haven't been able to figure that out yet,' Julie answered. 'It certainly isn't a tomb. In fact it doesn't seem to serve any practical purpose. Yet, it was an important place. Look at the size and depth of the ditch around it. People were not meant to come here. There was a concerted effort to ensure that people stayed away from this place. That's probably why the stone steps leading to this chamber are so irregular. Whoever built this structure wanted to ensure that people would not come snooping here. Imagine trying to climb down those steps in darkness, without the handrail to support you and with a steep drop both at the top and the bottom of the pit?'

'I think it's time to get some air,' Vijay suggested and started climbing back up to the top.

At the landing midway between the two flights of steps, he paused to examine the two galleries Julie had mentioned.

The lower gallery was around one and a half feet above the landing, with a width of barely more than a foot, extending backwards in a shallow arc for around eight feet.

The upper gallery was at a height of around four and a half feet above the landing and was much wider than the lower one. Almost three feet in width, it extended to about nine feet in length. Its height increased with its depth, reaching to a little less than four feet at the inner end. This gallery ran above the roof of the lower flight of steps and the corbelled roof of the underground chamber.

'What purpose could these have served?' Vijay wondered aloud.

'All part of the mystery,' Julie replied.

Vijay began the final ascent to the top of the shaft, knocking his helmet against the lintel that supported the roof of the shaft as he climbed the last few steps. He was thankful for Julie's suggestion regarding the helmet; he would otherwise have had a nasty bruise and, perhaps, more.

'So there you are,' Julie said, as they got back into the car. 'The three knots on your map. Did that help?'

'It certainly did,' Vijay answered, as Harry pulled away from Mine Howe. 'It most certainly did.'

87

August, 54 B.C.

Present-day Britain

Julius Caesar sat across his archenemy and studied him. Cassivellaunus was a tall man, well built, with a thick mane of red hair and a bushy red beard. With full battle armour on, he would have been a fearsome opponent in battle. Caesar had fought many wars alongside his troops but even he would have thought twice about plunging into battle against this man.

Just as well, Caesar thought, that he had been able to bring Cassivellaunus to the negotiation table through subterfuge.

He was satisfied with the way things were progressing. On the one hand, he had been able to win over the Trinovantes and their allies, the Cenimagni, Segontiaci, Ancalites, Bibroci and Cassi, which substantially eroded the support that Cassivellaunus had counted upon. This had played a large part in convincing the young chief to join the peace talks. Of course, the fact that the Romans had crossed the Thames, where the largest battle of this expedition had been fought, and won a decisive victory, had played no mean part in persuading Cassivellaunus that his best option was to sue for peace.

On the other hand, Caesar finally had the opportunity to find what he had come for. If he couldn't get it any other way, he would get it through negotiation. He was looking forward to this conversation.

Before the formal negotiations could begin, Caesar had instructed that Cassivellaunus be brought to his tent, unarmed and unaccompanied. He had wanted a private conversation with the young Celtic chief. The only other person in the tent was an interpreter, since neither Caesar nor Cassivellaunus could speak the other's language.

'There is something you have that I want,' Caesar came to the point immediately. 'And if you give it to me, then our negotiations will be easy. It is in your hands to decide if your people are to face the entire might of my legions.'

Caesar had realised that, notwithstanding the power of the secret that the Druids harboured, there had to be a reason why he had encountered its mysterious effects only once the previous year and not at all on this expedition. He didn't know what that reason was, but it gave him leverage.

Cassivellaunus held Caesar's gaze. 'And what might that be?'

Caesar leaned forward, trying to disguise his excitement at finally being in the moment when he could talk to a Celtic chief about his deepest desire.

'The secret of your Druids,' he said softly. 'The power that they have exercised in battle against my legions, both here and in Gaul. I want that power. It must be mine!'

Cassivellaunus flinched at the last words, which were barked out by Caesar. The ferocity of Caesar's demeanour was not lost on the Celtic chief. Clearly, this was something that the Roman wanted dearly. And he was intelligent enough to realise that the Roman general would go to any extent to acquire it.

'You don't know what that power is, Caesar,' he responded. 'It is not something that you can carry back with you to the provinces or empires that you wish to conquer. Even though that power is much weakened over time, it can only be exercised here. In Britannia. Or in Gaul. This is where it has rested for thousands of years. It cannot leave this sacred soil.'

Caesar pondered these words. 'I do not wish this power to win battles,' he scoffed. 'You have seen that I can win battles without it.' He lowered his voice to almost a whisper. 'But I have seen what this secret can do. And I know I can use it in Rome.'

Cassivellaunus shook his head. 'You cannot use it in Rome, Caesar,' he said.

'Why not?' Caesar demanded.

Cassivellaunus told him.

When he had finished, Caesar's face sagged with disappointment. But not for long. A thought had occurred to him.

'I will build the machines that are needed,' he said. 'I will do what is required. Your Druids will help me. Now, tell me how I can find this secret.'

Cassivellaunus shrugged. 'Only the Druids know,' he said. 'But since you have promised me moderate terms of settlement, I will speak to them. I will not promise anything. But I will do my best.'

Caesar nodded and called out to the guards outside his tent. As Cassivellaunus was led away, Caesar sat lost in thought.

How much longer did he have to wait?

88

February, present year

Day 4

Ayre Hotel, Kirkwall

Harry knocked on the door of Vijay's room. After returning to the hotel, Vijay had locked himself up, telling Harry he needed some time to check some facts for himself. Vijay had also borrowed a ruler from the reception, which puzzled Harry, but since Vijay was not forthcoming about it, Harry thought it wiser to not ask.

Only now had Vijay called Harry to his room.

The door opened and Harry entered, to find that Colin, Alice and Goldfeld were looking out at him from the laptop screen. Next to their video image were Patterson and Imran, who had joined the videoconference.

'I've spent the last couple of hours researching Orkney and the sites, and reading through a visitor's guide that Julie Dickens gave us,' Vijay began. 'And I tried to link it with everything we've learnt so far about the Druids. And here's what I found, starting with the assumption that the three knots on the coin correspond to three physical locations on the Orkney Islands, as Alice and Saul suggested earlier today. 'He briefed them about the three possibilities that Julie had told them about and brought everyone up to speed on what Harry and he had seen on the island.

'And you've figured out the location?' Patterson asked when Vijay had concluded.

'I think I have. I wanted to share my thought process with you to see if it makes sense, because I'm not sure if I am correct. It really is the weirdest riddle I've come across and I've seen some really strange ones by now. If I am correct, then we need to move fast to beat the Order to it.'

'Go on,' Patterson told him.

'I found the first clue at Mid Howe,' Vijay explained. 'It has twenty-four stalls. I wondered if it had anything to do with one of the inscriptions: *Twenty-four to four is the first of the squares.*'

'You think the inscription refers to Mid Howe?' Imran saw the connection Vijay was trying to make. 'I get what "twenty-four" means. But what is the "four" in the inscription?'

'That's what threw me at first,' Vijay replied. 'Then, I tried to use the same logic. If "twenty-four" referred to one of the dots—Mid Howe—then "four" should also refer to a location represented by one of the dots. And we did see a location where the number four stood out like a sore thumb.'

'Maes Howe!' Harry exclaimed, excitedly. 'That's why you were asking Julie about the four cornerstones in the chamber!'

'Exactly.' Vijay described the interior of Maes Howe to the others and brought up an image of the chamber on the laptop to show them what he meant.

'That's interesting, but not conclusive,' Patterson pointed out. 'What is the third location? And where do the "squares" in the inscription come in? Explain that and I'll buy your argument.'

Vijay smiled to himself. Patterson was the best devil's advocate one could ask for. He would challenge everything until he was absolutely convinced. It was this reason that had prompted him to get the task force leader on the call, even though protocol didn't necessitate a briefing at Patterson's level at this stage. He would scrutinise Vijay's theory like no other.

'I'll come to that,' Vijay responded. 'Using the same logic, I figured out that the third location was, indeed, Mine Howe. According to Julie, this was anyway the only location that corresponded unquestionably to the dot on the coin, since there are no other major sites in that area—none that have been discovered so far, at least.'

'Twenty-eight is the key number here,' Colin murmured. 'What did you find in Mine Howe?'

Vijay brought up an image of Mine Howe on the laptop screen. 'Mine Howe has two flights of steps,' he explained. 'The first flight has seventeen steps, not including the metal stairs at the top, which are modern. And the second flight has eleven steps, not including the last couple that allow you to reach the chamber floor without jumping for almost a metre. That's a total of twenty-eight steps. Actually, I was confused at first, because all the websites mention twenty-nine steps at Mine Howe. But, then, I counted and there are really only twenty-eight steps. I even found an archaeological report corroborating this.'

'So the three dots represent Mid Howe, Maes Howe and Mine Howe,' Imran summarised. 'What about the "squares"? Where do they come in?'

'There's a perfectly simple explanation for that,' Vijay smiled.

89

The Squares

'I found a useful map inside the visitor's guide,' Vijay held up the guide to the camera, showing the inside of the back cover which had a scale map of the Orkney Islands, showing all the major tourist attractions. The group on the videoconference could see markings on the map in different colours.

'I took shots with my phone camera as I worked, so you can see what I found,' Vijay continued, and pulled up an image of the map.

The map on the screen was criss-crossed with blue, black and red lines, connecting different sites.

'Before I figured out what the numbers in the inscriptions meant, I wondered if there was any connection on the map between the sites,' Vijay explained. 'I thought that maybe I would find that I could connect them using squares, or something like that. As you can see, there are quite a few combinations of geometric figures that are possible when you start connecting the different sites. And, as I am sure you notice, there are only triangles that emerge. No squares. Fascinating, but it didn't lead me anywhere. It was *after* I worked out which sites the dots represented that I found something really amazing. I still can't believe it.'

He used the cursor to outline a triangle with Mid Howe, Maes Howe and Mine Howe as the apex points.

'See this triangle? I didn't have a protractor with me to measure the angle, but I measured the sides. And guess, what?' He waited.

Colin was the first to react. 'Oh my god!' he gasped. 'You don't mean Pythagoras?'

Vijay beamed. 'The sum of the squares of the two sides is equal to the square of the hypotenuse.'

Patterson raised his eyebrows. 'That is amazing. Though that does explain the "squares" in the inscriptions. Mid Howe to Maes Howe is the first side to be squared. Maes Howe to Mine Howe is the second. And Mid Howe to Mine Howe is the hypotenuse—the sum of the squares. Incredible.'

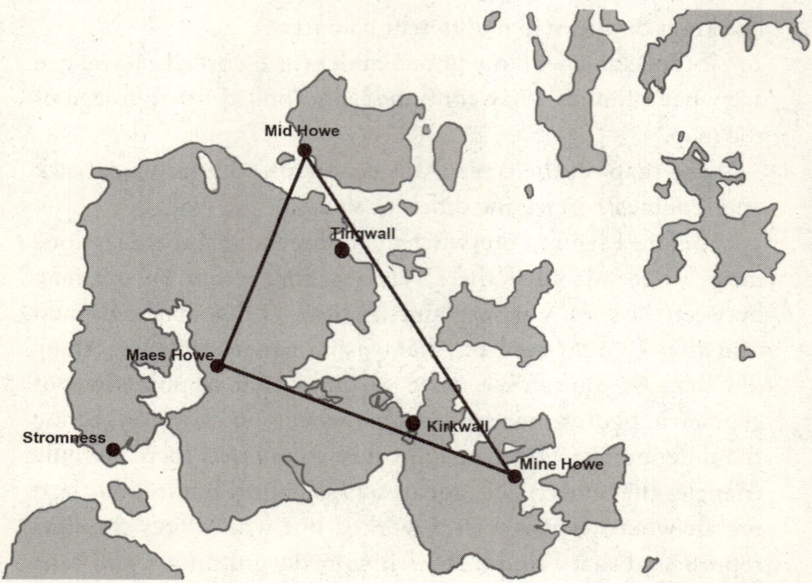

The right-angled triangle connecting the three megalithic sites on the Mainland and Rousay

'And, according to Clement of Alexandria,' Colin interrupted excitedly, seeing another connection here, 'Pythagoras had been influenced by the Gauls and the Brahmins.'

'Exactly,' Vijay said. 'I remembered you briefing us on that, Colin. It had seemed like a very minor, almost irrelevant, point when you first mentioned it, but it made a lot of sense once the inscriptions were deciphered. Knowing what we do now about the link between the Druids and the Vedic people, it is possible that they knew about the theorem long before Pythagoras did.'

'There is a legend,' Goldfeld said slowly, 'that Pythagoras visited India. This legend, of course, is unfounded, but ancient writers like Eusebius and Philostratus have clearly stated that Pythagoras derived a lot of his knowledge from the Brahmins or gymnosophists in India. That knowledge included his philosophy regarding the transmigration of souls, which, as we have seen, is also applicable to the Druids.'

'So, where is the weapon hidden?' Imran asked. 'If we take the first location to be Mid Howe, the second to be Maes Howe and the third to be Mine Howe, this still doesn't tell us the location of the weapon. Weren't the coins supposed to tell us where the weapon is hidden?'

Vijay was unfazed. 'I don't think so,' he countered. 'According to the Quintus Codex, the Druids told Caesar where the weapon was hidden. He didn't really need the coins. So why did he have them minted? I think Caesar had the coins minted to remind him of the location, not to pinpoint it. I don't think that he would have taken the chance that someone might solve the riddle and find the location, if they saw the coins. He was not familiar with the geography of the Orkney Islands or the megalithic sites on them, never having been that far north. Caesar didn't know when he would return for the weapon. It could be years before he went back to Britain. He needed an aid to remember. That is why there is a map of the Mainland and

Rousay along with the three dots. Their only purpose was to remind Caesar about the meaning of the riddle, when he finally returned to Britain.'

Patterson's brow furrowed. 'So how do we locate the hiding place?'

'I have an idea about where it might be,' Vijay said.

90

Ayre Hotel, Kirkwall

'I spent most of the last couple of hours researching all three sites,' Vijay explained. 'Let's go one by one in the order of the inscriptions. I won't go into detail but I'll give you just the key findings. Mid Howe was a communal tomb. The bones of twenty-five individuals were recovered from it. The site has been well excavated and if anything had to be found, it would have been discovered by now. Maes Howe is more mysterious. It is supposed to be a tomb but when it was excavated in 1861 only a few bits of human skull were found. Mysterious, certainly, but nothing indicates that this could have been a possible hiding place for the weapon. That brings us to Mine Howe.'

He took a deep breath. 'While I saw nothing at Mine Howe, this is the most intriguing of the three sites. Actually, it is the most mysterious of all megalithic sites in the UK—I'd venture to say anywhere in the world. While archaeologists have been able to attach labels to all other sites—"place for rituals", "burial tomb" and so on, no label has been found to be appropriate for the underground chamber there. The only attempt, and a weak one at that, in my opinion, is to call it a possible well, based on the similarity to another underground chamber at the Gurness Broch, which Harry and I have not visited. But even the so-called well at the Gurness Broch is an approximation—nobody can say for sure if it was a well; just that it is suspected to have been one.'

'So you feel the weapon is hidden at Mine Howe,' Patterson said. 'But you found the chamber empty.'

'The chamber was empty,' Vijay agreed, 'but I found something very interesting in the archaeological records for Mine Howe. It is the least investigated of the three sites. While Mid Howe was fully excavated and Maes Howe restored, the only excavations done at Mine Howe have been at the ditch and the area surrounding the mound. The mound at Mine Howe, in which the underground chamber was built, has not been excavated at all. A geophysical survey utilising magnetometry, resistivity and ground-probing radar was carried out on the mound. This survey led to the discovery of the ditch around Mine Howe, which suggested the possible presence of other chambers within the mound. And if you recall what the Quintus Codex said, the Druids had hidden their weapon away before Caesar's invasion of Britain. The dating of Mine Howe coincides quite neatly with the time that this could have happened—a few centuries before Caesar. Mine Howe, after all, is an Iron Age structure, according to the archaeologists. So it could have been built around 300 B.C. to 100 B.C. and that could also have been the time when the Druids hid the weapon away.'

'You think that one of these hidden chambers contains the weapon,' Patterson concluded. 'Your logic is sound but if that is the case then why didn't the weapon show up in the geophysical survey?'

'I think I can answer that one,' Colin spoke up. 'The weapon is obviously ancient—from a time much before the Druids. I think we've established that. We also know, from our personal experience, that there was technology available to cloak devices and make them invisible. We found evidence of that in India two years ago. If the weapon was covered with a cloak that made it invisible to microwaves then there's no way that it could be discovered through a geophysical survey.'

'That's exactly the thought that struck me,' Vijay said. 'Moreover, the report I read also said that the ground-penetrating radar results were limited by extensive deposits of clay, random internal voids and irregular stonework. If the Druids didn't want the weapon to be found, maybe they deliberately built the chambers in such a manner that no technology could penetrate through to the weapon.' He paused. 'Of course, all this could be just conjecture. There's only one way to find out.'

'I think it is worth checking out,' Imran opined.

'I can't find any fault with your argument,' Patterson admitted. 'But we have to move fast. I'll start pulling strings in London. We should have back up for you within three hours.'

'Great. Harry and I will head out to Mine Howe and see if we can get a lead on how to access the underground chambers mentioned in the geophysical survey.'

'Good idea,' Patterson said. 'That will save us time. We don't know what resources the Order will marshal for recovering the weapon. Orkney is fairly remote, so it is easier for them to mount a large-scale operation there, away from media attention.' His eyes bored into Vijay, through the camera and across thousands of miles. 'Be careful, Vijay. You've done a great job so far. There could be worse dangers ahead that you have to be mindful of.'

'I understand.' Vijay knew the risks. 'We won't go there immediately. We'll leave after an hour or so. That way, by the time the reinforcements arrive, we'll hopefully have something for them to take back.'

'Colin, you'll take charge of the Special Forces who will be travelling to Orkney. We don't want to brief them in too much detail. All they're going to be told is that they have to secure this site in Orkney.' Patterson waited for Colin's confirmation.

'Sure thing,' Colin replied, delighted that he would be in on the ending of this mission. While he had accompanied Vijay on the journey of discovery in India two years ago, he had been unable to accompany Vijay last year. Apart from the risks involved and the imminent danger, he relished the opportunity to visit an ancient site once more.

'Let's get to work, folks,' Patterson signed off.

'Good luck, Vijay,' Imran said and the others joined in the chorus.

Vijay smiled. Inwardly, he was having a hard time controlling the trepidation that he felt.

What was he going to find at Mine Howe?

91

48 B.C.

Alexandria, Egypt

Julius Caesar stood at the window of the palace and gazed at the ships anchored in the Alexandrian harbour. He knew what Achillas was trying to achieve. There were thirty-five Roman galleys—his ships—in the harbour of Alexandria and reports had reached him that the Egyptians were trying to mobilise more than seventy Egyptian quadriremes, quinqueremes and warships that were moored there. If they succeeded in their attempt, they would bottle up his own fleet like rats in a hole.

For a moment, a fleeting feeling of dread took hold of him.

Had the Egyptians guessed what he had done to their precious treasure?

After all, they must have wondered what Caesar was doing in Alexandria, participating in this internecine war with just four thousand soldiers against the might of the Egyptian army, which was five times larger.

He shook off the feeling just as quickly as it had materialised. Even if they had worked out his true intentions, they were too late. Two Roman galleys had departed a week ago and were, doubtless, now safely in the Roman port he had designated as their destination. Once there, arrangements had been made to transport their precious cargo under the cover of night to a secret destination that only he, and a handful of trusted soldiers commanded by the faithful Paulinus, knew about.

The siege of Alexandria had lasted for months, with Caesar controlling the palace, the Bruchion area— which the Romans had fortified—and the harbour; while the Egyptian general, Achillas, controlled the surrounding city. Achillas had been convinced into collusion by Ptolemy's regent Pothinus and had marched on Alexandria with twenty thousand men. Hard street fighting had ensued as a result of the siege but neither side was able to gain the upper hand.

No, the Egyptians were still ignorant of what he had done.

It was far more likely that the Egyptians, tired of besieging the Romans, had decided to wrest control of the harbour from him in order to cut off his supplies and, more importantly, his potential escape route.

'Achillas is a smart man,' the beautiful woman at his side remarked as she gazed out to sea, divining Caesar's thoughts. Her lustrous black hair was draped over her shoulder, reaching almost to her waist. She wore the raiment of the Pharaoh, except for the Atef crown, which she had not had occasion to wear since it was more ceremonial than practical in nature.

Caesar cast an admiring look at her. Not only was she beautiful but he had also come to respect her intelligence in both governance and warfare. A rare combination in a man, he had not expected to find it in a woman. He was proud of her in a way that a hunter is proud of his trophies.

'That he is, Cleopatra,' he grudgingly admitted. Caesar had defeated his great rival, Pompey the Great, who represented the Senators in the civil war that had wracked the Roman republic, at Pharsalus. The battle, decisively won by Caesar, was the turning point in the history of the Roman Empire, marking the phase when it transitioned from a republic to an autocracy, eventually leading to a long line of emperors.

Caesar had pursued the defeated Pompey to Alexandria; arriving there just after Pompey's death, which had been instigated by Pothinus, the most influential person in the court of the Egyptian King, Ptolemy XIII. Egypt was nominally under Roman guardianship and Caesar felt it imperative to intervene in the Alexandrian War between the two siblings, Cleopatra VII and Ptolemy XIII. Not that his passion for Cleopatra had less influence on his decision to settle the dispute. After meeting Cleopatra, Caesar had helped her detain the young King Ptolemy, which had led to the siege of Alexandria by the Egyptian army and the sight he was witnessing today.

But he had no regrets. Quite apart from his affair with Cleopatra, the intervention in the war served another purpose. It had provided the perfect cover to carry out his plans, which had been executed to perfection. The risks had been great and the plan's success had been achieved at great cost, not the least of which was the prospect of being embroiled in a battle for the better part of the next twelve months.

But it was worth it. He had the prize within his grasp. And the instructions to Paulinus were clear. He would assemble the scholars and oversee them. By the time the war in Egypt was over, Caesar would have what he was searching for.

He smiled grimly. If the Egyptians thought they would strike terror into his heart, they were mistaken. In fact, they had just provided him with another opportunity to cover his tracks and disguise his real motives for visiting Alexandria.

'Maybe not smart enough, then,' Cleopatra observed, as she saw his smile and immediately discerned that the Roman dictator had a plan in mind. What she didn't know was that the plan had two objectives.

First, destroy the Egyptian ships.

Second, destroy the only evidence of his secret mission in Alexandria; a mission that the world would never learn about.

Caesar laughed. 'You are perceptive, my dear,' he remarked. 'You will be the divine Queen of Egypt. I promise you that.'

Cleopatra turned and kissed him. 'I know,' she whispered, smiling at him. 'With you by my side, how can I lose?'

92

February, present year

Day 4

Surveillance

'They're on the move,' Harper reported, looking at the laptop screen. They were in Dee's hotel suite, where they had set up their equipment, which included a state-of-the-art GPS tracking system. After getting the GPS details for the Land Rover that Harry had rented from Hertz, it had been a cinch for Harper's team to track the movements of the vehicle.

'Good.' Dee was comfortably ensconced in a high-back chair, sipping her single malt whisky. 'Get the choppers loaded and ready to go. Let's see where they are going.'

She sat back and reflected. While he hadn't described the coins in his diary, Caesar had been quite explicit about the purpose of the map that he had crudely represented on the coins along with the inscriptions. It had been put there to help him remember the exact location when the time came for him to return to Britain and retrieve the weapon.

Dee hadn't worried about how she would figure out which region of Britain the map represented and which megalithic sites were depicted on the map. She had decided to cross that bridge when she came to it.

And now, Fortune had presented her with the answer.

It was almost as if she was destined to achieve victory.

'They're going east,' Harper reported.

'Mine Howe,' Dee said, jumping to her feet. 'That's where they're going.'

She was intrigued. Owing to her late arrival at Kirkwall, she hadn't been able to visit any of the sites on the coins, but she had read up on them. It had puzzled her to think that the weapon could be hidden in any of those sites. Surely it would have been discovered by now if it had been there?

But Vijay was on his way to Mine Howe. Did that mean the weapon was buried there? Or was there a clue there, which would lead to another hiding place?

Whatever it was, she knew it was time to end this cat and mouse game. She was going to find out what Vijay knew.

Then, she was going to kill him and locate the weapon herself.

Back at Mine Howe

Harry pulled into the Mine Howe car park. It was a dark night and, once the car headlights were switched off, the mound in which the underground chamber lay was barely visible.

Vijay hopped out and opened the boot, pulling out two helmets and torches. He had asked Harry to pick them up before locking himself up for his research. He had a hunch they would need these accessories tonight.

The gate leading to the mound was locked. Both men vaulted over the gate and made their way to the top of the mound, where they stood over the manhole-sized opening in the ground that led to the stairway below.

It was cold and windy. It would not be pleasant down there.

Vijay took a deep breath. 'Okay, let's do it.'

Harry took a look around. The night was pitch black. A heavy cover of clouds hid the stars and the first few drops of rain had begun to fall.

'Great,' he said. 'What timing.' He shone his torch down the pit as Vijay started climbing down into the abyss. 'All clear. No vehicles around for miles. We haven't been followed. Looks like time is on our side.' He checked his watch. 'Just an hour or so to go before the heavy artillery gets here.'

He chuckled. 'I'd love to see the face of whoever is leading this mission from the Order, when they finally get here.'

'Okay, I'm on the landing,' Vijay's voice came up to him, slightly muffled by the acoustics of the shaft and the wind blowing across the mound. 'I need some more light here.'

Harry clambered down the iron ladder and sat on the last iron stair, his feet resting on one of the stone steps from the original structure. With one hand, he held on to the iron handrail and with the other, he shone his torch down the shaft.

'Thanks,' Vijay said, shining his own torch into the upper gallery. He had discussed the layout of Mine Howe with Harry and they had both agreed on two things.

First, if there were more underground chambers housing the weapon, then it would not be possible to access them through the main chamber. The walls of that chamber, though built with dry stone piled in layers without mortar or cement, seemed to be too solid to have any openings in them.

Second, the only other option for accessing the hidden chambers would be the upper gallery. The lower gallery was much too narrow for anyone to manoeuvre through. The upper gallery, though, was just wide enough for a man to wriggle through on his stomach, and the height at the inner end was sufficient for someone to crouch or even kneel.

While both galleries had been explored by others, Vijay

wasn't sure if anyone had specifically looked for an entrance to a chamber beyond the walls.

'I'm going in.' Vijay stepped up to the upper gallery, using the sill of the lower gallery as a foothold, and pushed the torch inside, lighting it up.

He then half pulled, half pushed himself through the entrance of the upper gallery, and lay there, panting.

Breathing today was going to be a problem, with the wind whipping across the surface of the mound.

Grasping the torch, Vijay crawled forward, until he was fully inside the passage.

A sudden cold fear gripped him. What if the structure were to collapse? What if he got stuck? Help would be at hand within an hour, but would he survive till then with the poor air quality down here?

Brushing these morbid thoughts aside, he forced himself to focus on the inner wall.

Part of the masonry had collapsed, exposing the midden deposits which made up the mound. Clearly, there wasn't anything beyond the wall here.

'I'm in!' Vijay called out to Harry, who climbed down and stood on the landing. He could see Vijay's boots through the gallery opening.

'Blimey!' was all Harry could say as he shone his torch into the gallery to aid Vijay.

Vijay turned his attention to another part of the wall, a cold doubt forming in his mind.

What if he had been wrong about this and there was no entrance to an underground chamber from here?

93

In the helicopter

Dee's mood was as dark as the night outside and the tension was building up within her like the electrical storm brewing tonight.

Peals of thunder rolled across the heavens and the odd flash of lightning cleaved the darkness as the five helicopters made their way to Mine Howe.

The pilot shouted something to Harper.

Dee raised an enquiring eyebrow.

'Storm's getting bad, he says,' Harper told Dee.

'Is he worried about lightning?' Dee asked. 'I thought our helicopters were designed to withstand a lightning strike.'

'Air turbulence,' Harper said. 'He says the forecast isn't good and, especially if we're carrying a payload, control may be a problem. He wants us to finish fast and leave before it gets too bad.'

Dee nodded. 'Tell him it won't take too long. I want to finish this as fast as possible.'

In the gallery

Vijay suppressed his misgivings and put the torch down, feeling along the wall, looking for loose stones that might conceal an opening. Most of the stones seemed to be tightly fitted together and would not budge.

His breathing came in short bursts now and he felt distinctly uncomfortable. But he couldn't give up.

Not now.

Not when they were so close.

A thought struck him. He picked up the torch and began shining it across the wall in a sweeping motion, slowly covering every stone that made up the walls of the gallery.

Then he saw it.

A single stone with a mark on it.

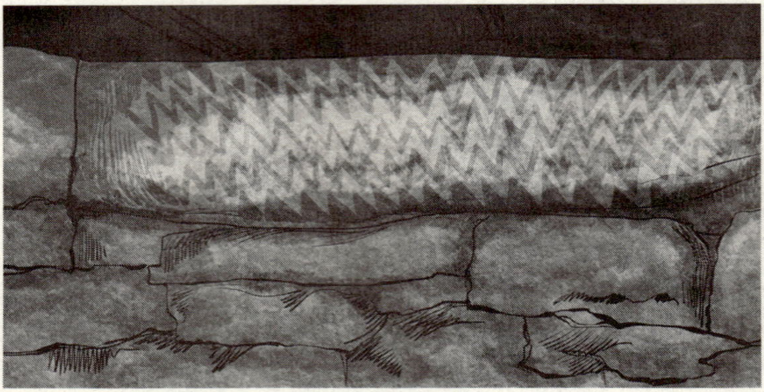

Mark on the stone in the upper gallery

He didn't know what the mark meant, but none of the other stones were marked in the same way. He swept his torch across the other stones once again, just to be sure.

No other stone was marked.

Putting the torch down, he held the stone at its edges with both hands, ensured he had a good grip on it, and pulled.

The stone moved slightly. It was right at the top of the wall, just under the capstone that formed the roof of the gallery.

Encouraged, he shifted slightly to give himself more room and tugged once more on the stone.

It wiggled slightly. It was definitely loose.

Abandoning brute force, he slowly jiggled the stone around, gently prying it loose from the others surrounding it.

Slowly, reluctantly, the stone slid loose and came away in his hands.

Beyond it was darkness.

Vijay was elated. There was no midden deposit behind the stone.

He tugged at the other stones in the wall. They came off easily, one by one. He realised that the stone with the inscription was a keystone, locking the wall in place. Once the keystone was removed, the other stones were fairly easy to remove.

In a matter of minutes, he had taken apart enough of the wall to reveal an opening similar in width and height to the entrance to this gallery.

'I've found something!' he shouted out to Harry. 'There's an opening here. I'm going in.'

'Roger,' Harry shouted back. It had been a while since Vijay had last spoken and Harry had begun to feel a little anxious.

Vijay pulled himself through the gap in the stone wall and found himself on another landing.

There were stone steps leading down from the landing into an underground chamber, probably a twin of the one that had been excavated.

The chamber was deathly silent. No sound from the surface penetrated through this far.

Vijay swung his torch around the chamber as he descended the stairs. It was a larger chamber than the main chamber of Mine Howe, in which he had stood with Julie Dickens not so long ago.

But it wasn't the size of the chamber that caught his attention and held him spellbound.

It was the contents that astounded him.

He had not come prepared for the sight that greeted his eyes.

94

48 B.C.

Alexandria, Egypt

Caesar stood at the window of the palace, sipping his wine and watching the glow that lit up the night to the north. He smiled. His plan was working. The fires were raging.

He had already received word that the surprise attack on the ships had been successful. In their confidence that they had the Romans pinned down, the Egyptians had relaxed their guard.

The sudden attack by the Romans, under the cover of darkness, had taken the Egyptians by surprise. Within no time, the ships were ablaze, the fires lighting up the harbour for miles around. The tarred rigging and waxed decks of the ships were quick to feed on the flaming firebrands hurled at them.

A similar sequence of events had taken place at the docks and warehouses, most of which were unguarded. No one had imagined that the Romans would have the least interest in attacking these buildings when they, themselves, were besieged.

The fires from the docks had spread quickly to adjoining buildings, the embers fanned by the sea breeze, and the warehouses and ship-houses soon joined in the general conflagration.

Including the one building that Caesar wanted burned down. The great Library of Alexandria.

Caesar put down his glass of wine. It was time for his next move. His legionnaires, having accomplished their task of setting fire to the ships and the buildings along the shore, would have begun the task of garrisoning the Pharos, the famous lighthouse, on an island. This was to be his retreat.

And his access to the sea.

95

February, present year

Day 4

Inside the chamber

Vijay slowly climbed back up the stairs. If breathing outside had been a problem, it was worse here, where the air was stale, having been sealed in for centuries.

He longed for the clear, crisp air outside. Just a short while more, he thought to himself, and this would be over.

'I'm through. I've found the chamber,' Vijay yelled out, poking his head through the hole in the wall. 'Call Imran and inform him. Get a status update on the reinforcements. I'll join you in a minute.'

'Roger.' Harry made his way up the top flight of stairs, as Vijay took a last look around the chamber, marvelling at the sight before him.

He crawled back through the upper gallery, then dropped back to the landing.

Mine Howe

Harry pulled himself up the iron ladder and emerged from the pit, scrambling to the surface of the mound. As soon as he stood up, he knew something was wrong.

Instinctively, he switched off his torch, dropped to the ground and rolled down the mound, presenting himself as a moving target in case anyone out there wanted to take a shot at him.

But no shot came.

He crouched, supporting himself on one knee, looking around in the darkness, trying to sense what was happening here. He had no way to warn Vijay, other than crying out. Even then, he didn't know if the cry would actually reach Vijay's ears.

Without warning, a huge shape came lumbering out of the darkness and hit him like a ton of bricks.

Harry went flying several feet and landed on his back. He had lost his hard hat while rolling down the mound and the torch now flew from his hand and disappeared into the darkness.

He rose slowly to his feet, disoriented. Suddenly, the shape materialised again out of the darkness, but this time Harry was prepared. He still couldn't fathom how his attacker could see him in the darkness when Harry himself was unable to see more than a foot in front of him.

An enormous fist, as hard and heavy as a blacksmith's hammer, hit him on the chin, then in the head, followed by a blow to his stomach, knocking the wind out of him and doubling him up with pain.

His attacker picked him up as if Harry was a bundle of cotton, and hurled him to the ground, a few feet away.

Harry landed hard on his back, despite rolling over on landing to reduce the impact of the fall. His opponent was strong. Harry had never been hit like this before. The man seemed to have superhuman strength.

The attacker, an indistinct shape in the darkness, lunged at him but Harry managed to roll away just in time. His head was spinning both from the punch as well as from the fall but he got to his feet unsteadily.

His attacker flew at him again. Harry's eyes had adjusted better to the darkness now and he sidestepped, landing a few good punches of his own to the man's head and face.

It didn't seem to make a difference.

Only now did Harry become conscious of the size of his attacker. The man was huge, well over 7 feet tall, and he towered over Harry.

Harry heard a growl of anger. A fist slammed into his face, splitting his cheek.

A hook to his head made him see stars.

Before he could recover, his attacker had picked him up again and slammed him to the ground.

Harry was tough, but he was taking a beating that few men could endure.

He tried to get up, fighting the pain and the darkness that lurked on the edge of his consciousness.

He had to get back into the fight.

An enormous boot crashed into his face, breaking his nose.

The man kicked him again, this time in the ribs.

Harry flipped over with the force of the kick and landed on his face.

He clawed at the ground.

The darkness was threatening to engulf him. He couldn't allow that to happen.

Before he knew what was happening he was roughly pulled up by his collar.

An uppercut to his chin, swiftly followed by a cross punch to his head, staggered him.

'Don't kill him.' A woman's voice. Hard and cold. 'Not yet.'

Harry's head lolled limply as he veered between consciousness and insensibility.

He was flung to the ground, like discarded trash.

The light from a torch blinded him.

The last thing he remembered was the rain falling on his face.

And the woman's voice saying, 'He isn't the one.'

There was a jolt of pain, then a cool blackness enveloped him.

Out of the frying pan…

Vijay pulled himself out of the pit leading to the underground chamber. Where was Harry?

'Harry?' he called out.

In response, a dozen torches were switched on simultaneously, blinding him. He held up his hands to shield his eyes.

A grim realisation hit him.

The Order had reached here before the reinforcements.

A young woman walked up to him. Her face glistened in the rain.

'So,' she said, her eyes fixed on him. '*You* are Vijay Singh.' Her eyes gleamed with a malevolence that sent a shudder through Vijay.

'I've waited for this meeting for a long time. I am Dee.' She smiled, a cold, venomous smile that never reached her eyes. 'What did you find down there?'

Vijay said nothing. He stood there, silent, sullen. He was worried. What had they done to Harry?

96

The Secret of the Druids

Dee impatiently paced the length of the road as Harper and his men unloaded and set up the searchlights and trained them on the mound.

The helicopters had landed a short distance away. A group of men had set up a secure perimeter so that they wouldn't be disturbed. Until Harry had emerged from the pit, they had waited silently in the darkness.

Dee had wanted to ensure that whoever emerged from the mound was caught off guard and captured in such a way that he would be unable to warn anyone else who might be with him.

The searchlights would ensure they could see what they were doing.

'Are we done yet?' Dee demanded as the large wooden crates were deposited at the base of the mound.

Harper nodded. Everyone was wet and it was cold but they knew that Dee would not let up until they had got what she wanted.

'Good,' Dee said, sounding satisfied. 'Switch the lights on.'

The searchlights came on, illuminating the mound.

'We have to hurry,' Harper told Dee. 'Aberdeen just informed me that police helicopters have taken off a while ago, bound for Kirkwall. And a private jet just landed in Kirkwall.'

He jerked a thumb towards Vijay, who had been trussed up and made to sit on the road. 'His back up is on its way.'

'Load them up,' Dee instructed. 'I want to be out of here before they arrive. How much time do we have?'

'Twenty minutes,' Harper said. 'I'll get the men to work faster. But it isn't easy. There isn't much air down there.'

Even as the searchlights were being put up, Harper's men had moved into the pit. They had quickly found the hole Vijay had made in the inner wall of the upper gallery and had reported on the contents of the second hidden underground chamber.

Vijay's thoughts turned to Harry. There was no sign of the former SAS trooper.

It galled him that he would have to watch as this woman, who was evidently in charge, had the contents of the chamber loaded onto the helicopters.

He had been unable to believe his eyes when he first saw the weapons in the chamber. There were at least twenty of them, maybe thirty, down there. Exactly like the description in the Semiramis story. Resembling clubs, thinner in the middle than at both ends, where they expanded into bulbous heads, they stood upright in the chamber, resting in receptacles especially carved to hold them.

Dee's men had set up a system of pulleys at the mouth of the pit. It seemed that a team of men were passing the clubs through the gallery to a man on the landing, who fastened them to one end of the rope around the pulleys, making it easier to haul them out swiftly.

As Vijay watched despondently, the clubs were packed into crates and carried to the helicopters. It was like a bad dream come true. A repeat of the last mission. The Order was going to get away with the weapons just like they had got away with the *amrita*. And there was nothing he could do except pray that Colin arrived with the reinforcements in time.

Dee walked up to him. 'You thought you would get away with these, didn't you?' She indicated one of the clubs being carried from the pulley to a crate that was being packed nearby. 'But what would you do with these? You don't even know the *mantra* to operate them.'

'And you do?' Vijay scoffed.

Dee laughed. 'Of course I do. Caesar was very helpful.'

'Caesar?' Vijay was puzzled.

'Julius Caesar,' Dee clarified. 'How do you think we got to know about the coins in the first place? Caesar wrote a diary, which we got our hands on. Everything was there—the story of Semiramis, the two halves of the puzzle that would lead to her grave, his deal with the Druids, the riddle of the Druids, the coins and the *mantra*. Everything we needed to know.'

'They probably don't even work after all these centuries,' Vijay ventured.

'They don't need to,' Dee retorted. 'We will simply reverse engineer them and then make our own weapons. Perhaps even improve on the technology.'

Vijay didn't like the sound of that.

'Just what do you intend doing with the weapons?' he asked.

'Why, control the world, just as Caesar wanted to,' Dee replied, then realised that Vijay's question meant that he didn't know what the weapons were. 'You don't know how they work, do you?'

Vijay shrugged. 'Did Caesar explain that, too?'

Dee laughed again. 'Caesar wouldn't have understood the science behind it. But he was smart enough to know that this technology could do wonders. He saw the application of the science behind the technology first hand in the battles against the Celts. That gave him an idea of how powerful the weapon itself could be.'

Despite himself, Vijay was now curious. What *was* it that the weapon could do?

'I know that the weapon has something to do with the stone circles and the burial chambers,' Vijay said.

Dee considered this for a moment. 'That's a pretty good deduction, you know. And I guess it won't hurt to tell you a bit more about the weapon. After all you aren't going anywhere. I don't claim to understand the science behind it, but I will tell you how the weapon works. After all you've been through, perhaps you deserve to know. Before you die.'

Vijay listened as Dee explained, his mind spinning as he realised the enormity of this discovery.

No wonder the Druids venerated the weapon. It was one of the most powerful weapons mentioned in the Mahabharata and other Vedic scriptures.

Now, the Order was going to use it to control the world.

And Vijay could do nothing but look on.

And wait for his imminent death.

97

Into the night

'We're all packed,' Harper reported to Dee, who was still talking about the weapon to Vijay.

'Time to go,' Dee said in response. She looked at Vijay. 'Your mates are arriving soon. Too bad you won't be around to greet them.' She laughed and walked off, Harper following her.

Vijay watched her walk away. He wondered how he was going to die. Would they shoot him? Break his neck? Stab him?

A sudden thought struck him. He hesitated for a moment.

Should he…?

Then he made up his mind.

He would do it.

'Wait!' he called after the retreating figure of the woman.

Dee stopped and turned.

'Don't do it,' Vijay said to her.

'Don't do what?' Dee walked a few steps towards him.

'The weapons. Don't carry them in the helicopters. I've heard what you told me and I've figured out the science behind it. You—'

'Don't tell me what I should or shouldn't be doing,' Dee spat at him. 'You're a dead man. I know what you're trying. This is a last-ditch attempt to stop me from taking these away. Well, you're not going to succeed.' She nodded to Harper. 'Put him in the hole.' She strode away towards the helicopters.

Two men came over and untied his legs even as a huge man came lumbering towards Vijay. He was well over 7 feet tall, almost 8 feet by Vijay's estimate, with knotted muscles that bulged and rippled under his shirt. He seemed oblivious to the rain and cold and wore neither a jacket nor an overcoat.

'He's all yours, Yeti,' one of the men sniggered. The giant picked Vijay up like a sack of potatoes and carried him to the mouth of the shaft where he deposited Vijay inside the pit.

'Down,' one of the men who had accompanied Yeti said to Vijay. 'Into the underground chamber.'

Vijay made his way slowly down the steps, climbing down sideways, since that was the only way he could hold on to the iron railing with his hands tied behind him. A cold fear gripped his heart as he realised what they were going to do.

The big man called Yeti picked up an enormous piece of wood—the remains of the structure that had sheltered the mouth of the shaft until a gale had torn it apart—and slammed it over the mouth of the pit.

Darkness immediately flooded the shaft. Vijay had reached the landing. He heard a few sharp thuds against the wooden door to his prison and realised they were dumping rocks on the wood to keep it in place.

As if he would have been able to move the wooden plank by himself with his hands tied behind him. He was in a hopeless situation.

Vijay knew that the danger to him was not from the lack of oxygen but from the build up of carbon dioxide. Already, the carbon dioxide levels down here would have been high because of the men working in the chamber and the shaft. Very little fresh air would have entered the chamber thanks to the rain and the wind on the surface. As the carbon dioxide became more concentrated, it would become more toxic. Eventually, he would die, not from oxygen deprivation but from carbon dioxide poisoning.

How long could he last down here?

He decided to sit on the landing and wait. There was no way he could climb down the second flight of stairs with his hands tied behind him. Colin would be here soon with the reinforcements. Until then, he had to conserve the air and reduce his intake of carbon dioxide. And the best way to do that was to slow down his breathing. No exertions.

There was no way he could get out of here on his own. Rescue would have to come from outside.

But one thing gave him satisfaction. In his short conversation with Dee, he had figured out something about her. And he had put that insight to good use.

Whatever happened to him, Vijay had ensured one thing.

They would never get the weapons to safety.

This time, the Order would not win.

98

Outside Mine Howe

Colin surveyed the scene. The searchlights had been left in place and still lit up the mound. He was crestfallen. They had arrived too late.

From the sky, as the helicopters began their descent towards Mine Howe, they had seen the glare of the searchlights, indicating that the Order had reached before they could.

After landing, a cursory search of the area around the mound had led to the discovery of Harry's lifeless body, his neck broken and his body bearing the evidence of the savage assault on him. Colin had struggled to keep his emotions in check. He had already come to think of Harry as a friend during the short time they had known each other.

They had also discovered an immense wooden plank weighted down by large rocks. The special forces officers who had accompanied Colin set about removing them. Colin guessed that the Order had covered up the mouth of the shaft leading to the underground chamber.

Vijay was nowhere to be seen.

Had the Order taken Vijay with them? Colin was perplexed. Did that mean that Vijay had found the weapons? How had the Order found Vijay so soon?

There were too many questions and no answers.

A shout went up at the top of the mound, where the mouth

of the shaft had now been uncovered. One of the men had climbed into the shaft and discovered the limp body of Vijay, on the landing.

Colin rushed to the opening and watched as the men hauled Vijay out, his head and hands hanging limply as they carried him down the mound.

'Is he alive?' Colin enquired anxiously. He could only hope.

In the sky over Aberdeen

Dee hummed a little tune to herself. She was exultant. Things couldn't have gone better. Her hunch had been correct, her plan had worked and the weapons were in her possession. Vijay Singh would be dead by now and she would now turn her attention to Van Klueck.

She had to admit that the man had his uses for the Order. He had had a good run so far. Until he got in her way.

Now, she had a bigger prize than the *amrita*. Oh, sure, the virus conferred longevity. But it was a complicated process, which was still not understood perfectly.

When the Order had acquired the virus, it was initially thought that immortality would automatically follow.

It hadn't been so easy. She was a case in point. The Order believed that people with the true bloodline stood a better chance of benefiting from the virus because of their genes. And, to some extent, that belief had been correct. Volunteers had been called for and she had been one of them—eager young things, trying for a shot at immortality.

But no one had reckoned for certain less understood effects of the virus. It had given her an unnatural glow on her face. Her skin tone and texture had changed after she had been given a dose of the virus. It had also impacted her vocal chords, giving her the steely voice that she now had. But what really bugged her since she had been dosed with the *amrita* was the uncomfortable feeling that something was happening inside her. It was nothing obvious but an unpleasant sensation would wash over her at times. No pain, no aches, no symptoms of anything wrong. Just an uncanny feeling that she had. And she hated it.

No, the *amrita* was not all it was supposed to be.

This prize was the ultimate one.

If the Order was able to control every human being on the planet, who would oppose it?

A shudder ran through the helicopter.

Dee looked around. 'What the hell is happening? I thought we were out of the storm?'

They had managed to successfully navigate through the turbulence of the electrical storm. The helicopters had been bumped around, their engines and rotors strained to the maximum, but they had made it. What was happening now?

'I don't know!' the pilot shouted back. 'It isn't the engines.'

There was another shudder, followed by a deep-throated rumble. A sound like thunder.

Dee looked back at the crate that was stowed at the back of the helicopter. It seemed to be coming from there.

But why?

Each of the five helicopters had a crate like this one. Each crate contained six weapons. Thirty in total.

Without warning, a spark seemed to emanate from the crate. It arced out like a lightning bolt, visible for a fraction of a second, then disappeared.

'What was that?' Harper asked nervously.

Before anyone could answer, there was another spark; then another; a flurry of sparks, arcing out in different directions. The sound that was now emanating from the crate was deafening as it reverberated around the helicopter.

Bright flashes of light from the other helicopters told Dee that they were experiencing the same thing.

What was happening? She couldn't understand.

'Electronics have been hit!' the pilot shouted. 'I've got rotor damage. I'm losing control!'

The crate continued to spark like a faulty electrical transformer, striking different areas in the helicopter, which went into a nosedive.

'Electrical discharges!' Harper's face was pale as he looked at Dee. Only he, apart from Dee, knew the true nature of the weapon and what it could do.

But they had not expected it to act in this manner. Not when they were supposed to have it under their control. After all, *they* had the mantra to activate it. No one else knew how to deploy the weapon!

'If it hits the fuel tank...' Harper left his sentence unfinished. He could not bring himself to state the worst possibility. He looked at Dee, cold fear in his eyes. 'What have we done?'

Dee cursed. Caesar had only mentioned the *mantra* to activate the devices.

He had not said anything about turning them off.

Aberdeen

The skies were clear, the storm having blown over. A few clouds hung over Aberdeen but the stars could be seen in patches. It was a rare winter night in Scotland. Yet, the sound of thunder rumbled across the heavens.

Startled residents, planning to retire for the night, looked up in surprise at the sky.

Against the black canvas of the sky and the faint starlight, there were flashes of lightning, short bursts of light, accompanied by the sound of thunder.

But the lightning was confined to five small spaces in the sky. There was no major discharge between the earth and the sky.

As the onlookers watched, one of the balls of lightning transformed into a massive fireball, its centre glowing red and orange with the heat of the blast, spewing flaming debris in all directions, as the sound of an explosion rocked the heavens.

The horrified residents of Aberdeen watched, transfixed as a second explosion followed.

Streaks of light shot out in every direction from the exploding fireballs, like fireworks on New Year's Eve; and residents ran for cover as bits and pieces of metal rained down on them.

A third explosion shook the skies, followed simultaneously by two others.

Silence reigned above the city. The night sky returned to normal and the stars resumed their twinkling amid the gossamer clouds, as the last of the debris clunked to the ground.

99

A week later

Intelligence Bureau Headquarters, New Delhi

Patterson looked around at the group around the conference table. They had all gathered here to review and debrief the recently concluded mission.

After his rescue from the underground chamber at Mine Howe, Vijay had spent a few days in hospital in London, recovering from his ordeal. He had then flown back to New Delhi to join the rest of the team for the review.

Colin was there, with Shukla and Imran. Alice and Goldfeld had been invited as part of the review, given their respective roles in helping the task force achieve success in the mission. Even Patterson had specially flown in for the review.

The only person missing from the group was Harry. The mood was grim as Patterson made it a point to mention the former SAS Officer's contribution to the mission. Despite an undercurrent of quiet satisfaction, everyone looked sombre.

Like the previous year, they had lost a member of the team. But, unlike last year, the Order had not succeeded.

'We know from eyewitness reports in Aberdeen, that there were five massive explosions in the sky,' Patterson announced. 'The timing of the explosions roughly corresponds to the time that the helicopters of the Order would have been flying over Aberdeen. And since they had five helicopters in which the weapons were loaded, it certainly sounds like their helicopters blew up. There would have been no survivors. We're lucky that no one on the ground got killed.' He looked at Vijay. 'So what happened up there? The eyewitness reports mention flashes of lightning in the sky minutes before the explosions, even though the skies were fairly clear over Aberdeen and there definitely was no electrical storm in the area at that time.'

'It was the nature of the weapons,' Vijay told them. 'When Dee, the woman leading the group from the Order, told me how the weapons worked and what they had been used for, I realised what they actually were. She didn't have a clue about the science behind the weapons, but I'm an electrical engineer, so I was able to work out the technology behind them—or so I thought. So I used reverse psychology on the woman. I told her not to carry the weapons on the helicopters. And I *was* being honest. I knew what would happen if I was right about the technology. But I also knew that she would not take kindly to advice from me. She had a strange arrogance about her. Like she felt that something about her entitled her to certain privileges. It worked. She refused to listen to me.'

'And you were correct about the technology,' Imran interposed. 'Vijay, if you know what the weapon is, why don't you start from the beginning. Fill us in on all the gaps, starting with what the Druids were doing with the weapon.'

Vijay flushed. He had kept both Patterson and Imran in the dark about the prisms, sharing that information only with Alice, Colin and Shukla. And, of course, Goldfeld.

Now, he realised, he would have to reveal the source of the Semiramis story. He couldn't possibly explain what he knew about the history of the weapon without talking about the story in the inscriptions on the prisms.

He took a deep breath and began. 'Twenty-five years ago, my father, who worked with the Archaeological Survey of India, discovered an artefact during an excavation in Kishangarh.' He proceeded to tell them the story that his father's colleague, KS, had shared with him during their meeting almost a year ago. He told them about the prism that KS had given him, which had led to his visit to London where he had tried to gain access to the second prism at the British Museum.

'Alice helped me by getting Kurt Wallace to recommend us to the Museum Director,' Vijay concluded. 'Wallace also helped us get a reference from a Trustee of the museum and we were finally able to examine the second prism.'

There was silence when he finished. Vijay looked at Patterson and Imran. 'I'm sorry; I should have shared this with you earlier. But I had no idea that this was connected in any way to the Order. There was no way I could have guessed the connection. I just wanted to know why my parents had been killed.'

Patterson looked at him. 'I understand, Vijay. And I'm sorry about your parents. I think it is obvious now that the Order had a hand in their death. We'll re-open the case and investigate. I'm not very hopeful that we'll get any clues after the passage of so many years, but we'll try.'

Imran nodded his agreement.

Vijay was grateful and appreciative. Patterson would have been justified in being angry at having these facts hidden from him. In this situation, and with this particular enemy, any information could be crucial. And this link had eventually turned out to be a vital piece in the puzzle that finally led to locating the weapons.

Patterson's response left Vijay emotional.

'Go on,' Imran prodded Vijay, sensing his feelings. 'Fill us in on the details.'

Vijay pulled himself together. 'Here's what I understand of the story.' He looked at Alice and Goldfeld. 'Jump in anytime you feel I'm missing anything.'

They nodded back at him.

'At some time before recorded history began,' Vijay resumed, 'someone—call them the *Tuatha de Danann* or the *Danavas;* it doesn't matter—built the stone circles and the so-called burial mounds that dot the UK and Ireland. Incidentally, during my research, I discovered that there are stone circles and other megalithic monuments all over the world, including in India. This was a global phenomenon. And while archaeologists have tried to give these stone structures a date, no one really knows exactly when they were built because you cannot reliably date a stone structure.'

'Who are the *Tuatha de Danann?*' Imran wanted to know.

Vijay indicated to Colin that he should explain, and Colin briefed the group on the results of his research into the Druids and the Lords of Light, including the connections between the *Tuatha de Danann* and the Vedic people that he had discovered.

'Interesting,' Imran remarked. 'But we don't know why they built these structures.'

Vijay shook his head. 'We can speculate all we want but there's nothing conclusive because these are folks who inhabit the world of mythology. But based on what we've discovered, I think I can safely guess what the Druids did with them. Saul, can you please share the story on the prisms?'

Goldfeld obligingly narrated the story of Semiramis and the Druids; the war she waged to retrieve the celestial weapon from India and her death and burial in Britain.

'But we now know that she didn't bring back one weapon,' Patterson observed. 'She brought back a whole bunch of them.'

'Correct,' Vijay said. 'This would have been around 2000 B.C. We don't know where the Druids came from but they probably descended from the Lords of Light who started the Druidic tradition. The knowledge of the weapons was passed down to the Druids, along with their religion and philosophies, as the prism tells us.

'And where did the weapons come from?' Patterson asked.

Vijay requested Shukla to reiterate the explanation he had given the others earlier, regarding the origin of the weapons in the Mahabharata.

'The weapons that Semiramis handed over to the Druids,' Vijay resumed, when Shukla had explained the connection with the Mahabharata, 'were, I believe, distributed across the sites in Britain. I think that each device was erected at a specific site, so there couldn't have been more than thirty sites all over Britain where these were installed.'

'Is that a conjecture or is it based on something you discovered?' Imran quizzed.

'A bit of both,' Vijay replied. 'After Dee told me about the device, I did some research while I was in hospital, to see if my theory about the weapons was correct. To understand this, I'll have to explain how the weapons worked.'

100

The science behind the weapons

Vijay looked around the table. 'Let me start by explaining the piezoelectric effect,' he said. 'When pressure is applied to certain crystals, for example quartz crystals, an electric voltage across the material appears. As pressure is applied, each side of the crystal takes on an opposite charge, resulting in a drop of voltage across the crystal. The direct piezoelectricity of quartz can produce potential differences of thousands of volts. That's the technical explanation. What this means in simplistic terms is that pressure applied to a quartz crystal, for example, results in the generation of electricity from that crystal. Another way of putting it is that piezoelectric materials generate electricity if you bend, stretch or apply another mechanical force to them. This electric current is usually a high-voltage and low-amperage current. An example is your kitchen gas lighter. The spark that is produced to light your gas stove is a high-voltage current that is generated using the piezoelectric effect. The reverse is also true. If you apply a voltage across piezoelectric materials, they will deform accordingly. Piezoelectric materials are used in loudspeakers, as another example, to convert electrical signals to mechanical vibrations which create sound waves to produce the desired acoustic signal.'

He paused to see whether he had been able to explain the concept that was critical to understanding the nature of the celestial weapon.

'Go on,' Shukla said. 'If I can understand what you are saying, anyone can.' He laughed and the others joined in.

Vijay smiled and resumed. 'The second concept that we need to understand is the principle of resonance. Waves originate from vibrations. Sound waves, for example come from mechanical vibrations in solids, liquids and gases. Light and other electromagnetic waves come from the vibration of charged particles. All objects, charged particles, and mechanical systems have a certain frequency at which they tend to vibrate. This is called their resonant frequency, which is their natural frequency of vibration. Now, when sound or light waves strike an object, those waves are already vibrating at a particular frequency. If that frequency matches the resonant frequency of the object the waves are hitting, we get resonance. Resonance is when the amplitude of an object's oscillations is increased by the matching vibrations of another object. If a wineglass is exposed to a musical tone that matches the resonant frequency of the wineglass, it will shatter. Another example is the so-called sound of the sea that you hear if you put a seashell to your ear. We are surrounded by sound waves with a range of frequencies, many of them inaudible because of their low intensity. This background noise fills the seashell causing vibrations within it. Now, if one of the frequencies around us forces air within the seashell to vibrate at its natural or resonant frequency, a resonance situation is created and you hear the amplification of that background frequency.'

'Got it,' Goldfeld gave Vijay a thumbs up. 'What you're saying is that an external vibrating force can make another object oscillate at its resonant frequency with a greater amplification.'

'Exactly. Now let's combine the piezoelectric effect and resonance. If a voltage or a mechanical force is applied to a piezoelectric material it creates vibrations in the material, which means that a wave of a particular frequency is produced. If the vibration frequency is the resonant frequency of the material, the piezoelectric effect causes a higher output voltage across another section of the material. And, at a certain frequency, these materials become efficient radiators and can be potentially used as antennas.'

'I get the physics,' Imran said, as Vijay paused once more. 'Are you saying that the weapon uses the piezoelectric effect to generate electricity and that explains the flashes of lightning that people in Aberdeen saw before the helicopters exploded?'

'Hang on, Imran, you're going too fast,' Vijay laughed. 'I'll come to the weapon soon. Right now, I'm trying to explain the connection between the device and the megalithic monuments.'

Alice looked puzzled. 'I still don't get that connection,' she stated flatly. 'Even if the weapon discharged electricity somehow—and I have to admit I'm not clear how that could happen—of what use would that be in a stone circle or a burial mound?'

'Let's forget about the weapon discharging electricity for a moment,' Vijay said, holding up his hands. 'That isn't the important bit when it comes to the stone structures. Let's first see the connection between the weapon and the stone monuments. To understand that connection, let me tell you what a piezoelectric transducer is. It is a device that vibrates at a given frequency when a radio frequency wave is applied to it, generating an acoustic wave. Conversely, if an acoustic wave is applied to the transducer, it converts the acoustic wave into a radio frequency output. Basically, electromagnetic radiation generated from an acoustic source.'

The expressions on the faces of his audience told him that they still didn't get the connection. But he wasn't finished with his explanation yet.

'I guess the last piece in this puzzle,' Vijay explained, 'lies in the acoustic properties of the megalithic structures. Several studies have been conducted on a number of megalithic sites including Stonehenge and startling results have emerged, especially if one considers the physics that I have just explained. Many of the monuments, including Stonehenge and some of the burial chambers, have resonant frequencies of 10 to 12 hertz. In other cases, in chambered cairns like Maes Howe, where there are smaller chambers leading off the main one, the resonant frequencies of different chambers have been found to have resonant frequencies of 95 to 110 hertz. This is important because the difference between the two frequencies is 10 to 15 hertz. I'll explain why this particular frequency is important in just a moment. But consider this. If you had a source that could produce an acoustic wave at the same resonant frequency as the stone structure, imagine the effect that could be achieved through resonance! It has been conclusively demonstrated through several scientific studies that beating a certain kind of drum at a certain speed can actually generate acoustic waves corresponding to the resonant frequencies of these monuments.'

He paused to look around. 'And Dee told me that Caesar first realised the power of the Druids when the Romans in Gaul started falling apart during skirmishes with the Gallic resistance. Each time they failed, they heard drum beats for a long while before the battle began.'

Colin began to see where Vijay was going with this. 'So you're saying that the acoustic properties of these monuments had something to do with the effects experienced by the Romans?'

'Correct.' Vijay beamed. 'Look at the stones that were used to build these monuments. Granite in Salisbury, sandstone in the Orkney Islands...stones with a high quartz content. Stones that could experience the piezoelectric effect.'

Colin connected the dots. 'So what you are saying is that, an acoustic wave at the resonant frequency of the stone structure could make the structure act as a piezoelectric transducer, making the stones generate radio waves or electromagnetic waves?'

'That's right,' Vijay affirmed. 'And that's where the weapon comes in. According to what Dee told me, the weapon was installed within the megalithic structure and was used as the source of the energy or force required to create the piezoelectric effect in the stones. Of course, she didn't understand the science behind it so what she really told me was that the weapon was the source of energy for the stones to radiate waves that could control people.'

'But that still doesn't explain the effect on the Romans,' Imran pointed out. 'How can the stones radiate waves that control people?'

101

The real secret of the Druids

'So here's where I am making an inference based on all the facts I've explained to you so far,' Vijay replied. 'I haven't found anything to support my theory because no scientific experiments have ever been conducted to see if the stones do radiate a signal and, if they do, at what frequency. But when Dee made this remark about controlling people, I figured there is only one way to control people. And that is by controlling their minds. So I googled the terms "resonant frequency" and "human brain" and guess what I found?'

There was an expectant silence in the room as everyone waited for the answer.

'Brainwaves are produced by many neurons firing at the same time. Sometimes the firing is often, at other times it is less—and this determines the activity's frequency or wavelength, which is measured in hertz and recorded through a process called electroencephalography, commonly known as EEG. I also came across an article in *Scientific American* that described how rhythmic sound coordinates the thinking of people in a group by synchronising the mental processes of individuals in a group. According to the article, experiments showed that the waves of brain activity—alpha and beta waves—became synchronised around an external auditory rhythm. The conclusion was that rhythmic sound synchronises brain waves. What's more, the effect is nearly instantaneous. Almost immediately, on receiving the impulse, the brain waves start to get in synch with the rhythm.'

'What are alpha and beta waves?' Alice asked.

'That's exactly the question I asked myself,' Vijay smiled. 'I learned that there are five types of brainwaves. Gamma waves have a frequency range of 40 Hz to 100 Hz. Beta waves range from 12 Hz to 40 Hz. Alpha waves, from 8 Hz to 12 Hz. Theta waves range from 4 Hz to 8 Hz; and Delta waves from 0 Hz to 4 Hz. What intrigued me was the fact that the alpha and beta waves, which were also mentioned in the *Scientific American* article, are in the same frequency range as the resonant frequency of the megalithic structures. Beta waves are commonly observed when we are awake—when we are thinking, analysing, like right now. They have a stimulating effect and the right frequency of beta waves helps us to focus on our tasks and activities with ease. Too much beta leads to stress and anxiety and too little can lead to depression. Alpha waves are supposed to bridge our conscious thinking and the subconscious mind. They help to calm us down and help us relax deeply. Too little of alpha waves can lead to anxiety and high stress.'

'Let me see if I've understood this,' Patterson boomed. 'What you're saying is, in effect, that the Druids could control the minds of the people they lived among, by manipulating their brainwaves? Because brainwaves tend to synchronise with external impulses? And I guess the logic used for sound waves can be extended to electromagnetic waves?'

Vijay nodded. 'That's exactly what Dee told me about mind control. And it makes sense. If you remember what we learned about the Druids—the fact that they settled disputes, that they were more powerful than kings—one has to wonder how they were able to achieve all that, especially with the Celts who were great warriors, while the Druids were, at best, scientists and astronomers.'

'Don't forget,' Colin chimed in, 'the descriptions of how Druids could stop battles by simply walking between the two warring sides who would then quietly retreat.'

'I think,' Vijay continued, 'that different megalithic sites had different purposes. If you look at the tombs, different tombs had different resonant frequencies. The larger chambers generally had lower frequencies. Some sites were tuned to generate alpha waves to calm people down, get them in a state of relaxation. The Druids probably used these when settling disputes or stopping wars. And other sites were tuned to generate beta waves at higher frequencies to create panic, anxiety and stress. Beta waves can block out the alpha waves, so, hypothetically, a situation could be created where people who were calm and focused would suddenly panic and feel anxiety. I think this is what they used against the Romans. According to the research I did, there's been a fair amount of study done on the effects of microwaves and other forms of electromagnetic radiation, including ELF or extremely low frequency waves—which correspond to the alpha, theta and delta waves. Studies have shown that people subjected to external ELF waves become almost hypnotised—they are just about aware of what is happening but cannot do anything about it. Just imagine the Druids using this against the Romans! No wonder Caesar wanted this technology; he could have got anything that he wanted with it.'

'Hold on a moment.' Patterson looked puzzled. 'There's a flaw in this hypothesis.'

The others looked at him, wondering what he had discovered in the logic that Vijay had presented so far.

'If the Druids used waves generated by their megaliths to control their people or the Romans,' Patterson said slowly, 'then how come they weren't affected? After all, their brains should also have been under the control of the waves generated—whether alpha or beta.' He looked at Vijay. 'Take the example of the Celts fighting the Romans. The Druids generate beta waves, which create fear and anxiety among the Romans. Fine. The Romans fall apart. I understand that. But how come the Celts remained unaffected? Shouldn't they also have been gripped with panic? How were they able to stay immune to the effect of the waves generated by the megaliths?'

Vijay was silent. He had no answer.

'Er… I have a thought regarding this,' Colin ventured. 'Just a thought, based on some stuff I saw during my research on the Druids.'

'Go ahead,' Imran said.

'I came across two things during my research,' Colin said. 'At that time, I didn't think they were linked. But now that Director Patterson has brought up this point, I think I see the link. At least enough to speculate.'

He referred to his notes for a moment then looked around. 'The first thing I discovered,' Colin resumed, 'was something about the Druids that seemed to be a mythical fact, if you know what I mean. Part of the myth around them, created by classical writers, but not based on fact. Apparently, this myth is rooted in the writings of Pliny the Elder, whom we spoke of earlier, who lived in the first century A.D. According to Pliny, the Druids gathered mistletoe with great ceremony, especially on the sixth day of the moon. He wrote that the Druids believed that the mistletoe, if given as a drink, would grant fertility to any barren animal and that it was an antidote against all kinds of poison.'

'That's right,' Goldfeld observed. 'I've heard of the association of the Druids with mistletoe as well. It's a fairly strong tradition, actually.'

Colin nodded. 'I didn't mention it at that time, because it didn't seem relevant. But I also came across another reference to mistletoe, not connected with Druids. Apparently, mistletoe extract has been used since ancient times to treat many ailments. It has been shown, in laboratory experiments, to kill cancer cells and to affect the immune system. Animal studies have suggested that mistletoe may be useful in reducing the side effects of anti-cancer therapy like chemotherapy and radiation. And, it seems that mistletoe tea—made from European, not American, mistletoe—was used since ancient times as a sedative, and to control hysteria and other mental disturbances. It was also used to reduce symptoms associated with high blood pressure, including dizziness, headaches, loss of energy and irritability. It is believed that European mistletoe has the ability to reduce blood pressure and act as an antispasmodic and calming agent. It is used to promote sleep, ease anxiety, relieve panic attacks, headaches and improve concentration.'

'So you're saying that the association of the Druids with mistletoe is not accidental or mythological,' Patterson mused, 'and that they used mistletoe or a preparation from the leaves of the mistletoe plant to ensure that the Celts were not affected while the Romans, not having access to the medication, experienced the effects of the megalithic radiation.'

Colin nodded. 'Perhaps they served it up to the soldiers before they went into battle. The mistletoe potion would have had a calming effect on them, counteracting any effects of the waves from the stone structures.' He held out his hands. 'Look, this is just a theory.'

'But a plausible one,' Goldfeld said. 'The Druids were respected for their medications and potions—you told us that when you researched them. Perhaps their knowledge of herbs and plants was really good and this was just one kind of medication that they used?'

'It also ties in with their link to the Vedic people,' Shukla added. 'Remember that Vedic medicine, as propagated by Susruta and Caraka, was based on herbs. The Indian system of alternative medicine, Ayurveda, is based completely on herbal sources.'

'I'm curious about one thing,' Imran said. 'You said that selected sites had the weapon installed. And some sites were used for generating alpha waves while others would enhance the beta waves. I'm no physics expert but from what I recall of school physics, at these frequencies, you are talking about extremely long wavelengths. And long wavelengths require large transmitters. Granted that some of the stones are quite tall, but still, I'm not sure they would transmit these signals across such large distances.'

'Good point,' Vijay observed. 'And I think I can explain that. The wavelengths would, indeed, be very long—approximating the circumference of the earth, for example. And that would require a transmitter with a length of several kilometres. So you're spot on there. But just look at the landscape where all these structures are. Take Salisbury. The megalithic sites are within a few kilometres of each other. It is the same in Wales. In Orkney, too. In most cases, these sites are situated on hill tops and, in Orkney, some of them actually face each other. The only analogy I could think of was that of a transmitter and receiver system, in which the receiver also doubles up as a transmitter. So, the structure with the weapon transmits the signal; another structure picks it up and, through the piezoelectric effect, generates another signal which gets picked up by another site, and so on. The signal could travel huge distances this way. And if you look at the network of megalithic sites around the world, who knows if this signal could have been transmitted thousands of years ago, across distances of thousands of kilometres?'

'I have to sound a discordant note here,' Alice said, ruefully. 'As an archaeologist, I cannot let this pass. Almost all the megalithic sites are in ruins and could have been that way even two thousand years ago. The roofs of the mounds in Orkney were all broken in. You saw that for yourself. That doesn't make sense, if the weapon was being used in the manner we've just been discussing. This would require all the megalithic sites to be in their pristine state.'

'I have my own theory about that,' Vijay said. 'There's no scientific evidence to show exactly when the sites were abandoned. I know the accepted dates are around 2500 to 2000 B.C., depending on which site you are talking about. But how can you possibly date that? I believe that the sites were in working condition when Caesar invaded Britain. The Druids planned to retrieve the weapons and use them against the Romans.'

'But there were burials in the tombs,' Alice pointed out. 'Skeletons were found. Even at Stonehenge. How do you explain that if they were working machines to generate these mind control waves?'

Colin jumped in. 'Remember, I told you guys about the campaigns against the Druids in the first century A.D., first by Paulinus and then by Agricola?'

Everyone nodded.

'I've been thinking about this Agricola guy ever since I read about him. He seemed to be the sincere, committed, loyal type of Roman, dedicated to his Emperor. Which was fine as long as Vespasian was Emperor. But when Domitian came to the throne, he didn't like Agricola. In fact, from everything I read, the guy hated Agricola. He recalled him from Britain just as Agricola crushed the Druids in their final battle. I'm wondering if Agricola was the one who buried those coins in Inverness. After all, he went all the way there. Suppose Vespasian gave Agricola the coins with the instruction to find the hiding place of the weapon? We don't know that Caesar's secret had not survived down the line of the Emperors of Rome. It is possible that Domitian didn't know about what had transpired between Vespasian and Agricola, once the coins were out of Rome. I wouldn't be surprised if Agricola had managed to figure out that the weapon was hidden on the Orkney Islands but decided to bury the coins and go back because he didn't want Domitian to get his hands on the weapon.'

'Colin, that still doesn't explain the skeletons,' Alice protested.

'I was coming to that,' Colin said. 'I think that the Druids got wind of the fact that Agricola was coming for the weapon and they decided to destroy all the tombs on Orkney just in case. They knew they were doomed anyway. Why let their sites fall into enemy hands? Remember, no one, including the Druids, knew how to build these structures. The precise geometry, the careful alignments—this knowledge would have disappeared with the *Tuatha de Danann* centuries before. And the skeletons could just be a cover up; drama on the part of the Druids. What better way to keep people away from a dangerous weapon that can control minds than put a few dead people in there and create hype around a ritual centre for the dead? Who would dare go into those tombs, knowing that there were corpses decaying in there and the spirits of the dead floating around?'

102

Caesar's Secret

'So how was Caesar going to use the weapon?' Alice demanded. 'Where would he find the right kind of megalithic site in Rome? I know there are standing stones and other megalithic sites in Italy, but how would Caesar know which sites were the right ones for the weapon he found? And if the Druids didn't know how to build the structures, they couldn't teach him how to build one either.'

'Dee gave me the answer to that,' Vijay replied. 'She said that Caesar, in his diary, mentioned that he was going to look for the secret to building the right kind of structure in the Library of Alexandria.'

'But he burned down the Library,' Goldfeld pointed out. 'There's a lot of confusion about the Library, even speculation about whether it really existed or not, but many sources mention that it was burned down when Caesar tried to break the siege of Alexandria by the Egyptians, by burning their ships in the harbour. The fire spread from the ships to the docks and to buildings along the docks, including the Library.'

'Maybe I'm getting good at creating conspiracy theories,' Vijay laughed, 'but I think that, if you want to steal a national treasure—like the contents of the Library—the best way to do it would be to secret away its contents and then burn it down so no one would ever know that you've stolen anything.

I think that is what Caesar did. He spirited away the scrolls in the Library, probably put them on a ship to Rome before the siege, and then used the burning of the ships and buildings in Alexandria, including the Library, to cover his tracks. I'm quite impressed with the cunning of that man and wouldn't put this past him.'

'Given all that we now know about Caesar,' Alice said soberly, 'what you say could be likely.'

'We're digressing,' Patterson interjected. 'The mystery of the Library of Alexandria can wait. If Caesar's diary says he was going to look for the secret there, then let's take his word for it. What I want to know is how the weapon worked. I mean, how was it the source of the energy or power to generate the signals?'

'I can explain that,' Vijay answered. 'Once the weapon was activated, it generated acoustic waves which matched the resonant frequency of the structure it was installed in. These acoustic waves were converted, through the quartz crystals in the stone acting as a piezoelectric transducer, into the signals that we discussed earlier.'

'And how was the weapon activated?' Patterson pressed Vijay.

'Like I said, Dee didn't have a clue about the science. Everything I'm telling you is inferred from what she told me about the weapon.'

Imran grinned. 'But I think you have an idea of how the weapon was activated.'

'Actually, I do,' Vijay hid a grin. 'Given the importance of acoustics in this entire process of generating the signals, I think the key lies in sound. The weapon was activated by sound. I've always wondered how the weapons of the Mahabharata were operated by *mantras*. Perhaps the *mantras* were passwords for a voice-controlled security system that activated the weapons?

Or, as in this case, maybe the way the *mantras* were chanted created an acoustic wave at the resonant frequency of the device, which activated it. I think each device was built to create sound—acoustic waves—which were the same frequency as the resonant frequency of the stone structure in which it was installed. That would explain how each device would fit a specific structure. This would trigger the piezoelectric effect in the stones, generating the signal, as we've discussed earlier.'

'But that doesn't explain what happened with the helicopters,' Imran countered.

'No it doesn't,' Vijay admitted. 'But we can take an educated guess, based on the description provided by the prisms. Remember that the weapon was described as the "sceptre of light", not the "sceptre of sound". So, while it possibly generated sound, it also generated light. And, light being more visible and more impressive than sound, the name stuck. I couldn't figure this out until I remembered some recent experiments that have created voltage out of sound. You start with a device that contains a magnetic material to produce a spin current, using sound waves as an energy source. The spin current gets injected into a metal structure, which detects the spin current, and then by using the reverse spin Hall effect in the metal, the spin current can be converted into an electrical voltage. If a high voltage is produced with low amperage then a spark can result, which dissipates almost immediately, like a flash of lightning. The interesting thing is that the device itself can potentially produce both the sound waves and the voltage. Here's how it could work. The *mantra*, maybe combined with another acoustic source like drums, produces the sound waves that produce the initial voltage, which is then used to feed into a piezoelectric material within the device that produces sound waves leading to generation of a spin current and so on—the cycle continues. With the continuing generation of voltage, visible as arcs of lightning, the device could live up to its name of the "sceptre of light"'.

'And that's why they chose Mine Howe to hide the weapons,' Alice said. She had seen sketches of Mine Howe and Vijay had told them about the silence and the darkness in the chamber. 'The architecture of the site ensured that no sound could reach the weapons to trigger them off. The perfect hideaway.'

'I have a feeling that they were first stored in the main underground chamber, probably when they were in use,' Vijay observed, 'but they removed them to the hidden chamber when they decided to hide them away permanently.'

'No wonder the Order was so keen to get its hands on them,' Colin observed. 'They would be able to control the world with this technology. Even if the original stone circles and chambers are not functional, they could always build new ones using better materials and newer technology.'

'I still can't figure out which weapon from ancient times the term "sceptre of light" refers to,' Imran commented. 'I'm sure something like this would have been mentioned in some ancient text.'

Vijay shrugged. 'I haven't the foggiest idea,' he admitted. 'Nothing I've ever heard of corresponds to this description.'

'I think I can guess,' Shukla said slowly. He had been lost in thought ever since Vijay had started describing the science behind the weapon. 'There *is* a weapon mentioned in the ancient texts that might correspond to this description. Now that we've discussed the science behind it and the working of the weapon, it seems more obvious.'

All eyes turned to Shukla. What weapon was this?

103

Weapon of the gods

'This weapon is mentioned in the Mahabharata several times,' Shukla said. 'It is also mentioned in the Rig Veda. The Mahabharata describes it as a six-sided weapon. The Rig Veda describes it as a weapon with a hundred joints; a weapon with a thousand points. It is described as bright, hard, and—in more than one part of the Rig Veda — as made of iron.' He looked at the keen faces before him. 'It is called the *Vajra*. The Thunderbolt. The weapon of Indra. Moreover, in the Mahabharata it is said that Arjuna was given *Vajras*, which means that he was given more than one of these weapons.'

There was stunned silence at this revelation. This was more than anyone could have even conjectured. Yet, it made sense. The thunderbolt, common across mythologies as a weapon that created lightning and thunder.

'The woman didn't stand a chance,' Vijay said sombrely. 'In some of the experiments on the acoustics of the stone structures, it was found that thunder could set off the resonance in the air within the chambers as a result of what is known as Hemholtz Resonance—the same principle that causes a sound to be made when you blow across the mouth of a bottle. It is possible that the thunder and the sound of the helicopters' engines combined with the chop of the rotors could have triggered the resonant frequency of the *Vajras* the helicopters were carrying.'

They all digested this, thinking of the horrible fate of the people in the helicopters. Vijay was right. None of them stood a chance with a weapon as powerful as the mighty thunderbolt of the legends.

'All right, folks,' Patterson said. 'Good job, everyone. This round goes to us. But be warned. The Order will not be sleeping. They will have figured out by now that there is an organised opposition to them, which didn't exist earlier. The Nine were passive and didn't really go after the Order—they were more interested in defence than attack.'

Imran nodded. 'We already have operations in place, as a result of the task force morphing into a full-fledged covert organisation. I can't brief you on these operations now, but you will get to know in due course.'

'And,' Patterson added, 'I have great pleasure in inviting Dr Goldfeld and Ms Turner, along with Dr Shukla to be a part of the new organisation. Given the fact that we will need to delve into archaeological mysteries, their expertise will be valuable. I'm happy to announce that they have all accepted my invitation.'

Vijay and Colin cheered at this news. This team had gone through so much in the last one year that they had all become close friends. It was good to know that they would be working together to defeat a common enemy.

Patterson dismissed the meeting, promising them that they would get their next brief soon. There was much work to be done and the sooner they started, the better.

Vijay had mixed feelings. While he was elated at their having bested the Order this time, he also felt a deep sorrow. He had knowingly sent a human being to her death. He had known what would happen in the helicopter when the weapons were being transported away from Orkney. And, while he could console himself that he had legitimately tried to warn Dee of the danger, he couldn't get away from the fact that he had deliberately ensured that she would disregard the warning.

It was a cold-blooded decision. And he felt sick with himself for having done that.

He tried to console himself. Radha last year and now Harry had both been killed in cold blood by the Order. And he had failed to deliver on his promise to find Radha's body and retrieve it from the clutches of the Order.

Did that really justify what he had done?

He knew one thing, though. Over the last two years, he had changed.

Vijay only hoped that he was not becoming like the people who were a part of the Order. Not afraid to kill. Not afraid to send people to their death. Not worried about sacrificing lives as long as the end goal was met.

On the other hand, he reflected, did he really have a choice?

Epilogue

2002 B.C.

Near the River Indus, modern-day Pakistan

Ninus, upon his death, had bequeathed Semiramis the throne of Assyria. With her son by Ninus still a minor, Semiramis had begun what would turn out to be a reign that would vie with the fame of Ninus.

The reports of her lasciviousness had shocked Sthavarapati. But it wasn't these accounts of how she slept with any of her warriors whom she found attractive that surprised him. He knew that she would not wish to re-marry for fear of losing the power that she had gained for herself. Neither did it surprise him that these warriors were put to death after she received favours from them.

The true surprise was how Semiramis leveraged her position and situation to fulfil her long-standing ambition to elevate herself beyond the clutches of society.

Stories reached his ears of how the people of Assyria had begun revering Ninus as a god. He was told about the common belief that the son of Semiramis had been conceived through the spirit of Ninus after his death. And he learned of how the Assyrians had, believing that Ninus had re-incarnated as his own son, begun worshipping Semiramis as a goddess. For, they reasoned, if she was the mother of a god, wasn't she more powerful than the god himself? He heard about the legend that had spread about her birth—that Semiramis was the daughter of an unholy liaison between the goddess Derceto and a Syrian, and was brought up by the doves of the goddess when she was abandoned, only to be found by Simmas. Associations with Ishtar, the Akkadian goddess, were being created and cemented. Sthavarapati knew that the victories that Semiramis achieved in Persia, Egypt and Ethiopia were the result of the conviction of her soldiers that they were following a goddess. Her licentious ways had already firmly established her association with Ishtar, the goddess of love and fertility; and her victories in battle reinforced that association.

For, Ishtar was also the goddess of war.

Her sign became the moon and Sthavarapati knew that the fifteen-year-old girl who had left the lands of the Indus had finally achieved what she had yearned for all her life.

He had, therefore, never believed there was anything more she could do that could surprise him.

Until today.

When the messenger from Semiramis had ridden into his camp, asking for a conference, he had been surprised. Very surprised.

And confused. What was happening? Where had Semiramis been the last one week? And what did she want now?

Sthavarapati instinctively knew that she wasn't asking to meet him to negotiate a surrender of arms or discuss peace. But he couldn't guess what she was planning now. He found it hard to believe that she had actually unearthed the celestial weapon that she had claimed to be seeking.

So, when she had met him with a small group of soldiers, and no army in sight, he had realised that she possessed something that gave her strength. And confidence.

Semiramis had revealed the contents of the wagon with a dramatic flourish. The priests accompanying Sthavarapati were, like the king himself, flummoxed.

Not only had Semiramis proven the ancient legends true, but she had also found what the legends had spoken of.

A powerful celestial device that would give its owner the power of the gods.

The *Vajra*.

And it was now in the possession of the Assyrian queen.

Semiramis smiled, observing Sthavarapati's reaction. But it was a sad smile. There was no happiness there that Sthavarapati could discern.

'Leave this here,' Sthavarapati requested. 'It belongs to us. To this land.' He appealed to her with pleading eyes. 'To you. You, too, belong to this land.'

Semiramis shook her head. 'I don't belong here anymore,' she said. Her smile was gone and her face looked weary and worn. 'And I cannot leave this here. I will go back to Nineveh today. And I will take this treasure with me. I must. I have made a promise.'

'Surely no promise can be more powerful than your loyalty to the land of your birth?' Sthavarapati persisted.

Semiramis looked the king in his eye. 'News has reached me from Nineveh that my son is conspiring to overthrow me when I return. I have already suppressed a rebellion by two sons.' Sorrow showed in her eyes. 'They had planned to kill me, goaded on by the eunuch Satibaras, and I had to execute them. But, this time, it is a prophecy that has come to pass. I must return and abdicate in favour of my son.' She compressed her lips, trying to hide her emotions.

'You can stay here,' Sthavarapati argued. 'Send your army back to Nineveh. Let them announce to your son that you have decided to return to the land of your birth.'

'And destroy everything that I have created so carefully?' There was still fire in the queen. 'No. I will not give up everything I have worked so hard to achieve. The only way is to go back. And, after abdicating, disappear.' The shadow of a smile flickered across her face. 'That way, I will truly become the stuff of legends. A goddess, gone back to the land of the gods. Immortal. Living in the memories of men forever.'

'Then return to Nineveh but come back here after that,' Sthavarapati would not give up. The priests with him wondered why he was being so insistent. They had been listening to the conversation with great bewilderment. The two mighty enemies were conversing as if they had known each other their entire life.

'I cannot do that,' Semiramis replied, with a sigh.

'Why not?' Sthavarapati wanted to know.

'Here, I will be a mortal. A disgraced queen, overthrown by her own son. A prodigal who has returned without achieving anything.' Semiramis took a step forward, her hands outstretched, as if she were going to clasp Sthavarapati's hands. Then, abruptly, she checked herself, stepped back and withdrew her hands. 'More than that, I have given my word. The priests of the island have helped me all these years. It is time for me to repay them. They need this.' She indicated the contents of the wagon. 'And I have promised to bring this back to them. I will go with them to their island, where I will live out the rest of my years as a goddess to be worshipped as part of their rituals. And, when I die, I will be buried secretly in an unmarked grave, so that my legend and worship live forever.'

Sthavarapati pondered this for a few moments. 'I understand,' he said, finally. 'And I will not stop you from achieving what you desire. May the gods be with you.' He glanced once more at the wagon. 'A word of caution. You know the legends. This is a dangerous thing to possess. The priests must use it, if they will, with care.'

'I know,' Semiramis replied. 'Another good reason for me to go with them.' She half turned to go.

'One more thing,' Sthavarapati extended one hand as if trying to hold her back. 'You may not wish to die in your native land. But we will value the knowledge of where your tomb stands. We are proud that you are a daughter of our kingdom.'

Semiramis' eyes glistened.

Were those tears? Sthavarapati wondered.

'My final resting place must stay concealed forever,' Semiramis countered. 'But this much I will promise you. You will have half the knowledge of where I rest. The other half will remain with the priests. And neither of you will know the language in which the story is told.'

She approached Sthavarapati and whispered something in his ear. Then, she turned and, without a backward glance, strode away to mount her horse. Her soldiers followed.

Sthavarapati looked upon the departing riders with sorrowful eyes. The priests gathered around him, curious, wondering. What had Semiramis whispered to Sthavarapati? What great secret had she shared with him?

But Sthavarapati would not tell them. Only a few people in his court knew the true secret of Semiramis. And only they could have guessed the parting words that Semiramis had whispered to him.

She had said, 'Goodbye, Father.'

LAST NOTES

As is my wont, I've provided additional information on the science, history and mythology in *The Secret of the Druids*.I hope you will find this section helpful and that it will enrich your reading experience.

While writing *The Secret of the Druids,* I read over one hundred books and articles—too many to list down here since that would run into several pages. I have mentioned only a few key books in these notes. In case you wish to access more information about these facts, please register, or, if you are already a member, log on to The Quest Club where I have included more details (including photographs).

THE SCIENCE

Earthquakes and strange lights: The mystery of the strange lights accompanying the earthquake in the Prologue, at Cairnpapple Hill, which so amazed and stupefied McGregor and his men, is rooted in very interesting news reports suggesting a scientific basis for these sightings. It is a fact that strange flashes of light have been witnessed around earthquakes throughout history. Earlier, these lights were attributed to birds, planes, even UFOs, or—as in the case of McGregor and his crew—to the devil or an ancient goddess! Recent research, however, has revealed that these lights are caused by electrical properties of certain rocks in specific settings. Essentially, scientists believe that the tension caused by the movement in the Earth's tectonic plates (that cause the earthquake) creates an electronic charge which turns into light when it reaches the surface. Even now, scientific studies are being conducted to try and understand this mysterious phenomenon.

Piezoelectricity and the piezoelectric effect: I won't go into too much technical detail here because Vijay has already explained the piezoelectric effect quite well in the book. Suffice it to say that the piezoelectric effect does explain the flashes of lightning that were the nemesis of Dee and her henchmen. Piezoelectricity was discovered by Jacques and Pierre Curie in 1880 during studies on quartz crystals. A more detailed explanation of the science (with diagrams) will be available on The Quest Club for those who want to know more. For the purpose of this note, it is scientifically accurate to state that quartz crystals and, therefore, stones which contains these crystals, are perfectly capable of generating the piezoelectric effect.

Resonance: While Vijay has already explained this, I will provide a few more details for those readers who, like me, were not science students in secondary school or college. The root of the word "resonance" is Latin and means to "resound". Many musical instruments produce sound because of resonance. This is how wind instruments or brass instruments produce music. These instruments are simply metal containers (the hollow metal tube) with a column of air inside. When we blow into the mouthpiece of the instrument, the vibration of our lips against the mouthpiece produces a range of frequencies. One of these frequencies matches one of the natural frequencies of the air column inside the metal tube, forcing the air inside the tube into resonant vibrations. It is these vibrations that produce the sound we hear in the form of music.

Effect of microwaves on physiology and brain functioning: While many experiments have been conducted and research undertaken into the very real effects of microwaves on physiology and the human (and animal) brain, there is a commercial aspect to this controversy leading to a clear divide in the opinions of people. Thus, this remains a very controversial subject.

I will start with a brief introduction to Schumann Resonance, which refers to naturally occurring rhythmic signals that travel around the globe, in the cavity between the planet's surface and the ionosphere. These electromagnetic standing waves, discovered by Professor WO Schumann of the Technical University of Munich in

1952, were found to have a frequency of 7.83 Hz, which is similar to the alpha waves of the human brain. This is the frequency that controls performance, stress, anxiety, creativity, and the immune system. Circadian rhythm experiments were conducted by the Max Planck Institute to determine the association of Schumann resonance with human physiology. Volunteers were placed underground, in this experiment, where Schumann Resonance was absent and only the transverse magnetic fields from the earth were present. These volunteers reported headaches, sickness and their circadian rhythms were disrupted. When the 7.83 Hz frequency was reintroduced, these complaints disappeared. The effect of ELF (extremely low frequency) waves on the Romans, as described in this book, is a very real possibility based on real science, even though this book is a work of fiction.

Mistletoe and its therapeutic properties: A study by German scientists has shown that the mistletoe plant can halt the growth of malignant melanoma, when it is combined with the diabetes drug Rosiglitazone. This discovery was made at the University Hospital of Hamburg, where it was shown that this combination reduced the rate of growth of cancer cells by upto 79 per cent. An article in the Daily Mail, UK, on 28th December, 2010, also reported that it is believed that mistletoe helps the body's immune system fight tumours and speeds up the disposal of the toxic substances left in the body by chemotherapy.

While the use of mistletoe may not be yet approved for the treatment of cancer, multiple institutes of repute, and centres for research do concur that it may be useful in alleviating the side effects of chemotherapy and radiation based on studies of its effect on animals. In fact, The National Cancer Institute in the U.S states that mistletoe extract has been shown to kill cancer cells in the laboratory and to affect the immune system.

It is also true that Pliny the Elder is credited with creating the belief about the tradition of the Druids with respect to their reverence for mistletoe and the gathering ceremony described in this book. Did they use mistletoe tea as an antidote, as mentioned in this book? That is my invention and is pure fiction. Interestingly, a study did reveal that drinking black tea showed an increase in alpha waves , indicating that ingredients in some beverages can have a measured impact on brainwaves.

The dating of megalithic sites: A quick word on this subject because this, too, is a controversial topic. Writers like Graham Hancock and others have questioned traditional dating techniques and, with them, the dates traditionally ascribed to megalithic sites. The conversation between Alice and Vijay in this book regarding the dating of Stonehenge and other megalithic sites mirrors a very real conversation I had with an archaeologist when I was trying to understand the merits of dating stone monuments.

Creating electricity out of sound waves: For the experiment Vijay refers to, please see this video: https://www.youtube.com/watch?v=9ODOZggDIFI

The Acoustics of megalithic sites: When I first thought of the theory outlined in this book—how megalithic sites could have been used as generators of electromagnetic waves, using sound waves as a trigger—I had based it on the extensive research I had done on the piezoelectric effect, resonance and the nature of the stones used in megalithic monuments (for more details of how I came up with this theory—an interesting story in itself—please log on to The Quest Club). At that time, I had no idea that there had been so much research conducted on the acoustics of megalithic sites or that there was actually a branch of archaeology dealing with this, called Archaeoacoustics. When I finally turned to validate the scientific principles with actual research on the stone monuments, I was amazed to find that there was data available that established that many megalithic sites actually had acoustic properties. None of the studies proposed the theory that I have outlined in this book—that is fiction and a product of my imagination.

Archaeoacoustics is the study of sound in archaeological contexts and is carried out by exploring natural sounds and acoustics at monuments or by using electronic instrumentation to explore the acoustic properties of a monument. It is also interesting that many such studies indicate that the acoustic properties of ancient structures may influence human brain function, stimulating an area of the brain that is believed to relate to mood, empathy and social behaviour.

Magnetometry: Soil is created through the build up of material resulting from all kinds of past activity, one of which is burning—either accidental or deliberate—in a specific location or across an area (forest or crop). The magnetic properties of the surrounding soil are changed permanently by burning, through the alteration of the magnetism of miniscule iron particles. If the soil is moved (or a stone embedded in the soil is removed) through activity such as ploughing, earthwork construction or filling in a ditch, this activity can be traced by tracking variations in soil magnetism against the background of the earth's magnetic field. An area in which the soil has a slightly different magnetic orientation to the surrounding earth can indicate the presence of sub-surface archaeology. Archaeological features show up as either higher or lower readings. Deposits with a lot of burnt material are usually higher. Stone walls are usually lower. Magnetometry is the technique of measuring and mapping these patterns of magnetism in the soil that can reveal buried features like ditches and stone structures now underground (including foundations of walls). However, where there is non-archaeological magnetic contamination such as metal fencing, iron refuse or traces of extensive modern burning, magnetometry does not work.

THE HISTORY

The Library of the Nine: Strictly speaking, this is not history or even a legend. But I'm including this in the History section because of the association with Asoka the Great, a historical figure, who is said to have founded the Brotherhood of the Nine Unknown Men. The legend of the Nine (as mentioned in many books and websites) says that they wrote nine books on different topics (more details at The Quest Club). However, I never felt comfortable using the legend in its commonly accepted form and decided to create my own version of it when I wrote *The Mahabharata Secret* in 2006. In my version, Asoka the Great created the secret brotherhood to hide away a discovery, a secret that he didn't want the world to know about, because were it to fall in the wrong hands it would spell destruction for humankind. Part of this discovery was an ancient secret from the Mahabharata. The other part of the discovery, in the version of the legend that I created, was a storehouse of knowledge—the Library of the Nine, a vast repository of scientific knowledge from ancient times that was discovered by the Nine/Asoka, which they were sworn to protect through the centuries. Since I invented the concept of the Library of knowledge, it was a natural extension to include, as part of the knowledge in the Library, the blueprints of the megalithic sites.

Julius Caesar in Egypt: The timelines and events described in this book regarding Julius Caesar's presence in Egypt are historically accurate. Of course, the conversations between Caesar and his centurion, and between Caesar and Cleopatra are all imaginary. I thought it might help if I shed light on the events that preceded Julius Caesar's presence in Egypt. As explained in the book, Caesar created an alliance with Crassus and Pompey in 59 B.C. This was the world's first triumvirate. Pompey also married Caesar's daughter Julia. In 54 B.C., Julia died and in 52 B.C., Pompey was elected as the only consul. This weakened the alliance with Caesar and led to the two men becoming bitter rivals. Caesar had realised by now that control of his army was critical to his survival, since Pompey, in Rome, had an army at his command. Caesar also knew that, if he ever returned to Rome as an ordinary citizen, his enemies in the Senate would have him imprisoned. In 50 B.C., the Roman Senate passed a resolution that required Caesar to relinquish his command of his army. A brief period of politicking followed where Pompey and Caesar, through their proxies, attempted to ensure that they did not have to give up control of their respective armies unless the other man did so simultaneously. In 49 B.C., Caesar brought his army to the border of Cisalpine Gaul and camped on the banks of the Rubicon river, which was the boundary of his province. This eventually gave rise to the saying "to cross the Rubicon". He decided to take his army across the river and confront his opposition, thus violating a law that prohibited a provincial governor from commanding troops outside his dominion, and effectively declaring the start of a civil war in the Roman Republic. Pompey and the consuls fled Rome and took refuge in Brundisium. Caesar marched against Pompey's generals in Spain and defeated them. He next pursued Pompey into Greece where he finally routed him in the battle at Pharsalus in August of 48 B.C. Pompey fled to Egypt, hoping to find refuge there since he had once donated soldiers and gold to the Egyptian ruler Ptolemy XII. But Ptolemy XII had recently died, leaving his four children to fight for the throne. The young king, Ptolemy XIII, was now on the throne but the real power lay with Pothinus, his guardian, and Pompey was murdered on his arrival in Alexandria. When Caesar landed in Alexandria, Pothinus was openly insolent and insulted Caesar. Cleopatra saw her chance and arranged for a secret meeting with Caesar. Plutarch narrates the well known story of how Cleopatra had herself smuggled into the palace in a carpet (or in a sleeping bag, depending on which translation you read), which was unrolled to reveal her in all her beauty. Caesar, charmed by her courage and charisma, or smitten by her beauty, immediately decided to reconcile Cleopatra and Ptolemy and have them rule Egypt together. At a banquet to celebrate the reconciliation, Pothinus conspired with Achillas to kill Caesar, who learned about the plot. After he successfully secured the harbour of Alexandria, Caesar had Pothinus executed. Achillas was later killed by Arsinoe, Cleopatra's sister, who also had amibitions to the throne. Ptolemy XIII later drowned in a battle with the Romans, while Arsinoe was taken prisoner and paraded in Rome when Caesar returned after the war.

The *Commentarii de Bello Gallico*: All the facts mentioned about the *Commentaries* are historically accurate, except for the ninth book, which is fiction. The eight books that make up the *Commentaries* are:

Book I: *The Helvetian War and the War with Ariovistus*

Book II: *The War with the Belgian Confederacy*

Book III: *The Alpine Campaign and War with the Veneti*

Book IV: *The Campaign against the Germans and the first Invasion of Britain*

Book V: *The Second Invasion of Britain and Rebellion in Northern Gaul*

Book VI: *The Second Passage of the Rhine*, with some notes on the Druids and the remarkable animals found in the Hercynian forest

Book VII: *The War with Vercingetorix*

Book VIII: *The Supplement of Aulus Hirtius*

Before the advent of printing, copies were made by hand, many of them in monastaries in Europe, especially France. These are our primary sources for Caesar's work, since the original is lost. All extant manuscripts were catalogued by Virginia Brown in the 1970s. There are three manuscripts from the 9th century, and the others are generally from the 11th century onwards.

Semiramis: While I've included Semiramis under the History section, she really is not a historical figure. Or, at least, if there was a historical Semiramis, there is no clear consensus on who she was. The story of Semiramis narrated by Goldberg in Chapter 14 and the events described in Chapter 31 pertaining specifically to her marriage to Onnes, and subsequently Ninus (including the Bactrian adventure) are part of the legend described in the surviving books by Diodorus Siculus, the Greek writer from the first century B.C.—*Bibiothēkē*. Diodorus Siculus (based on his own claims) borrowed the essentials of the story from the Persian history by Ctesias. However, this is a legend that is not taken very seriously by historians—especially the explanation for Semiramis' birth and death.

If you have read my earlier books, you are familiar with my penchant for taking existing legends and remodelling them to create my own versions. Likewise, I have changed the legend of Semiramis in places to suit my purpose. While Strabrobates is mentioned by Diodorus, the relationship I have shown between Semiramis and the Indian king, also known as Sthavarapati, is my invention. Similarly, while the legend of Semiramis talks about her journey through the Makran desert, there is no mention of a divine weapon in any of the legends I have come across. Neither does Semiramis leave her army for a week in search of this weapon. In the legend, Semiramis is very much part of the battle with Sthavarapati and even sustains grievous injuries from an arrow and a javelin of the Indian king. Finally, according to Nicolaus of Damascus, a Greek historian, the episode of her sons (by Onnes) Hyspates and Hydaspes conspiring against Semiramis occurred while she was returning from India, whereas, I have shown this episode happening *before* she came to India. Their fate, however, is not described by Nicolaus because the fragment of his work describing this event breaks off after Semiramis confronts her sons and accuses them of conspiring to kill her. However, from the fragments of Cephalion, a Roman historian, we can gather that Semiramis executed her sons for their crime of plotting against her, as she discloses to Sthavarapati in the Epilogue. Finally the historical references to Semiramis are based on factual attempts by historians to ascribe a specific timeline for her existence as a historical figure.

Cicero: Marcus Tullius Cicero was born in 106 B.C. and died on December 7, 43 B.C. He was an active voice in the Roman civil wars, often speaking out openly against Julius Caesar. Interestingly, Caesar had invited Cicero to join the political alliance of Caesar, Crassus and Pompey since Cicero considered it unconstitutional. Cicero disapproved of Caesar's dictatorship and, in an interview with Caesar in 49 B.C. told him of his intention to propose in the Senate that Caesar should give up the war with Pompey. In addition, Quintus Cicero was also a historical figure exactly as described in the book. His letters to his brother, Marcus Cicero, mentioning Semiramis, the Druids and the weapon, of course, are fiction.

Julius Caesar in Gaul: The details about Caesar's years in Gaul and his exploits there in Chapters 8 and 43 are historically accurate. To summarise:

58 B.C.: Caesar defeated the Helvetii, a Celtic tribe of Switzerland, and then the Teutonic tribe of the Suebi led by Ariovistus.

57 B.C.: Caesar subdued the Belgae—the Belgic tribes in northern Gaul.

56 B.C.: Caesar annihilated the Veneti, a Celtic tribe of Southern Brittany.

55 B.C.: Caesar defeated two Germanic tribes which had invaded

Gaul and then crossed the Rhine to invade Germany. He also invaded Britain for the first time.

54 B.C.: Caesar returned to invade Britain for the second time. A serious revolt brewed in northeastern Gaul and Caesar stamped it out with a firm hand.

52 B.C.: Vercingetorix began uniting the tribes of Trans-alpine Gaul and started cutting off the supplies of the Roman forces. Caesar's forces attempted to capture Gergovia, where Vercingetorix was camped but suffered great losses and failed in their endeavour. Subsequently, Caesar attacked Vercingetorix in Alesia, northwest of Dijon, and captured him.

51 B.C.: Caesar besieged the Celtic rebels holed up in Uxellodunum and finally defeated them after cutting off their water supply. Caesar ordered his soldiers to cut off the hands of the rebels.

50 B.C.: Caesar organised the rule of his conquered territories in Gaul. Peace prevailed finally.

Divitiacus: He is a real historical figure, mentioned by name, by Quintus Cicero in one of his letters to his brother. Caesar never mentions Divitiacus by name but all the details provided about Divitiacus are historically accurate and based on information provided in several academic research studies on the Druids and Gaul. Of course, the conversations between Caesar and Divitiacus are fictional.

Caesar's invasions of Britain: All the historical facts presented in this book about Caesar's two invasions of Britain and the Roman outlook on Britain, in Chapters 43, 46, 48, 57, 65, 78 and 86 are based on documented historical accounts. The drums in Chapter 57 are fictional (though that particular battle is not) and the Quintus Codex is also fictional.

Suetonius Paulinus: After Julius Caesar left Britain in 54 B.C., never to return, the gaze of Rome, inexplicably, never turned back to Britain—as a land to be conquered—until 43 A.D., when Emperor Claudius decided that Britain was worthy of Roman attention, and sent Aulus Plautius to invade it for the first time in almost one hundred years. Emperor Caligula (37 to 41 A.D.) did plan an invasion of Britain in 40 A.D. but his army refused and the invasion was abandoned. In 60 A.D., General Suetonius Paulinus arrived in Britain, during the reign of Nero, with a clear objective of destroying the Druids who retreated to Anglesey. Paulinus invaded Anglesey and finally defeated the Druids and razed Castell Ior to the ground. In Britain, Paulinus was accompanied by a young officer called Gnaeus Julius Agricola.

Gnaeus Julius Agricola: He returned to Rome with Paulinus and married Domitia Decidiana. He was appointed *Quaestor* of Asia and later became Tribune, followed by *praetorship*. After Nero's death, Galba, the new emperor, chose him to check on treasures stolen from the temples, in which he achieved a lot of success, according to Tacitus. In 69 A.D., Agricola learned of Vespasian's bid to become emperor and joined him. His reward was being made commander of the 20th Legion in Britain, after which he was appointed governor of Aquitania. Finally, in 78 A.D., he was sent to Britain and immediately set about subduing the Ordovice tribe and establishing control of North wales, where he established the fort of Segontium just outside Caernarfon. He next marched upon the island of Anglesey and defeated the remaining Druids. He then consolidated his hold on northern England, marched into Scotland and established a line of forts from the Firth of Forth to the Firth of Clyde. Interestingly, Tacitus says here, 'The enemy had been pushed into what was virtually another island.' Was this a reference to the Orkney Islands? And, yes, Agricola did go all the way to the Moray Firth and Inverness.

The Library of Alexandria: Who destroyed the Library of Alexandria? And why? This is an enduring mystery. There are enough clues, though, that Julius Caesar was the culprit and I have used these indications from several ancient texts—including *Civil Wars* by Julius Caesar, *The Alexandrian War* by Aulus Hirtius, *The Pharsalia (Civil War)* by Lucan, *Life of Caesar* by Plutarch, *Epitome* by Florus, *Geography* by Strabo and *Roman History* by Dio Cassius—and historical records to create my theory that Caesar had the Library of Alexandria burned because he stole the manuscripts and shipped them away. Destroying the Library was the best way to conceal the theft. Irrespective of the historical facts, once again, I decided to create a legend of my own about Caesar's motives and actions in burning down the Library of Alexandria.

Octagonal Prisms: These were used as media to describe, through inscriptions, reigns of kings, important events, rituals and battles. There are several such prisms, made of clay, in the British Museum, and I based the prisms in the book on these artefacts. Photographs of the actual prisms are available at The Quest Club.

The Aedui: They were a Celtic tribe of central Gaul (occupying most of present-day Burgundy). They were Roman allies since 121 B.C. and were awarded the title of "brothers". In 60 B.C., they were defeated by Ariovistus, as described in this book, and appealed to Rome for help. The Aedui supported Julius Caesar. In 48 B.C., the Aedui elite, increasingly Romanised, became the first Gallic community to be allowed to provide senators for Rome. (source: Encyclopaedia Britannica).

The Inverness Hoard and Roman coins minted in Alexandria: This is a fictional discovery, inspired by the true-life mystery of the Fetter Lane hoard. In 1908, workmen excavating foundations for a house in Fetter Lane, in the City of London, unearthed 46 coins in a pot. This hoard was purchased by the Reverend FD Ringrose who also published an account in 1911, describing the coins. In 1914, the coins were bequeathed to the British Museum, by which time the pot had disappeared. The hoard remains a mystery. The coins in this hoard were all minted in Alexandria between 58 A.D. and 284 A.D. Coins had first been minted in Alexandria under the Ptolemaic dynasty (c 312-30 B.C.), which continued after Egypt became a Roman province in 30 B.C. However, coins in Alexandria were initially made of debased silver before declining into a mainly copper alloy coinage. These coins did not form part of the official Roman denomination system but circulated in the eastern Mediterranean. Coins used in Britannia were from official Roman mints. The mystery behind the Fetter Lane hoard is this: why were these Alexandrian coins brought to Britain where they formed no part of the currency system? The gold coins minted in Alexandria, depicted in this book, are also fictional, but the mystery of the Fetter Lane hoard has been captured, and explained, in the case of the Inverness Hoard.

THE MYTHOLOGY

Ishtar: Was an Akkadian/Babylonian goddess of healing, fertility and war. She was often depicted with a bow, quiver and sword, riding a lioness. Her symbol was the dove—another link with Semiramis. The Akkadian Ishtar is also associated with the planet Venus.

Tuatha de Danann: Were a race of people who achieved mythical status after being deified by later generations. Their name means "people of the goddess Danu". They were reputed to have come to Ireland from the Northern World. Some have suggested a Middle Eastern origin for them, or at least an association with the Middle East. Their name is associated with the Goddess Dana or Danu and they were identified with an intellectual class, the Druids, who were trained in religious, legal and astronomical skills among others. Their system was later adopted by the Celts. Several Celtic scholars believe that Druidism in its most basic form was imposed on the Celts by the earlier megalithic populations of Europe. I used this analysis as the basis for the theory that the Tuatha de Danann were the megalithic builders who used the *vajra* in their stone monuments and created Druidism which was then passed down to the Celts. Needless to say, this theory is fictional.

Gwydion ap Don: The Welsh *Triads of the Island of Britain* tell the story of a Druid called Gwydion ap Don who is introduced as a "master of the movements of the heavens". He is said to be buried near the Welsh town of Caernarfon, which I visited, under a "Stone of Enigmas". In *Uriel's Machine* by Christopher Knight & Robert Lomas, the authors are told by a Welsh historian that the name Gwydion means: man of learning, Druid, magician, philosopher, wise man or even scientist; and there are older meanings—giant, monster, wizard, sorcerer or woodland deity. "Ap" means son of, so Gwydion was the son of Don. In the *Mabinogion*, an old collection of Welsh legends, Don is the mother of a group of children who are known in myth as the Children of Light or the Lords of Light, of which Gwydion was the eldest and renowned as an astronomer and a "master of light". He is also described as "one of the men of science". Celtic scholars consider Don to be a variant of the name Danu, who is the Irish mother of the sacred tribe of the Tuatha de Danann. (source: *Uriel's Machine*).

The shlokas from the Mahabharata: All the Sanskrit shlokas in this book are real and original and taken from the M.N. Dutt translation of The Mahabharata. The English translations of each shloka are also from the same source.

Pronunciation Key

Reading gives so much more pleasure when one knows the pronunciations of strange words, especially words in a different language, when one encounters them in a book. Since this book has many names in a range of languages including Welsh, Scottish, Greek, Classical Latin and French, I thought it would be useful to include a glossary for the pronunciation of these names of places and people. I have tried my best to provide the best phonetic guide, but I will request you to bear in mind that expressing the phonetics in English, and in words, is often very difficult since the original pronunciation has nuances that may not be captured in this manner. Nevertheless, here you are…

NAME	PRONUNCIATION
Achillas	A - **kill** - ass
Aedui	**Aye** - doo -ee
Anglesey	**Angle** - see
Barclodiad y Gawres	Bark - **lod** - yah - uh - **gow** - res
Belgae	**Bell** - jee
Bellovaci	Bell - oh - **hah** - see
Broch	Brock
Brodgar	**Broad** - yeur
Bryn Celli Ddu	**Brin keth** - lee… thee
Cairnpapple	**K - air** - rrn Papple
Cassivellaunus	**Cassy** - vel - **aw** - nus

Celts	Kelt
Cicero	**Kick** - kair - oh (Classical Latin) **Sis**- a - row (English)
Commentarii de Bello Gallico	Kaw -mmen - **tari** Dee **Bel**- low- **Gaa** - liko
Ctesias	**Tee** - zee - us
Danu	**Daa** – noo
Diodorus Siculus	Die - oh - **door** - us **Sick** - you - liss
Diogenes Laertius	Die - **a** - gin - eez Lay - **ur** - she - us
Divitiacus	**Di** - vee - tee - **aa** - ko - us
Dumnorix	**Dyum** - know - ree
Galatae	**Gal** - a - tay
Gnaeus Julius	**Nee** - us **Joo** - lee - us
Agricola	Uh - **grik** - uh - luh
Gwydionap Don	**Gwid** - yon Aap Don
Helvetii	Hel - **vee** - shee - ahy
Maes Howe	Mayz - **how**
Mid Howe	Mid - **how**
Mine Howe	Mine - **how**
Ninus	**Nine** - us
Ninyas	**Nin** - yus
Onnes	**Ons**
Orgetorix	Awr - **jet** - uh - riks
Quadrireme	**Kwod** - ruh - reem
Quinquereme	Kwin - kwi - **reem**
Rousay	**Row** (rhymes with cow) - see
Semiramis	Si - **mee** - ruh - miss, *though* Semi - **ram** - is *also seems acceptable*
Sequani	**So** - caan - ee

St. Gildas de Rhuys	**Saan** - jildaas - **doh**rwees
Suebi	**Sway** - bee
Suetonius Paulinus	Sway - **toe** - nyus Poul - **ee** - nus
Taversoe Tuick	Tai - **ver** - sow **Too** - ack
Tuatha de Danann	**Too** - uh - huh Day **Daah**-nuh-n. The "Too" is like the Hindi "tu"
Wiltshire	**Wilt** - sheer

Acknowledgements

A book is never the result of the effort of a single person. While a writer may toil in solitary confinement, nothing can be accomplished without the support and help of others.

I know for certain that none of my books would have been successful if it had not been for the unstinted love and support of my wife Sharmila and my daughter Shaynaya. This is especially true of this book, where, for the first time, I stayed up several nights, writing and researching into the early hours of the morning and disrupted our normal household routines. Not only did they look up sites in the UK which could help me in my research and accompanied me to many of the locations, but they were also most understanding when I decided to spend more than a week travelling by myself to research additional locations in the UK.

Sharmila and Artika Bakshi were, as usual, my first draft readers, reading and cross-checking facts, locations and historical references to ensure that I stayed accurate.

I am grateful to my schoolmate and friend, Arjendu Pattanayak, Professor of Physics at Carleton College, Minnesota, who spent a lot of time fielding my (silly) questions on the science in this book, patiently explaining concepts in physics that I had left far behind me in school and pointing out the inaccuracies and implausible aspects of my hypothesis so that the science in this book was correct and supported by scientific evidence. His help, and endorsement of the plausibility of the scientific hypothesis I have presented in this book in no way implies that he necessarily agrees with any of my theories, applications or interpretation of the laws of physics and their correlation with the Mahabharata.

I owe a lot to the archaeologists and guides who accompanied me on personalised tours of many of the megalithic sites that I visited while researching for this book. Not all the sites finally made it into the plot (I visited over forty in the UK) but the field research helped enrich the final story. I would like to mention Dave Lawrence, who runs Orkney Archaeological Tours, Kirkwall, in particular. Dave is a professional archaeologist living in Orkney and he also runs a tour company that offers genuine archaeological tours. He gamely spent a wet, rainy, squelchy day with me in Orkney, crawling through tunnels, burial chambers and the amazing but mysterious shaft at Mine Howe that is part of the book. He answered all my questions patiently, including the ones that challenged archaeological traditions, and was a cornucopia of knowledge about the Orkney Islands. Two other gentlemen in the UK who also accompanied me on personal tours of archaeological sites are David Hutchison of Heritage Holidays, and Patrick Macguire of Rousay Tours. David spent a day with me visiting the Wiltshire sites and demonstrated his expansive knowledge, which was invaluable for my research. Patrick also spent a day with me on the island of Rousay (Orkney Islands), climbing hills and wandering through burial chambers.

Anand Prakash, my friend and designer extraordinaire, continued his tradition of designing brilliant covers for my books by creating a cover that combined all the critical elements of the plot, for which I am grateful.

My thanks go out to Jacqueline Schumann, Humberto E. Ricci Jr., Patricia MacEwen, Elizabeth Gilligan, Berry Kercheval, Phyllis Irene Radford, Christy Marx, and John C. Bunnell—

fellow scribes in my writers' research group, who answered all my questions on topics that were hard to research.

Priyankar Gupta did a great job with the illustrations, helping to bring descriptions in the book to life so that readers could see what I saw both in my mind and around me.

A big thank you to all the people at Westland, especially Gautam Padmanabhan, Krishna Kumar Nair, Sarita Prasad and Varsha Venugopal, who have been tremendously supportive in the last one year with all my endeavours.

As usual, Sanghamitra Biswas, my editor, did a wonderful job of polishing my writing, making changes that ensured that the narrative was smoother and true to the plot.

I did a lot of research for this book. Apart from the field research, I read hundreds of books and articles and viewed videos on history, mythology, and the scientific laws that underpin my hypothesis. Without the wealth of information that I was able to gather from these sources, it would have been very difficult to present theories backed by evidence and published scientific research or connect the dots between history, mythology and science in the manner that I have done in this book.

My acknowledgements cannot be complete without expressing deep gratitude to my parents, who inculcated the joy of reading in me and ensured that I always had a ready supply of new books to read. Without that foundation, I would never have dreamed, as a child, of someday being an author.

Finally, while I acknowledge the contribution of everyone who has supported me, I take full responsibility for all errors and omissions of fact or detail in this book.

HAVE YOU JOINED THE QUEST CLUB YET?

A word about The Quest Club, in case you haven't registered as a member yet. Membership is free and gives you access to Quest Club events—where readers interact with me both online and offline—that are held all over India. There will be free ebooks over the coming years, in addition to quizzes, puzzles, contests and exclusive previews of my future books for members of the club. Finally, you can join me, as I research my books, and gain free access to images, videos and my research notes. You could even learn more about characters, locations and events in my books. An exciting journey filled with adventure and mystery beckons all Quest Club members. You can register for free at: www.christophercdoyle.com/the-quest-club right away for free.